SMART GIRL SWEPT AWAY

Denise Swanson
P.O. Box 371
Wilmington, IL 60481-0371

SMART GIRL SWEPT AWAY

Change of Heart Series

Denise Swanson

http://www.DeniseSwanson.com

For MW,

Hope you're Swept Away!

Best,

Denise Swanson

Smart Girl Swept Away

Smart Girl Swept Away

When feminist author Sheridan Davis is forced to return to Sutton Falls, Illinois to care for her estranged father, the last person she wants to run into is Ridge Sutton. Meeting Ridge, who has matured from handsome to gorgeous, while she looks as if she's spent the night in a cardboard box is so not how Sheridan pictured seeing her high school crush again. Especially not after what he and his friends did to her the night of their senior prom.

Ridge is stunned that he didn't recognize Sheridan. As often as he's thought about her, her image should be permanently imprinted on his brain. Then again, she doesn't look like the eighteen-year-old girl he daydreamed about in high school. Or even the woman in the photo on the dust cover of her books. Has she really changed that much, or is it him?

Ridge is tired of being dependable. Tired of trying to live up to his mother's expectations. And most of all, tired of the life in which he'd allowed himself to become trapped. Tricked into a disastrous marriage that ended in a divorce and stuck in the role of Sutton Falls' mayor, Ridge is ready for a change.

However, now is not a good time to abandon his responsibilities. With the town under the threat of a flood, and the levee that could save it owned by the Davis family, Ridge must balance his personal desires against his duty to the citizens of Sutton Falls.

Although neither Sheridan nor Ridge trust each other, sparks fly whenever they're together. The sex may be terrific, but Sheridan questions whether Ridge's interest is genuine or due to his desire to buy the levee, while Ridge wonders if Sheridan's sudden sentimental attachment to the land is sincere or just a way to drive up the price.

While floodwaters creep higher and higher, can Sheridan and Ridge make peace with their past? Or will their growing love be swept away in a sea of doubt?

Praise for *Good Girl Overboard*, book number one in the Change of Heart romance series.

"*Good Girl Overboard* is a wonderful start to a promising series. I loved it and could not help rooting for Darcy to find love with the handsome captain. ... Mishaps, interesting characters, witty banter, ulterior motives, passion, secrets, a shipboard romance and love intertwine to provide readers with an entrancing story that will leave them feeling good. ... I cannot wait to see what else Ms. Swanson has in store for her readers with the next Change Of Heart novel."
— Dottie, RomanceJunkies.com

Publisher's warning: This book contains sensual consummated love scenes.

Series description:

The Change of Heart series is about a group of small town friends who all need a fresh start and a change of outlook in order to find their forever loves.

Good Girl Overboard: **978-0-9861017-0-0**

Lucky Girl Hits the Jackpot: **978-0-9861017-1-7**

Smart Girl Swept Away: **978-0-9861017-2-4**

Sweet Girl Undone: **978-0-9861017-3-1**

For more information, please visit www.DeniseSwanson.com

Dedication:

To my sorority sister Geraldine Cox who allowed me to borrow her thoughts on what being a lifelong member of Alpha Sigma Alpha truly means.

CHAPTER ONE

Sheridan took a quick look over her shoulder. *So far, so good.* No one was paying any attention to her. She snagged a gallon of milk from the refrigerated case of Sutton's Supermarket, stowed it in her cart, and sucked in a lungful of air.

How long had she been holding her breath? Probably since the produce department, when she'd almost bumped into Mrs. Bunson near the rutabagas. Mrs. B was one of the biggest tsk-tskers in town, and she didn't want to be seen in this condition by anyone, let alone that not-so-sweet old lady.

Sheridan bit her lip so hard that she tasted blood. How had she ended up like this again? Back home less than a day and already cowering next to the cottage cheese. This wasn't who she was. She was Sheridan Davis, the successful author of cutting-edge books about women's empowerment.

Yeah. She was Sheridan "Hear-Me-Roar" Davis, all right. That was, until she crossed into the city limits of Sutton Falls, Missouri, then every bit of hard-won confidence was sucked out of her soul faster than a Hoover could vacuum up a dust bunny.

She scowled at a nearby carton of yogurt. This was all her father's fault. *No.* That wasn't fair. For all his failings, she couldn't blame Errol for his ill health. But he was definitely responsible for Sheridan's presence in the grocery store.

Despite the fact that Sheridan had explained to her father that she couldn't go into town looking like she had spent the night in a cardboard box next to the railroad tracks, he had insisted that he couldn't wait twenty-four hours for her suitcase to arrive to have a meal. And he had refused to be satisfied with a supper consisting of potato chips and leftover Easter candy.

In the end, Errol's complaints of starvation had overcome

1

DENISE SWANSON

Sheridan's resistance, and here she was at the supermarket trying to finish up the shopping while doing an imitation of the Invisible Woman. At least there was only one item left on her list. She might actually escape without seeing anyone else she knew. A minor miracle in a town with a population of 4,253.

"Sheridan Davis?"

Shoot! Someone had spotted her. Sheridan turned slowly, ready to deny her identity, then grinned. Standing a few feet away was the one person in her hometown who had encouraged her writing talent.

"Ms. Wilson." Sheridan hurried over to her favorite teacher. "How are you?"

"Just fine." The attractive middle-aged woman clasped both of Sheridan's hands in her own. "But I think you can call me Lucille now that you're no longer my student."

"You'll always be Ms. Wilson to me"—Sheridan squeezed her mentor's fingers—"but I'll try."

"Good." Lucille stepped back and examined Sheridan. "I've enjoyed your books very much."

"I appreciate you saying that." Sheridan blew out an audible sigh of relief. "I'd hoped you'd like them, but I know not everyone agrees with the issues they address."

"I found them well-written, engrossing, and thoroughly researched."

"All skills I learned in your freshman English class and polished in your senior honors seminar." A weight lifted from Sheridan's shoulders. "Thank you."

"You had the talent. It was my pleasure to help you acquire the tools to use that ability to its best advantage." Lucille's expression grew serious. "I heard your father was taken to the hospital this morning. Is he okay?"

"We don't know yet." Sheridan barely stopped herself from making a face.

2

Every household had a police scanner, and very few of the town's citizens understood the words "none of your business." Although it was nice that the people cared what happened to each other, after living for so many years in the anonymity of a big city, it was disconcerting to be the target of their scrutiny once again.

"They didn't find out what was wrong?" Lucille's eyebrows drew together.

"The ER doctor wanted to run more tests, but Errol insisted on getting a second opinion from his own physician first."

"Tests?" Lucille tilted her head. "I heard he'd fallen down the porch steps."

"That's right. He broke his wrist and ankle." Sheridan leaned against the freezer. Clearly, this would take a while. "But what they're really worried about is *why* he lost consciousness."

"Naturally." Lucille nodded. "It was a good thing you were able to get here so fast. If I remember correctly, you live in St. Louis."

"That's right."

When Sheridan didn't elaborate, Lucille prodded, "Did your aunt call you?"

"No." Sheridan hid a frown. "The hospital contacted me."

While Lucille might be one of the few folks in Sutton Falls who she liked, the teacher wasn't above turning her chance encounter with Sheridan into grist for the rumor mill.

"It was a blessing that they were able to reach you." Lucille continued her fact-finding mission. "Were you at home?"

"No."

"On a book tour?"

Sheridan had hoped her short answers would discourage her former teacher, but clearly, her plan wasn't working. Maybe it was better to tell someone the real story before the gossipers put their own spin on the incident.

"Actually I was helping build a Habit for Humanity house," She gestured to her frizzy ponytail, torn jeans, and baggy sweatshirt, "which is why I look like this."

"Not too different than how you dressed in high school." Lucille winked. "Right?"

"I suppose." Sheridan's cheeks warmed.

Her appearance as a teenager had been her way of rebelling against her late mother. Vivian Sheridan Davis had been a stunningly beautiful woman who had always taken pride in being flawlessly dressed, made up, and coiffed whenever she was in the public eye. Sheridan bore her mother's family name, and Vivian had been determined to turn her into the pretty and popular daughter who would live up to the honor.

"But that was a long time ago." Lucille's brown eyes were sympathetic. "I'm sure it was just a phase you were going through."

"I like to think I've changed since then." Feeling compelled to explain her dishabille, Sheridan said, "Unfortunately, I was over an hour away from my condo when I got the call, so I drove straight from the construction site to the hospital."

Now that she had an image as an up-and-coming author to maintain, she never even went to Walgreens without doing her hair and makeup.

"You poor thing." Lucille moved closer and patted Sheridan's arm. "You must have been so frightened. I'll bet all you could think of was getting to your dad, and now you're stuck without any of your things."

"Uh-huh." Sheridan swallowed hard, remembering her panic when she'd realized that she might not reach the hospital in time. "Luckily, since I'd only been working a little while, I wasn't too dirty. And my assistant was part of my construction team, so I was able to give her my keys and ask her to pack a bag and overnight it to me. By tomorrow I should look more like myself again."

"So you're going to be around town for a while?" Lucille asked.

"Just until I can hire a home health care aide."

Sutton Falls had its charms, but growing up there was like being on a reality TV show. Everyone watched their neighbors and discussed any missteps. Nowadays, they probably tweeted about the slipups and posted pictures of them on Facebook. Sheridan had needed to leave the omnipresent eyes of the townspeople in order to become her own person.

The combination of her experience the night of her senior prom and discovering Errol's secret a few weeks later had been the perfect motivation to put Sutton Falls on her list of been there, done that, and will never wear the T-shirt.

"Have you—"

"It was great to see you, Ms. Wil— I mean Lucille." Sheridan hurriedly gestured to her watch, determined to avoid any more questions. "But I need to get going."

"Of course, dear." Lucille looked pointedly at the contents of Sheridan's cart. "I don't want to keep you from making supper. Your father's probably thrilled at the idea of a home-cooked meal since he so often eats at the diner."

"Oh, I don't know about that." Sheridan fought to keep her expression neutral. "His sister takes good care of him, and then there are all those casseroles that the single women from church make for him."

"Ah, yes. An eligible widower is a rare and wondrous commodity around these parts." Lucille's tone was droll. "At least, that's what my aunt keeps telling me."

"Oh?"

"Yes. After my great aunt started to develop dementia, I moved out to the family farm to live with her. Her opinion of my single status is ever-present in our dinner conversation. It's fortunate that she thinks that I'm still twenty-five, or she might take out an ad to get me a husband."

"Believe me, I understand." Sheridan smiled sympathetically. "My happily married sorority sisters have a lot in common with your aunt, and they know exactly how old I am."

After hugging Lucille good-bye, Sheridan headed for the pain relievers. She'd developed a headache during the three-hour drive to get to the hospital. The pain had gotten worse when the ER doctor had informed her that her father would be confined to a wheelchair for several months. And increased tenfold when she'd realized she was stuck in Sutton Falls until she could hire someone to take care of Errol.

As she stared at the empty space where the bottle of Tylenol should have been, her temples throbbed. Her father's medicine cabinet only contained aspirin, which upset her stomach, and ibuprofen, which gave her hives.

She whimpered in frustration. How the heck could they be out of something as basic as Tylenol? Another drawback of small-town life. Lack of choice.

"Do you need some help?"

Sheridan turned to answer but was struck speechless as she gazed into familiar green eyes. Her belly dropped like she was on a free-falling elevator. It couldn't be.

She darted a glance at the rest of his face.

But it was.

The sexy voice belonged to Ridge Sutton, owner of the grocery store. And the gas station. And the car dealership. And a whole lot of other businesses in the area. He was a descendant of the town's founding father, and Sutton Falls's version of the unreachable star.

Not to mention the guy Sheridan had been infatuated with since they were both in seventh grade.

When she continued to stare at him, Ridge repeated, "Is there something I can help you with?" He smiled encouragingly, and faint lines formed around his eyes and mouth.

"No, thanks." Sheridan shook her head, distracted by her attempt to mesh the memory of the eighteen-year-old she'd had a crush on with the thirty-one-year-old man standing in front of her.

He'd grown a couple of inches and gained some muscle in his chest and shoulders, but the other changes were subtler, almost imperceptible. Instead of cocky, he seemed confident, and his features had somehow matured from handsome to gorgeous.

Great! He was even more attractive than before, and she looked like crap.

In her fantasies, if she ever met Ridge again, she was dressed in Prada and surrounded by admiring readers. Just her luck, in reality, she was wearing a pair of K-mart Blue Light Special jeans, and there wasn't an adoring fan in sight. Where was a good sinkhole when you needed one?

Sheridan stepped back, her heart hammering in her ears as she studied his expression. He didn't seem to recognize her. Which, considering her current appearance, should make her feel better but instead caused a dull ache in her chest.

How could he not know her? They'd attended twelve years of school together—thirteen if you counted kindergarten. There were less than a hundred kids in their class, and she'd tutored him in English twice a week for an entire semester. But apparently, she'd been just as invisible as she always felt.

Damn it all to hell! It was silly to care about something that'd happened so long ago. She straightened her spine and attempted to walk away, but a tanned arm with an attractive sprinkling of golden-red hairs shot out and gripped the handle of her shopping cart.

"Wait a minute, were you looking for a bottle of Tylenol?" He indicated the empty shelf.

"No." His nearness made her nearly incoherent. "Uh, yes. I mean, it's not important." She tried once again to get by him.

"I can get you one from the back." He smoothed down the crisp white shirtsleeves that had been folded back to mid forearm. Fastening the buttons at his wrist, he added, "It'll only take a second."

"Uh...okay...thanks."

She watched his long-legged self-confident stride as he disappeared toward the storage room, then she deliberately shut out her awareness of him and planned her escape. The store was small. It was only five aisles with a few coolers and freezers along the rear wall and two cash registers by the front door. Maybe she could get away while he fetched the medication. Then, if they met again, she'd be her usual well-dressed and polished self.

She was nearly around the corner when a hand on her shoulder stopped her. Without turning, she knew it was Ridge. The warmth of his palm through the material of her sweatshirt sent a shiver down her spine, and she had to force herself to move out of his reach.

"You look familiar." He flashed an irresistible grin, the one that had won her heart in junior high and kept it securely in his pocket for the next six years. "Have we met before?"

If anyone else had said that, it would have sounded like a pickup line, but Ridge's voice resonated with sincerity.

Fighting his charm, she put a snip in her voice and said, "Weren't you getting me some Tylenol?"

"Sure." He sounded taken aback at her chilly response.

This time, she made it to the checkout counter before he came back. Jamming his hands into the pockets of his black wool pants, he said, "I remember you from somewhere. Maybe college?"

"Again, no." Why didn't he recognize her? Sheridan
clamped down on her disappointment and, with a cool stare,
said, "How about that Tylenol?"

As soon as he left, she paid for her purchases, then, hoping
he wouldn't pursue her outside the store, hastily pushed her
loaded cart into the parking lot. She had to get away from him
before she said something she would regret.

Yes. He had been the big man on campus, and she'd been at
the bottom of the pecking order. But really, he should remember
her name. If only because of what his then-girlfriend and current
wife had done to her throughout their senior year. Especially the
awful woman's coup de grâce the night of their prom.

Sheridan hurriedly tossed the grocery bags into the trunk of
her Lexus. Storm clouds had rolled in while she'd been in the
store. The nearly constant rain of the past month might be about
to start up again, and she wanted to get home before it did.

"Wait!" She was opening the driver's door when Ridge ran
up to her, the wind barely moving his short auburn hair. "I know
who you are." He shoved a bottle of Tylenol at her and said,
"Jessica, from the county court house, right? You asked me to
the Fireman's Ball, but I was going to be out of town and
couldn't go. Maybe we could do something this weekend if
you're still interested."

Okay. Now she was really mad. Any points she had given
him for thinking she looked vaguely familiar were forfeited. Not
only had he confused her with some pathetic loser who he'd
rejected, he thought she was the kind of woman who would go
out with a married man. Fury almost choked Sheridan as she slid
into the soft leather seat.

Ridge beamed at her, clearly confident that she'd be thrilled
at his offer of a pity date. It was all Sheridan could do not to slap
him.

She knew she was overreacting. Her teenage crush notwithstanding, Sheridan had always been aware that he was out of her league. Still, there had been that one time when he'd noticed her. That golden day when there had been a look on his face that she'd never seen before. A look she hadn't fully allowed herself to recognize. A look of a man interested in a woman.

When Ridge had told her that he was planning to break up with his girlfriend, Alexis, the next day and once he was a free agent, he had a question he wanted to ask Sheridan, an intense flare of longing had zipped through her body. It had started in her chest, making her breasts ache, and moved south, causing other parts of her to tingle.

But nothing had come of it, and he'd returned to treating her as if she were a stray kitten that occasionally crossed her path—an absentminded pat on the head and quickly forgotten. Then a couple of months after Sheridan had left for college, Ridge and Alexis had gotten married.

The memory of that high school disappointment formed a painful knot in the pit of her stomach, and Sheridan slammed the car door. She started the engine, but before she could pull away, Ridge knocked on the window and gestured to her to lower the glass. As she reluctantly complied, she wondered why she didn't just leave. Why was she prolonging this agonizing encounter? Was it just to gaze into his gorgeous green eyes for a few seconds longer?

"Oh. My. God! You're Sheri Davis." Ridge's expression was dazed. "You tutored me in Honors English for a good part of our senior year. You really saved my ass in that class. Without your help, I wouldn't have gotten the A that I needed to get into Wash U."

Had that been a flicker of guilt darting across his face? Sheridan curled her lip. *No. Of course not.* Ridge Sutton wouldn't recognize that emotion, let alone experience it.

"What was all the mystery about?" His brows formed a perplexed vee over his nose. "Why didn't you tell me who you were?"

"Why should I? It's not as if we're old *pals*," Sheridan emphasized the last word. "Because if you had truly considered me a friend—not just some smart girl whose help you needed to keep your straight A average—you would have known me right away."

Before Ridge could respond, Sheridan put her Lexus in gear and shifted into reverse. As she squealed out of the parking lot, she looked in her rearview mirror. Ridge stood exactly where she'd left him, an unreadable expression on his handsome face.

CHAPTER TWO

Sheridan gripped the steering wheel as though it were Ridge Sutton's neck. She was dismayed that she had so quickly reverted to the prickly, insecure girl she used to be. She'd thought she'd laid that part of her to rest, but the waves of self-doubt washing over her said otherwise.

It was as if she were a rubber band that had been stretched and let go. The elastic loop always went back to its exact same shape. And no matter how hard she tried, when she was in Sutton Falls, she would always be who she had been before. At least until the rubber band broke. And if that happened, would she be able to handle the fallout?

Her reaction to Ridge was exactly why, on her brief trips home, Sheridan visited only her family. It was also the reason she never read the local paper or listened to gossip about any of the townsfolk. After what had happened at the end of her senior year, she had tried to close off her emotions and wipe the entire place from her memory. Clearly, she had failed.

With the exception of her cousin Merry, Sheridan hadn't had any close friends in high school. She hadn't been athletic, so she didn't fit with the jocks. She wasn't musical, so she didn't fit with the band or chorus kids. And, although she was smart, she wasn't a genius, so she didn't fit with the brains. All she'd ever been good at was writing. And that wasn't a group activity.

Frustrated, Sheridan blew a wayward curl out of her eyes and made a face. She couldn't wait until she kicked the dust of this suffocating town from her shoes and resumed her life back in St. Louis. Although she didn't participate in the kind of exciting social whirl that people expected, at least she had her critique group, her self-esteem, and her privacy.

Was it too late in the day to contact the home health care employment agency? She glanced at her watch. *Damn!* It was already after five, and the Tag Heuer on her wrist kept perfect time, so she couldn't even hope it was actually any earlier.

Sighing, she turned on her Bluetooth and said, "Dial Darcy."

She'd tried to call her three best friends on the drive from St. Louis to the hospital, desperate to hear their reassuring voices. But Lucy was a teacher, so she'd been in class, and Delaney was on a delayed honeymoon with her new husband and hadn't answered her cell. Thank goodness Darcy, who was also a writer, had answered her phone and helped Sheridan make it through the long trip.

Knowing that once Sheridan got to the hospital, she would be busy with her father, Darcy had promised to let the others know about Errol. Now that she had a second, Sheridan wanted to update her friends.

Sheridan, Darcy Simons Starr, Lucy Wheeler Campbell, and Delaney Smallwood DeWitt had been inseparable in college. The four of them had pledged Alpha Sigma Alpha together and been suitemates for the three and a half years afterwards. Around the university's campus, they'd been known as the Four Seasons. Lucy was summer—always cheerful, living for the moment. Delaney was spring—ever hopeful and ready for a new beginning. Darcy was fall—crisp, with a hint of sadness. And Sheridan was winter—cool and a bit aloof.

"How's your dad?" Darcy's voice broke into Sheridan's reminiscing.

"He seems okay," Sheridan answered slowly. "He has a broken wrist and ankle, but he'll need to have further testing to figure out why he lost consciousness."

The tension eased from her shoulders as she spoke. It was

so good to have friends she trusted. She hadn't realized how much she yearned for that type of relationship in high school until she'd gone to college and found lifelong friendships in her sorority.

"Are you still at the hospital?"

"No." Sheridan turned onto the blacktop that led to her family's house. "We've been home for about three hours. Once I got my father settled, I had to run to the grocery store. The only things in his pantry were salty or full of sugar."

"Sounds about right for a widower." Darcy laughed, then her voice lowered in concern. "How was your trip into town?"

Darcy, Delaney, and Lucy were the only three people, other than her therapist, with whom Sheridan had shared what had happened just prior to her departure from Sutton Falls. Without her sorority sisters, she would have never worked through the trauma of those events.

When she'd first arrived at college, Sheridan had felt as if she were a Christmas tree ornament that someone had deliberately crushed under their foot. She'd had to pick up all the tiny fragments and reassemble them, bit by bit. With the help of her friends, she'd eventually been able to patch herself up and get on with her life.

But she knew that if she ever allowed herself truly to feel again, the glue would come apart. And if that happened, she'd shatter into so many pieces that, this time, she'd never get herself back together again.

"As you can imagine," Sheridan finally answered her friend, "I wasn't too thrilled to have to go to the supermarket dressed like a refugee from a tractor pull."

"I can imagine, Miss Always-Perfectly-Dressed," Darcy teased. "Did you see anyone you know?"

"My old English teacher."

"The one who encouraged you to pursue writing as a

career?"

"Uh-huh."

Sheridan glanced out her side window and frowned at the sight of the pond-size stretches of water filled with ducks and geese. By late April, the land should have already been plowed and planted.

Poor Mick. Her cousin farmed with Errol and had a considerable amount of property of his own. He must be going nuts with the unending rain keeping him out of the fields. At this rate, forget the Fourth of July. The corn wouldn't be knee-high until Labor Day or maybe Halloween.

"Was it nice to see her?" Darcy's voice brought Sheridan back from her reverie.

"It was." Sheridan realized how much she missed the folks in town whom she had liked.

The cliché about throwing out the baby with the bathwater certainly applied to Sheridan's scorched-earth policy where Sutton Falls was concerned.

"So going back there wasn't as bad as you thought."

"No," Sheridan said, her voice breaking. "It was a hundred times worse."

"Why?" Darcy's own voice rose in alarm. "What happened?"

"I also ran into Ridge Sutton." Sheridan paused to gather herself together. "And he was just as gorgeous as I told you guys."

"Oh?" Darcy's tone was cautious. "What did he do? Was he cruel to you?"

"Not at all." Sheridan tried to force some humor into her tone but failed. "Actually, he asked me for a date."

"What?" Darcy squealed. "Didn't you say he got married a couple of months after you left town?"

"Yep." Sheridan swallowed hard. Thinking about Ridge

married to Alexis always caused a lump to form in her throat. "But that's not even the worst part."

"Seriously?"

"Sadly, yes." Sheridan brushed a single teardrop from the corner of her eye. She would not cry over that man again. "He didn't even recognize me. Back in high school, I truly was nothing more than a flyspeck on his windshield."

"I'm so sorry," Darcy murmured softly. "I know what happened to you froze your heart, and you've always shown the world your professional face. But I had hoped that finally being home, you could come to grips with your past and reclaim who you really are deep inside."

"I—"

Darcy cut off Sheridan's protest, "I know it's not the image you have of yourself, but you *are* a warm, loving person. It's a shame you never let anyone but Delaney, Lucy, and me see that side of you."

"That's..." Sheridan stuttered to a stop, unsure how she meant to finish her sentence.

"Look, just think about it." Darcy filled the silence, then changed the subject. "Oh, before I forget, Delaney and Lucy said to tell you how sorry they were about your dad's illness, and that you should call them when you have time to talk."

"Okay." Sheridan nodded, still thinking about Darcy's assessment of her personality. "Thanks." She paused, then, feeling guilty for not asking earlier, added, "How are the babies and Mitch?"

"We're all fine. The kids are growing like weeds, and Mitch seems to have adjusted beautifully to captaining a desk rather than a ship."

"That's great." Sheridan smiled. After what Darcy had been through with a vile ex-fiancé, she deserved a happy ending. "Maybe we can set up a Skype session with the Four Seasons next week."

"That would be awesome. Michelle and Michael are usually asleep by eight, so for me, evenings work the best. During the day, if I'm not writing, I hate to ask the nanny to take care of them."

"Eight your time is fine. I'll text you about a specific day. Talk to you then."

Hanging up, Sheridan tried to concentrate on her mental to-do list, but unhappy memories of her teenage years kept popping into her mind.

She snarled in frustration and hit the dashboard with her palm. The last thing she wanted was for Errol to see that she was upset. It was a good bet that he wouldn't offer the comfort she craved, and if by some miracle he did, after what he'd done, she couldn't accept it.

Fighting the urge to pass by the white gravel drive leading to the house that had been in her mother's family for over a hundred fifty years, Sheridan made the turn and stopped the Lexus a few feet from the back door. Before exiting the car, she studied her childhood home.

The white paint was peeling, a post on the wraparound porch was broken, and one of the attic's dormer windows was cracked. Had the upkeep become too much for her father? Or maybe, with her mother dead, he just didn't bother.

In either case, before she left, she needed to hire someone to do the repairs. Her mother had cherished this house, and Sheridan's guilt wouldn't permit her to let Errol neglect it.

Growing up, she'd been closer to her father than to her mom. She'd always sided with him. Then, by the time she saw his true colors, Vivian was dead, and there was no chance for Sheridan to admit how wrong she'd been about her dad.

Wishing she could go back and rewrite history, Sheridan dragged herself out of the Lexus and into the house. Her cell started ringing while she was in the utility room toeing off her shoes. She hurried into the kitchen, dumped the grocery bags on the worn Formica counter, and snatched the tiny red device from her purse.

Catching her breath, she swept her finger over the screen and said, "Hello?"

"Why aren't you answering your phone?" Grace Kaplan's nasal voice blared in Sheridan's ear.

Grace was her agent. And although now that her books were so successful, Sheridan should feel in control of the relationship, she didn't. She'd accumulated two hundred and seven rejection letters from other agents before Grace had agreed to represent her, and she was still a little intimidated by the gruff businesswoman.

"Sorry." Sheridan frowned. Her phone had worked just fine while she was talking to Darcy. Mentally shrugging, she said, "Sutton Falls is a black hole for cell reception. I must have been in a dead zone when you tried me."

"What in the hell are you doing in Hooterville?" Grace bellowed.

"I got a call from the local hospital informing me that my father had been admitted with a suspected coronary."

Sheridan walked over to her father's bedroom to check on Errol. He was asleep with the TV blaring. The nurses had warned her that the pain medication would make him drowsy.

"Is he okay?" Grace asked.

Before she responded, Sheridan eased Errol's door shut. "We don't know yet. It turns out it wasn't a heart attack after all."

She returned to the kitchen, put the phone on speaker, and opened the bottle of Tylenol. Shaking out two caplets, she reconsidered and added another one to the pair in her palm.

"What do you mean?" Grace's voice hardened. "Was it one

of your dad's tricks to get attention?'"

Early in their relationship, Sheridan had mentioned to Grace that Errol often pretended aches and pains to gain sympathy from the neighborhood ladies. Once she'd learned that her agent was her business partner, not her pal, she tried to keep her professional and private lives separate. It wasn't always possible, but she made an effort not to overshare. Especially anything negative.

"Not this time." Sheridan dry-swallowed the pills, then started putting away the groceries as she described Errol's refusal to allow the ER doctor to run more tests. When she was finished explaining, she said, "So I have to take him to his regular physician to find out why he lost consciousness. Unfortunately, I couldn't get him an appointment until Monday."

"You don't sound like your usual calm and collected self." Grace's tone was suspicious. "If your dad's okay, why are you so agitated?"

"I'm not agitated," Sheridan lied.

"Look, it may be a million miles from Podunk to New York, but now that I finally got through, this phone connection is crystal clear, and I can tell something's bothering you. What happened?"

Sheridan dropped into a kitchen chair. She suddenly felt dizzy and slightly disoriented. "It's just upsetting being away from my routine.

"You manage on book tours."

"That's different." Sheridan thrust a curl behind her ear, counting the minutes until her flat iron arrived and she could get her hair into its usual smooth chignon.

"What aren't you telling me?"

Sheridan's mind raced. She didn't want to admit to her agent what a loser she'd been as a teenager. In the publishing business, showing any kind of Achilles' heel was akin to

bleeding in shark-infested waters—dangerous at the best of
times, suicidal if you were in a weakened state.

"It's not a big deal." Sheridan answered quickly.

"What isn't a big deal?"

Shoot! Sheridan's agent was like a terrier. If she thought
something might slow down her client's writing or cause her to
miss a deadline or be less productive, Grace wouldn't rest until
she had shaken every last scrap of information loose. What could
Sheridan say to satisfy her?

"I was just reliving some high school angst." Sheridan
chuckled.

"About what?"

"Nothing that will interfere with my work." Sheridan got up
and walked over to the fridge.

She needed to eat something before low blood sugar made
her blurt out something stupid.

"Good." Grace, evidently not quite satisfied that there
wouldn't be a problem with the next book, added, "Since it's
been over a decade, it's time to get over whatever this nothing
is."

"I thought I had." Her appetite gone, Sheridan shut the
refrigerator door.

"Sounds like you thought wrong."

The tendrils of the depression she'd fought all through
college crept into her psyche, and she struggled to banish them.
Shit! She had to take charge of both this conversation and her
emotions.

"Maybe." Sheridan infused a chill into her voice. "But since
you're my agent, not my therapist, and I told you I don't want to
discuss it, I'm going to hang up."

"Not so fast." Grace's tone was irritated. "The reason I
called was when your editor couldn't get a hold of you, she
phoned me. *New York Times*'s best-seller statistics are in. *Good-*

bye, Gloria Steinem, Hello, Kim Kardashian is number one on next week's list. I know you've hit the list before, but number one is a huge deal."

Sheridan took a deep breath and grinned. It had taken her a year to research her theory that women had lost ground since the seventies feminist movement. To do so, she'd talked to hundreds of teens and twenty-something girls about their aspirations. A disturbing majority's only goal in life was to find some man to buy them the newest Louboutin shoes and Louis Vuitton purses.

Supporting this impression were the facts that Sheridan had gathered regarding the professions young women were entering and the amount of their average starting salaries. None of the data had been encouraging.

"I have a ton of interview requests," Grace broke into Sheridan's thoughts. "And your publisher wants you out on tour ASAP. Where's the nearest airport? How fast can you get to New York?"

"I thought my editor agreed that since I have such a tight deadline for the next book, I didn't have to do signings this time."

Sheridan had missed Lucy's wedding due to the last promotional tour. Her friend had understood, but Sheridan still felt bad. At least she'd been there for Delaney's big day, and she'd made it to Fort Lauderdale for both Darcy's baby showers.

"That was before the Democratic presidential candidate read the book," Grace interrupted Sheridan's stroll down memory lane. "When she gave it a thumbs up and it took off, the publisher decided you needed to cash in on the publicity."

"I understand, but it's going to take a little while to get things set up for Errol." She hadn't called him Dad since she'd learned of his perfidy. "Marketing isn't a part of my contract, right?"

"No." Grace bit off the single syllable. "But this is a chance of a lifetime, with a narrow window of opportunity." She paused, obviously allowing time for Sheridan to comprehend the importance of her words. "Since the *NYT* print list doesn't come out until a week from this coming Sunday, that's how long you have. After that, unless the book stays at number one for a second week, the offers will dry up."

"I should be able to leave way before then." Sheridan crossed her fingers. "I just need to find a home health aide to take care of him. I'll phone you Monday afternoon."

"Fine." Grace hesitated, then said, "In the meantime, stay away from whoever upset you."

After Grace hung up, Sheridan stood for a moment before stuffing her cell in her pocket. Her agent was right. She had to get away from Sutton Falls before she lost all her hard-won self-confidence *and* the chance to spread her book's cautionary tale to all the women who needed to hear its important message.

Straightening her shoulders, Sheridan pushed her distress aside and opened a can of tomato soup. While it heated, she made toasted cheese sandwiches and a salad. When everything was ready, she brought a tray into her father. He was awake and watching the weather on the six o'clock news. It had rained nearly every day since the beginning of March, but it looked as if tomorrow might be dry.

"Thank God you're back." Errol glanced up from the weather map on the TV set. "My stomach was beginning to think my throat had been cut."

"How are you feeling?" Sheridan was used to her father's dramatic pronouncements and didn't respond to his theatrics. "Any pain?"

"No." He held a pencil, deftly threading it through the slender white fingers of his right hand while he spoke. "You can leave tomorrow morning. One of the ladies from church will help me get to the doctors and such."

"I'll stay until I can hire someone who can live-in while your wrist and ankle heal." Sheridan kept a neutral look on her face. Errol would go to his grave with women fighting to take care of him. "Meantime, we need to find out why you passed out and keep it from happening again."

He nodded, and they ate their supper in uneasy silence watching the meteorologist point out the ever-increasing areas of flooding.

CHAPTER THREE

Ridge Sutton sat behind the desk in his study staring out the Palladian window at the stars studding the dark sky. Questions tumbled through his mind like pebbles caught in a hubcap. How could he have failed to recognize Sheri Davis? He thought about her often enough for her image to be permanently imprinted on his brain.

Then again, she didn't look like the eighteen-year-old girl he remembered from high school. Or even the woman in the photo on the dust cover of her books. Had she really changed that much, or was it him?

When he'd come out of the storage room hunting for the grocery store manager, she was the last person that he'd expected to see in the aisle. As far as he knew, and he'd kept an ear out for any word of Sheri, she rarely returned home. And when she did, she never came into downtown.

Her shunning of Sutton Falls was legendary. And a lot of folks were offended that she never did an interview for the local paper, a talk at the library, or a signing at the bookstore.

Ridge suspected that Sheri avoided her hometown not because she was a snob but because of something that had happened to her at her senior prom. And although he'd never quite found out what had taken place, he'd heard that the big dance hadn't had a happy ending for Sheri.

His own experience at the prom hadn't been much better. He was never exactly sure what had happened that night to either of them—his memories ended at the pre-prom party—but if Sheri's experience had been half as bad as his, he understood why she'd turned her back on Sutton Falls.

Early in his marriage to Alexis, he'd tried to question her about the dance, but she'd claimed that she had no idea what had caused the gaps in Ridge's memory or why Sheri had been so upset. Now that he knew that his ex-wife rarely told the truth, he doubted her declarations of ignorance.

Pushing aside his thoughts of Alexis, he returned to contemplating his encounter with Sheri. Clearly, she hadn't been happy to see him. Would she have behaved differently toward him if he'd recognized her right away?

Back when she tutored him, he'd thought she liked him. But judging from this afternoon, he'd been dead wrong.

At the sound of someone clearing their throat, Ridge flinched, sure that it was his mother with another of her ridiculous demands.

He cursed himself for allowing the controlling woman back into his household. But when Alexis had literally abandoned their twelve-year-old daughter on his doorstep, Evelyn had pointed out that for the past five years, his ex-wife had only allowed Ridge to see his daughter once or twice a month.

On the other hand, Evelyn emphasized, she had been permitted to see her granddaughter on a regular basis, so the girl would be more comfortable with her grandmother in residence. His mother's argument had seemed valid, and wanting to do what was best for his daughter, Ridge had reluctantly agreed to Evelyn moving in with him.

She had promised to stick to her wing and respect his privacy. But as she had so many times in the past, she had lied.

Relief washed over Ridge when he looked toward the open French doors and, instead of Evelyn, saw Odell Voss standing at the threshold. He wasn't up to dealing with his mother tonight.

He motioned to the older man to come inside and said, "What's up?"

"I need to know if you decided on a color for the shutters

and trim." Odell tucked a limp gimme cap in the back pocket of his gray work pants. "I got 'em all scraped and ready."

Odell had been the Sutton groundskeeper and jack-of-all-trades since Ridge was a boy. He was the one who had taught Ridge how to change a tire, bait a hook, and shoot a rifle. He was also the one with whom Ridge had shared his hopes, dreams, and troubles.

"I haven't given it much thought." Ridge got up and walked toward the other side of the room. "How about a cold one?"

"Don't mind if I do." Odell licked his lips. "A Bud would hit the spot."

Ridge bent down to the small refrigerator underneath the wet bar and grabbed two cans. He didn't particularly like Budweiser, but he always kept it around and drank it with Odell, who was a rabid fan of the "King of Beers."

Ridge handed one of the cans to the older man and said, "Have a seat."

"Thanks." Odell sat on one of the two matching wing chairs that faced the desk and gestured to his boot-clad feet. "These old dogs are sure barkin' tonight."

"Which is why I told you to shorten your hours." Ridge settled back behind his desk. "Why didn't you knock off at three o'clock like we agreed?"

"You're paying me for an honest day's work." Odell's expression was stubborn. "So that's what I'm giving you." He popped the top of his Budweiser, took a long swallow, then smirked. "I hear Sheri Davis is back in town. You still got the hots for her?"

Ridge choked on the swig of beer he had just taken. *Shit!* He loved Odell like a father, but the older man was too long on memory and too short on tact.

"What are you talking about?" Ridge protested. "Of course not."

"Old Lady Bunson said she spotted you this afternoon chasing that girl through the grocery store and out into the parking lot like a kid running after an ice cream truck," Odell cackled. "Sounds like the hots to me." His thick white eyebrows met over his nose. "Seems I remember you mooning about her back when she was over here tutoring you."

Ridge froze, as a picture of Sheri in his bedroom popped into his mind. She always had a streak of ink across her cheek and a red pen between her moist pink lips. What would have happened if he had replaced that ballpoint with his mouth?

They had spent hours alone together as she helped him write the numerous papers the senior honors English classes required. But Sheri's natural gift with words and her unflagging good humor had made the minutes disappear.

"You didn't fool me back when you were eighteen, and you don't fool me now," Odell snorted. "Hell, Sheri was all you could talk about. I never did understand why you didn't just ask her out."

"I was already in an exclusive relationship with someone else." Ridge's tone was stiff.

The memory of his then-girlfriend, Alexis, whining that he didn't pay her enough attention made him squirm. He hadn't dared to tell her that he'd been so captivated by Sheri's wit and intelligence he couldn't stop thinking about her. Maybe he should have.

Blinking himself back to the present, Ridge mentally shook his head. There was a lot he *should* have done.

"And that relationship worked out so well," Odell muttered under his breath, then asked, "So, is Sheri like you remember her?"

"No. Not at all." Ridge thought about the woman in the supermarket.

It was hard to believe she was Sheri Davis. She had been

angry and unforgiving, totally unlike the shy, warmhearted girl he'd known in high school. The one who'd always been happy to see him. She'd been hurt by someone, maybe more than one someone, and he suspected his name was on that list. He just wasn't sure why.

"Oh?" Odell drained the last drops from his can, crushed it, and tossed it into the trash can by the desk. "She's not good-looking anymore?"

"No. If anything, she's even prettier." Ridge shook his head. How was she different? "It's... I don't know..."

He frowned. It was hard to put it into words, but this Sheri had a brittleness that made him think she might shatter into a million pieces if he said the wrong word, and she had stared at him with such disgust in her eyes.

"Maybe she was in a hurry to get back to her dad." Odell stood up. "After all, she'd just gotten him home from the hospital."

"Could be." Ridge shrugged, then, eager to change the subject, he said, "White."

"Huh?"

"Just paint the shutters and trim white like they've always been."

"I thought you wanted something different," Odell said, raising his bushy white eyebrows. "You know, to finally put your own stamp on the place."

When Ridge had finished college and he and Alexis had returned to town, they had moved into the main house on the Sutton property. Evelyn had relocated to a smaller place about a mile away, and they'd all settled down to live their lives exactly the same way that their ancestors had for the past hundred or more years.

"Maybe next time." Ridge shrugged.

Odell started toward the door but stopped and said, "Afraid

your ma will throw a fit if you change something from the way your dad did it?"

The denial on Ridge's lips died before he uttered it. Odell had a point.

"You know, your ma isn't always right, especially about you." Odell put two fingers to his forehead in a salute and said, "See you tomorrow."

Thirty minutes later, Ridge threw down his pen and shoved back the massive leather chair that had been his dad's throne. He never felt comfortable sitting in that seat, and his mother continually reminded him that he didn't fill it nearly as well as his father.

Frowning, Ridge drained the now warm beer and threw the can into the recycle bin. He still hadn't made a dent in the files stacked on his desk. He usually spent several hours each evening handling the unending paperwork generated by his position as mayor, as well as his family's numerous businesses. People's livelihoods depended on him, and he was determined not to fail them.

Ridge rubbed the back of his neck. He'd never had trouble staying on task before. Even during his divorce six years ago, his attention hadn't wavered from his duties. Why couldn't he focus tonight?

Giving up on the idea of working, he rose from his seat and strode outside onto the stone patio. It had finally stopped raining, and he prayed that it wouldn't start up again. Much more water would result in flooding that could be devastating to Sutton Falls.

Thankful that Odell had dried off the furniture earlier in the day, Ridge took a deep gulp of the damp night air and sank onto the nearest chaise lounge. Staring at the imposing lawn that ended at the edge of the cliff overlooking the river, he relaxed against the tan and black plaid cushions.

When Ridge's great-great-great-grandfather had homesteaded the area, he'd claimed the highest spot for his estate. The symbolism wasn't lost on his descendant.

Ridge yawned. Maybe his lack of concentration was because he was bone-tired. Tired of being dependable. Tired of trying to live up to his mother's expectations. Tired of being a Sutton. But most of all, tired of the life in which he'd allowed himself to become trapped.

Sighing, he finally admitted to himself that seeing Sheri that afternoon had disturbed him. It had brought back the pain of a past he didn't often let himself contemplate. A time when he'd made mistakes that couldn't ever be fixed.

Surrendering to his memories, he thought about the last two months of his senior year in high school. Sheri had haunted his teenage fantasies. Whenever she'd looked at him with those big brown eyes, he'd lost his train of thought. Both her curves and her long golden-brown hair had been so soft and inviting it had taken all his self-control to stop himself from constantly touching her.

And although he'd dreamed of her almost every night, it had taken him until classes were nearly over to admit that he wanted to be with Sheri, not Alexis Byrnes. But as usual, his timing had sucked.

Alexis had begged him not to break up with her until after the prom—refusing to give him back his high school ring. She had tried everything from crying to carving her name into the leather seats of his brand-new BMW, but he'd remained immune to both her pleading and her threats.

Sheri was leaving for college at the end of June—some pre-freshman writing practicum—and he'd wanted to ask her out before it was too late.

After the car-slashing incident, Ridge had grabbed the damn ring off Alexis's finger. Free at last, he had intended to ask Sheri out when she came to tutor him the next day.

Instead, his mother had overheard an argument between Ridge and his best friend, Beau Bunson, and thrown a monkey wrench into his plans.

Ridge and Beau had been playing pool in the Suttons' game room when Beau had said, "Gwen told me today that she won't go to the prom with me if you don't take Alexis."

"Gwen will change her mind."

"No, she won't."

"Ask Merry McIntyre." Ridge sunk a ball. "You've always had a crush on her. This is your chance to do something about it."

"Merry's going with Rick Trunkey." Beau shook his head sadly, then took a swig from the silver flask he kept in his back pocket. "And you better watch your dick. I hear Alexis is out for blood. Maybe you should take her to the stupid dance, then, in a few months, when you go to college, you can just sort of let things fade away."

"No!" Ridge jerked, missing an easy shot. "I'll ask someone else out."

"You're taking another girl to the prom?"

"I'm not going to the prom." Ridge had considered the idea but rejected it. Asking Sheri now would seem like he thought she'd been waiting around for him. "Just a regular date."

"Who's so important that you have to mess up everyone's night?" Beau took another pull of vodka.

"Sheri Davis." The minute the name slipped out of his mouth, Ridge knew that he shouldn't have told Beau.

"That cow!" Beau jeered.

"Never." Ridge whirled on Beau. "Ever." He poked his friend in the shoulder. "Call her that again." Ridge was nose to nose with Beau. "I'm cutting you some slack because you're drunk, but next time you insult Sheri, I'll shove this cue stick up your ass."

"You've got to be shitting me." Beau backed away, his expression a mixture of confusion and fear. "You never minded what I said about Alexis."

Ridge stared at him without speaking.

"Guess I better get going." Beau staggered toward the door. "See you tomorrow at school."

Ridge turned to rack the balls, stiffening when he heard his mother's voice. "I forbid you to take out that Davis girl. What will people say?"

Evelyn Sutton took her position in Sutton Falls society seriously. When her husband had died the year before, she had immediately started grooming Ridge as his successor.

"Why should they care?" Ridge faced his mother, the Ice Queen, as he privately referred to her.

"You know very well that everything a Sutton does in this town is scrutinized." Evelyn adjusted the cardigan of her pale blue cashmere twin set. "Sheri Davis is unsuitable for someone of your social position. Her family barely ekes out a living on the little farm of theirs."

"It's a date, not a lifetime commitment." Ridge slumped on one of the barstools. Dealing with his mother always exhausted him. "Besides, even you aren't that much of a snob. What's the real reason you don't want me dating Sheri?"

"A gentleman would never leave a lady without an escort." Without missing a beat, Evelyn sidestepped his question and changed tactics. "Poor Alexis is devastated that you aren't taking her to the prom."

"She's ticked off." Ridge glanced at the paneled walls, wishing there was a secret exit. "Nothing devastates Alexis."

"You know your father was always a perfect gentleman." When he wouldn't budge, Evelyn always brought out the big guns. "He'd be extremely disappointed in your behavior."

"Dad would understand." Ridge wasn't sure that was the truth, but he'd never admit that to the Ice Queen.

"I wonder if the Davis family has a mortgage on their farm."

"Why?" A flicker of unease crawled up Ridge's spine.

"Alexis's father is the bank president." Evelyn fingered the strand of perfectly matched Mikimoto pearls around her neck. "How far do you think he'd go to retaliate if his little girl doesn't get what she wants?"

"You can't do that!" Ridge shouted, leaping off his seat.

"Of course not, dear." Evelyn put her hand on the doorknob. "But Mr. Byrnes can. He and I have often discussed how happy we are that you and Alexis are together."

Up until that moment, Ridge had never allowed himself to recognize how much his mother manipulated his relationship with Alexis. He'd ignored the warning bells that rang whenever she pointed out that the Byrnes' wealth was second only to the Suttons' fortune. And that Alexis would be the perfect wife for Ridge.

Now it dawned on him that she had been pushing Alexis at him since they were children. *Son of a bitch!* Whether he'd loved Alexis or not, and despite any obstacle he'd put in her path, his mother had intended to unite the Sutton and Byrnes dynasties.

"I won't be blackmailed into taking—"

"Since you weren't intending to invite Sheri to the prom anyway, have one of the boys in your circle invite her. That way you can have a few dances with her but do the honorable thing where Alexis is concerned. Then, in a few days, you can ask Sheri out yourself."

"But—"

"Think it over," Evelyn cut him off again. "As you said, it is only one night."

Ridge hadn't wanted to see Alexis ever again, but he wasn't

willing to risk Sheri's family farm. So he'd done what his mother had suggested. He'd asked one of his friends to escort Sheri, given Alexis back his ring, and taken her to the prom. A decision that had changed the course of his life forever.

CHAPTER FOUR

Monday morning, Sheridan woke slowly. Her sleep had been restless. For the fifth night in a row, she'd dreamt of the time when everyone in school had pretended she wasn't there. That day, with the exception of Ms. Wilson, even the teachers hadn't called on her in class. She'd never quite figured out how Alexis had managed that feat.

Sheridan told herself that the recurring nightmare was due to her lack of progress in securing a home health aide for Errol. But in her heart of hearts, she knew it was a result of her encounter with Ridge last Wednesday.

Stretching, she almost rolled off the mattress. When was the last time she had slept in a twin bed? She sat up and looked around. White French Provençal furniture, pink walls, and lace curtains. Nothing had changed since her mother had fixed up the room as a surprise for Sheridan's eleventh birthday. She hadn't been overly fond of the girly design then, and it definitely hadn't improved with age.

Why had her father kept it just as it had been the day she'd left for college? Had he expected her to live there again someday? *No.* More likely, he rarely thought about her or her room, and it hadn't even occurred to him to redecorate.

Sheridan fought the urge to lie back down and pull the covers over her head. The past four days had been a complete waste of time. Although her suitcase and laptop had arrived late Thursday afternoon, she'd been too distracted to write.

And none of the home health agencies had anyone available for interviews until Wednesday morning. Even her Aunt Flora, who usually could produce a distant cousin with the required skills for any job, hadn't known of anyone looking for work caring for an older housebound man.

Sighing, Sheridan threw back the pink satin comforter and swung her feet over the edge of the mattress. Lying in bed wouldn't solve her problem. Things would look better once she'd showered and dressed.

There was no way she would let anything keep her in Sutton Falls. Somewhere within a reasonable driving radius, there was the perfect person available to take care of Errol. And Sheridan was determined to find him or her in the very near future.

The *beep, beep, beep* of her father's video poker machine greeted her when she took in his breakfast tray. His glasses were pushed up on his forehead, and a frown of concentration bracketed his mouth.

"Here you go—coffee, grapefruit juice, oatmeal, and toast. Do you need anything else?"

Errol pushed a few more buttons on his game before putting it aside. "How about some marmalade?"

"Coming right up."

When Sheridan returned from the kitchen with the jelly jar, she reminded Errol, "Your doctor's appointment is at ten thirty, so we should probably leave about quarter after."

"Thursday, when Flora stopped over to see how I was doing, she said that she could drive me there today."

"That was sweet of her to offer her help." For a moment, Sheridan grasped at the idea of her aunt taking over Errol's care. But his sister was seventy, ten years his senior, and had her own health issues. "Then again, why should she when I'm here?"

"I heard you on the phone the other day with your agent." Errol took a sip of his coffee. "You said you'd call her back this afternoon. If they need you in New York, you don't have to stick around to baby me."

"Everything's under control." Sheridan's tone was brisk. "Grace just wanted to let me know my book was number one on

The New York Times best-seller list."

"That's wonderful. Congratulations." Errol reached out a hand, but Sheridan pretended not to notice. "Why didn't you tell me right away?"

"I didn't think you'd be interested." She stared at a space above his head.

It was hard to believe that, growing up, she had adored her handsome, talented, devil-may-care father. She had been convinced that a man with his artistic ability shouldn't be stuck farming in some one-horse town. But he'd insisted he was happy as long as he was with his wife. And Vivian refused to leave the land that had been in her family since before the Civil War.

"You've accomplished everything you set out to do, Sheri Berry— I mean Sheridan." Errol picked up his serrated spoon and scooped out a grapefruit section. "I'm so proud of you, and, God rest her soul, your mother would have been, too."

Sheridan bit her lip. "Would she?"

Her mother hadn't seemed very interested in Sheridan's academic achievements. Vivian had wanted her daughter to be popular and marry a local boy willing to take over the farm. Errol had always been the one to curtail his wife's nagging for Sheridan to dress better and be more social.

It had saddened Sheridan that she and her mother were so far apart in both what they wanted out of life and personality. Vivian had possessed a droll sense of humor and a self-assurance that came from knowing she was the center of her husband's universe. Sheridan had never had that kind of confidence.

Ignoring his daughter's question about her mother, Errol said, "Even though it'd be nice having the company, I don't want you to stay if it interferes with your success or stirs up bad memories."

"Don't worry about my career." Sheridan stepped into the open doorway. "And as for the other, I'm a big girl now. I know how to handle bullies a lot better than before."

Errol didn't look convinced.

"Besides, there's no reason I have to see any of those people," Sheridan murmured, more to reassure herself than her father, then added, "Although it's wonderful that my aunts and cousins help you on the everyday things, with something as important as your health, it's up to me to sort out matters."

"If that's how you feel." Errol's smile was hopeful. "You know that I'm happy you're here."

Edging out of the room, she said, "Enjoy your breakfast. I'll be back in a little while to get you ready for our trip to the doctor."

Sheridan had finished her coffee and toast and was tidying up the kitchen when she heard the back door open and her cousin Mick's voice shout, "Anyone around?"

"In here." Sheridan finished wiping the table and hung the dishrag over the faucet.

Mick McIntyre walked up to Sheridan and put an arm around her. "Good to see you."

"You, too." Sheridan returned his hug. "How are Nan and the kids?" Mick and his wife had just celebrated their twentieth anniversary, and their twin sons were freshmen in college.

"Everybody's fine." Mick rested his hip against the counter. "How's your dad?"

"So far, so good," Sheridan answered. "I'm taking Errol to the doctor today."

She studied her cousin. He was in his midforties and looked a lot like a younger version of her father. They both had deep tans from all the time they spent outdoors, as well as the same blue eyes, lean body, and attractive face.

"Doc Brown will get to the bottom of it." Mick shoved his hands in his pockets. "Ma told me you were looking to find someone to fix up the outside of the house." His mother was

Errol's sister Flora. "If you want, I could do it for you. I can't get into the fields until they dry out, which they'll only do if the rain has truly stopped." He stared down at the buttons on his flannel shirt. "I could sure use the money."

"You wouldn't want to let me hire you to take care of Errol?" Sheridan asked, a flare of hope flickering in her chest.

"No, sorry. That's one job I won't tackle." Mick held up his hands. "I'm not good around sick folks."

"I understand." Sheridan forced a smile. "But I will take you up on your offer to do the repairs." She picked up her purse from the kitchen chair. "How about I give you my credit card for the materials, then you let me know what I owe you for labor?"

"No need." Mick grinned. "This isn't the city. The hardware store will run a tab, and you can settle up with them when we're finished."

"Terrific."

Mick had started to leave but turned back and said, "Oh, one other thing. Tell Uncle Errol that we have had some more vandalism. This time, they broke all the windows on his tractor shed. With the rain and all we need replace them ASAP. I already called the glass company, the police, and the insurance agent."

"Who would do something like that?" Sheridan asked.

"Probably just some drunk kids."

Sheridan nodded and waved good-bye to her cousin. Another flaw in small-town living was nothing for the kids to do. Boredom drove them faster than a Corvette to alcohol, drugs, and trouble. Which was why, when her friend Delaney had won the lottery, she'd built a youth center for her rural community.

Maybe Sheridan should think about organizing something like that for Sutton Falls. *What? Where had that come from?* She had no investment in the community. It wasn't as if she lived there or anything. Why should she try to help a place that had caused her so much pain?

She paused. To be fair, she shouldn't be upset with the whole town—just a handful of its meaner residents. And maybe it was time to let go of old resentments, at least the grudges concerning people only peripherally involved in the incident.

As she considered the idea of forgiving and forgetting her past hurts, Sheridan helped Errol dress. Up until now, he'd been wearing his pajamas or a sweat suit. But the cast on both his wrist and ankle made it hard getting him into real clothes.

Once Sheridan finished, there were only a few minutes to put herself together. She smoothed her hair into its usual chignon but didn't have time for her complete makeup routine. She had to settle for a hasty application of mascara and lipstick. With just a few seconds left, she hurriedly changed into a pair of khaki slacks and a black V-neck sweater.

Then, winding a silk scarf around her neck, she slipped into loafers, grabbed her purse, and ran back to her father's room. After getting him into his wheelchair, she headed for the back door. Thank goodness Errol had installed a ramp during her mother's illness. Without it, Sheridan wasn't sure how she'd get him out of the house.

As she pushed him toward her Lexus, Errol said, "I think it'd be easier for me to get in and out of the station wagon."

"Sure." The old car sat a few feet away, its dull blue paint faded and cracked with age. "Whatever you want."

She would much rather drive her considerably more swanky pearl-white Lexus, but she resignedly turned the wheelchair toward the ancient Oldsmobile. She probably wouldn't see anyone she knew, anyway. Certainly, no one she needed to impress.

* * *

The doctor's office was crowded. Every seat in the waiting area was taken, so Sheridan leaned against the wall behind Errol's wheelchair. As she scanned the room, she noticed a girl sitting beside an expensively dressed older woman.

The woman, who seemed vaguely familiar, flicked a glance in their direction, then stared at the wall to her left, pointedly ignoring both Sheridan and her father. Which was odd, since women rarely gave Errol the cold shoulder.

The preteen caught Sheridan's eye, stared for a second, then got up and walked over to Sheridan and Errol and said, "Hello, Mr. Davis."

"Hi, Sally." Errol's blue eye's twinkled. "What are you doing here? You don't look sick. Are you playing hooky from school?"

"No." Sally pointed behind her. "I'm waiting with my grandmother. It's Teacher Institute so she's taking care of me." She peeked at Sheridan through her lashes. "Not that I need anyone to babysit me, but Dad insists."

"I'm sure your father knows what's best." Errol nodded his head at Sheridan. "And when you get older, you can return the favor like my daughter is doing for me."

"Uh-huh." The girl studied the floor, then lifted her gaze to Sheridan. "Can I ask you something?"

"Sure."

"Well, uh, are you Sheridan Davis? The author?"

"Yes I am." Sheridan smiled at the girl. "Have you read one of my books?"

"Yes, I love them." The girl's face glowed. "I can't wait to read your new one."

"Isn't the subject matter a little old for you?" Most of Sheridan's fans were over twenty.

"At first my mother said I couldn't download them, but when I moved in with Dad, he said it was okay." Sally stopped abruptly.

"Did he read them to make sure the content was appropriate?"

"I doubt it." The girl's voice cracked. "He just doesn't care what I do."

Sheridan remembered all the books her mother hadn't thought she should read but Errol had allowed her to have.

"Did you understand them?" Sheridan asked.

"Most of the stuff, but some of it was a little confusing."

Sheridan had always claimed to have no maternal instinct, but there was something about this girl—maybe it was because she reminded Sheridan of herself—that made her say, "I'll probably be around until the end of the week. If you want you come out to the farm some afternoon, we could talk."

Sally's face lit up. "That'd be great."

Before the girl could add anything, a nurse stepped into the waiting room and announced, "Errol Davis."

Sheridan pushed her father's wheelchair into the examination room, then stepped into the hallway to give Errol some privacy. She'd join them once the doctor was ready to discuss his findings.

While she waited, Sheridan found herself thinking about the past few days, especially her run-in with Ridge. She squirmed. Why couldn't she stop thinking about him?

Yes. His fingers had been warm when he touched her. And she couldn't deny the spark that danced between them. But it was stupid to feel like the same breathless girl of eighteen who had nearly died of excitement when she'd thought Ridge might ask her out. What she needed to remember was the crushing pain when he hadn't.

Ridge had always been attractive, with an inherent strength of character in his face. The touches of humor that had constantly played around his mouth and near his eyes were still there, but there was a new expression, as well. She couldn't put her finger on it, although she saw it in her own mirror often enough. Could it be regret?

CHAPTER FIVE

Monday morning, Ridge found himself holding a receiver in his hand listening to an automated voice repeat, "If you'd like to make a call, please hang up, and try again."

With no clue as to whether he was picking up the phone to make a call or putting it down, having completed a conversation, he sank into his chair and buried his head in his hands. Was he developing early-onset Alzheimer's disease? The only other explanation was that Sheri's presence in town was driving him crazy.

Where had that stupid idea come from? He hit his palm against his forehead. So he'd had a crush on her back in the day. That didn't mean he still had any feelings for her. Puppy love couldn't possibly have lasted thirteen years. That was a hell of a long time to moon over a girl he'd never even kissed.

Ridge hastily returned the receiver to the base, and although he knew he was alone and there were no witnesses to his lapse in focus, he groaned and rubbed his eyes with his fists. His ex may have voluntarily given him custody of their daughter, but Alexis had never been one for consistency.

All he needed was for her to get wind of his odd behavior and add memory loss to the list of transgressions she'd try to use against him at their next court appearance. Who knew that divorce was the gift that kept on giving?

Frustrated, Ridge swept the papers that covered his desktop to the floor, then looked around for another target. His office at the city hall was a far cry from the study at his house. When he'd been elected mayor, he'd sold off the expensive antiques and rare Persian carpets that his father had purchased.

After replacing the furniture with serviceable pieces, he'd returned the remainder of the money to the town budget. A decision his mother still complained about whenever she dropped by to enumerate his lengthy list of faults.

Finding nothing else on which to vent his aggravation, Ridge buzzed his administrative assistant. "Where are those contracts I asked for?"

A cool voice answered from the intercom, "On your desk. Upper right corner."

He looked at the debris surrounding him and grimaced. Forcing an even tone, he responded, "Thanks, Wendy."

After cleaning up the mess he'd made, Ridge checked his watch. Nearly noon. He grabbed his trench coat and told his admin that he was going out. Maybe lunch would clear his mind and he could get some work done this afternoon.

For the first day in a long time, there were no thunderstorms in the forecast, so Ridge walked the couple of blocks to Pinky's Diner. Other than the Rocket Man Drive-In, it was the only place in town to eat, and he made a mental note to look into luring another restaurateur to Sutton Falls.

Taking a breath of the fresh washed air, he was grateful no one was around to ask what he would do if the rain started up again. How he would save the town from flooding. It was a relief to make the short stroll to the café in peace. The constant questions about a situation that he had no control over and few answers for were exhausting.

Nabbing the last free table in the busy restaurant, Ridge settled into the booth and looked over the specials. A few minutes later, when the sleigh bells above the entrance jingled, he automatically glanced toward the door.

Sheri was pushing her father in a wheelchair over the threshold. It was as if his previous thoughts had conjured her up, and his heart kicked into high gear.

While she stood scanning the crowded diner, Ridge studied her from behind the menu. Her hair was coming loose from her bun, and errant curls caressed her cheeks and throat. The silk scarf around her neck was sliding off, and her efforts to get her father inside had stretched her black sweater tightly across her breasts. The V neckline was pulled down, revealing an amount of cleavage that made his throat grow dry.

Before he could reconsider, he was out of his seat and standing in front of her. "Hello, Errol." Ridge forced himself to look at the older man instead of stare at Sheri's décolletage. "I heard you'd hurt yourself. How're you doing?

"Not too good." Errol tapped the arm of his wheelchair. "Doc says I'll be in this contraption for a couple of months, and he wants to run more test to see what made me pass out."

"That's a shame." Ridge patted the older man's shoulder. "But I'm sure the doctor will figure it all out."

"Uh-huh." Errol's nod was noncommittal.

"All the tables are taken." Ridge gestured at the bustling diner. "Why don't you two join me? I'm by myself."

Errol and Sheri both shook their heads, but Errol spoke first, "We can wait—"

"You could," Ridge cut off him off, "but why should you?"

"No thanks. We wouldn't want to impose." She started to wheel her father away. "We'll just eat at home."

It was suddenly important to Ridge that she sit with him. He tugged the handles of Errol's chair from her grasp. "It's no bother. There's some business I want to discuss with your dad. This will save me a trip."

She regarded him silently, clearly suspicious of his motives.

Prepared to turn on the Sutton charm, he opened his mouth. But when his gaze met hers, his heart jolted and the air around them became electrified. Did she feel it? He tried to assess her expression, but it was unreadable.

Clearing his throat, he croaked out a word he didn't usually have to utter to women. "Please."

*　*　*

Watching Ridge help her father onto the booth's bench seat, Sheridan knew she shouldn't have agreed to have lunch with him. So why had she? She didn't want anything to do with Ridge Sutton. Was she trying to show everyone that she was no longer the bullied teenager who had fled her high school tormentors? Did she think the classmates who had mistreated her would see her with Ridge and suddenly like her?

No! Of course, not! In a small town, you were forever who you'd been in high school. Chewing her thumbnail, she wondered why, after all these years, she still cared.

Sitting with Ridge was a mistake. He represented the past. She liked who she was now a whole lot better than who she had been back then. So why, despite her reservations, despite the fact that he was a married man, had she followed him to his table?

Because when he'd looked at her and said please, she'd been unable to resist the sparks flickering between them. His gorgeous green eyes had stared into hers with an intensity that reminded her of being hit in the stomach during a seventh grade volleyball game. Stunned, winded, and like she might throw up.

Sheridan jumped when Ridge put his hand on her elbow. Even through the material of her sweater, his touch set off a flare of warmth inside her chest that spread through her stomach as if she'd gulped down a shot of single malt whiskey. Meeting his gaze, she could tell he felt something, too. His pupils were dilated, his lips slightly parted, and his breathing uneven.

"Have a seat." He spoke into her ear, sending a shudder down her spine. "It looks as if Errol is ready to order."

Sheridan freed her arm from Ridge's grasp and moved to

the table. She tried to join her father, but Ridge guided her to the opposite bench.

"I think Errol would be more comfortable with the seat to himself," Ridge said smoothly as he slid in next to her, blocking her escape.

Sheridan closed her eyes. Would she be able to get through this lunch without making a fool of herself? She was already hyperalert to Ridge's presence. The inches that separated their thighs sizzled with heat, and he kept scooting closer.

If she was this turned on by someone who had hurt her so badly in the past, it had obviously been too long since she'd had sex with any guy besides Mr. Vibrator. Battery Operated Boyfriend only scratched a part of the itch. Once she got back to St. Louis, she needed to start seeing someone other than B.O.B.

The waitress appeared before Sheridan could study the menu, and when she automatically asked for a salad and iced tea, both her father and Ridge rolled their eyes.

After their orders had been taken and the server had poured coffee for Errol, Ridge asked, "Why do all women eat like rabbits?"

"Perhaps because most men demand that women go through life thirty pounds underweight," Sheridan said more loudly than she'd intended. Moderating her volume, she added, "You all expect us to look like a *Playboy* centerfold, while most of you could barely make the pages of *Mad Magazine*."

"That's quite an attitude problem," Ridge drawled.

"No." Sheridan turned slightly to put some distance between them, then, mostly to annoy him, said, "It's a male perception problem."

This was better. As long as she could keep up the persona she donned when promoting her books, she could fight her attraction. Although she believed every single word she wrote, in real life, she was nowhere near as snarky or critical as she was when she played the part of Sheridan Davis, feminist author. Still, she sustained that role for hours at appearances. Surely the thirty minutes or so it would take them to eat lunch would be a snap.

Maintaining a haughty expression she certainly didn't feel, Sheridan stared at Ridge. She was surprised and a bit nonplussed that he didn't appear the least taken aback by her pronouncement. Most men would be either cowering or fuming by now.

Instead, Ridge seemed truly interested when he asked, "Then why did you order a salad?"

There was no way she would admit the real reason—that his presence muddled her so much she couldn't even figure out what she wanted to eat—so she said, "Because I felt like it."

As she spoke, she tucked in the tendrils that had escaped their hairpins and adjusted her sweater. Feeling more in control, she sat with her spine straight and looked down her nose at Ridge. The transformation from Sheri back to Sheridan was complete.

Ridge narrowed his eyes, clearly understanding her message.

Sheridan hid her triumphant smile, then noticed that their table had become the center of attention. Every diner was avidly watching them.

Ridge followed her gaze and his lips momentarily thinned. A nanosecond later, he pasted an affable expression on his face and waved at a table of older women wearing bright red hats.

Putting his mouth next to Sheridan's ear, he whispered, "Welcome back to Sutton Falls, where you can kiss your privacy good-bye."

"Another thing I *didn't* miss while I was gone," Sheridan muttered, fighting her desire for another kind of kiss from him.

Ridge nodded in agreement, then turned his attention to

Sheridan's father. "Errol, have you given any more thought to selling Sutton Falls the part of your land that contains the levee?"

Sheridan shot a quick glance at her father. This was the first she had heard of him disposing of a huge piece of their property.

"Some." Errol took a sip of his coffee. "I'm not getting any younger, and Mick has enough of his own land to tend. Not to mention, his fields are way the heck on the other side of the county from that parcel, so it's a real pain for him to move the machinery back and forth between the two places."

"Errol, why haven't you ever said anything to me about this?" Sheridan's voice was thick with disbelief.

She never wanted to live on the farm, but the land had meant so much to her mother. And by rights, since Vivian had left her a thirty percent interest in the property, Errol couldn't sell it without Sheridan's signature.

Not that she'd ever claimed any of the income. Even when she'd been struggling to get published and needed the money, she'd returned the checks her dad had sent to her.

"I didn't think you'd care." Errol didn't look up from his cup.

"I didn't think I would, either," she admitted, surprised by her reaction. "But it's the last tie I have with Mom."

It was probably the guilt talking. She still felt responsible for not having a closer relationship with her mother. She had always hung out with her dad, escaping Vivian's attempt to make Sheridan the pretty, popular daughter she desired.

Ridge's expression was thoughtful. "Sentiment aside, what would you do with the farm, Sheri?"

"Sheridan. I prefer to be called Sheridan now." She frowned at Ridge. "I don't know, but I sure want a chance to think about it before you get your hands on our land. Why do you want it, anyway?"

"Not me personally. The town needs it for flood control. You probably didn't know that I'm the mayor."

"What a surprise." Her tone was sarcastic. "The mayor is almost always a Sutton. And if the river floods, the Suttons have more to lose than anyone else around here does. Don't try and pretend this is only to save the town."

"I'm not saying my family doesn't have a lot at stake."

"I bet you want to buy our land for pennies, then the next thing we know, there's a house on every acre."

"I would never do that. I love Sutton Falls." Ridge scowled at her. "Which is more than I can say for you. How long has it been since you set foot in this town?"

She glared at him. "How are my visits home any of your business?" Her voice was taut. "I doubt you even noticed I wasn't around. Heck, you barely recognized me a couple of days ago."

"It's been thirteen years and you've changed a lot." Ridge's usually assured voice held a note of uncertainty. "Tell the truth. Did you know me right away?"

Sheridan was silent, not wanting to admit that she would recognize him at midnight during a lunar eclipse.

"You didn't, did you?" Ridge crossed his arms. "Maybe if you'd have come to the ten-year reunion—"

"I'm sure you and Alexis were too busy reigning over the festivities to spare a thought about your less popular classmates."

"What are you talking about?" His expression was puzzled. "Alexis and I—"

"Forget it." Without waiting for him to make his excuses, Sheridan pushed on him and demanded, "Let me out."

He stood and she slid across the bench. Making her escape, she rushed into the ladies' room and locked the door. Barely stopping herself from kicking over the trash can, she gave a muffled scream. The diner was too small to allow herself the luxury of really letting go.

Ridge acting as if he'd cared, whether or not she ever came back to town was contemptible. But then pretending had always worked for him before.

He'd pretended he wasn't aware of the cruel pranks his girlfriend had played on Sheridan—and anyone else she thought was weak enough for her to get away with tormenting. He'd pretended to like Sheridan when he'd needed her to help him get an A in English. And now that he wanted her family farm, he was pretending to have noticed her absence.

This time, she wasn't falling for it. Sure, the electricity that had always zinged between them was still there, but that was only lust. It definitely didn't indicate she had any kind of genuine feelings for him.

She sat on the closed toilet seat for a long time, waiting for the anger and the hurt to recede. Her emotions had been more out of control in the last five days than in the last thirteen years.

It was time to get off of the Tilt-A-Whirl and reclaim her serenity and self-confidence. She couldn't allow Ridge Sutton to tear down her defenses and let out all the feelings she'd worked so hard to repress and forget.

Taking a deep breath, she went to the sink, splashed her face with cold water, and smoothed her hair. She squared her shoulders and made sure her expression was serene, then emerged from the restroom. Relief washed over her when she spotted her father sitting by the door in his wheelchair with her purse and a to-go bag on his lap.

Glancing nervously from side to side, Sheridan walked swiftly over to Errol. If she was quick, maybe she could get out of the restaurant without having to have another strained conversation with Ridge.

"Ready to go?" She asked her father, proud of how detached her voice sounded.

"All set. Sorry about—"

"Let's talk about that after we get home. Okay?"

Errol nodded and she pushed him out the door and helped him into the car.

As she steered the old station wagon down the asphalt, she clutched the wheel so fiercely her fingers ached. Was her tightly controlled world starting to fall apart?

CHAPTER SIX

Much like the past thirteen years, Sheridan and her father maintained a strained silence while they drove out of town. She needed time to gather her thoughts so that she could present a calm and reasonable case rather than an emotional plea.

Finally, as they neared their house, she said, "I don't want you to sell the farm. It should remain in the family for the next generation. Perhaps one of my cousins' kids will become a farmer."

Her mother's only sibling, a brother, had taken a job in California. But that didn't mean his children or his grandchildren might not want to come back and claim the family land. Granted, it was highly unlikely, but anything was possible.

"I know you think your mom wouldn't want me to sell, but she isn't here."

"Surprisingly"—Sheridan didn't bother to keep the sarcasm from her voice—"I hadn't forgotten that little fact or what happened after she passed away."

In early March of Sheridan's senior year in high school, Vivian had been diagnosed with congestive heart failure, and by the middle of June, she'd been dead. The morning of her mother's funeral, Sheridan had received a letter telling her that her father was having an affair.

Enclosed had been a picture showing his reflection in a mirror alongside a naked woman. The woman's head had been turned away from the camera, and Errol had torn up the photo and refused to identify her. He'd also refused to talk about the letter.

To Sheridan, it had seemed as if she'd lost both parents that day. Now, with her father thinking of selling the land, it was as if her sense of home was also being stolen away, too. No matter that she would most likely never live there again, the family farm would always be what she considered her homeplace.

"You never believed me when I told you, it was just a sitting for a portrait. That whoever wrote that letter was lying." Errol touched her arm. "I thought maybe now that you're older, more mature, you'd realize that just because someone says something, it isn't necessarily the truth."

"I begged you to tell me who the woman was, and if she was just modeling for a painting, why I had never seen the canvas, but you refused to explain. You insisted that I trust you. You never gave me one good reason that someone would accuse you of an affair if you were innocent." She shook off his hand. "Tell me now, who and why, and let's get this behind us."

"You didn't see the canvas because she insisted the work be done at her house." Errol held out his hands. "When I was commissioned to do the portrait, I agreed to never reveal her identity. She made me sign a confidentiality agreement."

"How convenient." Sheridan pulled into their driveway.

For months after receiving that photo, Sheridan had prayed that Errol would tell her something that would allow her to forgive him. He never had. Instead, he'd asked her to have faith in him. But by that point, with everything that had happened to her—her mom dying, her classmates turning on her, and proof of her father's infidelity—she was fresh out of trust for anyone.

"Honey, do we have to do this again?" Errol rubbed his temples.

"Just give me one good reason why someone would accuse you of cheating," Sheridan repeated, ignoring his obvious desire to end the conversation. "It's not as if you were rich and could pay blackmail."

"I have my suspicions, but I truly don't know," Errol

sighed. "I'm not even completely sure who sent the letter and photo. But I can tell you I was not having an affair."

"Name the woman and I'll let it go at that." Sheridan's head felt like it was going to explode. They'd had variations of this conversation for the past dozen years, and Errol always refused to answer her questions. "Surely you can see that a confidentiality agreement only matters if I was going to make the information public, and I'm not."

"I can't." Errol grimaced. "I gave my word, and a gentleman doesn't go back on a promise."

"What is more important, being a gentleman or being a father?" Sheridan's voice cracked, and she swallowed back the tears that always threatened when she thought about her dad's betrayal.

"That's not a fair question." Errol's handsome face twisted in anguish.

"Then how about this one? Who is more important to you, the woman in that picture or me?"

"You, of course, but..." Errol trailed off, then scrubbed his eyes with the heels of his hands. "Look, let me contact her and see if she'll release me from my word."

"Fine." Sheridan got out of the car, fetched the wheelchair from the back, and helped her father into it.

"I'm sorry, sweetheart, but it's the best I can do." Errol was quiet for the few minutes it took for them to get into the house, then, out of nowhere, said, "The town's isn't the only offer we've had for the land."

"Who else wants it?" Sheridan was happy to let Errol change the subject.

Until he could tell her who the woman was and why someone would falsely accuse him of adultery, there was nothing more to discuss. She unpacked the to-go bag from the diner, heated her father's meatloaf and mashed potatoes in the microwave, and helped him onto a kitchen chair.

"It's an anonymous bid through a broker." Errol took a bite of his food, swallowed, and added, "The money was good."

"You do recall that I would have to sign off on any deal?"

"Of course, but since I wasn't interested and refused the offer, there was no need to discuss it with you."

"Oh." Sheridan's tone was grudging.

"Although, with the recent spate of vandalism and my fall, maybe we should talk about what's going to happen if I can't farm anymore." Errol wiped his mouth with a paper napkin. "The insurance isn't covering the whole cost of repairs, and we've had to make so many claims our premiums will be sky-high. You know at the best of times, we barely make a living from the crops, and these haven't been the best of times."

"Won't Mick take over if you feel you aren't able to do the work?" Sheridan's stomach clenched. Errol *was* getting older. She closed her eyes. She couldn't bear the idea of giving up her mother's land or the thought of her father changing from the vital man she remembered to someone too weak to continue working. Retirement was one thing. Declining health was another matter entirely.

"It depends." Errol shrugged. "Maybe when the twins finish college, *if* they decide to farm, Mick may want to buy our land."

"That might be the solution." Sheridan brightened. "Mick is just Mom's nephew by marriage, but at least he's still family."

"His boys won't graduate for three more years," Errol said. "Right now, the only reason I would ever consider selling the property would be to save people's homes from flooding. I figured you'd go along with that."

"I have to think about it." Sheridan glanced at her father through her lashes.

Giving up the land for the greater good sounded so much like the man she'd admired when she was growing up that she blinked back a tear. Which was the real Errol? The betrayer or the hero?

After they finished their lunch, Errol said that the outing had exhausted him. He planned to nap and watch the Weather Channel until supper.

Sheridan helped her father into bed, then phoned her agent. Grace was not happy that she was still in Sutton Falls, but Sheridan appeased her with a promise to be on a plane to New York by Sunday afternoon at the latest.

Hanging up from the conversation with her agent, Sheridan was too agitated to write. Instead, she wandered from room to room trying to distract herself from her thoughts. The house was small—two bedrooms, a tiny den, a living room, and a big kitchen—but it had been just the right size for Sheridan and her parents to share.

She paused at the door of the den, remembering that when she was six, she'd wanted to fix up this room as a bedroom for a brother or sister. Her mother had explained that she wasn't able to have any more children.

Being an only child had put all her parents' dreams onto her shoulders. Vivian had wanted Sheridan to marry one of the heirs to the land adjoining their acreage. Errol had hoped that she would go to New York and become the famous artist he'd always wanted to be.

Both of her parents had chosen to ignore Sheridan's own ambitions. While she wanted to eventually get married and have a family, the role of farm wife didn't appeal to her. And although she was a reasonably talented painter, her true passion had always been writing.

In the living room, Sheridan sat in her mom's rocker and put her feet on the embroidered footstool. The wood shone from years of loving care. Her mother had sat in this chair every afternoon, her needle flashing as she worked her latest cross-stitch project.

It was here that Sheridan and Vivian had discussed life, love, and clothes. Not that they'd ever agreed much on any of those three topics.

Why had she argued so vehemently with her mother? Why hadn't she tried a little harder to make her mother happy? Would it have been so bad to wear the pretty outfits her mom had bought for her?

Sheridan pushed down the lump of regret wedged in her throat and stiffened. Was she doing the same thing with her father? Maybe she should let the matter of his infidelity go and forgive him for whatever had happened in his past.

No! That was an entirely different situation than what had happened with her mom. With Vivian, it was a matter of compromising her individuality, not overlooking a man cheating on his dying wife.

Sheridan checked her watch. It was only three thirty. She closed her eyes. Maybe sleep would make the time pass more quickly.

Half an hour later, her nap was interrupted by her cousin Merry's cheerful shout from the kitchen, "Yoo-hoo, anyone home?"

Few people in Sutton Falls locked their doors, and it was common for family and close friends to walk in without knocking or ringing the bell. Usually a verbal announcement was the only warning of impending visitors.

"I'm in the living room," Sheridan yelled.

Beyond being cousins, Merry had been one of Sheridan's few friends in high school. They were the same age and had been classmates. They still talked on the phone several times a week.

Merry rushed into the room and, hugging Sheridan, said, "Long time no see, cuz. We've missed you."

"Hey, we were together over Christmas break." Sheridan

shook her head in mock dismay. "Did you already forget spending a week with me in St. Louis?"

Merry ran her fingers through her curls. Her short hair formed tight spirals that sprang from her head like silky black ribbons. "How could I forget? You had us on such a tight schedule we never had time to just sit around and gab. Now that you're back in Sutton Falls, that shouldn't be a problem. Nearest we get to a social whirlwind is Independence Day weekend, and that's not for a few more months."

"Well, I certainly won't be here in July." Sheridan shuddered at the thought. "I need to be out of here by Sunday, so if you want to visit, how about now over some hot tea?"

"Great." Merry headed toward the kitchen. "I'll get the kettle. For some reason, our dad stores it in the oven."

Frowning, Sheridan followed Merry. Her cousin's words had invoked a tiny stab of regret. It shouldn't have bothered her that Merry was more at home in Errol's house than she was, but somehow it did.

Sheridan placed some store-bought cookies on a plate, then took a seat on a stool at the counter that divided the kitchen from the dinette.

Once they were settled with steaming cups, Merry asked, "How's Uncle Errol?"

"Other than his broken wrist and ankle, he seems fine." Sheridan took a sip of her Earl Grey. "The doctor ordered more tests, but we have to wait for the hospital to call and schedule them."

"Did Doc have any guesses as to why your dad fainted?"

"He said it could be anything from low blood sugar to something with his heart."

"I'm sure it's nothing serious." Merry patted Sheridan's hand.

"I hope so." Sheridan bit her lip, then changed the subject.

"So, how's sixth grade English this year?" Merry taught in the local junior high.

"Not bad. Although we do get a few difficult ones, most of the kids from around here are good. But there are always the families who move to Sutton Falls from the city thinking they'll escape the problems their children are having at those schools."

"Doesn't work, I'll bet." Sheridan bit into a gingersnap. It wasn't as good as her aunt Flora's, but it would have to do. Sheridan certainly wasn't learning how to bake.

"No, and then the parents are ticked off at us for not magically fixing everything."

"Teaching sounds way too hard for me." Sheridan pulled a face. "I'll have to remember this conversation the next time I get writer's block."

"Actually"— Merry leaned toward Sheridan, her eyes twinkling—"that's one of the things I wanted to talk to you about."

"Oh?" Sheridan could smell a trap.

"I talked to my principal, and she thought it was a good idea."

"And this good idea is what?" Sheridan scooted her stool away from the counter, prepared to make a run for it.

"To have you come and speak to my classes about being a writer."

Sheridan froze. The thought of facing a roomful of twelve- and thirteen-year-olds scared her to death. She had little experience with children.

"Uh…my books are aimed at adults and are pretty controversial. I don't think most of your students would understand them." Sheridan knew she was rambling but couldn't stop. "I'm sure a lot of parents wouldn't approve of the subject matter. Sutton Falls is still fairly patriarchal. Isn't it?"

"That's why I talked to my principal and cleared it with her before I came out here." Merry's expression was earnest. "Her only restriction is that you talk about writing, not about content."

"Well, I'm going to be busy with Errol." Sheridan thought of excuses as fast as she could. "And I have to leave for New York as soon as I hire someone to take care of him. Maybe next time I come home for a couple of days."

"When will that be?" Merry snorted, choking on her tea. "The next millennium? I could be retired by then. This is the first time I can remember that you've stayed in town for more than a few hours."

"Very funny." Sheridan narrowed her eyes. "You know why I don't visit very often."

"Actually, we've never talked about it." Suddenly serious, Merry patted Sheridan's hand. "At first, I thought it was because home reminded you of your mother and brought back the grief of her passing."

"That's a part of it." Sheridan chose her words carefully, trying not to allow the hurt to seep into her voice. She didn't want to reveal her father's duplicity to his niece. The family knew Errol was a flirt and a ladies' man, but she was fairly certain they were unaware that he had stepped out on his wife. "But since Errol and I aren't as close anymore, it seems hypocritical to play the doting daughter."

"Hmmm." Merry's tone was quizzical. "That's so weird. You were his shadow when we were growing up, and he's so proud of you now."

Sheridan ignored her cousin's implied question and continued, "But mostly I don't spend much time here because I just never felt a part of Sutton Falls. I always seemed to be on the outside looking in. I never felt accepted anywhere until college, when I joined my sorority."

She remembered seeing the Alpha Sigma Alpha creed posted on a bulletin board. The line, to find a dominant beauty in art, literature, nature, and friendship, had struck a chord deep inside of her.

Then when she'd gone through rush and one of the older sisters had assured her that ASA was a sisterhood that didn't require conformity, Sheridan had known she had found a place she could be herself and still have friends. The indescribable loneliness that had weighed her down for years had disappeared as she'd experienced the joy of true friendship.

Even now, when she traveled on book tours, there were sisters in every city who came to her events. And the sorority had taught her how to break the ice, to be the first to say hello, to open herself up and reach out. All skills she'd been sorely lacking in high school.

Sheridan came back to the present when Merry leaned over, hugged her, and said, "I'm glad you found that sisterhood. I wish I could meet Darcy, Delaney, and Lucy. You talk about them so often that I feel like I already know them."

"Maybe I can set up a Skype session next time you visit me in St. Louis." Sheridan returned the hug, then said, "You know, you were my only real friend here, especially after Alexis started targeting me our senior year. I never did understand what I had done to bring down her wrath."

"I wasn't your only friend, just the only one you couldn't push away." Merry tilted her head. "But you're right. Alexis did play some cruel tricks on you."

"You think?" Sheridan winced. "That one with the wanted poster with *NOBODY WANTS HER* written across my picture was truly heinous."

"Yes, it was. And she was lucky you didn't pull a Carrie on her after what she did to you at the prom."

"True," Sheridan muttered, then clamped her lips shut as a frisson of remembered fear shot up her spine.

Merry only knew a small part of what had happened that

night. And Sheridan didn't intend to enlighten her, or anyone else, about Alexis's pièce de résistance.

"Still, I don't think it was personal. She was sort of mean to everyone who wasn't a part of her inner circle." Merry filtered the truth through a kinder lens than Sheridan's memory allowed. "She was just insecure."

"What did she have to be insecure about?" Sheridan made an all-encompassing gesture. "She had money, was beautiful, popular, and dating the hottest guy in our class."

"She never felt rich enough or pretty enough or popular enough." Merry spoke with an unsettling conviction. "And most of all, she was never sure of Ridge, especially after he broke up with her that time."

"They were broken up for all of five minutes." Sheridan scoffed, keeping her expression scornful rather than allowing Merry to see her hurt.

Back then, Sheridan had been so glad when she'd heard that Alexis was no longer wearing Ridge's class ring. She had even dared to hope that Ridge would ask her out. But before their next tutoring session, Alexis had had his ring back on her finger and a smug look on her face.

It was then that Sheridan had learned not to allow herself to wish for things she couldn't have. The devastating pain of the inevitable disappointment was too high a price to pay for that all-too-brief moment of hope.

Shaking off her regret, Sheridan added, "And they ended up married, so it turns out Alexis didn't have to worry about him after all."

"They've been divorced for six years or so." Merry wrinkled her brow. "Didn't you hear?"

"No." Sheridan fought the urge to grin. She didn't care that Ridge was no longer married, so there was no cause to smile. "The only reason I knew about their wedding was I saw it in the paper."

"Didn't you see the divorce notice?"

"No." Sheridan shook her head slowly. "When I left for college, Errol arranged for me to receive the local newspaper, but after I told him I wasn't interested in anything going on in Sutton Falls, he cancelled the subscription."

"I'm surprised your dad never mentioned it."

"Even though Errol loves a good gossip, it's not something he would bring up in our monthly phone calls." Sheridan shrugged. "And you're the only one I talk to from our class."

"I guess because you never seemed to want to hear about anybody around here, I stopped telling you things." Merry bit her lip. "You always acted like you didn't care what anyone in town did."

"Which was true."

Sheridan was beginning to realize that she had allowed her own feelings of inadequacy, her anger at her father, and her guilt about her mother to rob her of not only her faith in men but also of her roots. She was starting to believe it might be time to take it all back.

"Was?" Merry pounced.

"Maybe I was wrong to run away from my past."

"Really?" Merry asked. "You're ready to put it all behind you and move on?""

"I'll think about it."

"Good, then I'll expect you at my room Thursday at eight fifteen for my first-hour class. They're my accelerated group, and I think they'd get the most out of your experiences."

"Wait, I didn't say I'd do this." Sheridan trailed Merry into the utility room and watched her cousin put on her shoes and jacket.

"Yeah, but you will." Merry stepped outside, yelling good-bye over her shoulder.

The slamming of the door sounded like a clap of doom, and Sheridan shivered. The idea of talking to a bunch of kids scared her more than diving into a piranha tank wearing a bathing suit made out of hamburger. But it was the thought of facing her past that really terrified her. What was it about the pain suffered in high school that lasted a lifetime?

CHAPTER SEVEN

After the scene at the diner, Ridge couldn't face returning to his office. He was restless and irritable. Suddenly his tie was choking him, and his suit felt a size too small. He needed a break from being mayor, from running the family business, from being a Sutton.

Avoiding the city hall entrance, he walked around back to the parking lot, got into his car, and drove home. Inside his unwelcoming empty house, he changed into jeans and stomped into his garage. Maybe a ride in the '95 Cobra Mustang that he was restoring would take the edge off of his restlessness.

Throwing himself into the driver's seat, he turned the key, and the Ford's powerful motor roared to life. Pointing the sports car toward the country, he told himself it was time to inspect the levees and see how high the river had risen. In reality, Sheri's outburst had unsettled him, and he needed to calm down before tackling the mountain of paperwork waiting for him on his desk.

All the rain had eroded the gravel roads, and they were like washboards. At first, Ridge had to concentrate on his driving, but once he fell into the rhythm of steering around the ruts, his thoughts went back to lunch. What the hell had happened?

He ran through the incident in his mind. *Okay.* He had practically forced Sheri to sit with him. Could that be why she'd gotten so mad? He knew she prided herself on her independence. Had he crossed the line?

No. That wasn't it. Her face had crumpled when he'd asked Errol about selling the land. But why would she care? She hadn't lived in Sutton Falls for years.

Damn it! She barely visited the area. If she was so emotionally attached to her family farm, why didn't she spend any time there?

After she'd marched off to the ladies' room, Errol had said something about Sheri never forgiving the town for the incident at the prom. *Shit!* That was nearly thirteen years ago. He never would have guessed she'd hold a grudge that long.

What in the hell had happened? With her mother's death and Sheri out of school for the remainder of the year, Ridge hadn't been able to talk to her. Then when he'd finally gotten up his courage and gone to see Sheri, he'd discovered that she had left for college nearly two weeks ahead of schedule. He'd asked Errol about that night, but Sheri's father had refused to discuss the matter.

The last thing Ridge could remember was going to Beau's house for a pre-prom party. The next thing he knew, he'd woken up beside Alexis in the Quincy Holiday Inn. Maybe he should ask someone what had gone on with Sheri. But who would still remember?

Then again, it might be best to leave the past in the past. It wasn't his problem. If Sheri wanted to be left alone, more power to her. In a few days, she'd lose interest in her family's land, go back to the city, and Sutton Falls would be back to normal.

Why did his chest ache at the thought of Sheri leaving again? He'd already had one disastrous entanglement with a selfish woman. Surely he wasn't fool enough to get involved with another one.

He put on his signal and turned at the next corner. Only after he'd gone several miles did he notice he was on the road that passed the Davis property. The annoyance he already felt with himself intensified.

Great! If Sheri caught sight of him, she'd probably accuse him of stalking her.

* * *

Ridge's head was pounding. The Tuesday afternoon city council meeting was not going at all well. The hostile stares and restless movements of the townsfolk had thrown off the council members' usual rhythm. They'd been discussing the Laundromat's request to increase its parking lot for two hours. Ordinarily, the matter would have been settled in a couple of minutes.

One more comment from Mrs. Bunson about maintaining Sutton Falls's green space and Ridge would go crazy. This wasn't exactly New York City. The whole area around the town was fields. How much greener could they get?

Pounding his gavel on the table, Ridge said, "Do I hear a motion to approve the expansion of the Wash n' Go's parking area?"

Mick McIntyre immediately said, "I so move."

Once the motion was seconded and passed, Ridge asked, "Is there any new business?"

"Yeah." A large man wearing overalls, a long-sleeved T-shirt, and a John Deere cap stood. "What are you all doing about the flood warnings?"

"We're in close touch with U.S. Army Corps of Engineers," Ridge answered. "They assure me that if there are no more heavy rains, Sutton Falls will be okay. As it presently stands, the system of locks and reservoirs, floodgates and levees, backwaters and cutouts, and pump stations and dikes are handling the excess water."

"How about if we get another storm?" a woman dressed in jeans and a sweatshirt asked. "Is there a plan in place if that happens?"

"We're looking into possible solutions should that occur." Ridge's pulse accelerated, but he kept his voice smooth.

He glanced at the council members. They all stared down at

their notepads. No one else appeared anxious to join the discussion.

The owner of the town funeral home rose. "How about blasting the levee?"

"That would be our last resort." Ridge resisted the urge to tug at his collar. "We can't sacrifice the hundreds of acres of farmland and fifty homes southeast of here until we know for certain there's no other choice."

No matter what he did or when he did it, he couldn't win. Breach the levee before they were absolutely positive it was needed and people would call him reckless. Wait until flooding was a sure thing and those same folks would brand him as indecisive.

"If it's that or losing most of the town, I don't see as there's much of a contest." The mortician remained standing.

"If that becomes the case, I agree," Ridge said slowly. "However, we don't own the levee. It's on private property."

"Eminent domain!"

Ridge wasn't sure who had started the shouting, but the rest of the audience soon took up the chant, adding, "Seize the levee."

Pounding his gavel until they were quiet, Ridge waited a beat, then said, "The eminent domain process isn't something that takes place overnight. Our best hope is to negotiate with the owner."

"And?"

"And I am doing so." Ridge injected confidence he didn't possess into his tone.

He thought of how he'd left things with Errol Davis after Sheri had left the table in the diner. Up until her return, he'd been certain that if flooding appeared imminent, Errol would sell the city the acreage containing the levee. Now he wasn't so sure. Sheri had seemed to value the property more than he'd expected.

Was it sentimentality or something else?

"Your father would already have that land secured." Mrs. Bunson shot Ridge a disapproving look. "You need to get tougher with Errol Davis."

Ridge ignored the older woman and asked, "Any other new business?" Before anyone could answer, he said, "Do I hear a motion to adjourn?"

Mick quickly made the motion, another council member seconded it, and after a six to one vote—Mrs. Bunson never cast her ballot with the majority—Ridge brought his gavel down and declared, "Meeting adjourned."

Of course, it wasn't that easy. Ridge was instantly surrounded by a flock of concerned citizens, and it took him another twenty minutes to escape.

After everyone had voiced their opinion, he hurried up the stairs toward his office. He needed a few minutes of peace before heading over to the car dealership or the gas station or one of the other Sutton businesses to solve the crisis du jour. Unfortunately, his administrative assistant nabbed him at the top of the steps before he made it into his inner sanctum.

Wendy Gibson was sure that Ridge's time was too valuable to waste moving from one location to another and insisted that he multitask as he walked down the long hallway. Trailing him, she ticked off items on her list as she brought him up-to-date on what he'd missed during the three-plus hours that he'd been held hostage at the Sutton Falls City Council meeting.

As they passed the U.S. and Missouri flags, she said, "At 1:05, Sutton Hardware's smoke detector was triggered, and the store had to be evacuated. The fire department responded but found no reason for the alarm."

"Uh-huh." Ridge scowled.

What was going on with the family companies? Did somebody have it in for them? It seemed as if lately one or more of the businesses had an incident every day. It was almost as if someone wanted to keep him busy. Too busy to spend time with his daughter. He shook his head. Now he was just being paranoid.

Ridge glanced at the portraits of the town's previous mayors that lined the hallway. His father's picture appeared to glare at him as he passed by it. Was the sneer on his old man's face even more contemptuous than usual?

"At 2:17, you texted me that the city council meeting was running long, so I rescheduled your appointment with the civil engineer for first thing tomorrow," Wendy reported.

She insisted on relaying his messages chronologically, rather than in order of importance, and except for that quirk, she was such a good assistant he gritted his teeth and allowed her to have her way.

"Good." Ridge nodded. "Thanks."

He paused and stared at the framed map of Sutton Falls that hung next to his office suite's door. It detailed the town and surrounding areas. He reached out a finger and traced the acreage that would be lost if they had to open up the levee.

"The police chief would like to have a word with you at your earliest convenience," Wendy continued to read from her notepad.

"Have him come in after the engineer." Ridge stepped into the reception area and made a beeline to the Keurig. "Did he say what he wanted?"

"No." Wendy shook her head, but her heavily lacquered bouffant didn't move. "Probably a budget increase. He's been getting a lot of those forensic equipment brochures in the mail again."

Ridge didn't ask how Wendy knew about the catalogues. Her husband was the postmaster. An unfortunate profession for the worst gossip in town.

"He knows we don't have the money or the criminal activity for our own crime scene investigations." Ridge looked at his admin. "Anything else?"

"The contracts for the city workers came from the attorney's office." Wendy went behind her desk and sat down. "Mr. Bunson would like them back by Thursday afternoon at the latest."

"Got it." Ridge pushed the button and waited for the French roast to fill his mug.

"The manager at Sutton Lumber called to inform you that someone sawed a hole in the hardwood's storage shed and several thousand dollars' worth of teak and oak flooring is ruined." Wendy crossed out an item on her legal pad. "You need to contact the insurance agent about the loss and make a police report."

"Great." Ridge grabbed his cup and took a sip, burning his tongue on the hot coffee. "Can you get started on those calls now?"

At times like this, he was almost sorry that he'd arranged to provide fifty percent of Wendy's salary and pay as part of the workplace expenses so that he could run the Sutton companies from one location. Evelyn had thought he was crazy to shell out money for something his father and grandfather had considered a perk of being mayor, but Ridge hadn't wanted the citizens of Sutton Falls to feel cheated. And although the arrangement was more convenient and efficient than maintaining a second office, a little separation of private business and government problems might be nice.

As he started to walk into his office, Wendy said, "And at 3:39, Sally's homeroom teacher, Mrs. Warner, called." Wendy leaned forward waving a slip of paper at him. "This is her cell phone number. She'd like to see you this afternoon."

"I guess it's too late now." Ridge tried to keep the relief out of his voice.

"She said she'd be available until five." Wendy turned back to her keyboard.

"Thanks." Ridge stepped into his office. What had Sally done this time?

* * *

Mrs. Warner sat at her desk, the words *Math is real life* in bright yellow letters on the wall behind her, and said, "Sarah Ann stormed out of Mr. Nolan's social studies class today."

"Is she okay?" Fear blew its cold breath on the back of Ridge's neck. Surely, Evelyn would have called if Sally hadn't come home after school.

"She's fine." Mrs. Warner's lips twitched. "She marched down to the principal's office to complain that Mr. Nolan was a sexist pig."

"He does tend to have a misogynistic attitude," Ridge said mildly. He'd had Mr. Nolan for sixth grade social studies, too. "What happened?"

"Ms. Boutte listened to your daughter's complaint and agreed to speak to Mr. Nolan about his disparaging remarks regarding women in politics." Mrs. Warner grinned. "Sarah Ann's punishment for leaving the room without permission is to write an essay on the Democratic presidential candidate and her past career in government."

"That sounds fair." Ridge relaxed. "Ms. Boutte seems to have handled the situation with her usual finesse and diplomacy."

"Yes. She did." Mrs. Warner nodded, then said, "But Sarah Ann's teachers are concerned that we aren't getting to the root of her problems. She's having difficulty adjusting to this school. It's been several months, and we haven't seen much progress in her attitude or behavior."

"Not quite three." Ridge squirmed in his seat, the attached desk cutting into his side. "And the private school that her mother had her in was a lot different than Sutton Falls Middle School."

"So Sarah Ann tells us." Mrs. Warner rubbed her temples. "Over and over again."

"She prefers to be called Sally." Ridge struggled to find a comfortable sitting position. "The abrupt change of custody has been hard on her."

"I'm sure it has." Mrs. Warner steepled her fingers and rested her chin on them. "And I understand you hadn't been an active part of Sally's life since your divorce, which means your everyday presence is new to her as well."

"That wasn't my choice." Ridge felt his ears redden. "Her mother moved her out of state. I had to fight to see her twice a month."

"I'm not judging you." Mrs. Warner leaned forward. "And despite how it may appear, I'm only trying to help Sarah Ann be more successful in her new circumstances." The teacher raised her palms. "For instance, if she prefers Sally, she needs to tell us. When Mrs. Sutton registered her, in the space for nickname, she wrote *none*, so we've assumed that your daughter didn't have one."

"Sarah Ann is my maternal grandmother's name, so my mother is unhappy that Sally doesn't use it." Ridge slumped. "I know the school's intentions are good, and I agree she needs to let you know how she feels. Sally's been extremely uncommunicative with me, too, and I'm not sure what to do about it."

"Unfortunately, we don't have a full-time school psychologist or social worker." Mrs. Warner shrugged. "We're part of a special education cooperative, so the only counseling available is for children who have IEPs or 504 plans."

"Would Sally be eligible for those services?" Ridge winced. His mother's reaction to a Sutton having a special education label would be ugly. But if Sally needed help, he'd do the right thing despite his mother's fury.

"No." Mrs. Warner sighed. "You could refer her, but her issues seem more situational than a true disability, so she probably wouldn't qualify. You might want to consider private counseling. Someone who specializes in children of divorce."

"I'm guessing there isn't anyone local." Ridge tapped the molded plastic armrest.

"Regrettably, the closest therapist is in Mt. Morrison." Mrs. Warner stood, walked around her desk, and handed him a business card. "Here's someone you could contact there."

"Thanks." Ridge got to his feet, shook the teacher's hand, and headed toward the door.

"Mr. Sutton." Mrs. Warner's voice rang across the classroom.

"Yes?" He turned, half tempted to pretend he didn't hear the teacher's summons.

"In the meantime"—Mrs. Warner smiled—"if you could encourage Sally to attend some extracurricular activities, she might make a friend or two, which could turn out to be all she needs."

* * *

After his conference with Mrs. Warner, Ridge went straight home. When he entered Sally's room and tried to discuss her problems at school, she answered him in monosyllables. Finally, he gave up, told her he wanted to see the essay she'd been assigned for her punishment before she turned it in, and retreated to his own bedroom.

Feeling frustrated with his own inadequacies as a parent, Ridge changed into jeans and a T-shirt, then went back outside and got into his car. He sat and stared out the windshield. He shouldn't have left his daughter. He should have forced her to talk. Too bad he didn't have a clue how to get her to communicate with him.

He couldn't say, *Sorry your mom is such a bitch that she wouldn't let me see you very often these past five years.* He couldn't say, *Sorry that your dad is such a mess that he doesn't know how to make things better for you.* And he certainly couldn't say, *Sorry that I'm such a failure as a father.*

Sighing, he started the BMW, pulled out of the driveway, and headed southeast of town. Once again, he told himself that he was going out to check the water level at the levee. But it hadn't rained since he was out there yesterday, and Sheri's pretty face kept popping up in his imagination.

No matter how much she had changed toward him, how much she seemed to dislike him, an undeniable attraction between them remained.

The image of her as she'd entered the diner interfered with his breathing. The sight of her sweater molded to her curves and her golden-brown hair coming loose from its pins had robbed him of his good sense. How could his feelings for her be anything more than the memory of a better time?

Exhaling, Ridge glanced at his speedometer. *Shit!* He was going nearly eighty miles an hour on a road with a speed limit of forty-five. All he needed was to be pulled over by a county deputy and be caught driving in a nostalgia-clouded stupor. That would certainly inspire confidence among his constituency.

Ridge eased his foot up from the gas pedal and pulled to the side of the road. He gazed at the house to his left. Another mile and he'd be in front of the Davis place.

Reaching over, he touched the folded silk scarf on the

passenger seat, then he turned on his radio and laid his head back. The weather report was good—no precipitation in the three-day forecast—and Ridge blew out a breath of relief.

Suddenly, he felt someone watching him, and he turned in time to see the lace curtains move behind the window of the farmhouse. *Hell!* Mrs. Prater doubtlessly thought he was some cat burglar casing the joint. She told anyone who would listen that her Hummel collection would make her rich someday. She was probably on the phone to the cops right now.

Putting the BMW in gear, he pulled onto the road. A minute later, just as he was approaching the Davis place, Shania Twain started singing "Forever and For Always." Abruptly, he swung the wheel and turned into their driveway.

Last time, he'd let Sheri go without ever asking her out; he wasn't making that same mistake again.

CHAPTER EIGHT

Sheridan and her father had a quick supper of tuna salad sandwiches and Campbell's chicken noodle soup, which, beyond a few breakfast dishes, pretty much maxed out her culinary repertoire. Afterwards, Errol retired to his room to watch the news, and Sheridan went outside.

The early evening air warmed her skin as she used one foot to push herself back-and-forth on the porch swing. Tomorrow would be better. Tomorrow, she'd hire a home health care worker and be free to leave. Tomorrow was another day. Unlike most of her peers who loved *Gone with the Wind* for the romance, Sheridan had always liked the story because Scarlet was such a strong woman.

Scarlett had been someone who rebelled against the limitations of her role as a southern belle. And after losing everything, she had survived despite the destruction of her entire world. True, she hadn't always played nice. But if a man had acted the same way, would anyone have even commented?

Sheridan paused in mid-swing. Could this be the theme for one of her books? She'd have to do some research. Look at other iconic novels with strong female protagonists who were criticized for being too aggressive. Women who would have been judged differently if they were men.

She needed to make some notes while the ideas were whizzing through her head. Her mind racing, Sheridan jumped to her feet, but before she could go into the house, a metallic red Z4 purred into the driveway and stopped next to the sidewalk. The door opened and Ridge Sutton stepped out of the car.

He raised his hand to wave at her. Then turned and bent down to reach across the seat.

Oh! My! God! Ridge still had that incredible butt she remembered drooling over in high school. The jeans he wore might also be from that era. They were threadbare and clung to his backside like caramel coating an ice cream sundae. The only thing better than the worn denim would be if he had on nothing at all.

Damn! The thought of him nude kicked her in the stomach, and she blinked. Where had that dangerous idea come from? And more importantly, what would she do about it? Because now she was picturing him stripped and on the king-size bed in her St. Louis condo.

Before she could clear her mind of that image, the man himself bound up the front steps. He grinned and held out a neatly folded silk rectangle. Her mouth still dry from the thought of a stark-naked Ridge, she silently stared at his offering.

His smile dimmed and he said, "When I had lunch at the diner today, Pinky said you'd left this in the booth yesterday. I told her that I'd get it to you. I hope you weren't worried that you'd lost it for good."

As he handed her the scarf, his callused fingertips brushed her palm and lingered there for an extra second, making her heart pound so hard it felt as if it might explode from her chest.

"Thank you. I hadn't even realized it was missing." Sheridan struggled to maintain a casual expression. "You didn't have to make a special trip out here to return it."

"No problem." Ridge stuck his hands in his back pockets, pulling his jeans as tight across his crotch as they had been earlier across his butt.

Sheridan closed her eyes, swallowed, and missed a few of his next words.

"Anyway, as I mentioned at lunch, the city council needs to control the levee." He gestured with his chin. "You want to take a ride out there with me and check the water level?"

"I shouldn't leave my father alone." Sheridan's skin still burned from the brief caress of his fingers. Alarmed at her reaction to his slightest touch, she edged away from him and said, "Maybe some other—"

"Come on." Ridge took her hand. "Errol will be fine on his own for an hour." He tugged her down the stairs. "It'll be easier to show you why the town needs the levee than try to explain it."

"What's to understand?" Sheridan reminded herself that Ridge's only interest in her was her family's property and freed herself from his grasp. "The levee comes down, the river floods our southeast fields, as well as the property of a lot of other farmers in that direction, and the town your family mostly owns is saved." Summoning up the memory of how he'd treated her after he'd gotten his A in English and he'd no longer needed her help, she clung to that hurt and asked, "Did I leave anything out? Oh, yeah. Once again you get to be the hero."

"That's a simplistic view of the issue." Ridge rocked on his heels. "Yes, the Sutton-owned companies will be among the properties that are protected, but there are also fifteen hundred homes and many other businesses that are in danger."

"Which I am very sorry about." Sheridan swallowed a bubble of sympathy, then rallied her arguments. "But the land you want us to hand over to the town isn't just my father's farm or my grandfather's farm. It was homesteaded by my mother's great-grandfather. For the past hundred and fifty years, a Sheridan—the family for which I am named—has worked those fields."

She paused to take a breath, then continued, "Generations of men and women have farmed that property, supported their children, and made a dignified living on that acreage you want us to turn over to you. You want me to agree to flood mine and my cousins' birthright."

Ridge was quiet, noticeably affected by her impassioned

argument.

Clearing his throat, he said, "God knows that I'm aware of how hard it is to live up to a family obligation." He reached out and stroked her cheek. "But you and I have to think of the greater good. All the folks who are at risk if you refuse."

Sheridan shivered at his touch. For a moment, she allowed herself to fall under his persuasive spell.

Gathering her defenses, she said, "But have any of those people helped out the farmers when their livelihoods were in danger? During the drought, did they offer to help with the irrigation efforts? When diesel prices soared, did the fuel companies give the farmers a break? After the hailstorm, did any of the businesses in town extend interest-free credit?"

"As a matter of fact, Sutton Supermarket did just that." Ridge stepped closer. "And many other stores did the same thing."

Sheridan stared at him. "Really?" His nearness made it difficult to concentrate.

Was he telling the truth? She supposed it was possible. It wasn't as if her cousins discussed those types of issues with her. And the closest she and her father had gotten to the subject was when she'd offered Errol money after his crops were ruined and he'd turned her down, saying that he had it covered.

"Really." Ridge took her hand again and caressed the inside of her wrist. "So will you at least take a ride with me to see the levee?"

Sheridan opened her mouth to make a smart-aleck comment, but Ridge's raised brow stopped her, and she said, "Fine." Then, unable to think straight when he was touching her, she jerked her hand from his fingers. "Let me tell Errol where I'm going."

"You might want to change your shoes while you're at it." Ridge glanced down at her white flip-flops decorated with little yellow daisies. "It's muddy out there, and you don't want to ruin your pretty sandals or chip the polish on your toes."

Sheridan's cheeks turned pink. "Will do."

Overcome with boredom, she'd given herself a pedicure, complete with the bright orange polish that she'd found in the drawer of her old desk. Who knew an unopened bottle would last that long? She hadn't expected anyone to see her feet, and she was a little embarrassed to have Ridge witness her more frivolous side.

Once she was indoors and safely out of his sight, Sheridan leaned against the wall. Why had she decided to go with him? She knew darned well what the levee looked like. She'd played there as a child. Of course, she hadn't seen the water level. *Yes.* That was the reason she'd agreed. It had nothing to do with how right her hand in Ridge's had seemed.

Sheridan found Errol dozing as a game show contestant won a trip for two to fabulous Bermuda, so she left him a note and went to change. Stripping off her khaki slacks, she put on the old pair of jeans she'd been wearing when she was called to Errol's hospital bed and laced up her running shoes.

She didn't have many options with her and had already had to do laundry twice in the six days she'd been home. If she had to stay much longer, she would need to either go shopping or have her assistant FedEx more clothing to her. Maybe she'd text her tomorrow with a list.

No! Sheridan shook her head vehemently at the thought. Any list would be for what she needed for her book tour, not her stay in Sutton Falls.

Tomorrow, she was hiring a home health aide, and by Thursday, she'd be on the road to St. Louis, and soon after that, she'd be boarding a plane to New York. Ridge would be firmly back in his place as an adolescent fantasy, and she'd return to her life as a successful author.

When she rejoined Ridge outside, he had the car's passenger door open for her. Once she'd slid into the seat, he closed it and ran around to the driver's side. He was silent as he reversed the Z4 onto the main road and headed south. Sheridan stole a peek at him as he drove. She admired the easy way he handled the BMW.

Sheridan didn't know much about automobiles, but even though it was in pristine condition, this one didn't seem new. She turned to him and asked, "Is this the same car you had our senior year?"

She remembered that he'd always had a thing for vintage vehicles. He'd been upset when his mother sold the '67 Camaro he'd restored and surprised him with the brand-new Z4.

"Yeah. Although, not the original seats. I had to replace them a few months after I got the car." The tips of his ears turned red. "I know I threw a fit when Mom bought her for me, but once I got to know her, I fell in love."

"And you hang on to the things you love," Sheridan murmured, frowning. Did that mean that although he was divorced, he still felt married?

"I try to." Ridge glanced at her with an indecipherable expression. "But sometimes they get away."

Was he referring to Alexis?

To distract herself from that disturbing thought, she ran her fingers over the soft beige leather and asked, "How do you keep your seats so immaculate? I've only had the Lexus a year, and mine already are scuffed and marked."

"Leather Honey." Ridge glanced at her. "They make a cleaner and a conditioner."

"I'll have to get some of that and ask my detailer to use it."

"I could do it for you." Ridge turned left onto a gravel road and slowed down to twenty miles an hour. "Bring your car over tomorrow night, and I'll give it the special Ridge Sutton treatment."

"Thanks"—she shook her head—"but I'll probably be on the road to St. Louis by the time you get off work."

Sheridan's heart slammed into her chest as hope blossomed in her heart. She gritted her teeth and ignored the spark of happiness his words had ignited. He didn't mean anything by his offer. He liked cars, not her.

"Oh." Ridge slowed even more as the low-slung Z4 bounced over the rutted surface. "Did you find someone to take care of you dad already?"

"I'm interviewing several candidates in the morning." Sheridan played with the buckle of her seat belt, then, trying to keep the defensive tone from her voice, added, "My publisher wants me on tour ASAP."

"Sure," Ridge said, his tone neutral. "By the way, congratulations on the debut of your new book. Sutton Falls is so proud of you." His voice deepened. "I'm so proud of you."

"Thank you," Sheridan whispered softly.

Those were intoxicating words to someone who had struggled most of her adolescence to measure up—first to her mother's expectations, then to her classmates.

"It's your fourth, right?"

"The fourth one that was published," Sheridan said, more than a little thrilled at his apparent knowledge of her writing activities. "I wrote several, including a couple of novels, before I got my big break."

Had he kept up with her successes? *No!* She mentally shook her head. He'd probably just Googled her. After all, now that he wanted to charm her into selling the levee property to the town, he'd want to know everything about her.

"In the face of so much rejection, it must have been hard to keep trying."

"I knew a career as an author wouldn't be easy." Sheridan

shrugged. "I gave myself five years to break into the business, and if I didn't have any luck by then, I planned to go to law school."

"That's my Sheri." Ridge pulled the BMW into a dirt path and shut off the motor. "Always thinking ten steps ahead. Always prepared."

"Sheridan." She frowned at him but was angry with herself for the pleasure she felt hearing her name on his lips. "I prefer Sheridan."

"Sorry. It's hard to break an old habit. I always think of you as Sheri." Ridge exited the Z4, walked around the hood, and opened her door. "We have to walk from here. The car can't make it any farther."

He thought about her? Sheridan refused to acknowledge the zing of happiness that idea created. All the feelings and dreams that she'd been denying for the past thirteen years were surfacing, and she didn't like it. She preferred to live her life without the messy tug of emotions or crushing disappointment of unfulfilled hopes.

Ignoring Ridge's hand, she got out on her own and headed toward the river. He joined her, and side by side, they carefully picked their way through the mud. Once they reached the levee, they climbed up the grass-covered embankment and stared down into the swiftly moving water.

The river was higher than Sheridan could ever recall seeing it. She shivered. Ridge was right. Much more rain, the water would flood the lower-lying town areas. If the weather got bad again, she and Errol would have to make a decision fast. Which way would she go?

"It's frightening, isn't it?" Ridge asked. "Seeing how thin the barrier is between us and nature's fury."

"In the city"—Sheridan watched the gray roiling waves— "from the balcony of my condo, it's easy to forget."

Did she actually miss country life? As a child, she'd loved spending summer days under the bright Missouri sun or winter afternoons strolling down a snow-covered lane. She'd gotten her best ideas for writing projects while walking along the rural roads.

"I remember during a blizzard standing at the window of my apartment at Wash U and wishing that I was back in Sutton Falls," Ridge murmured. "St. Louis is a nice place, but I never was comfortable there. I always felt so alone during my time in college."

Sheridan turned and met Ridge's gaze. His eyes were the pale green of her mother's prized jadeite dishes. He framed her face between his palms and said, "Are you truly at home in St. Louis?"

"I..." Sheridan stuttered to a stop, not sure anymore. Her chest hurt again, like it had the night Ridge had stood next Alexis and done nothing while their classmates tormented her. Finally, she said, "I don't think that I'm really at home anywhere."

"Sheri." Ridge stared into her eyes, his own both sad and fierce.

Before she could correct him about her name, he pressed a soft kiss to her mouth.

At the touch of his lips, all the previous heat between them flared to life, sending a zing of electricity through her. She jerked backwards and her foot slipped. In slow motion, she fell, tumbling down the embankment until she landed in a muddy, grass-stained heap at the bottom.

Terrific! A single kiss from Ridge and she was once again a total mess with him looking down at her from the top of the hill.

CHAPTER NINE

Evidently, Ridge still had the power to make her fall head over heels at his feet—and not just emotionally. A tiny little kiss and she was eighteen again. She really needed a good old-fashioned gabfest with her sorority sisters.

Sheridan checked her watch for the fiftieth time. It was a little past seven Central, which meant she could finally set up the video chat session with her friends. She quickly texted Darcy, Delaney, and Lucy to see if they were available.

As Sheridan waited for the others to get online, she filled the coffee machine with water, measured in the grounds, and switched it on. While it brewed, she put her laptop on the kitchen counter and signed into Skype.

Once Delaney, Darcy, and Lucy had logged on and hellos had been exchanged between the four women, Sheridan said, "Who wants to come to Sutton Falls and rescue me?"

Darcy's soft sea-green eyes widened, and she demanded, "From what?"

"From myself."

"Oh. No." Darcy twisted a strawberry-blond curl. "Did you run into Ridge again?"

"I thought you said you were going to avoid him." Delaney tightened her lips. "When we talked yesterday afternoon, you vowed that even though he was divorced and available, you would turn and run if you saw him again. What happened?"

"A few hours ago, he showed up in my driveway," Sheridan explained. "I should have gone inside the house and locked the door before he even got out of his car."

"Did he come to ask you out?" Lucy squealed. "Did you say

yes?"

"No and no." Sheridan fought the flicker of regret at those answers. "He wanted to take me to see the levee."

"So you'd agree to sell him the land?" Lucy bit the end of her dark brown ponytail. "I warned you when you called me last night that he wouldn't give up easily."

"You were right." Sheridan drew in a lungful of air, then added, "He told me all about how the town needed it and gave me the greater good speech."

She rolled her neck. It was so stiff she could hear it crack as she twisted her head from one side to another. She yearned for a massage.

"And?" Delaney's honey-colored eyes narrowed. "Did you go for it?"

"He made some good points." Sheridan wrinkled her nose. "But you all know how much that land means to me and how guilty I already feel about my mother. I'm not sure I can sell something that's been in her family for five generations."

"Good for you." Darcy leaned forward. "Don't let him pressure you into a hasty decision. You said that it hasn't rained in a few days. There's no need to make a snap judgment."

"Don't worry." Sheridan took a sip of coffee. "I'm going to think long and hard before I agree to anything."

"Then why do you need one of us to rescue you from yourself?" Lucy asked.

"Because…" Sheridan paused, considering whether to tell them the rest of the story.

"What?" Lucy frowned. "Don't even consider trying to handle this on your own."

Lucy was right. The three of them were far more than her friends. They were her sisters. Women who Sheridan could lean on and trust for the rest of her life.

"He kissed me."

"Oh! My! God!" All three images on the monitor shrieked in unison.

"And it felt so good that it scared me, so I tried to step away." Sheridan's cheeks warmed. "Which resulted in me falling down the levee."

"Are you okay?" Delaney's expression was sympathetic.

"The only thing hurt was my pride," Sheridan admitted.

"What did Ridge do?" Darcy asked.

"He helped me up and took me home," Sheridan stated.

Her voice quivered with something she couldn't quite identify. Maybe regret at the lost opportunity to be with Ridge.

"Did he say anything?" Lucy asked.

"He apologized for startling me and tried to make light of it, but I was covered in mud and in no mood to discuss the matter."

"So you gave him the famous Sheridan Davis Silent Treatment," Delaney guessed.

"Sort of." Sheridan crossed her arms.

"Like you always told us, handsome men can be dangerous," Darcy teased with a slight smile.

"Exactly." Sheridan's chest tightened. "They'll just use you and break your heart."

At least, that was what Ridge had done in the past and, given the slightest opportunity, would doubtlessly do again.

"But we're all married to gorgeous guys." Lucy's hazel eyes shone with happiness. "And they haven't hurt us."

"Yeah." Delaney nodded. "We all had to take that leap of faith."

"Now it's your turn to take a chance," Darcy encouraged.

Sheridan pressed her lips together so she wouldn't scream at her friends. Being the last single woman with all the others happily married was a challenge. Delaney, Lucy, and Darcy heard wedding bells whenever Sheridan went out with a guy more than once.

"Ridge isn't my Prince Charming." Sheridan ran her fingers through her hair. "His looks, charisma, and position in town make him incredibly popular. In high school, he was always surrounded by his admirers. He was never alone."

"A lot could have changed in thirteen years," Darcy pointed out.

"He's probably with a different woman every night," Sheridan said, the words actually hurting her throat as she spoke them.

"Or he's lonely because everyone thinks he's too popular to invite out," Lucy suggested softly.

"No." Sheridan shook her head. "I remember at a bonfire after a football game. Ridge had scored the winning touchdown, and everyone wanted to be near him. To bask in his glory. For some reason, Alexis wasn't there, I think she might have had strep."

"Your point?" Delaney raised a brow.

"Alexis's BFF, Gwen, who was supposedly going with Ridge's best friend, Beau, sat down next to Ridge." Sheridan took a breath, recalling how she'd wished she'd had the courage to take that seat. "Gwen started whispering in Ridge's ear, and the grin on his face widened every time she pressed her breasts into his arm."

"What happened?" Darcy frowned. "Did he go off with his best friend's girl?"

"Probably." Sheridan shrugged. "Everyone was drinking pretty heavily, and Beau had already passed out." She exhaled noisily. "I couldn't stand to watch anymore, so I left."

"Which means that he could have done the right thing," Lucy said thoughtfully. "You should have stuck around to see how it ended."

"I couldn't," Sheridan whispered. "It was so devastating. Seeing him with a girl like that, my heart was splintering into a billion pieces."

"Ah, sweetie," Darcy said. "I wish I was there to give you a big old hug. But what I will give you is some advice." She paused, then, clearly drawing from her own past experience, said, "The guy deserves a chance. Maybe he's innocent of everything you think he did. Including the night of your prom. It's time to confront him and ask if he was a part of what happened or not."

"Maybe," Sheridan said, then noticed the time. "Now let's talk about someone other than me."

Darcy filled them in on how her newest novel was coming along. It was the second in a three-book deal she'd signed with a major New York publisher. Delaney gave them an update on the progress of the youth center that she'd sponsored with her lottery winnings. And Lucy told them all about the Easter egg hunt at her husband's church. Someone had slipped booze in the punch, and one of the parishioners had propositioned the Easter Bunny.

After they finished laughing and said their good-byes, Sheridan shut off the kitchen lights and headed to bed. The sensation of Ridge's lips on hers as they'd stood on top of the levee still haunted her.

Resolutely, she pushed aside the memory. She wouldn't, couldn't think about that moment. She had too much else on her mind to daydream about a guy who would never be a part of her life.

Turning her thoughts away from Tuesday afternoon's mud-covered ride home with Ridge, she vowed to keep him out of her dreams. A promise to herself that she couldn't keep.

* * *

Wednesday afternoon, Sheridan sat nursing her fifth cup of coffee. She hadn't slept well. Then, just when she had been convinced that her situation couldn't get any worse, fate slapped her upside the head, showing her that she was very, very wrong.

As if yesterday's humiliation at having to peel her muck-covered butt off of Ridge's expensive leather seats wasn't awful enough, today's eight, nine, and ten a.m. health aide interviews were even more hideous. Contender number one was an emaciated young woman with long, greasy hair and dirty fingernails. She reeked of cigarette smoke, and her eyes were bloodshot. And when Sheridan asked her about her previous experience, she'd been unable to form a coherent sentence.

The second applicant was clean, smelled of vanilla, and seemed ideal. That was, until the woman stated that Errol would have to agree to go to her church. When Sheridan inquired where she worshipped, the answer had put her out of the running for the position. Although not close to her father, Sheridan wasn't allowing him to attend religious services where snakes were honored guests.

The third candidate hadn't even bothered to show up. When Sheridan phoned the agency to complain, she was told that the man had been apprehended by the county sheriff in a sweep of the Mt. Morrison bars.

Barely able to stop herself from banging her head against the kitchen wall, Sheridan immediately phoned the other home health care agency in the area. They told her they had only two possibilities, and neither candidate was available to be interviewed until late Thursday afternoon.

That last blow was almost too much. Sheridan wanted nothing more than to get into bed and pull the covers over her head. Too bad, she had to get ready for Errol's appointment.

The hospital had called that morning. They'd had a cancellation, and if Errol could come in at one, they could perform the tests his doctor had ordered. Happy to move forward on at least one front, she had assured the scheduler that they would be there.

After helping Errol to dress and getting him settled in the station wagon, Sheridan spent the twenty miles to the county seat listening to her father talk about their family. Errol was the youngest of four. His sisters had produced two, five, and seven children, so Sheridan had fourteen first cousins. Most of whom were married with kids of their own.

Growing up as the only boy, Errol had learned the fine art of gossip at his older sisters' knees. And during the ride, he gleefully recounted all of the juicy details of his nieces' and nephews' lives to Sheridan.

As the time flew by, she realized she missed hearing about the day-to-day activities of her relatives. Suddenly, she wished she could be more a part of that warmth and love.

Catching up on everyone's activities took the entire trip. And when Sheridan pulled into the hospital's drive to drop off her father, they were still laughing about his youngest sister's reaction to the news of her granddaughter's pierced eyebrow and the tattoo on her breast.

Once Sheridan unloaded Errol's wheelchair and got him into the building, she parked the car and hurried back to the entrance. As she jogged toward the doors, the memory of her arrival at this same hospital a week ago flooded back.

Her chest tightened as she recalled that when she'd arrived, she'd been thinking that if her father died, they'd never get a chance to straighten out things between them.

Last Wednesday, she'd been blinded by the blue-white lights of the ER. But once her vision had cleared, she could see that the waiting room, including the reception desk, was empty. For a moment, she'd stood bewildered, panting as if she had run all the way from St. Louis instead of driven. Where was everyone?

When a giggle had drawn her attention, she'd moved toward

the sound. It was coming from behind a swinging door marked *Authorized Personnel Only*. Sheridan had knocked on the metal, but no one had responded.

After receiving the call that her father had had a heart attack, she'd driven three hours at breakneck speed. If someone didn't show up soon, jobs were going to be lost when she got through complaining about the staff's incompetence.

Finally, an explanation for the deserted ER dawned on her. This was a small rural hospital with a limited workforce. Had her father died while she was on the road? Was that why no one was around?

Holding back a sob, she'd pounded on the door again. He couldn't be dead, not when the last words she had said to him were so hateful. Of course, they rarely made it through a conversation without one hurting the other.

The sound of laughter had snapped her out of her thoughts, and wiping away the tear that had escaped down her cheek, Sheridan had pushed through the door and marched down a short corridor until she'd come to a room filled with people. A coffeepot sat on one side, and lockers lined the rest of the walls. Every seat at the scarred wooded table was taken.

Sheridan had spotted her father sitting in the center of a ring of pretty nurses and other female medical personnel. He was wearing a blue hospital gown, and his left arm was in a cast propped up on a metal stand attached to his wheelchair. Not a strand of his thick white hair was out of place. Even in the florescent lights, his face had glowed pinkly.

Everyone at the table was concentrating on Errol. An attractive woman on his left was holding down a stack of printer paper as he'd deftly sketched a caricature of her. Others had clutched already finished portraits to their breast.

It had been difficult to keep from screaming, but Sheridan had managed to tamp down her anger, and once she was in control of her emotions, she'd said, "Errol, you seem fairly chipper for someone so recently at death's door. I take it your heart attack was a false alarm?"

One of the nurses' aides had let out a yelp, and Sheridan had watched as her dad reached out a hand to comfort the startled woman. Clearly, he was still attractive to cute young things.

Her father's voice had held a note of defeat when he said, "Sorry to trouble you, but the doctor insisted on notifying the next of kin."

Sheridan had paled at the image brought to mind by that phrase. One of the nurses had vacated a seat, and Sheridan had sunk into it gratefully.

"Sorry." Why were the first words out of her mouth always so cruel? Wouldn't she ever be able to forgive him? She'd taken a deep breath and said, "Let's start over. What happened?"

"I passed out and fell down the porch steps. I was brought to the hospital, and about a thousand strangers examined me, then someone called you. They aren't sure why I fainted and wanted to run more tests, but I said that I'd wait for my own doctor to decide on that." Errol paused, then added, "Oh, and I broke my ankle and left wrist." He gestured to the cast on his leg that was hidden from view by the tabletop. "These charming ladies have been keeping me company while we waited for you to come get me."

Sheridan had thanked the women and then asked, "Would it be possible to speak to the doctor?"

An older nurse frowned and reluctantly got up. "I'll have to wake him."

"So?" Sheridan had never been fond of doctors, having little faith in a profession that was said to *practice* their occupation. It seemed to her, after a few years, they ought to get the hang of it. "He isn't paid to sleep, is he?"

When the man had presented himself, she was less than impressed. His wrinkled coat and disheveled appearance had not alleviated her concerns regarding his competence. Nevertheless, she'd thrust out her hand and said, "I'm Sheridan Davis. You treated my father, Errol Davis, earlier this evening. What can you tell me about his condition?"

A puzzled look had crossed the doctor's features and he'd said with a noticeable accent, "I am sorry, miss. I have treated a great many patients this evening and do not recall all the names."

"Male, early sixties, you couldn't figure out why he fainted." Sheridan's words were clipped.

"Ah, Mr. Davis. Yes. None of the tests we ran were conclusive." The doctor had put his hand on her back and tried to steer her out of the room. "He needs further evaluation."

"That's all you can tell me?" Sheridan shrugged off his touch. "How about his ankle and wrist?"

"They are broken."

Sheridan hadn't missed the look of relief on the man's face when she'd walked from the room. And now they were back for the additional tests. At least this time, she was with her father and had some control over the situation.

*   *   *

It had taken three hours for all the procedures on Sheridan's father to be completed, and they'd have to wait several days for the results to be reported to them. Prior to getting into the car to drive home, Errol took a pain pill and fell asleep before they were out of the hospital parking lot.

Unwilling to think about her father or Ridge, Sheridan turned the radio to an oldies station and concentrated on the lyrics. When she pulled into their driveway, Mick was replacing the broken front porch post. After she got her father settled inside, she sat on the swing and chatted with her cousin as he worked.

"We haven't had any rain for a few days." She gestured around her. "Are the fields drying?"

"Some." Mick finished removing the old pillar and laid it aside.

"Have you heard that the mayor wants to buy the property we have southeast of town?" Sheridan was curious as to her cousin's opinion of the sale.

"Yep." Mick heaved the new post upright. "I'm on the city council."

"Do you approve?"

"Hard to say." Mick shoved the column into place. "If it floods, it's the town's only hope, but we lose a lot of acreage and farmhouses."

"Do you lean either way?" Sheridan tried to pin down her cousin.

"Not really." Mick worked in silence, then said, "But your farm's been having a run of bad luck lately and has been losing money."

"Errol mentioned that." Sheridan leaned forward. "What happened besides those broken windows in the shed?"

"Sugar in the combine's fuel tank." Mick squinted. "The ventilation system on one of the silos was damaged, and we lost some grain to mold."

"That sounds more like deliberate vandalism than a run of bad luck."

"Yep." Mick tested the post's stability and grunted his satisfaction.

"Has Errol called the county sheriff's department about all this?" Sheridan asked.

"Uh-huh." Mick wiped the sweat from his face with a red bandana.

"And the cops said what?" Sheridan asked, gritting her teeth.

She wished that her cousin would be a little more verbal. While she admired the strong, silent type as a character in a book, in real life, it was darn irritating.

"They said they'd file a report and he should contact his insurance company."

"So no investigation?"

"That's right." Mick shrugged. "The deputy thinks it's probably kids, and unless they catch 'em in the act, there's not much they can do about it. He offered to patrol more often, but they got lots of ground to cover and only two officers on duty."

"Which means we're on our own."

"Pretty much."

"Let's hope these so-called kids don't decide to turn to arson."

CHAPTER TEN

The next day at eight, Sheridan walked into the middle school. The halls were empty, but the floors were littered with broken pencils and crumpled papers. She stopped at the office, where she was given a visitor's badge and directions to Merry's room.

Sheridan had woken that morning drenched in sweat with her pulse racing. The panic attack was far from the worst she'd experienced, but it had been nearly ten years since her last one, and she'd thought she'd left those demons behind a long time ago. Evidently, they had been waiting for her at the Sutton Falls city limits.

After she could once again exhale and her heartbeats resumed their normal speed, she'd forced herself out of bed and into the shower. During college, she had sought help for her recurring nightmares, and the therapist had diagnosed her as suffering from a form of Post-Traumatic Stress Disorder. Back then, with the help of cognitive therapy, she'd learned how to cope with her feelings.

But clearly, spending so much time in Sutton Falls, where the assault had taken place, had retriggered the PTSD attacks. Either that or the touch of Ridge's lips on hers had brought back too many memories and emotions.

Why had he kissed her? After her humiliating fall down the banks of the levee, she'd been too embarrassed to look at him, let alone have any kind of conversation. Despite Delaney's accusation, Sheridan hadn't intentionally given him the silent treatment. It was just that she hadn't been able to think of anything to say. As soon as he'd stopped his car in her driveway, she had muttered good-bye and bolted out of the Z4.

Once she was inside the house, she'd peeked out the window and seen that his BMW was still there. Ridge had appeared to be staring in her direction. He was too far away for her to see his expression, but it was a good five minutes before he'd finally put the car in reverse and left. What had he been thinking as he'd sat there gazing at her front door?

Shoving her questions about Ridge out of her thoughts, Sheridan made her way down the long corridor. She noted that the orange lockers hadn't been painted or replaced since she'd been a student. She relaxed as she heard the soft murmurings from the classes, and the faint smell of sweaty adolescents was strangely comforting.

Merry was waiting for her in the doorway and ushered her into the room. Eighteen pairs of eyes followed her, and Sheridan practiced deep breathing as Merry introduced her. Looking down the rows of young faces, Sheridan smiled when she recognized her father's young friend from the doctor's office. Sally grinned back and gave a little wave.

That grin seemed familiar. She hadn't caught Sally's last name. Did she know someone with that same smile?

Shrugging off the distraction, Sheridan faced the students. "Hi, as Miss Mac said, I'm Sheridan Davis and I'm a writer. What she didn't say was that I started that career sitting exactly where you're sitting now. Actually"—she pointed to the front row—"it was in this seat right here that I wrote my first published piece."

The boy sitting in the desk she had indicated raised his hand. When she nodded, he asked, "What did you write? Where was it published?"

"I wrote a short story about a girl whose cat turned out to be a handsome vampire, and *Sweet Teen Magazine* published it."

"Wow," Sally breathed. "After that, you must have been

famous."

"Nope. I put it out under a pen name." Sheridan glanced at Merry. "With the exception of my best friend, I never told any of my classmates."

"And she didn't tell anyone?" A girl with a braid hanging nearly to her waist seemed to think this was an amazing feat.

"She was a pretty special person. In fact, she's still one of my best friends."

"What was her name?" a boy in the back yelled.

"Merry McIntyre."

After the students cheered their teacher, Sheridan spoke about her writing process, finding an agent, and working with an editor. Once she opened up the floor for questions, Sally declared she wanted to be a writer, too, and monopolized the Q and A.

Sheridan recognized a lot of herself in the preteen and tried to encourage her to pursue her goal. But she also advised Sally to have a backup plan to support herself until that dream came true.

When the class was over, Merry explained that she had the next period free and led Sheridan to the teachers' lounge. Handing her a cup of coffee, Merry sat down next to her at the table.

After taking a sip of her coffee, Merry said, "You were wonderful with those kids, especially Sally. I knew you two would hit it off. And that was really nice of you to say I was still one of your best friends."

"Well, you are."

"If that's true, I have one more favor to ask you," Merry said with no trace of her usual humor.

"Go ahead." Sheridan narrowed her eyes, wondering what else her cousin had in mind.

"Friday night, a bunch of us are getting together at my place for a housewarming celebration, and I want you to come."

"Why?"

"Because you need to see that not everyone in Sutton Falls is a monster." Merry leaned forward. "Look, it will mostly be teachers and their significant others and maybe a few close friends of mine."

"Does Alexis teach here?" When Merry shook her head no, Sheridan asked, "You haven't become pals with her?"

"No." Merry crossed her arms. "Alexis left town right after her divorce. Her parents moved away when Mr. Byrnes lost all their family money in bad investments during the recession. Alexis only comes back here to attend homecoming. As the only four-time queen, she gets to wear her crown and ride on one of the floats in the parade."

"The perks of being universally loved." Sheridan rolled her eyes. "Did you know that her father told Errol that Alexis was better than every other kid in school and that any complaint about her behavior was because the rest of us were jealous of her?"

"I'm not surprised." Merry sighed. "That was one of her problems. Mr. Byrnes idolized his little girl, which made Alexis feel entitled."

"Entitled to torment her classmates?" Sheridan asked, then answered herself. "Of course. Old Man Byrnes told Errol that being bullied builds character."

"What B.S." Merry slumped in her chair. "Poor Alexis never had a chance with that kind of parenting."

"Poor Alexis!" Sheridan nearly screamed. "Are you freaking kidding me?"

"Never mind." Merry patted Sheridan's hand. "Forget about her and reclaim your past. My party will be fun, and you'll see that Sutton Falls isn't how you remember it."

"Maybe." Sheridan thought about how Ridge's kiss had instantly melted her brain into dumbstruck goop and asked, "Did you invite the mayor?"

"You know around here we don't send out formal invitations. I just asked my friends and colleagues to come over for some food and laughs." Merry tilted her head. "Do you want me to call Ridge?"

"No!" Sheridan shouted, then modulated her voice. "I was just curious."

The last thing she needed was to see Ridge Sutton at a party. She was already overwhelmed and feeling way too much for him. Her skin still tingled from his thumb rubbing sensuous circles on the inside of her wrist. She could not allow herself to fall for him again.

"Okay then." Merry's expression was inquisitive, but she didn't pursue the subject. Instead, she asked, "So you'll come to my party?"

"Yes." Sheridan added, "But I'm only staying a little while, and if I need to leave, you don't ask any questions."

"Great! Seven o'clock." Merry leaped to her feet. "It'll be fun. You'll see."

Sheridan hugged her cousin good-bye, returned her visitor's badge to the office, and headed for downtown. Aunt Flora was keeping an eye on Errol, and the home health care interviews weren't until three p.m. Since it appeared that she was stuck in the area for at least a couple more days, she needed to pick up a few items.

There was a parking spot a few doors down from her destination, and Sheridan pulled her Lexus next to the curb. She was half a block from the car when she realized that she hadn't locked the doors. She paused, then, laughing at herself, she continued toward the store. In Sutton Falls, few people locked their houses, let alone their vehicles.

Smiling, she headed for the pharmacy. There were a lot of differences from the last time she'd walked down this street.

Several new businesses had opened up, and everything looked fresher, as if all the buildings had been recently painted. She counted three shops selling one-of-a-kind gift items and jewelry, a pet boutique, and an ice cream parlor. Exactly the kind of quaint main drag tourists from the city liked to experience when they visited a small town.

Sheridan stopped in front of a window with *The Well-Caffeinated Reader* stenciled across the glass. It was a bookstore and coffee shop combo, and as she glanced at the display, she caught her breath.

Front and center, next to a large pile of her new books, was her picture. In bright red, the words *New York Times Best-selling Local Author* blazed across the top of the poster. Underneath was a clipping of a glowing review from *Publishers Weekly* and a photo of the Democratic presidential candidate holding Sheridan's book. It was truly a once-in-a-lifetime moment.

Feeling giddy, she whipped out her cell and snapped a couple of photos. She selected the best one and texted it to Darcy, Lucy, and Delaney with the message: Who would have thunk it? Knowing how invisible Sheridan had felt growing up, her sorority sisters would get a kick out of her hometown fame.

Still smiling at the bookstore's display, she entered Doral's Drugs. As she pushed open the door, she noticed a flyer taped to the glass advertising an arts and craft festival in May.

Merry might be right. It appeared that in the years that she'd been away, Sutton Falls had changed. The whole town seemed spruced up and more vibrant. Was that Ridge's doing?

The guy who had taken over as mayor when Ridge's father died had wanted everything to stay exactly the same. Maybe, since he was one of the few non-Sutton mayors, he felt it was his duty to keep the community in a holding pattern until the heir apparent took over. And now that Ridge was at the helm, the town could move forward.

The drugstore was nearly empty, and Sheridan took her time wandering the aisles. She picked up a bottle of hand lotion, a pair of tweezers, and a package of makeup remover wipes. She was browsing the office supply section looking for a package of her favorite gel pens when she heard two women at the pharmacy counter discussing a third.

"Christine's dating that new guy over at the tractor supply."

"Really?"

"She goes on and on about him."

"That's the trouble with a lot of gals."

"Oh?"

"Yeah. They get all excited about nothing, and then they marry him."

Both women broke into gales of laughter, and one said, "I told her to get her butt into college and quit trying to find some guy to support her."

Sheridan grinned. When she'd left Sutton Falls, despite it being the twenty-first century, there'd been a 1950s mentality among the residents. It seemed that attitudes in town were changing along with the businesses.

After picking up a box of Russell Stover chocolates for Errol's sweet tooth, Sheridan headed home. For the first time since she'd arrived in town, she felt optimistic. Surely, one of the two interviewees this afternoon would be just who she was looking for to care for her father. Then tomorrow, instead of attending Merry's party, she'd be on a plane to New York.

* * *

As soon as Sheridan stepped into the house, it was obvious that the family grapevine was in full swing.

Aunt Flora greeted her as she walked into the kitchen. "Sheri, honey, I'm pleased as punch that you're going to Merry's little get-together tomorrow night. I'll be over at six thirty to take care of your dad. Don't you even think of backing out. My little girl would be real disappointed if you didn't show up."

Before Sheridan could respond, her father called out from the bedroom, "You tell Flora that I don't need a babysitter."

"Errol Davis, you hush up," Flora yelled at her brother. Then, kissing Sheridan's cheek, she said, "I've got to run. See you tomorrow."

She tried to stop her aunt, but Flora hurried out the back door, got in her Buick, and drove away. Admitting defeat, Sheridan poked her head into her father's room.

Errol glanced away from the television screen and said, "You are going to Merry's shindig, right?"

"I came home to be with you, not to run around to parties. I do enough of that in St. Louis," Sheridan hedged.

Errol needing her would be the one excuse Merry would accept.

"Come on in and sit down." Errol patted the mattress. "It's time we had a little talk."

Sheridan reluctantly complied but perched on the edge of a chair rather than the bed. The look in her father's eyes made her uneasy.

"I've had a lot of time to think about what happened to you after your prom."

"That's in the past." Sheridan stood, a feeling of panic rising in her throat. "We don't need to have this conversation."

"Yes, we do." Errol's voice was surprisingly firm. "I know we don't have as close a relationship as we used to have, but I'm your father, and we need to talk about it. I should have been man enough to do it that night."

"No," she whispered, edging away from her father. Her chest was tightening and she could hardly breathe.

"I shouldn't have let you pretend you were okay, but with

your mom sick and all, everything just seemed to be going to hell." Errol's voice was thick. "I couldn't cope with one more heartbreak."

Sheridan clutched the doorknob. Her throat was closed and she couldn't answer.

"We should have gone to the police and gotten it straightened out. Punished those who were guilty and cleared those who were innocent. You may have been surprised at what category some of those involved might have fallen into."

"Maybe." She forced the single word between dry lips, taking small sips of much-needed air.

Errol sighed. "A few days after you left, Ridge Sutton came by to talk to you. When he found out you were already gone, he tried to ask me what happened."

Sheridan made a choking sound. The one thing about that night she never had been able to face was figuring out exactly what part Ridge had played in the incident.

"I wouldn't tell him. I figured he was just pretending not to know what went on. Trying to cover his ass. That was probably a mistake. Ridge never seemed like the type of guy to go along with something like that. In hindsight, I doubt he was involved."

Swallowing her anger and heartache, Sheridan struggled to respond. "Even if you're right, it's been too long now to correct that error."

"Not—"

Sheridan cut off her father's protests. "I know it's not Christian, but I don't think I can ever get over it until they're all punished. I want everyone who laughed at me to suffer, and I want Ridge and Alexis to feel the agony I went through."

Although in her heart of hearts, she had always believed that Alexis had acted on her own, it had been easier to ignore that belief and continue to blame Ridge. Holding him responsible made it easier to let go of any stupid fantasy about him being her soul mate. Easier to forget the chemistry between them. Easier to stifle the laughable idea that they belonged together.

Errol cocked his head and said, "Oh, I think those two have had their share of misery."

"A lot of people get divorced."

"I wasn't only talking about that."

"Then what do you mean?" Sheridan frowned.

"Well, I don't have all the details," Errol said, settling back and getting comfortable. "And I'm not a gossip, but..."

"Seriously?" Sheridan bit back a chuckle. "You're the king of the rumor mill. You've refined gossiping into an Olympic sport."

"Fine." Errol narrowed his eyes. "Just for that, if you want to know about Alexis's and Ridge's lives, you ask him."

CHAPTER ELEVEN

Thursday afternoon, Ridge stared at the stack of legal papers in front of him, but he couldn't concentrate on the printed words. For the hundredth time, his mind wandered back to Wednesday evening at the levee with Sheri. He hadn't intended to kiss her. But she'd been so beautiful with the setting sun shining on her hair and that vulnerable look in her eyes that he'd leaned forward.

Something inside him had broken free when he'd heard her slight gasp. Then, before he knew it, his mouth was on hers. A tiny part of his brain had marveled that her lips were as soft and silky as he'd always imagined they'd be.

It had been a magic moment. The fulfillment of an adolescent fantasy. Even better than he'd dreamed. What he hadn't been prepared for was the surge of hunger or the flicker of possession that had blazed to life deep in his gut.

But before he could take her into his arms or deepen the kiss, she'd jerked back from him. Then, as if in slow motion, he'd watched in horror as her foot slipped, and she slid down the embankment. His heart had stopped as he'd seen her tumble all the way to the bottom and then lay there without moving. Was her leg broken? Did she have a concussion?

The flat, metallic taste of fear had erased the sweetness of her lips as he'd run to her side, barely avoiding falling himself. But by the time he'd reached her, she'd gotten to her feet. Her big brown eyes had blinked rapidly, betraying her embarrassment, then, and without a word, she'd marched off toward the car.

Her silence had torn at his heart as he'd driven her home.

And the good-bye that she'd flung at him before throwing open the car door and stomping into the house had sounded final. How had things gone so wrong so fast? It had taken him a few minutes to recover, and when he'd finally backed out of her driveway, he was still trying to figure out what he should do next.

Rubbing his temples, he tried to erase the scene that seemed to be playing on an endless loop in his head. He had to focus.

After signing the last of the city workers' contracts, he slipped them into a large envelope and glanced at the vintage wooden swivel clock on his desk. *Shit!* It was quarter to five, and the paperwork was due by the end of business.

Hurriedly, Ridge buzzed his admin to walk the package over to Beau's office. As he handed over the documents, he told Wendy to go on home after making the delivery.

Once she was gone, Ridge leaned his head against his chair, trying to relax before starting the next task. Staring at the ceiling, he thought about Beau Bunson. How had someone who drank as much as Beau managed to get through college, let alone law school? Let alone convince the good people of Sutton Falls to elect him city attorney?

Granted, the man was smart, probably too smart for his own good. But his drinking had always gotten in the way of both his studies and his personal life. He had somehow passed the Missouri bar exam, but he was on his third divorce and constantly broke. If his mother didn't allow him to live in her guesthouse rent free, he'd probably be homeless.

Ridge had often tried to talk to his friend about his behavior, but Beau had always waved him off, refusing to participate in any kind of serious conversation. And when Ridge had asked Doc Brown for advice, he'd been told that because functional alcoholics are able to maintain their lifestyles, they don't believe there's a problem.

For the past year, Beau had been doing pretty well—only drinking on weekends—but something must have happened to push his addiction into high gear. His car had been in front of the country club bar until closing nearly every night this month, and people were beginning to talk.

Ridge was worried about his friend but at a loss for what to do for him. Doc Brown had dismissed the idea of an intervention. He'd cautioned Ridge that alcoholics needed to reach out for help on their own, and Beau's drinking would have to reach a crisis level before he would be ready to accept Ridge's help.

Ridge sighed. He might not be able to do anything for his friend, but he could do his best for the town. And in order to do that, he had to finish the work in front of him before he could call it a day.

Straightening, he switched the office phones to voice mail and checked his cell. There was a text from his mother. He needed to be home no later than seven thirty or find a babysitter because she had a social engagement at eight.

Another thing to add to the unending to-do list in his head. He wanted to spend more time with Sally, but when he did, she barely spoke to him. He needed to find out when the next extracurricular activity was and make sure that she attended it. If she could only make a friend or two, she might be happier. Did he know anyone with a daughter her age? Was Sally too old for him to arrange a playdate?

Exhaling noisily, he grabbed the top folder from his inbox and began reading the contents. Two hours later, he initialed the last document, put everything on Wendy's desk, and drove home. The windows in his mother's wing were dark, but there was a glow behind the front door's sidelights.

Evelyn was waiting for Ridge as he stepped inside the foyer. She wore a blue dress and carried a matching purse with the prominent Yves Saint Laurent logo facing outward. Her mouth was pinched in a discontented moue, and Ridge braced himself for whatever he'd done to cause her displeasure.

"When I agreed to assist you with Sarah Ann's care, I did not mean that I would devote my entire life to those duties." Evelyn adjusted the gold cuff bracelet on her right wrist. "I have other obligations. Many civic and charitable organizations depend on me."

"Actually, I didn't ask for your help, you insisted." Ridge walked past his mother, down the hall, and entered his study. Knowing that she would follow him, he continued, "If you'd rather move back to your own house, I'll start searching for a nanny tomorrow morning."

"That's not what I meant." Evelyn managed to get in front of him and block his access to the desk. The tone of her voice changed from complaining to persuasive. "I just think you need to spend more time with your daughter. She's not conducting herself like a Sutton."

"And how is her behavior un-Sutton-like?" Ridge asked, his mild tone concealing his anger.

Evelyn might be right about him spending more time with Sally, but he was damned if he would make his daughter conform to whatever mold the Ice Queen had in mind for her. Over the years, Ridge had allowed his mother to maneuver him one too many times.

He'd given in to his mother's wishes when he should have stood up to her, and the outcomes had nearly always turned out badly for him. No way in hell was he making the same mistake with Sally. He'd protect her from Evelyn's manipulations or die trying.

"She needs to dress more appropriately." His mother's lips thinned. "Today, I wouldn't allow her to wear those awful baggy jeans and T-shirts she prefers. In retaliation, she burned all her

113

lovely designer garments in the fireplace. Her mother would be appalled."

"I'm sure she would be." Ridge hid a smile. "But as long as Sally is in compliance with the board of education's rules, I will not force her to dress differently."

He'd thought the expensive clothing that Alexis had bought for Sally was ridiculous for a twelve-year-old. Some of those outfits cost more than what a typical Sutton Falls family lived on for a month.

"We'll see." Evelyn crossed her arms, going on to the next item on her list of grievances. "Sarah Ann also needs to learn how to handle people better. She refuses to attend the parties of her social peers."

"While I'd like her to make friends"—Ridge knew exactly whom his mother considered Sally's equals; they were all the grandchildren of Evelyn's cronies—"she has the right to choose them herself."

He may not have been able to stand up to his mother as a teenager. And he still had some difficulty as an adult. However, he had no problem doing so as a father.

"A girl her age needs guidance in those kinds of matters." Evelyn tapped the toe of her Louboutin pump. "I shudder to think who you might have ended up with if I hadn't stepped in and supervised your social calendar."

"You mean"—Ridge rarely raised his voice, but his mother was pushing all the right or, more accurately, wrong, buttons tonight, and he thundered—"besides the psycho bitch I married largely due to your interference?"

There was a loud gasp from the doorway, and Ridge whirled toward the sound. Sally was standing just over the threshold. Her reproachful stare drilled into his soul, and the hurt in her big green eyes that were so much like his own was almost too much for him to endure.

"Sally." Ridge took a step toward her, but she ran down the hallway. "Sally, honey, I'm sorry. I should never have said that about your mother." He followed her up the stairs and to her bedroom. "Let me explain." The door slammed in his face and he heard the lock click.

After several attempts to persuade Sally to open up, he admitted defeat, leaned against the solid wood door, and shouted, "Sweetheart, I'll be in my study when you're ready to talk."

Son of a freaking bitch! Barely resisting the urge to punch a hole in the wall, he fisted his hands and stomped toward the staircase. He never spoke badly of Alexis for precisely this reason. What had come over him tonight?

More importantly, how would he mend his already strained relationship with his daughter?

He had no idea how Sally felt about her mother's abrupt decision to give him full custody. Since the day Ridge had answered his doorbell and found his daughter standing surrounded by mountains of suitcases and piles of boxes, neither he nor his daughter had mentioned Alexis.

His only contact with his ex-wife had been through their attorneys. And as far as he knew, Alexis hadn't seen Sally since she'd abandoned her on Ridge's doorstep. Maybe his ex was texting or e-mailing their daughter, but she certainly hadn't visited.

Another subject he should discuss with Sally. Trudging down the steps, Ridge felt as if his head were about to explode. The skeletons of his relationships were piling up like firewood.

First, there was his ex. He'd divorced Alexis after finding her in bed with her personal trainer. Talk about a clichéd end of a marriage. He hadn't been upset by her actions. By that point in their marriage, nothing she did could hurt him. But he had been surprised.

She'd gone to such lengths to become his wife. Why would

she risk it all with her blatant infidelity? Maybe she never thought she'd get caught. She'd always gotten away with her selfish behavior before. If you looked up narcissist in the dictionary, Alexis's picture would take up the entire entry.

Second, there was Sheri. She was still angry with him for whatever had happened to her at their senior prom. He'd thought that he was making progress with her on their field trip to the levee, but her reaction to his kiss had proven that theory wrong. However, unlike his teenage self, this time Ridge wasn't giving up.

Although there was every indication that she'd say no, he would ask her out. He just needed to figure out a good way to do it.

And tonight, he'd added a third name to his list of failed relationships. What was he going to do about the daughter he barely knew and who clearly didn't want to know him?

Whatever he did annoyed her. She'd hardly spoken to him *before* she'd overheard his stupid statement about her mother. Now, she wouldn't even let him into her room. He had no idea how to make things right between them, but he wasn't giving up on her, either.

He needed to talk to someone about both Sally and Sheri. But who? He paused, his shoulders sagging. No one came to mind. He had a lot of casual friends, but no truly close ones. He'd dated several women in the years since his divorce but had never really clicked with any of them. They'd all seemed more interested in his last name and his bank account than in him as a man.

He didn't have any relatives in the area. He was an only child, as were both of his parents. Despite his popularity, he'd never felt liked for himself. How would he have been treated if he weren't a Sutton and his parents didn't own most of the town?

Dragging himself back into his study, he was shocked to see

his mother sitting behind the desk. She was a stickler for punctuality, and it was already quarter to eight. She would be late for whatever social engagement she'd been so hot to attend. That couldn't be a good sign. Ridge sucked in a deep breath and straightened his shoulders. This would not be pretty.

"Finally." Getting to her feet, Evelyn spoke in an icy voice. "I am not going to allow you to bring this family down. Get that child of yours under control. And do whatever you have to do to buy Errol Davis's land and tear down that damn levee." She walked to the door, then turned and stared at him. "Start acting more like your father. He would've had both situations sewn up by now."

After his mother left, Ridge grabbed the brandy bottle and poured until the snifter was full. He didn't bother with the niceties of swirling the amber liquid or warming it with his palm; instead, he slugged the expensive cognac back as if it were cheap wine.

Then he opened the French doors, grabbed his father's chair, and threw it as far as he could. It was past time for him to man up and be who he wanted to be rather than a poor imitation of his dear old dad.

CHAPTER TWELVE

Oh. My. God! Late Friday morning, Sheridan sat on a stool at the kitchen counter and buried her head in her hands. The two home health aides she'd interviewed yesterday afternoon hadn't been any better than the candidates she'd talked to Wednesday.

The first man had somehow managed to get into a political argument with her father. Considering Errol's interest in government affairs was close to zero, it had been almost funny to see her father lose his famous cool and tell the guy exactly what he thought of the current administration's handling of farm issues.

And the second applicant had had her two toddlers with her. She'd explained that she had no one to watch the children and she would have to be able to bring them with her if she got the job. While the kids were cute, their behavior was so atrocious that Sheridan was sure that their mother would spend all her time running after them and have little energy left to take care of Errol. How that poor woman kept her sanity was beyond comprehension.

To top it off, the agency had said the next candidates wouldn't be available until Tuesday. Where were all the good employees hiding? Had they all moved to a bigger town? Didn't anyone around here need a job? Maybe the economy had improved more than she had thought. Who knew that a thriving financial atmosphere would have a downside?

Sheridan hadn't had the internal fortitude to call her agent until this morning, and she'd just informed Grace that she wouldn't be able to leave Sutton Falls for several more days, possibly another week. As expected, her agent had had a hissy fit. The call had ended with a dire prediction that Sheridan's refusal to abandon her father, hop on a plane to New York, and start touring would ruin her career.

Trying to shake off the feeling of hopelessness that was threatening to engulf her, Sheridan got to her feet and walked into her bedroom. Since it now appeared that she would be in town for Merry's get-together and would have no excuse to miss it, she needed to figure out what to wear. Opening the closet door, she stared at the few items hanging on the rod in front of her.

There were a pair of khaki slacks, a white blouse, the jeans she'd been wearing to build the Habitat for Humanity house—now torn and grass-stained from her tumble down the levee embankment—and a black skirt. Her drawers yielded even less—a black sweater, the sweatshirt she'd worn with the jeans, and a couple of T-shirts she'd left behind when she'd moved out.

Wanting to present a professional image, Sheridan had worn the skirt and blouse to speak to the sixth graders at the school. Afterwards, her cousin had mentioned that she looked like a nun, so those were out. She certainly couldn't go to Merry's party dressed as Sister Sheridan.

She held the sweater and skirt against her and gazed in the mirror. Now she looked like she was in mourning. Not exactly, the little black dress effect she was hoping to achieve.

Damn it all to hell! If only she had admitted to herself that she might have to attend this shindig, she could have had her assistant FedEx her one of her many beautiful outfits.

After the years Sheridan had spent in baggy denim rebelling against her mother, her interest in fashion had surprised her. And because she wrote books on women's empowerment, she'd felt a little hypocritical and kept that interest quiet.

She'd been a bit ashamed to devote any of her time or money to such a trivial matter. But Darcy had pointed out that how Sheridan dressed and presented herself influenced not only how others saw her but also how she was treated.

Sheridan had realized that this was especially true for her publisher and agent. New Yorkers expected a certain amount of polish, and if her appearance lacked sophistication, they would take advantage of her. If she was less than stylish, there would be financial consequences.

Sheridan had come to terms with the fact that although she was working to change the mindset that judged men by their actions and women by their appearances, she had to play the game to be in the game. She had made peace with her desire to have a great wardrobe, and there was no way she was going to her cousin's party in anything less than a stunning ensemble, complete with killer shoes and purse. And that meant she had to go shopping.

Errol had announced that he felt better and had moved from his bed to the sofa. The television in the living room was connected to a DVD player, and when Sheridan joined him, he was immersed in *The Monument Men*.

He stopped the movie and said, "Benny Anders just called. He's coming out to watch the Tigers game with me this afternoon. Could you run to town to pick up some snacks at the grocery store and a six-pack of Guinness?"

"Sure. Chips and dip, pretzels, and an order of hot wings from the deli coming up." Sheridan scooped up her keys from the coffee table. "I'm glad you'll have company since I need to drive to Quincy and get something to wear for Merry's party." She paused, then added hopefully, "Unless you'd like me to stay home with you tonight?"

"Flora's bringing me supper, and then we're going to watch our television shows together." He tilted his head. "Merry's shindig will be good for you. I bet you'll be amazed at how much fun you have there."

"Right." Sheridan rolled her eyes. "I'm sure it'll be thrilling."

"You may be surprised. Don't let the past influence how you see the present." Errol turned back to the movie, and over the sound of explosions, he added, "Get some of those frosted brownie bites while you're at the supermarket. Mrs. Henson is doing the baking there now, and her stuff is real tasty."

"Will do."

Sheridan shocked herself by planting a kiss on Errol's cheek. Why had she done that? Just because they'd had a pleasant conversation or two in the past couple of days didn't mean their relationship had changed.

Less than an hour later, Sheridan was heading for the Quincy Mall. During the forty-minute drive, she used her Bluetooth to talk to her assistant. Cara handled Sheridan's Facebook page, but there were always questions from readers that only Sheridan could answer. Once she'd dictated her responses, she gave her assistant a list of items that she wanted sent to Sutton Falls.

After thanking Cara and saying good-bye, Sheridan turned on the radio. She hoped the smooth jazz would take her mind off of Errol's health problems—the hospital still hadn't called with his test results.

Instead, the sexy instrumentals reminded her of Ridge. Tuesday, when he'd talked about Sutton Falls needing the levee, his devotion to the town had made her look at him in a different light. Then on the drive to the river when he said he was proud of her success, Sheridan had been breathless at his praise.

But it was when he'd shared his loneliness during his time in St. Louis that she'd realized that for all their differences, they weren't the polar opposites she had always believed.

Hitting the steering wheel, Sheridan struggled to forget the sensation of Ridge's lips on hers. She had to stop thinking about him. To stop fantasizing about him. To stop allowing him to monopolize her dreams.

The only way she could regain her rapidly diminishing self-control was to concentrate on something else. Straightening her spine, she called her assistant back and discussed business for the rest of the drive.

A couple of times during the trip, Sheridan sensed someone watching her. Was she being followed? She glanced in the rearview mirror. *No.* There wasn't another car in sight.

Great! Evidently, along with the panic attacks, the paranoia she'd felt after her prom experience from hell was returning as well. If this kept up, she'd need to start seeing a therapist again.

Pulling into the mall parking lot, Sheridan said good-bye to Cara and forced herself to shake off her gloomy feelings. She was on her way to buy a new outfit, and that was always fun. She exited the Lexus and was almost at the Bergner's entrance when she remembered that she hadn't locked the car. Nine days in Sutton Falls and she was already out of the habit. She switched directions and jogged back to the LS.

Just as she neared the rear of the Lexus, the back door popped open, and a slight figure cautiously emerged. A hoodie and sunglasses obscured the girl's face, and it took Sheridan a moment to place her.

Finally, Sheridan blinked and said, "Sally? What are you doing here? Did you want to talk to me about the books?"

Okay. That was a stupid question. The girl hadn't stowed away to discuss feminism.

"Uh." Sally's eyes darted around, and she edged away from Sheridan.

"Wait." Sheridan grabbed Sally's upper arm to prevent her from making a run for it. "I'm not upset with you, but you know I can't let you go off on your own, so talk to me."

"You could pretend you didn't see me." Sally hunched her

shoulders and put her hands in the sweatshirt's kangaroo pockets. "Most people don't notice me."

"Oh." Sheridan's throat closed. Did Sally feel as invisible as Sheridan had as a teenager? "Did something recently happen to make you think that way?"

"Sort of. I guess." Sally shrugged. "But it's nothing new. My parents are divorced. Mom dropped me at Dad's and took off before he even opened the door. And he leaves me with my grandmother most of the time. My folks wish I'd never been born, and Grandmother only notices me when I do something that doesn't *become* the family name. Like dress like a human being instead of a stupid Barbie doll."

"I see." Sheridan was way out of her depth.

While she empathized with Sally's wardrobe issues, having fought the same fight with Vivian that the girl was engaged in with her grandmother, Sheridan had little experience with kids—especially twelve-year-olds. Which issue should she address first? *None.* She should call Sally's family and turn the girl and her problems over to them.

"I sincerely doubt that you understand," Sally muttered.

Ignoring her own good advice to let Sally's father and grandmother deal with her issues, Sheridan said, "Let's go inside and have something to eat. I skipped lunch and I'm starved."

"You're not taking me home?" Sally's expression was a mixture of suspicion and hope.

"Probably." Sheridan loosened her grip on the girl's arm and took her by the hand. "But not right now."

There was a TGI Fridays near the Bergner's mall entrance, and once they were seated and had placed their orders, Sally said, "Please don't make me go back."

"Is anyone hitting you or touching you in places they shouldn't?" Sheridan asked, fear that the girl was being abused crawling up her spine. When Sally shook her head, Sheridan let out a relieved breath and said, "Then sorry, but I don't have much choice. Do you have a cell?"

"Yes." Sally reluctantly took a purple iPhone from her pocket.

"Call your dad or your grandmother, tell them where you are and why, then let me speak to them."

Sally's green eyes filled with childlike resentment, and she shook her head.

Sheridan waited a couple of seconds, then, when the girl still didn't comply, she said, "Either you do it or I do it."

She suddenly remembered that she didn't know Sally's last name but didn't let that realization show on her face. "And put it on speaker so I can hear."

"Fine. Be that way." Sally swept her finger across the screen and tapped the appropriate icons. When a voice answered, Sally said, "Grandmother, it's me."

"Why are you calling?" the woman demanded. "Did you get into trouble at school again?"

Sally explained where she was, then said, "Ms. Davis wants to talk to you."

"Sally is fine," Sheridan said, annoyed that the woman hadn't even asked about her granddaughter's well-being. "Would you like to come pick her up?"

"I just arrived at the spa for a mani/pedi and have a hair appointment scheduled after that. I can't possibly leave for at least three hours." Her tone brooked no argument. "And Sally's father is in an important meeting and can't be disturbed."

"So…" Sheridan was appalled at the woman's apparent lack of concern for her granddaughter. "What would you like to do?"

"It would be best if you drove her home." There was a pause as Sally's grandmother advised the manicurist of her color choice, then she said to Sheridan, "You may drop Sarah Ann at the Enchanted Forest Spa when you return to town."

"But I need to do some shopping." Sheridan gazed at Sally. The girl was certainly right about her family's attitude toward her. "I won't be back for a couple of hours, maybe longer."

Sheridan would have liked to lay into the woman about her callous attitude toward her granddaughter and her assumption that her and her son's activities were more important than anyone else's needs but bit her tongue for Sally's sake. The girl's miserable expression broke Sheridan's heart.

"That's fine, dear." The woman dismissed Sheridan and said, "Sarah Ann, be a good girl. Since our little Sheri is such a famous writer now"—disdain oozed from the woman's voice—"you don't want to end up as a bad example in one of her ridiculous books. If you behave, maybe I won't have to tell your father about this."

"I beg your pardon?" Sheridan's voice was low, but her blood pressure wasn't. "My books are not—" The woman hung up before she could finish. After taking a calming breath, Sheridan plastered a pleasant smile on her lips and said to Sally, "Well, I guess we're spending the afternoon together."

"Sorry about my grandmother." Sally's face was red. "She's just a stupid old lady. Your books are awesome."

"Thank you. But don't worry about your grandmother insulting me." Sheridan patted the girl's hand. "One thing a writer has to develop is a thick skin. People on Amazon and Goodreads have certainly called my books worse things than ridiculous."

"I know." Sally lifted her chin. "I go on Amazon, and on every bad review, I click no to 'Was this helpful?'"

"That's so sweet of you." Sheridan grinned. She loved Sally's spunkiness. "But back to you stowing away in my car. What was your plan? Were you running away or just playing hooky?"

"At first, I just wanted to avoid Mr. Nolan's social studies.

He's such a chauvinist." Sally took a sip of her triple-berry smoothie. "He never tells us about anything that women did or are doing. I find out more about the great women of history on Google Doodle than in his class."

"It was the same when he taught me." Sheridan made a mental note to find out if there was anything that could be done about the teacher's blatant sexism.

"Once they take roll call during homeroom, they never notice if you're gone, so I slipped away when we changed classes between first and second period," Sally explained. "I hung around the park for a while, but when some moms came with their little kids, since I knew they'd wonder why I wasn't at school, I headed over to the grocery store to get something to eat."

"Wouldn't the clerk notice that you were truant?"

"I told her that I had a doctor's appointment and my grandmother was waiting in the car." Sally grinned, clearly proud of her quick thinking. "Then I heard you mention that you were going to the mall, so before you came out of the store, I hid on the floor of your backseat. I pulled that blanket you had there over me and fell asleep. I only woke up when you turned on the radio."

"Since you were getting out of the Lexus when I saw you, how were you going to return to Sutton Falls?" Sheridan was intrigued with Sally's story.

She had often dreamed of running away. Only her concern about worrying her father had stopped her.

"By then I had decided to take a bus from here to Chicago."

"Is that where your mother lives?" Sheridan asked. "We could call her right now and see if she could arrange a visit for you."

Before Sally could answer, the server brought their food, checked if they needed anything else, then left. As Sheridan slid the rod from her hibachi chicken skewers, she kept an eye on Sally. There was a wounded look on her face, and a single tear slid down her cheek.

Sally flicked away the droplet and said, "I don't know where Mom is. We got kicked out of our apartment because she spent all the money Dad sent her on clothes and to go out partying."

"That had to be scary." Sheridan's chest tightened.

"A little." Sally nodded, then continued, "When Mom left me at my father's, she didn't say where she was going. Just that she had some important business to take care of and she'd be back to get me when my father finally realized how hard it was to raise a child alone."

"Could she be finding a job?" Sheridan asked.

"I doubt it." Sally snorted. "Mom said that until Dad was willing to marry her again or increase the amount he paid for child support, she was done with me."

"She was probably just freaked out because she couldn't provide for you." Sheridan tried to comfort the girl.

"Dad always said he wanted full custody." Sally's head drooped and she whispered, "But now that he has it, he seems uncomfortable being with me."

"Maybe he needs some time to adjust," Sheridan offered, afraid it sounded as lame to Sally as it did to her. "I'm sorry your mom said that to you, but the issue is probably more about your parents' relationship and less about how they actually feel about you."

"Yeah. I get that they hate each other." Sally picked up her burger. "They've been yelling at each as long as I can remember."

"They fought in front of you?" Sheridan was disgusted. She might not have much maternal instinct, but she'd never allow a child of hers to witness something as disturbing as an argument between his or her parents.

"Mom and Dad didn't know that I was there." Sally took a huge bite and talked around it. "I used to sneak out of bed and watch them from the top of the staircase." She swallowed. "Once Dad said to Mom that if she hadn't trapped him, they'd both be a lot happier." Sally twisted her napkin. "I supposed he meant that she got pregnant with me to make him marry her."

"Probably. But that doesn't mean your father isn't happy you were born, he's just mad at how it happened." Having no idea what else to say, Sheridan ate a piece of garlic-black pepper glazed chicken. Swallowing, she asked, "So why Chicago?"

"My best friend from my other school—the one where I went before I came back to Sutton Falls—moved there." Sally squirted a pool of ketchup on her plate, picked up a seasoned fry, and swirled it in the sauce.

"I doubt her parents would allow you to stay with them without your folks' permission." Sheridan forked some jasmine rice pilaf into her mouth.

"Probably not." Sally made a face. "Next time, I need to plan this better."

"Or instead of running away again, have a conversation with your dad and tell him how you feel." Sheridan frowned. *Wait.* That sounded like advice Merry would give to her. "Has your father ever said he didn't want you around?"

"Not exactly." Sally stared at her plate. "But we don't talk much."

"It might be time to change that." Sheridan silently added, *for both of us.*

"I'll think about it." Sally went back to her cheeseburger.

When they'd finished eating and were heading to Bergner's, Sheridan said, "I hope I can trust you not to go AWOL while I try on clothes. I need to find something to wear tonight to my cousin's party."

"I promise." Sally crossed her heart. "On the drive back to Sutton Falls, can we talk about your books?"

"Sure." Sheridan smiled. "I'll try not to take too long to find an outfit."

"That's okay." Sally shoved her hands in the pocket of her jeans. "Mom always made me shop with her. I'm used to waiting around. If I get bored, I can read a magazine on my phone."

"Good idea." Sheridan smiled.

Another thing they had in common. When Vivian had dragged Sheridan to the mall, she'd always brought a book to keep herself amused while her mother shopped.

Once they entered Bergner's, Sheridan made a beeline for the women's apparel section. She quickly had an armful of possibilities and headed toward the fitting rooms. Sally took a seat on a nearby chair, and Sheridan started the process of elimination.

She rejected garment after garment until she slipped on a Guess vintage print fit-and-flare dress. The sweetheart neckline was flattering, and she loved that it showed a bit of flirtatious cleavage without being slutty. The cutout details in back were unexpected, giving it the perfect wow factor.

Fifteen minutes later, she found a second possibility. The Anne Klein black-and-white diamond-print pants paired with a black crêpe de chine blouse was fun. The cascading ruffled vee neckline added a bit of zing, and the slacks fit as if they'd been tailored for her.

Stepping out of the dressing room holding her choices, Sheridan was surprised when Sally popped up beside her and said, "Get the dress."

"Why?" Sheridan planned to buy both outfits, but was curious to hear the girl's thoughts.

"It looks more like a party." Sally touched the fabric. "The pants and top are cute but would be better for something in the daytime."

"Good point." Sheridan was impressed. "Are you interested in fashion?"

"I read Tavi Gevinson's *The Rookie*," Sally explained as she followed Sheridan to the shoe department. "It's an online magazine for teenagers. It combines clothes with what's going on in today's world."

"I used to read her blog," Sheridan said as she browsed. "I'll have to check out Tavi's magazine."

"You'll love it." Sally brought the magazine up on her phone and showed it to Sheridan.

A few minutes later, when the clerk approached her, Sheridan asked to see the shoes she'd selected in a size nine. Both pair of sandals fit perfectly, and Sheridan brought them, a couple of purses, and the clothes to the register.

After making her purchase, she and Sally headed to the parking lot. On the drive home, Sally peppered Sheridan with questions, but a few miles from the turnoff to Sutton Falls, she finally broached the one she clearly had wanted to ask from the beginning.

Turning to stare at Sheridan, she said, "So why do you write the books that you do?"

Sheridan had answered that particular inquiry so often that she had a pat response, but instead of trotting out the usual rhetoric, she said, "I had an extremely bad experience in high school, and I didn't feel strong enough to handle it the way I should have. I want to empower other girls and women to be tougher and more resilient than I was and to make better choices than I did."

Sally was silent for a long time, then she muttered, "Boys have it so much easier than us."

"Not in all respects." Sheridan pulled the Lexus into the spa parking lot. "Many of them are no more at peace with themselves than we are. They have the same insecurities about their appearance, their performance, and their futures as we do. But what they do have is more professional and economic advantages, and that's what we need to work on improving."

"Yeah." Sally opened the car door.

Sheridan walked the girl into the spa, and the receptionist said, "Sally, your grandmother asked me to send you to the hair salon when you got here."

Sally thanked the woman, then turned to Sheridan and said, "I've been thinking about what we were talking about in the car. If Mom felt better about her own accomplishments, I don't think she'd be so mad at Dad about his."

"Any time a woman's whole identity is tied up with the man she marries, there's bound to be a problem." Sheridan hugged the girl good-bye and watched her disappear down a long hallway. She hoped that Sally and her father could work things out before they ended up in the same sort of cold war situation that she and Errol were battling.

CHAPTER THIRTEEN

Sheridan stood in her bra and panties in front of the full-length mirror on the back of her bedroom door. Her hair was styled and her makeup applied. She glanced at her watch. It was six thirty.

All that was left for her to do was to put on her clothes and jewelry, but Sheridan didn't move. Why should she go to Merry's party? She knew her cousin meant well, but really, what would she have in common with those people? Even if she knew one or two of them, it had been thirteen years. What would they talk about—the weather?

Of course, teachers were generally pretty interesting. As a group, they tended to read widely and keep current on what was happening in the world. Maybe they'd say something she could use in the book she was supposed to be writing.

Her working title was, *The Male Intellect: An Oxymoron?* It would be interesting to hear what the staff had to say about the imbalance of male administrators versus female teachers. As long as she thought of the party as work, she was willing to attend.

She slipped on her new dress, twisting her arms to fasten the back zipper, then stepped into the sand Vince Camuto sandals she'd purchased that morning. The high-cut ankle strap and chunky heel paired perfectly with the dress's vintage feel.

It was a shame that the only jewelry she had with her were the gold hoop earrings and tiny initial pendant that she'd had on when she arrived in Sutton Falls. It would be nice to have some of her more impressive trinkets to wear.

As Sheridan walked down the short hallway to the living

room, she heard her aunt and father talking. The homey sound of the sister and brother gossiping about their relatives warmed her heart. She really had missed being a part of a family. In St. Louis, she might go as much as a week without seeing anyone besides the mail carrier and the takeout delivery guy.

"Hi, Aunt Flora." Sheridan pecked the older woman on the cheek.

"Why, Sheri, honey, you look pretty as a picture. That color is perfectly delicious on you. But…" Flora's words trailed off.

"But what, Aunt Flora?" Sheridan wanted to smack her aunt. Every compliment came with a small dose of criticism, and she wasn't sure she was up to it tonight.

"Well…your hair."

"What about my hair?" Sheridan's hand crept up to smooth her chignon.

"Uh…nothing. Except, maybe you could wear it loose once in a while. That bun you wear it in makes you look old."

"It's not a bun." Sheridan shut her eyes and counted to fifteen. She knew her aunt meant well, but trust Flora to pop the balloon of self-confidence. "It's a chignon."

"Whatever fancy name you have for it, that style adds ten years to your face."

"I'll keep that in mind," Sheridan answered, employing the exact same words she used when readers confronted her about something they wanted changed in her books.

"You do that." Flora crossed her arms.

Sheridan eased toward the door. "I'll probably be home by nine."

"Don't worry about us. We'll just eat and watch TV. I brought over Errol's favorite pie, a lemon meringue. I'll have to give you the recipe. Now that you're back, maybe you could learn to make it."

"Great." Sheridan forced a smile, then muttered under her

breath, "I'll start baking when hell freezes over and the devil holds a cooking contest." She waved her fingers and escaped out the door, yelling, "Bye," over her shoulder.

* * *

Sheridan pulled her Lexus onto the side of the road. It was a couple of blocks away from Merry's place, but her cousin's driveway was already full of cars, as was much of the rest of the street.

As Sheridan walked toward the beautiful home, she admired Merry's nerve. In Sutton Falls, it was almost unheard of for a single woman to have a large house built just for her. Unfortunately, in order to afford the place on a teacher's salary, Merry had had to accept a piece of property from her parents. Which meant she lived smack dab between her folks and her brother, Mick.

It was a good thing Aunt Flora was at the farm and Uncle Whit turned his hearing aid off right after dinner, because the music and noise blaring from inside was loud enough to bring down the walls of Jericho.

Sheridan let herself in through the unlocked screen door and admired the open floor plan. The blueprints Merry had shown her at Christmas didn't do the house justice. It was gorgeous.

From the foyer, Sheridan could see that the great room was wall-to-wall people. As she focused on individual faces, trying to locate her cousin, her mind registered that a lot of them looked familiar. Too familiar. It appeared that a good portion of their senior class was present.

Shit! Sheridan's heart rate sped up. What had Merry done?

Abruptly the voices died down, and everyone's gaze fastened on Sheridan. The silence grew, and she wanted to run out of the room, but her legs wouldn't cooperate. Her chest constricted, and she couldn't draw enough air to come close to filling her lungs. Were they about to turn on her? Would they laugh and point like the last time?

Black dots danced in front of her eyes. Sheridan recognized the onset of a panic attack and prayed she wouldn't faint.

Suddenly Merry emerged from the crowd. She was carrying a large sheet cake, and everyone began to sing, "For she's a jolly good fellow."

Her mouth hanging open, Sheridan sank into the nearest empty chair, trying desperately to get her breathing back to normal.

The song ended, people crowded around her, and Merry put the cake down on the coffee table in front of Sheridan. On top was a reproduction of her book cover, and written in buttercream frosting were the words *Congratulations, Sheridan!*

She smiled weakly, thanked Merry, then grabbed her hand and pulled her into the bathroom. Locking the door, Sheridan stood blocking her cousin's escape route.

Sheridan clutched her chest—her heart was still beating much too fast—and asked, "What have you done?"

Merry grinned. "Well, I couldn't recreate the prom. I knew I'd never get you into the high school gym. So, instead I invited everyone I could remember being there to celebrate your success."

"Why?" Sheridan was somewhat comforted knowing that her cousin would never deliberately cause her pain, but Merry was so sweet that she had no concept how cruel people really were. "You knew I didn't want to see those people ever again. They all had to have been in on what Alexis did to me."

"That's probably true," Merry said calmly. "And, yes, it was mean to set you up as the target of a joke, but that's what high school kids find funny. Nice? No. Monstrous? I don't think so."

"You're right. It was probably just a hilarious trick to them." Sheridan had never told her cousin about the additional, more horrendous surprise Alexis—and possibly Ridge—had arranged for her later that night.

"Exactly."

"But why did you have to gather them all together? I really don't want to face their ridicule for a second time."

"Ridicule?" Merry took Sheridan by the shoulders. "You know I would never expose you to that. These people are proud to say they went to school with you. You're a *New York Times* best-selling author. For crying out loud, you've been on national television. They feel you've slighted them by never doing a book event in Sutton Falls. Sean told me that he saw you walk right by the Well-Caffeinated Reader, and you didn't even bother to go in and sign stock. All I'm trying to do is soothe everyone's hurt feelings."

"I don't understand." Sheridan stubbornly refused to hear what her cousin was trying to tell her. She didn't want to take the chance of being hurt ever again.

"Don't try to pretend ignorance to me. Of course you understand." Merry crossed her arms. "It's time to move forward. Go out there and mingle. You write about strong women. Be one. Pretend this is one of your big signing parties. A lot of them have brought books they want autographed."

"Some will make snide remarks." Sheridan shook her head. "You know that's going to happen."

"Sure, a few are undoubtedly jealous." Merry turned Sheridan to the mirror. "Look how beautiful you are."

"I'm not—"

"Yes. You are." Merry didn't allow Sheridan to twist away from her reflection. "Just pretend they're reviewers and charm them. I've seen you handle hostile interviewers on talk shows. I'm sure you can handle a few small-town bozos without breaking a sweat." Merry shoved Sheridan toward the door. "Get out there and knock 'em dead."

* * *

Sheridan smiled at a guy who had worked on the school newspaper with her during their senior year. "So, what are you doing now, Les?"

"I manage Sutton's Supermarket. I took over when Henry died."

"You must do a great job," Sheridan said. "I was in the store a couple of days ago, and everything was in terrific order and very clean."

"I do my best." The balding man smoothed his shirt. "Ridge is a good boss. He lets me handle the whole shebang and backs me up if there's a problem. Which, unfortunately, we've been having more and more of lately."

"Good bosses are important." There was that name again. Could no one in this town talk for five minutes without mentioning Ridge Sutton?

"Yeah. I was really worried for a while when he and Alexis were going through the divorce. It was such a relief that Ridge got the store." Les leaned forward, lowered his voice, and said, "I...uh...always wanted to say that I was sorry for my part in what happened during our senior prom. I hope you're not mad at me."

"No, that's okay." Sheridan patted Les's arm. "I know Alexis was behind it all."

"She was really hard to say no to. Not someone you wanted to cross. She would have made my life miserable if I hadn't cooperated. You were going away to college, but I knew that I would be staying right here in town the rest of my life." Les cleared his throat. "I'm glad you're not mad or nothing, but I had to get that off my chest."

"Don't worry about it," Sheridan reassured him, then chuckled. "Only people who have bad memories have a clear conscience."

"Well—"

"Let's forget it. A lot of people had a part in that prank, but Alexis and Ridge are the only ones that I really blame." Those last bitter words slipped from her lips before she could stop them.

"But Ridge—"

"Truly, Les, let's put it behind us. Tell me about your family."

* * *

It was nearly nine and the party was in full swing. Sheridan had signed dozens of books, and it had been nice to talk to her former classmates. It was interesting to find out what they had been up to and where their lives had led.

Since she was having a surprisingly good time, she decided to telephone her aunt to see if Flora would mind staying a little while longer with Errol. It was too noisy to make the call from the main floor, so Merry suggested that Sheridan use the office upstairs.

Once she was seated behind her cousin's desk, she fished her cell from her pocket. Flora answered on the first ring. Her aunt was thrilled that Sheridan wanted to stay longer and kept her on the phone, pressing for details.

No one noticed Sheridan when she returned to the party, and she stood against the wall feeling invisible. The old fears and insecurities crept back to haunt her, but before she could work herself into a full-blown panic attack, a loud burst of laughter in the center of the great room drew her attention.

Well, hell! Beau Bunson was sitting behind Merry's piano. Beau had been, and probably still was, Ridge's best friend. Her gaze frantically swept the room as she inched backwards into the foyer. Was Ridge here as well? She hadn't seen him since the kiss on the levee, and after her humiliating fall down the embankment, she sure didn't want to face him for the first time in front of a crowd.

Sheridan took a deep breath. She was being silly. Just because Beau was here didn't mean Ridge was, too. Surely Merry would have mentioned it if he were there. Still, Beau had never been very nice to her, so best to avoid him.

With the open floor plan, Sheridan could see a few people in the dining room, so she headed toward them. Once she was away from the crowd around Beau, she exhaled in relief.

As Sheridan took a step to join the folks filling their plates, Merry walked out of the kitchen and asked, "Everything okay with Uncle Errol?"

"Yes. Your mom assures me that she and my father are watching a movie, and I can stay as long as I like."

"Great." Merry gestured to the table. "I'm going to make plates for Mick, Nan, and my father. Dad dislike parties, and Mick came down with the flu last night, so Nan doesn't want to leave him alone."

"I wondered why I hadn't seen your brother and sister-in-law." Sheridan watched her cousin fill three dishes. "I hope he feels better soon."

"Me, too." Merry chewed her lip. "After I take over Dad's plate, I'll text Nan and leave the other two in their screen porch. I don't want to get Mick's germs, but at least Nan can have something good to eat while she takes care of him." Merry headed for the back door off the kitchen. "See you when I get back."

Sheridan waved her cousin off, then, as she grabbed a

deviled egg, one of the guys who she recognized from her senior history class smiled at her.

After they exchanged greetings, he said, "Do you remember what a hard time Mr. Smyth used to give you about women's rights?"

Sheridan rolled her eyes. "How could I forget? He used to contradict what was written in our texts in order to get a rise out of me."

A woman joined their conversation. "How about the time the guidance counselor didn't want to let us girls take shop?"

"I'd forgotten about that." Sheridan shook her head. "Didn't we build a miniature fence around his office?"

"We sure did." The other woman nodded. "And you put a big sign on it that read: *The Sty. Every chauvinist pig needs a home.*"

The group around her roared with laughter, attracting even more people to join them. Before long, they were all reminiscing about their shared past. Their acceptance gave Sheridan a warm glow, and she realized that she'd allowed the bad times to make her forget all the good ones. She'd been foolish to avoid her hometown for so long.

She was laughing at another anecdote when a loud, drunken voice from the great room drew everyone's attention. Sheridan craned her neck and saw that although Beau was still sitting at the piano, most of his audience had drifted toward the dining room.

With a mean look on his flushed face, he said, "I'm surprised no one's told the funniest story about our famous author."

Fear flickered up Sheridan's spine. Would they all turn against her again?

Someone yelled, "Go home and sober up, Beau."

Beau ignored the advice and continued, "I see now that

she's famous, everyone wants to pretend it didn't happen."

A murmur started among the crowd, and someone shouted, "Beau, you're a great example of what happens when idiots have unprotected sex."

"Come on, guys." Beau glared at the men. "Have you read her books? She hates us."

The muttering grew louder, and a woman said, "If you were any stupider, Beau Bunson, you'd have to be weeded twice a month."

Sheridan took a hopeful breath. Maybe this time her classmates would stand up to Beau's peer pressure.

Beau narrowed his bloodshot eyes. "Remember what we did to her the night of the prom?" He smiled cruelly and his voice took on a coaxing tone. "We were all in on it."

Sheridan's chest tightened. *Shit!* She was having trouble breathing. Beau's mention of that night had triggered the traumatic memory, and she was moments away from a true panic attack.

"Not everyone." Alexis Byrnes Sutton strolled into the great room from the foyer. She was as gorgeous as ever. Her long blond hair hung in a silken curtain down her back, and her size-two figure hadn't increased an inch.

"Alexis!" Beau let out a delighted shriek. "When did you get into town?"

"I'll never tell." Alexis blew Beau a kiss, then swept the room with her gaze and drawled, "But your memory is faulty, Bertie. Only the popular kids were actually *in* on Operation Shame Sheri. The other sheep just played along."

The painful reminder of the humiliation of that night slashed into Sheridan's chest and brought on a wave of dizziness. She glanced around and realized she was trapped. In order to get to the front door, she'd have to pass through the great room, which meant coming way too close to Alexis for comfort. And there was a solid wall of people between her and the door off the kitchen.

This was exactly like the nightmares she'd had right after the incident, but she couldn't lose it now. It would be too mortifying to pass out. She tried to think what her old therapist had said to do to stave off a PTSD attack. First, breathe. Second, remember that she was the one with all the power. Third, take control.

Sheridan could hear Alexis's scathing comments to the others as the awful woman made her way across the room. "Les, I see you're still hanging around the fringes of every party."

The poor man shrank back as if Alexis had slapped him, and he mumbled a reply.

A nanosecond later, Alexis poked a woman in the midriff and said, "Nice muffin top, Prissy. I guess now that you're married, you just let yourself go all to hell."

"You're right." Prissy's face turned a dull red and she hung her head. "I should get to the gym more."

"Christopher, nice Bieber hair," Alexis sniggered. "What are you, like, thirteen?"

Sheridan frowned at both Alexis's treatment of her classmates and their reaction to her insults. Why was everyone allowing her to torment them? Back in high school, Alexis had collected embarrassing information like a squirrel gathering nuts for the winter. Was she still using blackmail to control them?

The crowd parted as Alexis continued her grand entrance, and Sheridan used the distraction to edge backwards. If she were lucky, she would slip away while the nasty woman's attention was focused on the others. She knew she should stand up to Alexis, but she wasn't sure she was mentally prepared for that kind of confrontation.

Sure, she was stronger now. And she'd faced down a lot of bullies in her professional life, but this was different. Alexis was the boogeyman from her past, the monster hiding in the closet that she'd never faced. It was safer to retreat until she was better prepared to deal with her high school persecutor than to stumble for words and revert back to *Sheri*, the intimidated wimp who had allowed herself to be terrorized her entire senior year.

Nearly out of the dining room, with escape only a few feet away, Alexis emerged from the crowd and grabbed Sheridan's arm.

Sometime in the minute or two that Sheridan had lost track of the loathsome woman, Beau had joined Alexis, and now he sneered, "Leaving already?" He reached out and grabbed Sheridan's other arm. "We can't have the guest of honor taking off so early."

"The fun's just getting started." Alexis's voice was venomous. "And just like prom night, you're the entertainment."

"Wrong," Sheridan replied coolly, determined not to let Alexis see her distress. "Now take your hands off me, or this time, I *will* press charges for assault."

"I doubt it. You don't have the guts or the self-respect." Alexis raised a perfectly shaped brow. "If you had even a tiny bit of dignity, none of that night would have happened. You had to know that Chris only asked you to the prom because Ridge made him. After all, it was less than a week away, and everyone who was anyone had had their dates lined up for months before."

"But Chris said he hadn't been sure if he'd be in town that weekend, and that's why he waited to invite me." Sheridan stopped. She didn't need to explain herself to these people. Jerking her arms from Alexis's and Beau's grip, Sheridan demanded, "Anyway, why would Ridge care if I went to the prom or not?"

"He was grateful you had helped him with his English grade and felt sorry for you," Beau mocked. "Why else would he even notice someone like you?"

"I see." Sheridan swallowed the lump in her throat, then as she began to process the various pieces of information, she stared speculatively at Alexis and said, "But you know what I don't understand is why you hated me so much. What did I ever do to you?"

"Hey. It's not my fault you came up short in the looks, personality, and family connection lotteries. Don't blame the messenger who pointed it out to you." Alexis stared down her pert little nose.

Had Alexis had plastic surgery? Sheridan was momentarily distracted. She didn't remember the woman having quite such a movie-star-perfect profile in high school.

Forcing her attention back to the matter at hand, Sheridan asked, "Why would you go to all that trouble to target a nobody like me?"

"You needed to be taken down a peg." Alexis's nostrils flared. "You were getting above your station in life." She abruptly changed her tactics and asked, "So, don't you want to know how we accomplished our little prank? Or can't you face just how many of our dear classmates were willing to help me crush you?"

Sheridan had always wondered exactly what had happened. She hesitated, then smiled, realizing that she really didn't care anymore.

But before she could decline, Beau jumped in and said, "Alexis figured out everything to the last detail. And everyone did their part." He pointed to Chris. "You agreed to invite her but then, per Alexis's instructions, didn't pick her up that night."

Chris looked down at the floor.

"And you," Alexis gestured to Prissy, "pretended to be Chris's mother and told Ms. Loser here that there had been some big emergency and she was supposed to meet Chris at the dance."

"I would have sworn you'd be too crushed to actually telephone him." Beau shook his head at Sheridan. "But Alexis was right, you just couldn't let it rest."

"It meant so much to my mother." Sheridan spoke almost to herself recalling her mom's excitement that she was finally socializing with the in crowd.

"When you showed up," Alexis cackled, "and Les flipped on the overhead lights, I thought I would die laughing. Then when everyone held up their posters, and you just stood there like a dumbass, I almost peed my pants."

"My favorite sign was the one that said *Girl Most Likely to Be Ignored*," Beau hooted, then turned to the crowd. "Do you guys remember any other ones?"

No one spoke. The shame they felt for having participated in such a mean prank showed plainly on their faces.

"And that wasn't even the best part of the joke." Alexis's blue eyes glinted with vindictiveness. "The icing on the cake was what happened once Sheri here turned tail and took off for the parking lot."

"Stop!" Sheridan yelled, her heart pounding in her ears. "It was childish back then and it's even more juvenile now." She straightened her spine and stared at Alexis, daring her to continue. "That's enough."

"Who are you to tell us what's enough?" Beau jeered. "You may impress these small-town hicks with your scribbling, but I'm a little more sophisticated."

Sheridan opened her mouth to reply, but a voice from the foyer broke in, "No, what you are, Beau, is a little more drunk, which makes you mean."

All heads swung toward the speaker. Ridge stood by the front door, clearly having just arrived. His gaze met Sheridan's, and the look in his eyes made her feel as if he'd taken her into his arms to protect her from everyone.

"Aw, Ridge." The smug smile slipped off Beau's face, and he stared at the other man with a slack-jawed resentment. "Alexis and I were just having a little fun." He patted Sheridan's shoulder. "Maybe we were a little tough on you, but it all happened over thirteen years ago. What do you expect, an apology?"

"So I should get over what you and Alexis and Ridge did to me?" Sheridan's voice was icy. "Like it was the scratches Alexis's claws just left on my arms? Do you think I can rub some Neosporin on the memory of that night and it will heal?"

There was dead silence as everyone stared at the vignette being played out in front of them. Sheridan turned to the onlookers. "You all need to stand up to these trolls. It's clear that Beau and Alexis have never grown up, but surely you have."

Nauseated, Sheridan stalked out of the room, into the kitchen, and outside onto the deck. Clear of the crowd's view, she allowed her shoulders to sag, staggered down the wooden steps, and leaned against the wooded railing. She was determined not to fall apart, but it took every ounce of the energy she still possessed to remain upright.

After a long moment, she took a deep breath. Her heart wasn't racing anymore, and she no longer felt like she might vomit. She had staved off her impending panic attack and stood up to Alexis and Beau. Sheridan was shaken by the encounter, but she hadn't permitted them to bully her or to see her distress.

Still, it was upsetting to hear that so many of her classmates had plotted against her. And even more upsetting that they continued to be intimidated by Alexis. Sheridan felt so sorry for all of them. It seemed as if the only one who had really changed was her. And maybe Ridge.

He'd stood up to his friend. Did that mean anything? Or was it all an act to get on her good side so she'd sell the levee to him? Of course, that was it. Any other idea was pure foolishness.

146

CHAPTER FOURTEEN

Ridge stood frozen. Before he could move to follow Sheri, he noticed Alexis slip out of the room and through the front door. What was she doing in town? The last time he'd heard from her lawyer, the woman had told him that his ex was in Florida with her parents.

Whatever brought her back to Sutton Falls boded no good for him or for anyone else here. Alexis had been mad enough to summon the flying monkeys when the town had sided with him in their divorce, and she was not a person who tended to forgive and forget. Total recall and scorched-earth revenge were more her style.

Ridge hesitated, torn between concern for Sheri and a foreboding that Alexis's presence was a sign of the coming apocalypse. A split second later, he made the only decision possible and ran after the woman he cared for rather than the one he feared.

He'd deal with his ex-wife later. He needed to find Sheri right now. Along with making sure she was okay, it was past time for him to uncover exactly what had gone on the night of their senior prom.

When he slammed out of the back door, Sheri was perched on the edge of an Adirondack chair, staring at the house. She was spotlighted by the lamps attached to the deck's posts, and the mixture of sadness and defeat in her eyes brought a bitter lump to Ridge's throat. She looked braced for an attack, and it pissed him off to see her so devastated.

He hurried down the steps toward her, but when she shook her head, he stopped a few feet from where she sat to give her a chance to regain her composure. It was clear that she'd been more upset about what had happened inside than she'd allowed anyone to see.

While Sheri collected herself, Ridge thought about why he'd opted to come to the party. Beau had told him about Merry's plan to celebrate her cousin's success with their classmates. And although Merry hadn't formally invited either Beau or Ridge, in a small town like Sutton Falls, gatherings like this one had an open-door policy.

Still, Ridge hadn't planned to attend. But the restlessness he'd been battling since kissing Sheri at the levee had gnawed at him. All he'd been able to think about was the feeling of Sheri's soft lips under his. And after spending a useless hour aimlessly wandering around his house, he'd given up any pretense that he might get some work done, asked Evelyn to watch Sally, and gone to the party.

Having walked in on Beau and Alexis's attack on Sheri, Ridge was thankful that he'd decided to drop by. While he'd hoped to get Sheri alone and convince her to go out with him Saturday night, defending her during the vicious pair's assault was more important.

And now, all he wanted to do was wrap her in his arms. To offer her a safe haven, where she could let go of her tough-chick image and accept the comfort that he wanted to give her and that she deserved.

Before Ridge could formulate a plan to break through the walls she'd erected, Sheri sniffed and said, "Go away. If you told off Beau thinking that I'd be so grateful that I'd sell you our land, you wasted your breath."

He stiffened. The sorrow and suspicion in her voice hit him in the chest and like a tire iron. Did she really think that poorly of him?

Determined to conceal how much her distrust hurt him, he said, "This has nothing to do with business. I'm not here as the mayor. I'm here as Ridge Sutton, a man who would like an opportunity to get to know you better. A man who would like to see if there's something more between us than chemistry."

"Oh." Sheri let out a tiny puff of air, then her eyelids dipped down, hiding her thoughts. Finally, her shoulders straightened, and she shook her head as if convincing herself not to trust his words. "You and your friends fooled me once. It's not going to happen again."

Her words of rejection shot an arrow of alarm into Ridge's chest. Something inside him said that the next few minutes would be the most important in his life. Either he could straighten out what had happened in the past or his chances with Sheri were zilch.

"Please." Ridge moved closer and eased down until he was sitting on his heels in front of her. "Just hear me out. I don't know what Alexis and the rest of them did to you the night of our prom. Back in the house, when you included my name with theirs, I realized you thought I was in on it, but I wasn't."

"You expect me to believe that?" Incredulity dripped from her voice.

"Did you see me there?"

"Yes." Sheri jerked her chin up and down. "When I walked in, you were clinging to Alexis like a cheap T-shirt."

"I have no memory of that night. It's a complete blank from about six thirty until I woke up the next morning." Ridge rubbed his eyes. Sheri's pain almost brought him to tears. "Beau had a pre-party at his place and served martinis. I swear, I only drank one, but after that, I can't remember anything."

"You're claiming that you were drunk?" Sheri crossed her arms. "*That's* your excuse?"

"No. I'm pretty damn sure I was roofied." Fury and shame battled it out in Ridge's gut.

He'd never admitted to anyone, even himself, that he'd

probably been drugged. How had he been moron enough to get into that kind of situation? Talk about being a poster boy for bad judgment. His choice of friends had really sucked.

"Why would they do that?" Sheri's tone made it clear she thought he was feeding her a line.

"Because they knew that I wouldn't go along with what they had planned for you. In high school, I was never there when Alexis pulled any of those malicious stunts. And when I heard about them and confronted her, she always claimed that the incidents had been blown out of proportion by girls who were jealous of her." Ridge cringed at his gullibility back then.

"That sounds like her kind of excuse. And it's true that you were never nearby when she ambushed me." Sheri's expression went from angry to miserable. "I was eternally thankful you weren't around to witness my humiliation," she murmured, biting her lip.

"But if I'd been there, I would have put a stop to her bullying."

"Maybe." Sheri didn't seem convinced that Ridge could have changed things, but she admitted, "Actually, you did seem really out of it on prom night. It almost looked as if Alexis was holding you up."

"Which lends credence to the theory that I was drugged."

"Possibly," she agreed, then shook her head. "But it doesn't mean you weren't in on her plot."

The hesitation in Sheri's voice made Ridge hope that he could convince her of his innocence. Or at least that he'd been stupid rather than malicious.

Ridge took her hand, relieved when she didn't immediately pull away, and said, "Why would she drug me if I was a part of it? And why would I do that to you? Someone who had helped me so much. Someone who had been so good to me. Someone who I really liked."

"I..." Sheri's tone was uncertain. "To please your girlfriend?"

Ridge's heart lightened when Sheri's eyes softened and she stopped trembling. He took her other hand and said, "Absolutely not. Alexis never, ever meant enough to me to be cruel to you. I had fully intended to never see her again after prom."

"Then why, after you two broke up, did you get back together with her in the first place?" Sheri jerked her fingers from his grasp. "Why did you marry her?"

"That's a story for another time, and I promise to explain it all to you if you'll go out with me tomorrow night."

Although it would kill him to admit what an idiot he'd been, Ridge knew he'd probably have to tell Sheri the whole sordid tale, but he needed to consider all the ramifications before he spilled his guts to her.

"Okay." Sheri nodded solemnly. "But no excuses tomorrow night."

"Agreed." Ridge was so damn happy to see the slight curve of her lips. Although he hated to have to dim her tiny smile, he knew he had no choice. They needed to clear up things between them. "But right now, you need to tell me what Alexis and Beau did to you."

"Fine." Sheri sighed, then described how Chris had stood her up and what had happened after she'd walked into the gym.

When her voice took on a heartrending hesitancy and she stuttered to a stop, Ridge stood and tugged her up from the chair and into his arms. He hugged her silently for a moment, resting his cheek on the top of her head.

When she relaxed against him, he murmured, "I know a few mean signs would have never made the Sheri Davis I knew leave town for good and let the bullies win." He leaned away and looked into her eyes, trying to convey his unconditional support. "Tell me the rest."

"I ran out to the parking lot, but I realized that my father had dropped me off and I'd forgotten my cell so I didn't have any way to get home. Before I could get up the courage to go find a phone to call for a ride, P...Pe..." She took a breath. "A boy from our class came outside. He said he'd seen what they'd all done to me and asked if I needed a lift home. I was hesitant, but he seemed so nice that I accepted."

"And?" Ridge kept his tone even, but his gut suddenly hurt.

If she couldn't even bring herself to utter the guy's name, this story would end badly.

"I know it was foolish, but I wasn't exactly at peak intellectual functioning." Sheri buried her face in Ridge's chest, her voice muffled. "At first he was really sweet, but then he went the wrong way and wouldn't listen to me when I told him to turn the car around. Instead, he pulled to the side of the road. By that point, we were out in the middle of nowhere, and I knew that I was in trouble."

Ridge stroked her hair. "Take your time."

It was hard enough for him to hear the details. He could only imagine how difficult it was for Sheri to revisit that awful night.

"I tried to get out of the car, but he made a grab for me and ripped the front of my dress loose from the straps." Now Sheri's words were rushing out so fast that Ridge could barely understand her. "I wasn't wearing a bra, and once he'd torn away my dress, something changed in his eyes. Up until then, it was almost as if he'd been playing with me, but then..."

Ridge had to swallow his rage before he could ask, "Did he...?"

"No." She choked off the single syllable. "I remembered the self-defense class we'd had in PE and managed to poke him in the eyes with my fingers and shove my knee into his crotch. While he was doubled over, I made it out of the car and ran into

152

the woods. He followed me, and for a while, I could hear him thrashing through the trees, but he finally gave up. Just before he left, he shouted, 'Alexis and Ridge send their regards.'"

"Son of a bitch!" Ridge gathered Sheri closer, fighting the urge to immediately find the guy and punch his lights out. Instead, Ridge said, "You had to know I would never do that to anyone, and especially not to you."

"It was hard to ignore his parting words," Sheri whispered. "Or maybe I just wanted to believe you were in on it because I thought it would be easier to give up the idiotic hope that we'd ever be together."

"You felt the same chemistry that I did?" Ridge's heart soared, and he pressed a tender kiss to her cheek. "So you would have gone out with me back then?"

"Seriously?" Sheri leaned away from him and raised a brow. "You had any doubts that if you asked out the class ugly duckling, she'd accept?"

"Everyone has doubts." Ridge drew her close again, then added, "And you were not an ugly duckling. You were never anything less than pretty and smart and wonderful. The only one who didn't know it was you."

"Right." Sheri's tone was frosty with skepticism.

"It's true," Ridge assured her. Then, knowing it would take more than words to convince her, he let the matter drop and asked, "How did you get home that night?"

"I walked. It's a good thing Chris was so short." Sheri paused and Ridge raised a questioning eyebrow. Continuing, she explained, "Because I didn't want to tower over him, I wore ballet flats instead of heels. It was over five miles, and I had to wrap what was left of my dress around me like a sarong." She shivered and Ridge held her tighter. "My dad was waiting up for me, so I had to tell him what happened. He wanted to take care of the matter with his shotgun."

"Why didn't you at least go to the police?" Ridge wished Errol *had* dispensed a dose of rural justice to the bastard.

"My father finally agreed to let the matter drop because neither one of us were willing to let Mom know the whole story. She was the one who pushed me to accept Chris's invitation to the prom and then insisted that I meet him there when he didn't pick me up." Sheri closed her eyes. "If we'd gone to the cops, the whole incident would have become public knowledge, and Mom would have felt as if it were all her fault for making me go. She was too sick to handle that kind of guilt, and we didn't want her last days to be burdened with the knowledge of what happened to me. So we kept it our secret."

"The asshole got away with it?" Ridge tried to keep the frustration out of his voice but failed.

"Yes." Sheri's shoulders slumped. "And God knows what other women he's attacked since then. Not reporting my assault was a decision that I've regretted every day for the past thirteen years."

"Will you tell me his name?" Ridge asked gently.

He needed to check out the law regarding the statute of limitations for attempted rape. The time to prosecute may have expired, but the guy could still be watched by the police until he did something else wrong. If the asshole still lived in Sutton Falls, Ridge would make sure he never had another good day in his life.

After a long moment, Sheri took a deep breath and said, "It was Perry Newtsen." She blew out a breath and shook her head. "That's the first time that I've said his name out loud since that night." Wrinkling her brow, she murmured, "Why did I let him have so much power over me?"

"Don't be so hard on yourself." Ridge tucked an escaped strand of hair behind her ear. "You weren't ready until now."

"Maybe." Sheri lifted her chin. "But I hate being so weak.

What did I think, that if I said his name, he'd appear out of a puff of smoke and attack me again?"

"You don't have to worry about that anymore," Ridge said soothingly. "Three or four months after the prom, Newtsen was killed in a car accident. It's highly unlikely he had a chance to harm anyone else."

"I wonder why Errol never mentioned it."

"It happened in the next county and Newtsen's folks pulled some strings to keep it quiet since he was flying high on meth when his car went off the bridge," Ridge explained. "I only heard about it because I was there when his mother asked mine for help in keeping it out of the newspaper." Sheri raised a questioning brow and Ridge added, "Evelyn owns a controlling interest in the Sutton Falls Journal."

Sheri rested her head against Ridge's chest and said, "I'm sorry he died but so glad that my not turning him in to the police didn't get anyone else hurt."

"I always wondered why you weren't in school the last few weeks, but I heard it was because of your mother's illness."

"That was what my father told the principal when he arranged for me to finish up at home," Sheri explained. "And I left town right after Mom's funeral."

"I'm so sorry." Ridge spoke into her hair. "If I had asked you out like I wanted to, or not taken that damn drink at Beau's pre-party, none of that would have happened to you."

"But then I wouldn't be the person I am now," Sheri said slowly. "And although it's been a tough journey, I think it was one I had to take."

"Even if that meant turning your back on Sutton Falls?" Ridge said. When she nodded, he asked, "How do you feel about being here now?"

"Strangely, better than I ever imagined." Sheri snuggled closer to him. "Merry was right to arrange this party. Between

DENISE SWANSON

the warm welcome from our classmates and finally being able to confront Alexis, I hope a lot of my demons have been laid to rest."

"You didn't mention hearing my side of the story." Ridge's voice was ragged. Sheri's soft curves were pressed along the length of his body, and it was distracting as hell. "Are you happy to find out that I had nothing to do with Alexis's scheme, or do you still want to keep your distance from me?"

He felt her hesitation, and he prayed like hell she wouldn't back away from him.

"I'm not sure." Sheri reached up and cupped his cheek, her thumb caressing his slight stubble. "I'll have to let you know about that."

Sheri slid her lips along his jawline, and desire tore through Ridge with the primal force of a Missouri twister. He immediately hardened, and without thinking, he moved his hands from her waist, sliding them down to her sweet ass. He settled her more firmly against his erection, and with a delighted hum, Sheri tangled her fingers in his hair and slanted her mouth against his.

A desire he could scarcely control battered at his usual practiced smoothness, snapping his restraint, and he deepened the kiss. She made an inarticulate needy sound and opened her lips for his tongue. Ridge had always loved Sheri's curves; her rounded hips and lush breasts might not be fashionable, but they took his breath away. He skimmed his fingers down the sweetheart neckline of her dress.

Ridge had fantasized about being with Sheri like this since he was eighteen. But the reality was so much better than he had ever dared to imagine. This time, nothing would come between them.

* * *

As Ridge's fingers played over her breasts, Sheridan's entire world was reduced to the blissful sensation of his caress. She'd been numb for so long, blocking out any emotions that threatened to break through the barricade she'd built around her heart. For the past thirteen years, the only feelings she'd allowed herself were anger and ambition. She'd been going through the motions of living while she stood off on the sidelines watching everyone else move forward.

Ridge appealed to her in a way that no other man ever had. Something about his strength drew her. His commitment to the people of Sutton Falls and the sense of permanence that he exuded attracted her at an elemental level she couldn't explain. Of course, the fact that he was sexier than caramel-coated sin didn't hurt, either.

But it was more than his charisma or his looks. Maybe it was his tenderness. She had never felt as treasured as she did in his arms, and it completely undid her. She snuggled closer, delighting in his arousal. She leaned back, peeked downward, and grinned. The zipper on his khakis looked ready to burst.

When Ridge clasped her to him as if he couldn't get close enough, her whole body burned. His breath heated her flesh, and she felt feverish, as if her skin was too tight. A tear hovered on her cheek. She was finally in his arms—where she had always wanted to be—and the possessiveness of his embrace ignited her senses in a way she'd never dreamt was possible.

Relishing his heart beating against her cheek, Sheridan spread her hands over his broad shoulders. His muscles rippling under her palms were heavenly. Fully dressed, she was more naked with Ridge here tonight than with any man before in her life.

She saw the heat in his eyes and the raw need on his face; and when he groaned low in his throat, her body responded with a fire of its own. She sucked in a startled breath and Ridge cupped her cheek. His mouth covered hers, and suddenly she wasn't able to think of anything except how good it felt to be in his arms.

Back in high school, rumor had it that Ridge was a great kisser, but clearly he'd used the passing years to hone his skills to the point where Sheridan forgot to breathe. Forgot to be nervous. Forgot all her doubts.

No man had ever kissed her like this. As if he wanted to own her body, her mind, and even her soul. She had never allowed herself to surrender completely to anyone she'd ever dated, but Ridge took that control and made her feel as if her body and brain were no longer connected.

At first, he took his time; his mouth moved sensuously across hers, exploring the shape of her lips. Then, just as she started to relax, to enjoy, to savor, he went deeper, and the kiss transformed from wonderful to a place she hadn't been before. With each deliberate glide of his tongue against hers, he stole another sliver of her usual caution.

He tasted of brandy and coffee and passion. Caressing every inch of her mouth, he stroked, then licked, and finally sucked hard on her tongue, twisting her into a knot of desire.

Sheridan had been attracted to Ridge since she was twelve years old, and although she'd fought those feelings with her whole heart and soul, they'd been buried deep in her psyche waiting for this night.

Her heart crashed into her breastbone with the sudden powerful hope that she and Ridge might finally be together.

As he broke off the kiss and took a ragged breath, she watched his palm glide up her thigh. The sight of his tanned hand against her pale skin did crazy things to her insides. And the sound of his voice, husky with desire, murmuring what he wanted to do to her had her thankful that she hadn't worn slacks.

The proof of his hunger for her pressed against her stomach, and she reached between them, popped the button of his pants, and slid down the zipper. He immediately grew bigger and harder. Then suddenly he put his hand over hers, halting her caress.

"Not like this." Ridge's voice was thicker than usual, and she could sense the rough edge of his self-control unraveling. "I want our first time together to be special. Let's go somewhere we can take our time. Somewhere private, where we won't be charged with indecent exposure."

Sheridan knew he was right, but it was so difficult to stop. She leaned her forehead against his, then, through the haze of her desire, she heard footsteps and glanced over Ridge's shoulder.

In the glow of the garage's halogen light, Sheridan saw Merry crossing the lawn toward them. She waved a hand at Sheridan, winked, and hastily retreated.

Oh. My. God! Sheridan buried her face in Ridge's chest. They'd nearly had sex on her cousin's back deck while, a few feet away, fifty or so of their previous classmates and Ridge's current constituents were dancing to Pink singing "Get the Party Started." Were they both out of their minds? Did she care?

CHAPTER FIFTEEN

As Ridge lay in his bed staring at the ceiling, he thought about the past few hours. He finally understood the expression "roller coaster of emotions." While driving to the party, he'd had a feeling of pleasant anticipation, which was quickly erased by the gut-wrenching scene he'd interrupted when he arrived.

Then the bliss of having Sheri in his arms had disappeared when she'd shoved him away and declared that she needed to go home. The warmth had drained from her eyes so fast that he'd had to grit his teeth to stop himself from howling at the loss.

His disappointment at the abrupt end to their evening had been somewhat lessened by Sheri's promise to go out with him the next night. And she'd seemed sincere when she'd explained that she had to get back to her father so that her aunt could leave. Still, it was frustrating that she had refused his offer to see her safely home. He'd been hungry for one more good-night kiss. Clearly, she hadn't felt the same way.

Being caught making out on someone's back deck was mildly embarrassing. And considering what they'd been doing moments before they were busted, the situation could have been even more awkward, but Sheri had reacted as if the paparazzi had snapped a nude photo of them and the picture was splashed across the front page of the *National Enquirer*.

He'd been thrilled when she buried her face in his chest. By turning to him for protection, Sheri had given him hope that she saw him as someone she could count on. But less than a nanosecond later, she'd jerked out of his arms, her cheeks ashen and a stricken look on her pretty face.

Her shamed expression tugged at his heart. And when she

stuttered about her professional image and what people would say, it was all he could do to stop himself from letting loose a string of four-letter words. He understood about keeping up appearances. But was she that embarrassed to be seen with him? Afraid that whatever he might say would be wrong, he'd kept his mouth shut. He'd accompanied her inside while she'd said her good-byes, thanked Merry for the party, and found her purse.

Then, ignoring Sheri's protests, he'd escorted her to her car. As she'd dug through her bag looking for her keys, he'd firmed up the details of their Saturday night date. Once she had her door unlocked, they'd exchanged cell numbers.

He'd smiled when she quickly grabbed his picture from the Sutton Falls website and added it to his contact data. It was his official mayoral portrait and not his favorite photo of himself, but it pleased him to no end that she would see his face every time he called her. Which, if he had his way, would be often.

As soon as she was done entering the information on her phone, she'd tried to slide inside the Lexus. But years of racquetball had honed his reflexes. He'd inserted himself between her and the driver's seat, giving her a final searing kiss before allowing her to leave.

Sheri had seemed confused at his persistence, and he wondered if she had any clue as to how beautiful she really was. A woman like her who was constantly on guard against the world most likely didn't permit too many folks to get close to her. Maybe no one had breached the fortress she kept around her heart.

Devil that he was, that last thought made him grin, and he turned onto his side, punching his pillow into shape. He sincerely hoped that there was no other man in her life. Not that a little competition would stop him, but he didn't need something else in his way. Convincing Sheri that he might be the one for her would be tough enough.

There were already too many minuses next to his name in her ledger. He mentally ran his finger down the page. Number one, the issue of her family's land. The town needed to control that levee, and her sentimental attachment to it might be a problem for both of them.

Number two, his ex-wife. A woman who had nearly gotten Sheri raped. A woman she had every right to hate. How would Sheri react when he told her the sordid details of his ill-fated marriage to Alexis?

Then there was number three, his daughter. Sally might end up being the true deal breaker.

Would Sheri be able to overlook who his daughter's mother was and see Sally for herself? Would Sheri be able to have any kind of reasonably good relationship with Sally? No matter how much he craved Sheri, he couldn't be with a woman who was anything but loving toward his daughter.

Ridge's stomach clenched. Maybe all his worries about what could come between Sheri and him were a moot point. If she didn't have the same feelings for him that he had for her, the other stuff wouldn't matter. He wanted nothing more than to wrap her in his arms and spend hours kissing her senseless. Was that what she wanted, too?

Flipping onto his back, he resumed his examination of the bedroom ceiling. Was a happily ever after even a possibility or just a pipe dream concocted by romance writers? His doomed marriage to Alexis sure had never had a chance at that kind of conclusion. And he certainly didn't consider his parents' dynastic union as particularly joyful.

Come to think of it, he couldn't name one friend who wasn't on at least their second wife or husband. Most were on their third. What did that say about the possibility for a fairy-tale ending?

Maybe the smart move would be to have his one date with

Sheri, then bow out of her life. What right did he have to pursue her when all that he had to offer her were complications and problems? He was a big fish in a small town. Sheri was the real deal.

Damn it! He rocketed upright. *No!* He wasn't surrendering that easily. This was his second chance and he wouldn't blow it. His time with Sheri on her cousin's deck had been the happiest that he could recall in recent history. Had he ever experienced that kind of passion and pleasure with anyone else?

It wasn't just the hotter-than-sin kisses or the feeling of her soft, curvy body pressed against his. It was the sense of rightness and contentment he felt when she was in his arms.

Before he fully realized what he was doing, he reached for his cell. He was about to tap her photo when he glanced at the clock.

Holy hell! It was nearly two in the morning. Was he going insane? Waking her up in the middle of the night was not the way to win her heart. And despite everything, he wasn't prepared to give up his one opportunity to be with her.

* * *

What in the world had she been thinking? Sheridan paced up and down her bedroom floor. *Had she lost her freaking mind?* Apparently so, because after Beau and Alexis's ambush and the shock of Ridge popping up at the party in the nick of time, she should have just gone home.

And she would have. Except that when she'd run out the back door, she'd forgotten her car keys. Which had been in her purse. Which was still sitting beside one of Merry's fancy Bauhaus white leather chairs.

Sheridan had been gearing herself up to go back inside and retrieve her bag when Ridge had found her. And although she'd known it was a mistake to stay, there'd been something in his expression that'd kept her rooted to the spot.

What was there about him that always had her doing the foolish thing instead of the smart one? He seemed to steal the common sense right out of her brain.

Not that she'd ever admitted it to anyone, but in the first few weeks after she'd left Sutton Falls, she had held on to the fantasy that Ridge would show up at her college dorm, declare that he had broken up with Alexis for good, and say that he wanted to date Sheridan. He'd assure her that he hadn't been involved in what had happened the night of the prom and sweep her into his arms.

Of course that whole daydream had exploded in her face when she'd read that Ridge and Alexis had gotten married. Any hope she'd had about him had died with that wedding announcement.

That was, until tonight, when Ridge had cradled her face between his hands and run his thumb across her bottom lip. At that instant, the music from the party and everyone inside had disappeared from her thoughts. The soft spot for him in her heart that had opened up when he'd defended her against his best friend's attack grew exponentially with every word he spoke and every touch of his fingers.

Joy had swept through her, and it was as though they were the last two people on earth. The only sound she'd heard was his voice whispering what she'd always wanted him to say to her. In that precious moment, he was the Ridge she'd always imagined.

It filled her with an indescribable bliss. And no matter how much her good judgment had warned her that he'd end up hurting her or that her heart was already way more involved than was good for her, there had been no way in hell she could make herself step away from his embrace. One glimpse of his gorgeous green eyes and his addictive smile and she was hooked.

She tried to move back and take things slowly with him. Accept his invitation for a Saturday night date and see how that evening went before taking the next step. But the minute his mouth met hers, she lost both her caution and her mind.

Ridge had roused something deep inside her soul. He seemed to demand a response from her that she hadn't thought she was capable of experiencing with any man.

At that second, when she'd surrendered to his kiss, all the yearning and desire for love that she'd kept buried in her subconscious had broken free. A scorching hot flame had ignited inside of her, and she'd been willing to let the blaze consume her.

Sheridan stopped pacing and leaned against the windowsill. Since her books had become successful, she had met powerful politicians, popular celebrities, and even some hunky athletes. But beyond a few dates and a couple nights of enjoyable sex, none of them had made much of an impression on her. Truth be told, she could barely remember their names.

They certainly hadn't tempted her to lose control, take a chance, and jump blindly into the fire. So why was she even considering making that leap for Ridge? Was it his concern, no, his rage, when he'd noticed the deep gouges that Alexis's long French-tipped claws had left on Sheridan's arms, or was it his searing mouth branding hers?

Or maybe it was that when Merry had interrupted them and Sheridan had wrenched herself out of Ridge's arms, he hadn't given up. For a long moment, the silence between them had been full of his anger or maybe hurt at her withdrawal, but he'd quickly recovered and accepted her decision.

Unlike a lot of men who would have sulked, Ridge had threaded his fingers with hers and accompanied her inside the house. He hadn't let go of her hand the entire time she was saying her good-byes. She'd been touched by the sincere well wishes of her classmates, and as she felt the warmth and the reassurance of Ridge's palm against hers, she'd had to force herself to hold tight to her heart.

Because did what had happened between them on the deck really change anything? A few kisses, a sexy caress were all it had been. It was probably nothing more than the adrenaline from facing off with Alexis and Beau.

Most likely, it was the same with Ridge. Just his usual Friday night with the woman du jour.

The thought made her gasp in pain. It already hurt to think of Ridge being with someone else.

Sheridan turned away from the window. She didn't want to look at all the pieces of her soul that might be revealed in the moonlight's reflection. The parts she hid from everyone, especially herself.

Taking a deep breath, Sheridan slid between the sheets, turned on her side, and closed her eyes. In order to satisfy her curiosity about Ridge and Alexis's marriage, she'd keep her date with him tomorrow.

After she figured out that last piece of the puzzle, she'd be able to put the past behind her and move on with her life. She'd find a good man from her present world to love, and once and for all, she'd lay to rest her adolescent crush.

Ridge would turn out to be the same as any guy. Nothing special. Certainly not someone she loved.

CHAPTER SIXTEEN

Sheridan hadn't fallen asleep until nearly two a.m., and when she woke to the sound of breaking glass, it took her a few seconds to surface from her erotic dream. It took her another minute to figure out what was going on.

Shoving her feet into slippers, she stumbled into the kitchen and found her father surrounded by the remains of their dearly departed coffee carafe. She groaned. Not only had she barely slept all night, now she was she up at the butt crack of dawn, and there was no caffeine.

"Sorry, honey." Errol rubbed the bridge of his nose. "I was trying not to disturb you, but the dang pot slipped out of my fingers."

Errol's recovery had been going so well that he was able to get into and out of his wheelchair by himself. And thanks to the doorways that had been widened when Sheridan's mother was ill, he could maneuver his chair from room to room, making him a lot more independent around the house.

The results of the tests that he'd had at the hospital on Wednesday hadn't indicated any serious problems, and Sheridan was cautiously optimistic that her father was on the mend. Monday morning, when they visited his doctor again, she hoped to get a better idea of Errol's overall condition.

"Accidents happen," Sheridan assured her father, then bent to clean up the mess. "I needed to get up anyway. I have lots of writing to do today."

"How was the party last night?" Errol wheeled himself out of her way. "Flora was thrilled you wanted to stay later, but she was a little riled that you didn't tell her about it when you got home."

"I'll have to apologize to her for that. I had an awful headache and just wanted to take an aspirin and lie down."

Sheridan deposited the large pieces of glass in the trash. Her aunt's thirst for gossip was almost as legendary as Errol's, which was why Sheridan had avoided saying anything much to her the night before.

"But you had fun?" Errol asked, a hopeful note in his voice.

"Yes." Sheridan grabbed the broom and dustpan, touched that her father was so concerned for her feelings. "It was nice seeing everyone and catching up."

"Who all was there?" Errol leaned forward, obviously as eager as his sister had been to hear the details.

"I talked to Les from the grocery store and Prissy Webster." Sheridan deliberately avoided mentioning Alexis's and Beau's names as she swept the remaining slivers into the dustpan and threw them away. No need to open up that can of worms with her father.

"Who else?"

"Oh, just a bunch of my classmates. Merry probably invited everyone we went to school with who still lives in town."

"So Ridge Sutton was there?" Errol's gaze followed Sheridan as she opened and closed cupboard doors.

"He stopped by for a few minutes." Sheridan gave up on her quest for a spare coffee maker. "Actually"—she tried to sound casual—"I'm supposed to see Ridge tonight. Unless you want me to stay home with you."

"No. I'm fine." Errol grinned. "So you're going out on a date with Ridge. That's nice. Did you two talk about what happened the night of your prom?"

"Yes." Sheridan edged toward her bedroom. She could not discuss this without coffee. "He said he wasn't involved."

"Do you think he was telling the truth?" Errol wheeled after her.

"His explanation is plausible." Sheridan stepped over the threshold. "Whether I believe him is still up for debate." Before Errol could pursue the subject, she added, "I need to get dressed now."

After closing the door in her father's face, she threw on a pair of jeans and a sweatshirt and made an emergency run into town for a replacement coffee maker. She was pulling into the parking lot when she realized she hadn't bothered to fix her hair or put on makeup. Living in Sutton Falls was already changing her, and she wasn't sure how she felt about that.

While starting her day off un-caffeinated and with only a few hours of sleep had put her in a grumpy mood, discovering that Sutton Hardware sold Keurigs cheered her up considerably. She quickly bought her dad the newest model, then stopped at the grocery store to pick up several boxes of K-cups to go with it.

As soon as Sheridan got home, she set up the appliance at one end of the kitchen table. There, Errol could get to the machine from his wheelchair and was in no danger of knocking it over trying to reach the controls.

At first, her father had protested, saying that he didn't need such an expensive coffee maker. But Sheridan noticed that, throughout the morning, he sampled all the different flavors. Good thing some were decaf or he'd be too wired to sleep that night.

By the time Sheridan called Errol for lunch, he had already ordered several variety packs of the K-cups online. After he wheeled himself into the kitchen, Sheridan joined him at the table. They'd been getting along much better, and recently he had been talking about the past. As they ate, she steered the conversation to his senior year in high school.

"I really didn't have any interest in going to college." Errol squirted mustard on his ham and Swiss sandwich. "And back when I was growing up, no one around here considered art a viable livelihood."

"I can believe that." Sheridan concentrated on assembling the perfect forkful of salad—lettuce, tomato, and carrot slices dripping with creamy Italian dressing. "Even as recently as thirteen or fourteen years ago when I was in high school, the guidance counselor tried to talk me into majoring in education rather than pursing a writing career."

"Considering your success, I doubt you'll have to go back and get a teaching degree anytime soon." Errol winked, then sobered. "When your mom and I got married, my plan was to paint during the winter months when there wasn't as much work around the farm."

"Which I remember you doing." Sheridan recalled the smell of turpentine in the garage, where Errol had set up his studio. She'd spent hours out there with her dad as Errol sketched. She still associated the feel of the wall-mounted heater blowing warm air around her with happier times.

"I loved creating something beautiful from an empty canvas."

"But like writing, it's not just producing the material, there's the business part of the job." Sheridan tried to recall if her father had ever had a gallery exhibition and frowned when she realized that her only memory was of him selling an occasional individual painting locally. "Did you ever market your paintings?"

"The galleries were all in the city, and I never seemed to be able to get into even St. Louis, let alone Chicago or New York to try to drum up interest in my work." He took a sip of pumpkin spice coffee and smacked his lips in appreciation. "I'd make plans, but something always came up, and I'd have to cancel the trip."

"Because Mom didn't mind if you painted as a hobby,"

Sheridan said with a new understanding of her childhood memories. "But she didn't want you to become successful and move her off the farm."

"Probably," Errol muttered. "But it wasn't all her." He ducked his head. "If I didn't show my paintings, then I never had to hear that they weren't any good."

This was a side of her father she'd never seen or at least allowed herself to see. In her mind, Errol, like the movie star he'd been named for, was the epitome of the swashbuckling, heroic male. Sheridan had always considered him fearless.

"Mom's been gone a long time. Is the fear of failure why you haven't chased your dream?" Sheridan asked gently.

"That"—Errol shrugged—"and after she passed, it seems kind of disloyal to her."

Sheridan clamped her teeth together to stop from snapping at her father. Cheating on Vivian had been a lot more of a betrayal than trying to sell his paintings. Before Sheridan left for New York, she would have to make him tell her whatever secret he was keeping about the naked woman in that picture.

But not now. Today, they were getting along, and she didn't want to ruin this moment.

So instead of demanding an explanation or asking if he'd spoken to the woman about breaking his word to her, Sheridan changed the subject and asked, "What do you think about the streak of vandalism we've been having around the farm?"

"It's been tough on the finances." Errol frowned. "But it's probably just kids feeling their wild oats."

"If you need some cash to tide you over—"

"Nope." Errol's expression was stubborn. "You don't take any money out of the farm, so you shouldn't put any money into it."

"Still, if it comes down to it, you'll let me know." Sheridan waited for him to nod, then asked, "How about the lack of police response?"

"Not much they can do." Errol shrugged. "That's why we have insurance. Too bad it doesn't cover everything."

Frustrated, Sheridan let the matter drop. And after making sure her father was settled watching a DVD, Sheridan took her laptop out on the porch and sat on the swing.

She propped the computer up on her knees and stared at the empty white screen. She could swear that the blinking cursor was mocking her. She could almost hear its taunting high-pitched voice. *You're a fraud. Your other books were freak accidents. You'll never write another word that anyone wants to read.*

Fighting the urge to check her Amazon ratings and reviews, which was a sure way to throttle up her insecurity, Sheridan tried phoning her friends. The calls to both Darcy and Lucy went straight into their voice mail, but Delaney picked up. From the background noise, it sounded as if she was at the youth center that she had built with some of her lottery winnings.

After a brief hello, Sheridan announced, "I made out with Ridge Sutton last night. And I have a date with him tonight."

"Do tell," Delaney drawled. "Hold on a second, I'm going into the office so I can hear you better." A couple of seconds later, she said, "Okay, tell me everything."

"My cousin Merry had a party to celebrate my new book, and Alexis showed up." Sheridan took a breath to calm the flicker of panic at the thought of Alexis's verbal assault, then continued, "Ridge got there just as she started to really attack me." Sheridan outlined the entire series of events to her friend, then, with a flash of pride, said, "So I told her off and marched out the back door."

"Good for you." Delaney paused. "Then Ridge followed you and…"

"And he explained what he knew about prom night."

Sheridan could hear a tiny inner voice urging her not to expose her feelings even to Delaney, but she ignored it and told her friend Ridge's version of what had happened. "Should I believe him?"

"Do you want to?"

"Yes." Sheridan hesitated. Despite how chivalrous Ridge had been when he'd told off Beau and how sincere he'd seemed when he'd claimed to have no recollection of the prom, she needed to rein in her hopes. "But—"

"But nothing," Delaney cut her off. "For once, you need to jump into the pool without checking the depth of the water. Did you reward him with a kiss?"

"And more." Sheridan tingled with the memory of Ridge's fingers sliding under her panties.

"More? Did you...?"

"Not quite," Sheridan admitted, remembering the dangerous pull of her emotions as Ridge had caressed her. It was more than just a physical reaction, and that scared her to death. "But only because Merry almost caught us with our hands in each other's pants. What in the world was I thinking?"

"You weren't." Delaney giggled. "And it's about damn time you let your heart rule your head."

"Maybe I should call off our date. What if he's lying about prom night?" Sheridan hated that her voice cracked. Hated the weakness she felt. Hated the threat to her control. "Or just using me to get the levee?"

"What if he isn't?" Delaney's voice was soft. "And what if he's the one guy for you and you never give him a chance?"

"You're right." Sheridan sank back against the porch swing. The growing threads of affection in her heart for Ridge were hard to deny. "It's now or never."

They chatted for a few more minutes, then Delaney had to go. Her husband was picking her up, and they were driving into

Chicago for dinner and a night alone in the Drake Hotel. With Spencer's teenage daughter in their house, privacy was a rare and precious commodity.

After hanging up, Sheridan stared at the disturbingly blank monitor of her computer. She chewed on her thumbnail. What was going on with her? She'd never had a problem producing her daily page count before.

Was this the writer's block so many of her friends described? She'd always secretly thought they were being prima donnas or plain lazy when they talked about being unable to write. Now she felt their pain and sent a silent apology to them all.

She rubbed her eyes. Maybe it was the change in her surroundings. She missed her office and her spacious desk and her ergonomic chair. She'd been in Sutton Falls for ten days, and on one hand, it seemed much longer; on the other, it almost felt as if she'd never left. As if it really was home.

Her head snapped back. Where had that come from? She must be tired.

Sheridan closed the laptop and put it aside. Pulling her knees up to her chest, she daydreamed about what her life might have been like if she'd never gone to the prom, her mother hadn't died, and her father hadn't had an affair.

A few minutes later, she reached for the computer, determined to squeeze out at least a few hundred words, but before she could power it up, a bike turned into the driveway. Sheridan shaded her eyes and squinted. It was Sally. Was the girl AWOL again?

"Hi, Ms. Davis." Sally hopped off her bike and waved. "Are you busy?"

"Sadly, no." Sheridan smiled, glad for the chance to focus on something besides Ridge or her sudden inability to write. "I'm a little stuck on the chapter that I'm working on." She scooted over so the girl could join her on the swing. "Does your father or grandmother know that you're out here?"

"I'm not running away if that's what you mean." Sally plopped down on the seat. "Grandmother gave me permission to go on a bike ride as long as I'm home by three. Evidently, Dad has made an appointment to spend some 'quality' time with me then."

Sheridan ignored both the comment and the bitterness in the girl's voice and asked, "Do you have more questions about my books?"

"Not specifically, Ms. Davis." Sally pushed the swing with her foot.

"Call me Sheridan."

"Thanks. That would be awesome." Sally grinned. "What I'd really like to talk to you about is why girls seem to hide how smart they are from boys."

"There's no good answer to that." Sheridan wished she had some spectacular wisdom to offer the girl. "The easiest one is that they think boys won't like them if they're too smart."

"Is that true?"

"Well..." Sheridan considered her words carefully, afraid she'd send Sally onto the same wrong path she herself had followed for far too long. "Probably, for some boys, but they aren't the ones who you want to like you, anyway."

"I can see that." Sally nodded, then asked, "What's another reason?"

"People learn from example, and sadly, the girls often observe adult women covering up their intelligence, so they think they should do it, too."

"Did you ever play dumb?" Sally turned and sat on one leg, staring at Sheridan.

"Nope." Sheridan met the girl's gaze. "And before you ask, no, I was not popular. And although there were many other causes, refusing to hide my intelligence was probably one of the reasons I wasn't asked out much."

"But you're not sorry, right?" Sally worried her bottom lip.

"No. I'm not." Sheridan realized that although she'd had a difficult time, pretending to be someone she wasn't wouldn't have been the answer. "I just wished that I'd have been brave enough to reach out to the kids who were like me and make friends with them. Instead, I resented the in crowd and sulked because they gave me a hard time and didn't accept me for me."

Summing up her experiences to Sally, also clarified them for Sheridan, and as she and the girl continued to chat, Sheridan felt a certain peacefulness that hadn't been there before now. Before she could analyze the sensation, a flash of lightning made them both jump.

It was followed almost immediately by a boom of thunder, and Sheridan scooped up her laptop, got to her feet, and said, "We'd better go inside. Those clouds look like it's going to start pouring any second."

"It's quarter to three." Sally wrinkled her brow. "Grandmother will have a cow if I'm late."

"Okay. Put your bike in the back of the station wagon, and I'll drive you home." Sheridan opened the door. "I'll take my computer inside, let my father know that I'm leaving, and meet you at the car."

"Thanks!" Sally sprinted for the driveway. "You're the best."

A few minutes later, rain pelted Sheridan as she ran for the station wagon clutching her purse to her chest. She slid into the driver's seat and turned on the engine. She had already started to back out of the driveway when it hit her. She didn't know where she was going.

Applying the brakes, she looked at Sally and asked, "Where do you live?"

SMART GIRL SWEPT AWAY

"Twelve twenty-five East Cliffside Drive." Sally frowned.
"Can you hurry?"

"Don't worry." Sheridan aimed the car toward town.
"You'll be there in plenty of time."

Why did that address seem so familiar?

Sheridan's heart thudded to a stop. She glanced at Sally.
Oh. My. God! It couldn't be! But it was. The girl had the Sutton green eyes.

Sheridan had recognized the street and number because she'd spent three afternoons a week there for most of her senior year. Why hadn't she ever asked Sally her last name?

And how had she not known that Ridge and Alexis had a child? She immediately answered herself. Because she didn't read the paper, and no one talked about town news to her.

Hell! Until last night, she'd avoided Ridge as much as she could. And recently, when she and Ridge had been together, her conversations with him hadn't been along the lines of *tell me all about what you've been doing the past thirteen years.*

"Is something wrong?" Sally asked. "You have a funny look in your eyes."

"No." Sheridan pasted an impassive expression on her face. She had no idea how she felt about Sally's parentage and definitely didn't want to discuss those feelings, whatever they were, with the girl sitting next to her. "I just didn't realize that your father was Ridge Sutton."

Sheridan slowed for an old Buick Impala going ten miles under the speed limit and nearly screamed with frustration. She needed to get Sally home before Sheridan blurted out something she might regret.

"Do you know my dad?" Sally stared at Sheridan.

"We were in the same high school class." By sheer force of will, Sheridan kept her voice impersonal. "I tutored him in English our senior year."

"So you knew my mother, too?"

"I did." Sheridan gripped the steering wheel, her knuckles whitening with the effort to hide her loathing of Alexis. "But not as well. She and I traveled in different social circles."

"She was the most beautiful girl in school, and Dad was the handsomest boy."

"That they were." Sheridan wished the car in front of her would speed up. Either that or that a giant sinkhole would open and swallow her.

Thankfully, Sally stopped talking about her parents and silently stared out the window.

After a couple of minutes, Sheridan finally figured out a way to ask the question gnawing at her mind. "I'm interested in astrology. I'm a Capricorn, which makes me hard-working and ambitious. When's your birthday?"

"February second," Sally answered. "I just turned twelve."

"So you're an Aquarius." Sheridan was glad she'd recently researched the influence of astrology on women's behavior and knew the months and characteristics connected with the different signs. "That means you have an imaginative nature and are honest and straightforward."

"Sounds right." Sally tilted her head. "Is that important?"

"I guess not." Sheridan smiled reassuringly. "You know how it is. You read something and all of sudden you're curious about the subject."

"Uh-huh." Sally seemed doubtful.

A few seconds later, Sheridan turned into the sweeping lane that led up to the Sutton house. As she drove toward the imposing residence on top of the cliff, her chest tightened with thoughts of her past visits to the estate. The happy times when she and Ridge had really seemed to connect and the sad day when their tutoring sessions had ended.

Pushing aside those memories, Sheridan stopped the car and

helped the girl get her bike from the back of the station wagon. Sheridan forced herself to wait until she saw the garage door open for Sally, then she waved and sped away.

As Sheridan headed home, she rechecked her math. *Yep.* Sally had been born nine months after the senior prom. Obviously, whatever drugs Ridge might have been given hadn't impaired his ability to procreate. Her stomach clenched. Or worse, despite what he'd said, he and Alexis had continued to see each other after that night.

The events leading up to Sally's birth were doubtlessly part of the explanation that Ridge had promised to give Sheridan on their date. It shouldn't matter to her, but it did. She needed to know the circumstances of his daughter's conception.

Without a very good explanation for Alexis's pregnancy, all of Ridge's claims of innocence were highly questionable.

CHAPTER SEVENTEEN

After giving a speech at the Junior Women's Club luncheon, Ridge hurried home, changed out of his suit, and escaped to the garage. When Sally had shown some curiosity about the Mustang he was restoring, he'd come up with the idea that they might be able to bond over their mutual interest in classic cars.

As he tinkered with the Ford, waiting for his daughter to return from her bike ride, he heard a rumble of thunder and tensed. He glanced at his watch. It was two forty-five and Sally wasn't due back until three. Should he go look for her?

Nah. She'd be upset. One of her frequent complaints when he tried to take care of her was that he treated her like a baby.

Ignoring the uneasy feeling in his gut, he went back to loosening the bolt holding the oil pan in place. A few seconds later, the sound of rain hitting the roof had him sliding out from under the Mustang and pawing through the mess on his workbench.

He remembered tossing the keys to the 1940 Ford pickup there after the last test drive. It was another one of his restoration projects and the only vehicle big enough to hold a bicycle.

When the tempo of the drops increased, Ridge ground his teeth in aggravation. The town couldn't afford much more rain. He had to talk to Sheri about the levee tonight. Was there any way of introducing the subject without it seeming as if he'd only asked her out to get her to sell him her family's land?

Probably not. All he really wanted to do during their time together was to make her forget everything about their past misunderstandings. To show her how much he felt for her, needed her, wanted her. But he'd have to suck it up, ignore his own desires, and discuss the possible flooding situation with her. The welfare of Sutton Falls and its citizens had to come first.

When his fingers closed around the keys to the truck, he pushed his worries about Sheri aside and hurried toward the pickup. Before he reached it, he heard a car door slam and Sally's voice thanking someone for the ride. Relieved that she was safely home, he sprinted to the front of the garage and hit the automatic opener button.

Ridge caught a glimpse of an ancient station wagon as it drove around the circular drive. Was that the Davises' Oldsmobile?

Sally seemed surprised to see him, and she quickly said, "Am I late?"

"No." Ridge stepped out of her way. "Did you get caught in the downpour?"

"Sort of." She wheeled the bike into its assigned spot in the five-car garage, grabbed a threadbare towel from the stack of clean rags on the shelf, and asked, "Why didn't you tell me that you went to school with Sheridan Davis?"

Ridge's pulse accelerated, but he said causally, "Didn't I? I guess I thought you knew." So that had been Errol's station wagon driving away. "Did Ms. Davis see you out riding and give you a lift?"

"Not exactly." Sally ambled over to the two-ton engine hoist, sitting empty in a corner of the garage, and ran a finger along the chain. "I...uh...rode out to her house. When Grandmother and I saw her at the doctor's office, Sheridan told me to come out to the farm if I wanted to talk. And she said it again when she gave a speech at my school." When he opened his mouth, Sally hastily added, "She told me I could call her by her first name."

"That was nice of her." His mind racing at the various

possibilities, Ridge forced a smiled and said, "So, you stopped by her house to talk about her books, right?"

"Uh-huh."

"They're really good, aren't they?"

"You've read them?" Sally's voice rose in surprise. "You never told me that."

"The books were really interesting. Before I overruled your mother's veto and allowed you to download them, I had to make sure they were age appropriate for you."

Ridge mentally thumped his forehead. Why hadn't he thought to talk about the books with Sally? They would have given them something to discuss.

Sally turned away from the hydraulic floor jack she'd been examining and looked at him. "But they're really long and you're always so busy."

"It was something important to you, so I made the time." Ridge moved closer to his daughter and cupped her cheek. "You matter more to me than anything else."

"I... That's..." Sally stepped out of his reach. "So you liked Sheridan's books?"

"I thought the writing was smooth." It hurt Ridge's heart that his daughter rejected any show of affection from him. "Sheri made a lot of good points."

"Sheri?" Sally tilted her head and gazed at him. "You call her Sheri? Is that because she tutored you or were you two friends?"

"Both." Ridge gestured toward the Mustang, determined to deflect Sally's attention from his past relationship with Sheri. "How about helping me with this?"

"Okay." Sally shrugged. "I guess I don't have anything better to do."

"Great." Ridge grinned. Not exactly the enthusiastic response he'd like but better than Sally's usual cold shoulder. He

182

pulled a second dolly next to the one he'd been using, tapped the smooth wooden platform, and said, "Want to see what I'm doing?"

"Sure." Sally joined him. "But Grandmother will be mad if I get dirty."

"I'll take care of that." Ridge flinched at the reminder that he'd allowed Evelyn to bully his daughter. Vowing to straighten that mess out before it got any worse, he slid both himself and Sally underneath the car and said, "Things are going to change around here, starting with your grandmother's attitude."

"I'll believe that when I see it," Sally muttered, then pointed and asked, "What's that?"

"It's what holds the oil." Ridge handed her the wrench he'd been using. "We need to unscrew the bolt so we can take off the leaky pan and replace it with a new one."

They worked side by side for a couple of hours. Sally had obviously been reading about vintage automobiles and asked intelligent questions. Ridge's heart swelled. Maybe their mutual interest in restoring classic cars would bridge the gap that had formed in the years Sally had spent apart from him while living with her mother.

It was a bonus that Sheri seemed to have formed some kind of connection with Sally. Maybe he'd been worried for nothing. Sheri had to know that Sally was his and Alexis's daughter, and she wouldn't have been so nice to her if Sally's parentage were a problem for Sheri.

Feeling hopeful, Ridge allowed his mind to wander to their date that evening. Thoughts of Sheri had teased him throughout the day. If they could straighten out the levee issue, maybe their budding relationship had a chance.

Sheri was a sensible person. Even as a teenager, she had always been extremely logical in her thinking. Surely she'd understand that the needs of the many people who would lose their homes and businesses in a flood overrode any sentimental reasons she had to keep the land.

Ridge and Sally had finished working under the Mustang and were now leaning over the open hood. He had relaxed and was enjoying the time with his daughter.

Suddenly, out of the blue, Sally said, "Sheridan was surprised you were my dad."

"Oh." Ridge clenched his jaw as a frisson of unease snaked down his spine. "She didn't figure it when she met you?"

"I guess she never heard my last name, so she didn't know who I was until today when I told her where I lived." Sally passed Ridge a screwdriver, then she asked, "You know what was really odd?"

"What?" Ridge didn't like where this conversation was going.

"She asked me about my birthday." Sally bit her lip. "Why do you think she wanted to know that? She said it was because she was interested in astrology, but I think that was bogus."

"She probably wanted to get you a gift," Ridge said, struggling to keep his expression from betraying his alarm.

Shit! Sheri had been trying to figure out the date his daughter had been conceived. He'd been hoping to explain what had happened the night of their prom before that little nugget of information came to light.

Maybe he should have just told Sheri the whole story when they'd been together on Merry's deck. But he hadn't wanted his tawdry past to spoil their moment in the moonlight. There were also Sally's feelings to consider.

Although there was no hiding that Alexis was expecting before they'd gotten married, Ridge had never told another soul the entire truth behind that pregnancy. But if he and Sheri would have any chance at exploring their feelings for each other, he would have to make an exception for her.

He was confident that Sheri would keep his secret, but it still worried him. If Sally ever found out what her mother had done, he was afraid both her self-image and her opinion of Alexis would be permanently damaged.

"Why would Sheridan want to buy me a present?" Sally's question broke into his thoughts.

Before Ridge could come up with an answer, the door between the garage and the house opened, and Evelyn marched down the steps. "Sarah Ann, it's nearly five thirty. You need to take a bath and get dressed."

"For what?" Sally asked, wiping her dirty hands on her jeans.

"The Children's Clinic pajama party fundraiser." Evelyn raised a brow. "You do remember promising to go with me, right?"

"But—"

"Look, Mother," Ridge interrupted his daughter's protest. "Surely you recall that we discussed that I wouldn't allow you to force Sally to go to parties she wasn't interested in attending."

"How could I forget that conversation? You were extremely rude."

"When you told me she was spending the night with you, there wasn't any mention of this pajama party." He didn't even try to hide his annoyance from Evelyn.

"I wasn't aware that I had to clear every detail." Evelyn's expression was unreadable. "But if you insist, the party is at the country club, and we'll all go directly to church afterwards."

"Did Sally agree to this?" Ridge asked warily.

"Yes." Evelyn nodded serenely. "Yesterday afternoon at the spa, Sarah Ann said that if I did her a favor, she'd do this for me.

"I did promise to go." Sally slid a glance at her father.

"What favor did your grandmother do for you?" Ridge asked, concerned that his daughter was being manipulated by his mother just as he had always been.

"Uh..."

"Now, Ridge." Evelyn shook her index finger playfully in his face. "We girls need our little confidences with each other." She turned to her granddaughter. "Isn't that right, darling?"

"Yes, Grandmother." Sally ran for the door. "It's okay, Dad. I said that I'd go and I will." She paused at the top of the steps and added, "If you want, I wouldn't mind helping you with the cars again sometime."

"I'll count on it." Ridge let the matter drop but gazed suspiciously at his mother. How had she maneuvered Sally into going to a party with her? When Evelyn didn't follow her granddaughter into the house, Ridge asked, "Is there something else, Mother?"

"Yes." Evelyn crossed her arms. "I don't think you should allow Sarah Ann to spend time with Sheridan Davis. I saw that woman drop her off here this afternoon, and she isn't a good role model for a young, impressionable girl. She'll turn her into a lesbian."

"Are you out of your freaking mind?" Ridge shouted. "What in hell would make you think that, let alone say it?" His head was about to explode. "Even you must know that someone's sexual orientation can't be influenced by his or her environment. It's biological, not environmental."

"Those feminists all try to convert the next generation to their cause."

"By their cause"—Ridge's jaw was so stiff it ached—"do you mean securing a woman's rights and making sure that they have equal opportunities to men?"

"I—"

"Or maybe you mean becoming a woman who stands up for herself and doesn't depend on a man to define her whole existence," Ridge continued, his voice steel-edged.

"I just don't want Sarah Ann ending up alone like Sheridan Davis." Evelyn tilted her head up and looked down her nose. "She's never been married, and as far as I can tell from what her aunt has to say, she has never been seriously involved with a man."

"Maybe she just keeps her private life private." Ridge had difficulty keeping the smile off of his face at the news that Sheri wasn't in a committed relationship. Because, despite what he'd just said to his mother about Sheri's desire to be discreet, there was no way Flora McIntyre wouldn't know if her niece were seeing someone on an exclusive basis.

"Fine." Evelyn crossed to the steps. "But I would still advise that you seriously consider limiting Sarah Ann's contact with that woman." Evelyn narrowed her eyes. "It's common knowledge that Errol Davis is a degenerate."

His mother disappeared inside before Ridge could respond. Where did Evelyn get her weird ideas? Degenerate? Errol might be a bit of a flirt, but he'd never heard a negative word about the man's character. What in the hell could Evelyn be talking about?

CHAPTER EIGHTEEN

Sheridan gazed at her reflection in the mirror. She almost didn't recognize herself. Recalling Aunt Flora's criticism of her chignon, Sheridan had fixed her hair in a cascade of curls down her back. The smoky eye makeup was a dramatic change from her usual neutral palette, and the bright red shade of lipstick on her mouth was normally reserved for television appearances, where the lights washed out any less-vibrant color.

Once again, her clothing options were limited. Her only viable choice was the pants and blouse she'd purchased at Bergner's. Ridge had already seen the dress she'd bought there, and she certainly wasn't wearing the outfit that her cousin had described as a nun's habit.

Sheridan checked the bedside clock. Fifteen more minutes. Her stomach did an unpleasant flip, and a voice in her head began to list all the reasons she should call Ridge and cancel the date.

First, she was just wasting her time with a man with whom she knew there was no future. Second, she should forget about her silly infatuation with him. And third—

No! She stomped her bare foot. She would not chicken out. She'd listen to what he had to say about his marriage and daughter and finally be able to forget him.

Yeah, *right!* Sheridan couldn't lie to herself. It was true that she wanted to hear his explanation, but the real reason had nothing to do with the past and everything to do with right now.

All she could think about was the time she'd spent in his arms. Every few seconds, all day long, a montage of those golden minutes had played over and over in her mind until she thought she'd go insane.

She swallowed a bubble of hysterical laughter. Ignoring her feelings for Ridge would be about as easy as forgetting how to breathe. She just hoped that acknowledging those feelings wouldn't have an even more disastrous consequence.

Slipping on her new Adrienne Vittadini sandals, Sheridan strolled into the empty living room. A few hours ago, Errol had announced that he was feeling much better, and if he didn't get out of the house, he'd go crazy with cabin fever.

She'd wondered if all the coffee he'd drunk throughout the day was the cause of his restlessness. However, she'd kept quiet about his possible caffeine overload as he'd phoned his buddy Benny and the two men had made plans for a big night on the town.

Benny had picked up Errol at five, and they'd gone to the Methodist spaghetti supper. Afterward, they were heading to the Lion's hall for a poker marathon. The two guys intended to play cards all night and finish up at the Rotary pancake breakfast in the morning.

Pleased about Errol's rapid recovery, Sheridan perched on her mother's rocker. It felt weird to be alone. She hadn't spent a second by herself in this house since she'd left for college. As she set the chair into motion, she caught a faint whiff of Coty's Tubéreuse perfume, her mother's favorite fragrance.

Sheridan sighed. Would Vivian have been happy that her daughter had a date with someone as handsome and popular as Ridge Sutton? Or would she have considered his threat to her family's land an obstacle even his good looks and social standing couldn't overcome? If only her mother were here to speak for herself, Sheridan wouldn't have to carry the burden for both of them.

She had just glanced at the clock when the sound of gravel crunching under tires alerted her to Ridge's arrival. He was five minutes early. She liked that in a man. At least, she liked it when he was picking her up for a date. In more intimate circumstances, not so much.

When she opened the door, her heart skipped a beat. Ridge stood on the porch holding a vase filled with her favorite flowers. Where in the world had he found pink peonies? They generally didn't bloom in Missouri until early May.

"Wow!" His pupils dilated, and he sucked in a quick gulp of air. "You look gorgeous."

"Thank you." His words felt like a caress, and she self-consciously brushed a curl back over her shoulder. "You don't look so bad yourself."

His perfectly tailored gray wool slacks, black cashmere sweater, and checked shirt were straight out of *GQ*.

"Thanks."

Sheridan waited, and when Ridge continued to stare at her, she pointed to the flowers and asked, "Are those for me?"

"Yeah. Right. Sorry." He handed her the bouquet. "I hope you still like these as much as you did in high school."

Sheridan had written a paper about the meaning and symbolism of the peony. It had been selected to run in the newspaper and won her a savings bond.

"You remembered?" She had been half convinced Ridge's flower choice was a coincidence.

"Of course." Ridge traced her cheek with his thumb. "Winning that contest was something important to you. How could I forget?"

Her throat closed at his thoughtfulness. Sucking in a much-needed breath, Sheridan stepped away from his touch before she did something reckless like throw herself into his arms.

"Would you like to come in?"

"Next time." He held out his hand. "I have a special evening planned."

She put the vase on an end table, slipped her fingers into his, and, closing the door behind her, followed him to the car. Her mind raced at his words. They implied that he'd put a lot of thought into their date and was confident that it wouldn't end immediately after he answered her questions about his marriage to Alexis.

Once he'd seated her and gotten behind the wheel, Sheridan asked, "Where are we going?"

"My place. My mother and Sally are at a charity sleepover, so we have the house to ourselves." He gave her a sidelong glance. "The only restaurant around here with decent food is the country club, and I thought we needed some privacy if I was going to tell you all my secrets." He wrinkled his brow, clearly concerned she might misinterpret his choice. "It's not that I don't want to be seen with you or anything, but you know how easy it is to be overheard in the club."

"It's fine." Sheridan actually didn't know because she had never been to the Belladonna Country Club.

Her parents hadn't belonged. At the time, she'd felt left out since so many of the kids hung out there. Now that she was older and wiser, she wondered if the members realized that their facility was named for a deadly poison. Which, considering how many lives had been ruined by the toxic gossip that went on at that place, was certainly apropos.

They drove in silence until Ridge steered the Z4 between a set of impressive stone gates and up the hill. The cement driveway curved toward an enormous brick house, and the view reminded Sheridan of a Thomas Cole painting.

As Ridge brought the BMW to a stop, he frowned and said, "We could go over to Mt. Morrison if you'd rather. I don't want you to think that I don't want to take you out somewhere nice like you're used to."

"Really. The life of an author isn't all that glamorous." She smiled at his nerves, liking him even more for his uncertainty. "As long as you don't expect me to cook, this will be fine." She chuckled. "My only culinary talent is zapping something frozen in the microwave."

"I definitely didn't invite you over to cook." Ridge exited the BMW, came around, opened her door, and held out his hand. "That's not even close to what I want you to do for me."

The sizzling look he gave her sent a flicker of fire through Sheridan's chest. She needed to calm down. There were a lot of questions she needed answered before she could even think about getting naked with Ridge.

Taking a calming breath, she stepped out of the car, walked up the sidewalk, and went into the house. The only other times Sheridan had been inside the Sutton Mansion had been when she was helping Ridge with his English class.

On that last day, he'd given her a check to cover the final tutoring fee and told her he'd call her. He never had. His failure to keep his word had crushed her and left her feeling used.

Shaking her head at who she had been back then and her own naiveté, Sheridan looked around the huge foyer. She had forgotten the opulence—and the formality. While she continued to be impressed with the soaring ceilings and crystal chandelier, it lacked the warmth she associated with a real home.

Although her condo was nowhere near as grand, Sheridan realized that it, too, was anything but cozy. The decorator she'd hired had used a cold shade of white throughout the space, with lots of leather, mirrors, and glass surfaces that showed every smudge. By contrast, Sheridan's childhood home was full of comfortable furniture, Errol's colorful paintings, and family photos scattered throughout.

As Ridge led her down a long hallway, Sheridan wondered what it said about both of them that they chose to live in such sterile surroundings. Entering the brightly lit kitchen, she realized that, unlike her condo, at least one part of Ridge's house exuded relaxation and comfort. It had been remodeled since her last visit and was now painted a cheerful yellow with new cream cabinets and gleaming stainless steel appliances.

Seating her at the granite counter, Ridge said, "I mixed up a batch of white sangria. Would you like to try some?"

"Sure." Sheridan watched him take a pitcher of the potent concoction from the fridge and pour two glasses. She took a sip and said, "Nice. Sweet and tangy."

"Just like you." Ridge slid a fingertip over her bottom lip.

She fought the urge to lean into his touch, refusing to give in to his seduction. They had a lot to talk about, and she wasn't allowing him to distract her from such an important conversation.

"Tangy maybe." Sheridan raised a brow. "Sweet, I don't think so."

"Then you would be wrong. You're very sweet." Ridge leaned in for a kiss.

When she moved back, he shrugged, took off his sweater, unbuttoned the cuffs of his shirt, and rolled them up.

Sheridan swallowed. He was even more gorgeous this way.

"Hope you like pasta." He tied on a white chef's apron.

"Who doesn't?" Sheridan's heartbeat quickened.

What was sexier than a hot guy cooking? Ignoring her attraction until after Ridge had explained Sally's birth would be tougher than she'd imagined.

As he turned the heat on underneath a couple of pans and adjusted the oven temperature, Ridge said, "So you met my daughter?"

"Several times." Although Sheridan wanted to discuss Sally, she hadn't been prepared for him to bring up the subject so soon. Keeping her voice neutral, she commented, "Sally's a smart girl."

"Which, as you know from personal experience, can be difficult."

"Yes, I do."

The memory of just how tough it had been to be like Sally washed over Sheridan. She'd been unable to understand why it took everyone else so much longer to figure things out. And equally confusing was when the kids accused her of showing off when she answered questions in class. Not to mention, the feeling of being exploited when her classmates demanded to copy her papers or cheat off her during exams.

"I wish I knew how to make things easier for her." Ridge poured cream sauce into a pan, then filled a larger pot with water. "She's having a hard time adjusting to the new school."

"New school?" Sheridan frowned, then put all the bits and pieces she'd heard from Merry, Sally, and Ridge together and said, "Right. Sally hasn't always lived in Sutton Falls."

"Sally was only six when I divorced her mother." Ridge sighed. "Alexis retaliated by moving my daughter out of state." He took a small loaf of herbed focaccia bread, wrapped it in foil, and slid it into the oven. "Sally barely remembers the kids she went to kindergarten with and hasn't really been able to make any new friends."

Sheridan toyed with the stem of her wineglass, recalling how bad it had felt when classmates had excluded her. "That's got to be tough on her."

"Extremely."

"And I imagine if Sally wasn't in Missouri, you weren't able to see your daughter very often during the time she lived with Alexis. The adjustment of suddenly having full custody is probably rough on you, too."

"It sounds as if Sally has revealed our whole lurid history." Ridge grimaced. "I'm surprised she's talked that much to you. She barely speaks to me."

Remembering the relief of revealing her feelings to her sorority sisters, none of whom had ever heard of Sutton Falls or Ridge Sutton, she said, "Sometimes it's easier to share with someone not directly involved."

"I guess." Ridge's broad shoulders slumped.

"It must be hard for you both in this situation," Sheridan murmured, trying to comfort him.

"Oh, I have parenting down to a science."

"Oh?" Sheridan heard the smile return to his voice.

"Yep." Ridge winked. "Every day with Sally is an experiment."

"I think that's probably how most mothers and fathers feel."

"True." Ridge walked over to the counter and took Sheridan's hand between both of his. "But God only knows what Alexis has said about me to our daughter."

"I take it the divorce wasn't amicable." Suddenly chilled, she enjoyed the warmth of his fingers around hers.

"Hardly." Ridge gave a humorless laugh.

He couldn't hide the pain that talking about his ex-wife brought him, and Sheridan hated to keep poking that exposed sore spot, but she had no choice.

"More often than not, that seems to be the situation," Sheridan commented.

"Yeah." Ridge shook his head. "But in our case, neither was the marriage."

Sheridan fought to keep her lips from curving, ashamed that she was glad that Ridge hadn't been happy with his ex-wife. Then, remembering what was coming next, she frowned and squeezed his fingers supportively.

Knowing she was about to cause him even more hurt, but needing to understand, Sheridan said gently, "Let's start from the beginning. What happened all those years ago when you and Alexis broke up and then almost immediately got back together?"

"I ended things with Alexis because I finally admitted to myself that I was attracted to you, not her."

Sheridan's heart raced. She hadn't imagined the chemistry between them during their tutoring sessions. What would have happened if she'd been brave enough to act on her attraction to him back then?

Swallowing, she said, "You did?"

"I did." Ridge lifted Sheridan's hand to his lips and pressed a kiss into the center of her palm. "But Alexis and I were in an exclusive relationship, and it wouldn't have been right to ask you out until I was free."

"Which you were for about five seconds." Sheridan tried to keep the bitterness out of her voice.

"Actually, it was several days," Ridge corrected. "But Alexis did not take the breakup well, and I was waiting for her to calm down before asking you for a date." He rubbed his thumb in circles on her wrist. "I was afraid of what she would do if she found out that I was interested in you."

"So what happened?" Sheridan was having difficulty concentrating on his story while his fingers stroked the sensitive skin on her inner arm.

"I'm ashamed to say that I gave in to my mother's blackmail." A flush crept across Ridge's cheeks. "She overheard me telling Beau that I wasn't taking Alexis to the prom because I wanted to ask you out. And when Mother couldn't persuade me to change my mind, she threatened your family's farm." Ridge's jaw clenched. "She mentioned that Alexis's father, as the bank president, had the power to mess with the loan on your farm. And if his little girl was unhappy, he'd do just that."

"But we didn't have a mortgage." Sheridan frowned. "That land has belonged to the Sheridan family free and clear for over a hundred and fifty years."

"My mother was untruthful. What a surprise." Ridge mocked his own gullibility. "I've learned since then that my mother is the duchess of deception. I should have known she was lying."

"As teenagers," Sheridan murmured, thinking of her own father, "it's hard to believe our parents would betray us like that."

"Unfortunately, as adults, we know better." Ridge let go of her hand, turned away, and dropped the linguine into the now boiling water.

Sheridan watched him stir the sauce. Even though she knew his answer might end their budding relationship, she also knew that she needed to ask the tough questions in order to decide if there was any chance for them to be together.

"So I'm assuming you didn't marry Alexis to save my family's farm." Her chest tightened. *This was it.* Taking a deep breath, she said in as detached a voice as she could manage, "Tell me the rest of the story."

"The agreement with my mother was that I would get back together with Alexis and take her to the prom, then after I left for college, I'd allow the relationship to slowly fade away. Once it was over, I'd planned to contact you at your school and ask you out." Ridge took a bottle of olive oil from a cupboard and poured it onto a saucer. "Mother suggested I get one of my friends to invite you to the prom so that I could at least have a few dances with you."

"I see." Sheridan felt like an anchorless ship, drifting in the middle of the ocean without any idea of when, or if, she'd find a safe port. Taking a small sip of her sangria, she asked, "Do you think that your mother conspired with Alexis to humiliate me?"

"Possibly. But Mother's goal was to get me back with Alexis. I'm fairly certain she thought that I'd forget about you once Alexis had me under her control again." Ridge ground fresh pepper over the oil. "My guess is that Beau told his girlfriend, Gwen, that I was interested in you, and she told Alexis."

"And Alexis couldn't stand the fact that you preferred me to her."

"Exactly."

While Sheridan thought about his words, she watched him test the pasta. Finally, she said, "So Alexis, with the help of her clique, plotted to take me down a peg. And at the same time, she made sure that I blamed you and thus would never go out with you even if you asked me for a date."

"It was a diabolically clever plan, and it worked perfectly," Ridge said, the fury in his eyes refuting the mildness of his voice.

Sheridan had a lot more questions but remained quiet, allowing Ridge to regain his equanimity. She could sympathize with his feelings of betrayal. Someone who he'd thought loved him had manipulated and used him in the worst possible way.

His posture stiff, Ridge silently drained the pasta and added it, along with shrimp, to the sauce. After he was finished, he visibly relaxed his shoulders and appeared to recover his composure.

Smiling at Sheridan, he suggested, "I thought it would be nice to eat in front of the fireplace." He took two bowls of salad from the fridge and added them to the tray that already held the bread and entrees. "Grab our drinks and follow me."

"Right behind you." Sheridan knew there was still a lot to discuss but was willing to let him set the pace. At least, for a little while.

There were big pillows on the floor next to the low oak coffee table. Ridge arranged the food on the top of a massive table that already held napkins and flatware.

Putting the tray aside, he said, "Do you mind sitting on the floor?" When she shook her head, he helped her onto one of the large cushions. "The dining room is so cold and formal, and the kitchen is too casual for a special occasion like our first date, so I thought this would be better."

"It's terrific." Sheridan felt treasured by the care he'd taken to make their evening together memorable. She was trying not to get her hopes up or read too much meaning into his actions, but she was losing the battle. Still, they had to finish clearing the air between them if there would be any chance for them truly to explore their feelings for each other.

"I'm glad you think so." Ridge gracefully folded himself onto the pillow next to her.

"So," Sheridan continued her questioning, not ready to eat yet, "you asked Alexis to the prom to protect my family's farm and got one of your friends to invite me. What happened next? I need to know the rest of it."

"You're right. It's about time the whole story was revealed." Ridge grimaced. "With this conversation in mind, I questioned Beau today. He admitted that Alexis put Rohypnol in my drink at the pre-party. She told him it was to keep me from interfering with the prank they were going to pull on you."

"Was he aware of the Perry Newtsen part of her plan?" Sheridan had always wondered who was and wasn't in on that portion of the plot.

"He claimed to have no idea about that, and I want to believe him." Ridge twitched his shoulders. "Beau's not a bad guy when he's sober."

"And how often is that?" Sheridan snapped. Beau's treatment of her was hard to forgive. Taking a calming breath, she said, "So Alexis arranged the attack on me all by herself."

It was a relief that no one else had been involved. A practical joke was one thing; scheming to have someone assaulted was an entirely different matter.

"Yes. Or Beau was too drunk to understand what she

intended." Ridge took a gulp of his sangria. "But from what I learned about Alexis in the years she and I were married, that kind of disgusting trick had her name written all over it."

"Then I only have one more question." Sheridan looked into Ridge's eyes, needing him to understand how important the circumstances of his daughter's conception were to her.

"You want to know how Alexis ended up pregnant with Sally if I was no longer interested in her." Ridge's voice was resigned. "And did it happen prom night or soon afterwards?"

"Yes." Sheridan forced out the single word. The lump in her throat felt the size of a beach ball.

"Before I tell you, I need your word that you will never discuss this with anyone. Not your father. Not your best friend. Not even your therapist if you have one." Ridge stared back at Sheridan. "I've never said this out loud, and it would devastate Sally if she ever found out."

"I promise." Sheridan put her hand over her heart, touched he trusted her with such a huge secret. "After tonight, we won't speak of it again."

"Okay." Ridge took a deep breath and said, "I have *no* memory of that night. From my research this afternoon, when Rohypnol is taken with alcohol, it produces loss of inhibition and amnesia, so I assume that's how Alexis and I ended up having sex. I certainly never was with her after that night. At least, not until we got married."

"She was really determined not to lose you. She must have loved you a great deal." Sheridan nodded to herself. She could almost understand Alexis's obsession. Ridge was a once-in-a-lifetime kind of guy.

"No." He shook his head emphatically. "She just couldn't stand the thought that I didn't want her. If she loved me, I would never have caught her in bed with another guy."

"She cheated on you?" Sheridan gasped, unable to

comprehend why a woman would want to be with someone else when she had Ridge as her husband.

"Apparently, she slept around from the very beginning of our marriage." Ridge pressed his lips together. "If Sally didn't look so much like me, I'd wonder if I was really her father."

Sheridan's heart broke for him, for all the hurt he'd kept inside for so many years. It might have made him the strong, resilient person that he'd become, but she wished he hadn't had to shoulder the duplicity of someone who'd claimed to love him in order to become that man.

"Thank you for sharing. I know how hard it was to rehash all this, but I really needed to know about it." Sheridan regretted causing him pain, but she wouldn't have ever been able to get over their past if he hadn't told her everything.

"I understand." Ridge leaned forward. "You needed to hear this as much as I needed to tell you."

Sheridan hugged the concern and sincerity in his voice to her heart.

"Any other questions?" he asked.

"None that I can think of right now." Sheridan realized that he'd soothed all her concerns about the past, and she was ready to start a fresh chapter with him.

Ridge broke off a piece of bread, dredged it through the oil, and held it to Sheridan's lips. "Then let's eat."

CHAPTER NINETEEN

The food was delicious, and despite her overwhelming awareness of Ridge's every tiny movement, Sheridan was able to enjoy the meal. As they ate, and the conversation shifted to their present day lives, she was finally able to ease the tight grip she'd kept on her emotions and allow herself to admit the attraction she felt for Ridge.

A fragile strand of something real began to form between them. It was new and bright and full of possibilities. As if the past thirteen years had disappeared and she was back to a time when she trusted him. A time when she felt at ease with him. A time when she was so in love with him she could barely breathe.

Only now, instead of being frightened by her feelings, as she had been back then, she could admit them—at least to herself.

After they finished their dinner, Ridge carried the empty plates into the kitchen. When he returned, he pulled his pillow close to Sheridan's and slipped his arm around her. She stiffened, overwhelmed by how right it felt to be hugged to his side.

He caressed her bare shoulders and drew circles on the nape of her neck until she relaxed, then he kissed her temple.

Nuzzling beneath her ear, his voice dipped with innuendo, and he said, "Are you ready for dessert?"

Sheridan raised a brow, and he grinned back at her, clearly amused by his own clichéd line. She snickered, then gasped when he returned to nibbling on the sensitive cord along the side of her neck.

She didn't want to think about all the reasons they should

wait. His lips on her skin sparked a fierce longing inside of her. He pressed warm, openmouthed kisses all over her face and down her throat.

His lips drew all the stiffness from her body, and as the sensations heightened, she asked, "What did you have in mind?"

Ridge's answering groan was the most erotic sound she'd ever heard. She turned her head to find him gazing at her as if she were the last chocolate chip cookie on earth.

"This." His low growl sent tingles through her body.

Even as Ridge crushed her to him, a small part of Sheridan's mind continued to worry that they were going too fast. Maybe they should discuss their lives during the thirteen years they'd been apart, get reacquainted before taking the next step.

Sheridan admitted that she was attracted to him. That she wanted him. But she was afraid that if she weren't extremely careful, she would make the irrevocable mistake of falling in love with him again.

And this time, she wouldn't be falling for his charm and good looks, she'd be falling for the man. A man who would be hard to forget when he grew tired of her.

She needed to protect herself, to be prepared for the inevitable good-bye. Ridge would never leave Sutton Falls, and her life was in St. Louis.

But when his lips touched hers, thoughts of slowing things down, of being cautious, whirled away, leaving behind nothing but a longing for more. She was shattered by the hunger in his kiss. He probed the seam of her mouth, and she opened to his invitation. When he swept his tongue inside, shivers of desire spiraled southward.

He tasted so good. Better than she recalled from last night. Like creamy Parmesan, sweet wine, and hot, hot man. His lips were firm and silky, and his tongue licked fire into her mouth.

The kiss went on and on, until he broke it off to cup her cheek, his green eyes so dark they seemed black. He said, "I've never wanted anyone as much as I do you."

His hands skimmed down the front of her top, unfastening the buttons along the way and sliding it over her shoulders. He dropped the blouse to the floor, then popped the catch of her bra and slipped it off of her.

Stroking his palms down her ribs, along her waist, and over the slight curve of her stomach, he brushed her burning skin with his fingers, and Sheridan could see the desire in his eyes. The heat of his appreciative gaze swept away every last vestige of insecurity. Her body might not be perfect, but Ridge clearly didn't care.

As he filled his hands with her breasts, he said, "You are so damn beautiful. Feel how much you turn me on," he whispered, pressing his erection against her thigh.

Sheridan gasped. He was like steel, and she could hardly wait for that hardness to fill her.

"You have the sweetest pink nipples." His calloused fingers stroked and tugged them into stiff points. "I've been dreaming of touching them."

She squirmed, making inarticulate needy sounds.

"Of hearing you moan when I play with them." He teased the peaks until they were impossibly taut. "Tasting them." He dipped his head and drew the tip deep into his mouth.

The pull of his lips sent a shudder through her that traveled down her belly and between her legs. She writhed against his mouth and took a deep, shuddering breath. The familiar sexy scent of his citrus aftershave washed over her, and she inhaled deeply.

Leaning away from him for a scant second, she dragged his shirt off over his head. Sheridan was surprised by the tribal band tattooed around his right bicep and traced it with a fingertip.

Ridge hadn't struck her as the kind of guy who got inked, but then, as she'd learned earlier in the evening, a lot of her assumptions about him had been wrong.

He returned his attention to her breasts, and she scraped her nails down his back. The powerful muscular build she remembered from high school was still rock solid.

A yearning for more tugged at her center, and she slid her hands around his waist to unfasten his belt. Fumbling with his zipper, she let out a triumphant cry when it finally opened. He returned the favor, and in seconds, they were sprawled nude on the rug in front of the fire.

Sheridan had often fantasized of what it would be like to be with Ridge this way. But she'd underestimated everything. Her response to him. The pleasure his lips brought her. And most of all, her feelings toward him.

Before she could worry she was falling for him way too fast, Ridge pulled her on top of him, and the sensation of the coarse hair on his chest pressed against her sensitized nipples drove away any lingering doubts. She moaned as the heat of his body swept through her, then slanted her head and ravished his willing mouth.

Instantly, he took over. She frowned. She liked to be in charge of everything, especially during sex. But as Ridge kissed her hard and deep, his tongue thrusting and pulling back in a sensual simulation of what he would soon do with her, she gave up that control to a man who clearly knew how to handle it.

While his mouth seduced her, his fingers skimmed down her belly to the juncture of her thighs and stroked the wet folds. Circling the bundle of nerves at the apex, between kisses, he murmured exactly what he was going to do to her and with her.

His explicit words increased her arousal. It was too much, yet she wanted more.

Tearing her lips from his, she panted, "Not like this. I want you inside of me."

At the joy in his face, something deep inside her soul ignited.

He immediately reached for his pants and fumbled a foil packet from the pocket.

The erotic image of him sheathing himself made her gasp.

Her palm traveled down his erection, and as he grew even larger under her hand, she purred, "I love that you're so hard for me."

He settled between her legs and asked, "Ready?"

"Yes," she hissed through clenched teeth, almost too close to coming to speak.

Inch by inch, Ridge eased inside of her, filling her core with the heat of him, with his solid length. This was so much better than her fantasies.

He started slowly, drawing each stroke out and causing little jolts of electricity to pirouette all through her body. When she couldn't stand it any longer and grabbed his ass, he slowed even more, then began a rhythm that drove her mad.

As the sensation built, she wrapped her legs around his waist and tried to hurry him, but he kissed her neck and crooned, "I've waited thirteen years for this. We are not rushing it."

His smile suggested that buried deep inside of her was the only place in the world he ever wanted to be and he would take his damn sweet time enjoying the experience.

"We'll see." Sheridan met him thrust for thrust, feeling her internal muscles start to tighten.

Ridge's pupils dilated at her movements and his eyes closed. He gasped and pistoned his hips, matching her pace. As he arched his back, the tendons in his neck and arms bulged. Reaching between them, he swirled his thumb on her sweet spot until she whimpered.

Every part of her concentrated on the stroke of his fingers

and his thrusts inside of her. The pressure building in her core took her up to a level she'd never experienced before. Then, with one final plunge, she was flung into an orgasm, the intensity of which she'd never imagined. He'd taken her, making her forever his.

Riding wave after wave of pleasure, Sheridan was shocked at the power of the heat and light that enveloped her body and consumed her soul. Every time she thought she was finished, there was another surge, until she cried out his name and held him as he lost himself inside her.

When the fireworks behind her eyes finally stopped exploding, she lay spent. Ridge was draped over her, his lips caressing her eyelids, nose, and cheeks. Instead of feeling suffocated by his weight, she welcomed the sensation. It reassured her that this was real. That they had truly just made love. When he rolled to his side to remove the condom, she felt abandoned.

Ridge must have sensed her need, because he gathered her to his chest and wrapped her in his arms. As her eyes drifted closed, her last thought was that Ridge had been worth the wait.

CHAPTER TWENTY

A few minutes later, Ridge kissed Sheri awake, and they moved into his bedroom. Wanting to reassure her that the ghost of his ex-wife wasn't present, he murmured into her ear, "Alexis and I never shared a room."

"Good to know." Sheri's arms snaked around his neck, and her smile conveyed her relief.

"You're the only woman I've ever invited here." Ridge wanted to make it crystal clear how special Sheri was to him.

"Oh." Sheri's beautiful brown eyes widened.

Before she could say anything else, a need fisted in Ridge's gut. He had to taste her again, feel her body move against his one more time.

His desperation must have been obvious, because Sheri tugged him toward the bed, pushed him onto his back, and straddled him. He liked that she was taking charge and relaxed. He enjoyed every caress and stroke of her talented fingers until he couldn't stand it one second longer and took over guiding them both to the pleasurable ending they craved.

After a quick shower, they crawled under the covers, and he held her, stroking her back until she fell asleep. As he trailed his fingers down her silky skin, he remembered that he needed to talk to her about the levee.

He'd do that in the morning, after they'd shared a leisurely breakfast and he told her how much he cared for her. Then, if he could just make himself stop looking at her for half a moment, his brain might work well enough for him to be able to form a cohesive sentence and explain to her how much the town needed her property.

He closed his eyes and replayed making love to Sheri for what he hoped was the first time of the rest of their lives. It had been a bit embarrassing after dinner when he'd put his arm around her and his raging erection had grown clear out of the waistband of his pants.

Still, she hadn't seemed to mind. He smiled at the memory, and as she sighed in her sleep, he drew her closer. She was a natural fit. Her long lashes lay on her pretty pink cheeks, making her seem so heartbreakingly vulnerable that he could scarcely swallow past the lump in his throat. This was such a different face from the one she showed the world.

His chest tightened at the hurt she'd already endured at his hands and the hands of his so-called friends. Barely able to breathe at the thought of Newtsen's filthy paws on Sheri and of what he might have done to her if she hadn't gotten away, Ridge vowed to protect her from any future pain.

He looked down at her head lying on his chest, and there was something so utterly beautiful about her sleeping in his arms every hair on his body stood at attention, and he was instantly hard again. He wanted to wake up every day with her beside him.

Throughout the night, she molded her body to the contours of his. And each time Ridge woke, he grinned like an idiot to find Sheri in his bed rather than just in his dreams.

* * *

When the phone rang at six a.m., Sheridan bolted upright. Where was she? Memories of the night flooded back, and when Ridge tugged her down beside him, she went eagerly into his arms.

A few seconds later, with a muttered curse, Ridge grabbed his insistently ringing cell from the nightstand. He checked to see who was calling, then said to Sheridan, "It's Sally. I've got to take this."

"Of course." Sheridan patted his arm and swung her legs over the mattress.

She pushed aside her disappointment and went to fetch her clothes, then took them into the bathroom to freshen up. It would have been nice to wake to a leisurely round of lovemaking, but considering the relationship that Ridge had described between him and his daughter, Sheridan doubted Sally was phoning to say good morning. There must be some emergency, and Sheridan could hardly fault him for answering his daughter's call.

By the time Ridge came to find her, Sheridan was dressed and prepared to leave. As long as they had been interrupted, she might as well try to make it home before Errol. It would save a lot of embarrassing explanation. She so didn't want to discuss her sex life with her father.

"Sally had some sort of argument, and her grandmother took the other girl's side," Ridge explained, zipping up his jeans as he thrust his bare feet into a pair of loafers. "She's hysterical and refuses to get into the car with her grandmother. I'm sorry, but I have to go get her."

"I understand." Sheridan looked around for her purse. "Can you drop me at my house first? I'd like to get home before my father. It's not a big deal, but he's already way too excited about our date."

"Would you mind taking one of my cars?" Ridge shoved a hand through his hair. "I've never heard Sally so upset, and I promised her that I'd be there as fast as I could."

"No problem." Sheridan nodded. "I'd offer to wait until you got back, but it sounds as if you'll have your hands full, and my being here might make things a little awkward."

"Thank you for being so sweet about this." Ridge pulled her

into his arms and rested his forehead against hers. "I had dreamed of us spending this morning very differently."

"Ah." Sheridan tapped his nose with her fingertip, smiling to herself that Ridge had obviously thought out their time together. "So you had last night's seduction all planned."

"Let's just say that I had high hopes. Just in case, I went all the way over to Mt. Morrison to buy the condoms." Ridge grinned. "I figured the word would spread too fast around here."

"Good call." A tiny flicker of happiness shot through her. If he'd had to make a special trip to buy protection, that meant he wasn't seeing anyone else. Even after his assurance that no other women had been in his bed, she'd been almost afraid to hope that he meant there weren't any others in his life.

"Sally and Mother were supposed to go directly to church from their pajama party." Ridge's lips brushed the sensitive cord beneath Sheridan's ear. "I was going to meet them there. We should have had the house to ourselves until ten."

"That would have been nice, but you need to rescue your daughter, and I'd like to beat my father home, so we'd better get going." Sheridan tried to step out of Ridge's arms, but he tightened his grip and gave her a scorching kiss.

When he released her, Sheridan was gasping for air and could barely close her fingers over the key ring he pressed in her palm.

"You take the Z4; I'll use my Mustang." Ridge put his arm around her waist and walked her outside. "I'll call you after I get things settled with Sally."

"Let me know if I can do anything to help." Sheridan slid into the BMW. "I don't have much experience with kids, but Sally and I seem to be on the same wavelength."

"Don't think I won't take you up on that." He closed the car door for her, and as she drove away, he shouted, "Last night was the best night of my life."

"Mine, too," Sheridan whispered to herself. "Mine, too."

* * *

Sally was quiet during the short trip from the country club to their house. Once they were inside, Ridge searched his mind for a way to break the silence. He liked to cook, and Sally seemed to appreciate his efforts, so he'd been trying to make Sunday breakfast their special time together.

Maybe continuing with that routine would help ease Sally into telling him what had happened.

Trying to sound casual, he asked, "Did you eat yet?"

"Nope." Sally shook her head. "Harper Webster started picking on me as soon as I woke up."

"How about you tell me about it while I make you that puffy French toast you like?" Ridge put his hand on his daughter's shoulder and guided her toward the kitchen. "Start at the beginning."

His heart warmed that she was talking to him. Now, if he could just handle this the right way, maybe it would be a turning point in their relationship.

While he waited for Sally to speak, Ridge sprayed the griddle with Pam, put it on the stove, and turned on the burner.

"Harper was giving me a hard time about how I dressed and said that I'd better stop showing off how smart I was in class or I'd never get a boyfriend." Sally worried her lower lip between her teeth. "So I told her that a famous author advised me not to worry about boys who were threatened by my intelligence. Then I casually mentioned that with Harper's crummy grades, the boys had better like her, because she'd never make it into college or have any kind of career."

Ridge hid his grin as he combined flour, sugar, baking powder, nutmeg, and cinnamon. "And she objected."

212

He was proud of his daughter for sticking up for herself. Hanging out with Sheri had obviously influenced Sally a great deal. Evelyn would have a fit, but he didn't care. He agreed with Sheri's advice.

Between his mother's treatment of Sally and her attitude toward Sheri, it was past time for the Ice Queen to move back to her own house. This morning, after church, he'd put the word out that he was looking for a full-time housekeeper. He was determined that neither Sally nor Sheri would be made uncomfortable by Evelyn's presence.

"Harper was so mad her face turned all red, and she yelled that she didn't want to be a brainiac like me." Sally paused and asked, "Do you want some help cooking?" When he nodded, she grabbed the bacon from the fridge and arranged the slices on a plastic tray, then continued her story. "Harper said her mom never went to college and she didn't need to, either. And at least her mother loved her enough to live with her, unlike mine."

"That wasn't nice." Ridge kept his voice mild as he mixed milk and eggs together.

Damn! There were a lot of children in Sutton Falls whose parents were divorced, but he couldn't think of any others who lived with their father instead of their mother. How would he explain Alexis's actions to Sally?

"So I said that my mom loved me but couldn't be here right now." Sally peeked at him from behind her bangs, clearly needing him to agree with her.

"That was a good answer. Your mom is going through a tough time, but she loves you more than anything."

Ridge didn't believe that for a second—Alexis only loved herself—but he knew the truth wasn't something Sally was ready to hear. She might never be ready to hear it.

"Maybe." Sally shrugged. "But then Harper said if that was how it really was, why had her mother seen my mother in Sutton

Falls on Friday night?" Sally covered the tray with a plastic dome, slid it into the microwave, and pressed start. "So I called her a liar and she slapped me."

As he placed the French toast on the hot griddle, he said, "That would have been a good time to go get an adult."

Hell! He should have realized that Alexis's presence would be the talk of the town.

"Maybe I should have gone to get someone." Sally took two glasses from the cupboard. "But I hit Harper back instead."

"Was that when your grandmother came into the room?" Ridge could just imagine his mother's reaction to her granddaughter brawling.

"Uh-huh. The other girls ran to get her." Sally poured juice into the tumblers. "Grandmother and Mrs. Webster pulled us apart. Then Grandmother yelled at me in front of everyone. She said no matter how badly provoked, a Sutton always acts like a lady."

"Did Mrs. Webster yell at Harper?" Ridge kept his back to Sally.

He didn't want her to see how angry he was at Evelyn. How dare she not support her granddaughter? It was bad enough Evelyn had never been there for him, but for her to treat Sally that way made him want to cut all ties with the Ice Queen.

"No. Mrs. Webster took Harper's side." Sally put napkins and silverware on the counter. "She said Harper was telling the truth about my mother being in town. And if I hadn't seen her, then clearly my mom thought attending parties was more important than visiting me."

Son of a bitch! Ridge gritted his teeth to stop from swearing out loud. Prissy Webster needed to learn to keep her big mouth shut. No doubt her attack on Sally was retaliation for how badly Alexis had always treated her.

"Did you know Mom was here?" Sally asked, interrupting

his thoughts.

"I saw her briefly Friday night."

Dammit! Ridge knew he should have told Sally that her mother was in Sutton Falls before someone else did. In fact, he had intended to tell her Saturday afternoon while they worked on the car. But they'd been having such a good time he'd put it off.

He hadn't had the heart to ruin their afternoon. To see the hurt in Sally's eyes when she found out that Alexis was in town but hadn't even bothered to stop by and say hello.

"I tried to locate your mother yesterday, but she must have already left," Ridge said, wishing he'd been able to find his ex and force her to visit their daughter.

"Without coming to see me?" Sally slid onto a stool, tears welling up in her eyes.

"I'm not sure what her schedule was like, honey." Ridge's mind raced, trying to find something comforting to say. "It was close to ten o'clock when your mom came to Miss Mac's party. Too late to see you. She probably left that same night."

"Why was she here?" Sally wiped at her cheek with a paper napkin.

"I don't know." Ridge took the French toast from the pan and slid it onto a pair of plates, then walked around the counter and hugged his daughter. "Your mom and I didn't talk."

"Is it true she was mean to Sheridan?" Sally whispered into Ridge's chest. "Mrs. Webster said that Mom really laid into Sheridan about something Mom did to her back in high school."

"Regrettably, your mother *did* say some unkind things to Sheri." Ridge wished he could lie, but there were too many witnesses.

He just prayed that Sally never found out the entire story of what Alexis had done to Sheri.

"Do you think Sheridan hates us because Mom was so awful to her?" Sally twisted a piece of hair and gazed at him worriedly.

"No." Ridge kissed the top of his daughter's head. "Sheri knows that we aren't responsible for what your mother does."

He turned his head so Sally couldn't see his grin. After all the incredible orgasms that he and Sheri had shared last night, he was pretty damn certain she didn't hate him.

"How can you be sure?" Sally demanded.

"As it happens," Ridge said slowly, "Sheri and I had dinner together last night, and she said how much she likes you."

He had hoped to ease into telling his daughter that he was dating her idol, but as soon as they were seen together in public, the news would get out. Which meant he'd better talk to Sally about his new relationship with Sheri sooner rather than later.

"You had a date with Sheridan?" Sally's green eyes sparkled. "Why didn't you tell me?"

"I wanted to see how it went," Ridge explained. "There was no use mentioning it if it was a one-time thing."

"So, was it?" Sally leaned forward, her face alive with hope. "Or are you seeing her again?"

"I think so," Ridge sighed. "I'll give her a call later and ask her." He put the French toast in front of Sally and handed her the bottle of maple syrup. "Now eat up. You have to shower and change. We don't want to be late for church."

CHAPTER TWENTY-ONE

"Seriously?" Sheridan stared at her father. "You want to go to church? Aren't you tired?"

"No. I feel wonderful." Errol grinned. "It was invigorating to be out and about, seeing people again."

Sheridan felt a twinge of remorse. She knew that Errol was a social being but hadn't realized how much being cooped up at home had affected him. She should have offered to take him to his club meetings and to visit his friends.

"You didn't mention going to services last Sunday," Sheridan said feebly, trying to lessen her guilt.

"I wasn't sure you'd be comfortable going there and facing everyone." Errol reached over and took her hand. He seemed pleased when she didn't immediately pull her fingers from his grasp. "But this past week, speaking to Merry's class, attending her party, going out with Ridge, you seem to have overcome a lot of your fears and resentment."

Sheridan was a little surprised her father had been so perceptive. When she was younger, she would have sworn he could read her mind, but after they'd grown apart, he'd appeared to have lost that ability. Maybe he'd just been hiding it from her.

"I guess I have." She shrugged. "Quite a few of the ghosts that have kept me away from Sutton Falls have been exorcised."

All but Errol's adultery. Maybe it was time to let that go, too. She leaned down and kissed her father's cheek. Would it be so bad if she never found out the truth? If she took his word and believed in his innocence?

"Great." Errol squeezed her fingers. "Then can we go to church?"

"Don't you want to get some sleep?" She certainly could

use a nap. She was happy to take her father to services, but she wasn't entirely convinced that his motive was purely religious.

"We can sleep when we're dead. And I have no plans to die anytime soon," Errol called over his shoulder, as he rolled his wheelchair into his room.

"Thank goodness for that." Sheridan blew out a relieved sigh. It was wonderful seeing her father feeling so much better.

"I'm going to put on my suit, and you'd better change, too. Those clothes look mighty wrinkled to me." Errol turned and winked. "Did you go to bed in them or were they just on the floor of someone else's bedroom all night?"

Shit! Sheridan ignored her father's teasing and marched into the bathroom. She hadn't had time to put on another outfit before Errol had arrived home. She'd barely managed to get Ridge's Z4 in the tractor shed and get into the house before Errol's friend had dropped him off.

Not that there really was any way to keep her relationship with Ridge a secret. That was, if they were going to have a relationship. He'd seemed interested in more than just last night, but he hadn't really said anything except that he'd call her. Which were often the famous last words at the end of many a date.

Her breath hitched at the thought of never being with Ridge again, and she frowned at her own weakness. How could she be falling for him so fast? Before this past week, she hadn't seen him in thirteen years. She really didn't know him at all.

No! a little voice insisted. *That isn't true. You know the things about him that really matter. That he loves his daughter. That he cares for the town's people. That he has been nothing but wonderful to you since you've been back. Not to mention that his touch makes you burn with desire.*

Sighing, Sheridan stepped into the shower. The water hadn't had time to warm up, which, considering her thoughts, was just as well.

* * *

Sheridan and Errol arrived at Sutton Falls's First Trinity Church only minutes before the service was scheduled. She was conscious of the entire congregation watching her as she pushed her father's wheelchair down the center aisle. Keeping a pleasant smile on her face, she said hello to the parishioners she recognized and nodded at the others.

Although she felt better about being in her hometown, she was still uneasy as the center of everyone's attention. It was one thing to be in the spotlight talking about her books. It was an entirely different situation coming to terms with her past.

She was nearly to the only open spots—the ones in the very front of the nave—when she saw Ridge and Sally in a pew a couple of rows behind the vacant seats. Her heart warmed when they both beamed and waved.

Sally was really a sweet girl, and Sheridan was happy to see that she appeared none the worse for whatever had happened to make her call Ridge for a ride home. Sheridan had never imagined herself as a mother, but a fleeting image of sitting down to dinner with Sally and Ridge in his cheery kitchen flashed across her mind.

Frowning, Sheridan flicked it aside. She couldn't allow herself to want something she'd never have. One night of mind-blowing sex did not equal a life together. Not when her life was in St. Louis and his was firmly anchored in Sutton Falls.

She glanced at Ridge again. He was staring at her with such intensity, with a look so hungry, that her lips tingled as if he'd kissed her. For a second, her breathing sped up, then she forced herself to look away. It was as if he was making off with her soul one heartbeat at a time, and that was something she couldn't

219

allow.

Forcing herself to focus on something other than Ridge, she noticed that Evelyn was not seated next to her son and granddaughter. Sheridan took a quick peek around and spotted the older woman sitting by herself, an outraged expression etched into the wrinkles of her face. What was that all about?

Mentally shrugging, Sheridan wheeled Errol the last couple of feet. She helped her father onto the bench, folded the wheelchair and leaned it against the side of the pew, then slid in next to him. As the minister started the service, Sheridan glanced at her dad. He was grinning from ear to ear. What was he up to now?

* * *

Ridge was surprised to see Sheri in church. She hadn't attended the previous Sunday, so he hadn't been expecting her today. But now that she was here, he couldn't tear his gaze from her sweet face.

He fought the urge to come to her assistance as he watched her maneuver her father out of his wheelchair and onto the pew. He was afraid that if he tried to help her, she might think he was being patronizing. He needed to reread her books and get a better handle on her views.

Blowing out a frustrated breath, he stared at her perfect profile. Sheri was completely unaware of her beauty. When he'd told her she was gorgeous, it was clear from her expression that she didn't believe him.

Although she'd always been pretty, she had matured into a knockout. Men who preferred emaciated Barbie dolls might not appreciate Sheri's curves, which was just fine with him. The less competition, the better.

The taste of her kisses was still on his lips. They reminded

220

him of silvery moonlight and twinkling stars. Of the softness of dusk and the warmth of a summer night's breeze. *Hey!* When had he turned into a poet?

Thinking of how they'd parted that morning, Ridge's stomach churned with anxiety and aggravation. He hadn't had time to tell her how he felt about her. They'd been hurtled back to earth from their amazing evening before they'd had a chance to talk. That certainly hadn't been fair to her. Or anywhere near how he wanted to treat her.

Hell! He'd practically thrown her out of the house. He hadn't even driven her home. Did she really understand? Or had her sympathetic acceptance of the situation merely been good manners?

The worship dragged on, and Ridge felt his mother's poisonous glares throughout the hour. As soon as she'd arrived home from the pajama party fundraiser, Ridge had informed her that he was taking over the care of his daughter and Evelyn had until Wednesday to move back into her own place.

When she'd protested, he'd added that sooner would be even better. Without giving her any chance to try her usual manipulation, Ridge had ended the conversation by telling her that in the meantime, she was to remain in her wing of the main house and to have only supervised contact with Sally.

Evelyn's icy silence had stiffened his resolve. And the slamming doors and squealing tires as she'd stormed away had convinced Ridge that he'd made the right decision. Now, he just had to get through this never-ending sermon, talk to Sheri, and make everything right.

An eternity later, with the conclusion of the benediction hymn, the congregation was free to make its way out of the nave. Ridge had to fight his overwhelming need to push everyone aside so he could get close to Sheri. When she and Errol headed toward the church hall for the after-service fellowship, he steered his daughter in that direction, too.

Just the thought of Sheri made him hurry down the corridor, only slowing when he noticed that Sally was skipping to keep up with him. His lips slid into an anticipatory smile, and his erection went to full mast as he entered the room.

However, when he saw a crowd surrounding Sheri and noticed that her hands were clasped into tight fists, the grin slipped from his mouth. Her nails were pressing into the soft flesh of her palms, and her mouth was clenched together almost as tightly. Would a kiss relax her lips? If not, he knew something else that would make her smile.

Shit! He was becoming a sex maniac. When had he turned into a complete pig? Instead of daydreaming about taking her to bed, he should find out what was upsetting her.

He guided Sally to the edge of the group and heard Mrs. Bunson haranguing Sheri and Errol about the levee. Ridge gritted his teeth. Between Beau and his mother, he wouldn't blame Sheri if she left town and never returned. Time to step in and stop it before she came to that same conclusion.

Before Ridge could make his move, he spotted Evelyn standing off to the side staring at Errol. Even from a distance, he could see the smile on her face wasn't a nice one. It was her patent lock-jawed social smirk and usually meant she was plotting someone's downfall. That couldn't be good.

Ridge shook his head. One problem at a time.

Bending down, he whispered in Sally's ear, "Can you push Mr. Davis's wheelchair over to a table and get him some coffee? I think he needs a break from everyone bothering him to sell his land, and I'd like to talk to Sheri for a minute."

"Sure." Sally drew herself up to her full height. "Don't worry, Dad. I'll take care of him."

"You're the best." Ridge hugged his daughter. The change in their relationship was amazing. It probably wouldn't last, but he sure intended to take advantage while he could.

"Ready?" Sally asked, the gleam of battle in her eyes.

"Ready." Ridge cupped Sally's elbow and shouldered their way through the throng.

Sally shot Ridge a grin and started whistling "We Are the Champions."

Once they reached where Sheri and Errol stood, he turned to Mrs. Bunson and said, "I'm sure Reverend Kael wouldn't approve of discussing business on Sunday morning. Let's leave those kinds of conversations for the city council meeting."

Before the old witch could object, Ridge jerked his chin at Sally, who whispered to Errol. When the older man nodded, she grabbed on to his chair and rolled him away. With Errol taken care of, Ridge laced his fingers with Sheri's and tugged her through the mob.

"What are you doing?" Sheri asked, a look of bemusement on her pretty face.

"Getting you the hell out of Dodge." Ridge kept a tight grip on her hand and lengthened his strides. "Sally will keep your father company and make sure no one bothers him about selling your land."

"I don't need rescuing." Sheri's voice was firm, but her breathing was rapid and uneven. "That type of peer pressure doesn't work on me."

"I know." Ridge made an abrupt right into a lounge used for evening Bible Study, closed the door behind them, and turned the lock. "I just couldn't wait another second to do this." He gathered her into his arms. "And this." He pressed his lips to hers. "And especially this." He sat on one of the armchairs and pulled her onto his lap.

"But—"

He cut her protests off with a searing kiss. The depth of his passion was terrifying—and exhilarating. His heart jolted and his pulse pounded. He'd never felt this way with any other woman.

Finally, when they were both breathless, Ridge murmured, "Now, instead of a frantic phone call, that is how our morning should have started."

"Mmm." Sheri nuzzled his throat, then lifted her head. Suddenly, every curve of her body radiated alarm, and she pulled away.

Ridge watched as an aloof mask settled over her features. Why was she so afraid of him and their feelings for one another? He'd thought that after last night, he'd put her doubts to rest. Was he pressing her too hard? He didn't want to freak her out. Maybe he should ease up. He'd already waited thirteen years; he could be patient a little longer.

Sheri stood, straightened her clothes, and asked, "How did it go with Sally?"

"Fine," Ridge answered without going into detail.

His daughter wasn't what he wanted to discuss at this moment. He needed to know why Sheri was trying to cool things off between them.

Getting up from his seat, he moved close to her, but she stepped back. Why was she determined to keep some distance between them?

He scowled. If he went too slowly, it would allow her to reinforce the walls around her heart. He couldn't give her time to reload her emotional ammunition and keep him at arm's length. Now that she'd finally returned to Sutton Falls, he wasn't about to let her run out of his life again.

"What did Sally and the other girl fight about?" Sheridan asked, crossing the room and pretending to study the notices pinned to a bulletin board.

Ridge clenched his teeth. She was determined to ignore what they'd shared last night.

Admitting a temporary defeat, he said, "The argument

started with Harper Webster ragging Sally about being too smart and not dressing right. But the tipping point was when Harper started in on Alexis not loving Sally enough to have her live with her."

"What a little b..." Sheridan trailed off, obviously remembering that she was in a church building. Her cheeks flamed and she revised her sentence. "What a little witch!"

Ridge loved to watch the color creep down Sheri's neck and into her cleavage. When she was a teenager, it had been easy to make her blush, and Ridge had been thinking about her creamy complexion tinged with that hint of pink for the past thirteen years.

He moved to where Sheri stood and said, "Then the girl told Sally that Alexis was in town."

"Well, heck," Sheri muttered. "I didn't see that one coming. I take it you hadn't mentioned your ex's guest appearance at Merry's party?"

"Nope. But I should have."

"Yes, that would have probably been a good idea," Sheri agreed. "But you wanted to protect her."

"Fat lot of good that did." Ridge scowled at his own inadequacies as a parent. "Anyway, Sally called the girl a liar, and Harper slapped her."

"So how did Sally take it when you finally told her everything?" Sheri raised a questioning brow. "You did tell her everything, right?"

"Yeah." Ridge smiled. "We had a really good talk, and it seemed like for once she didn't hate my guts."

"I'm sure Sally never hated you." Sheri reached out and patted his arm. "She was probably confused about what was happening to her."

"Maybe if I had explained what was going on that first day, when her mother dropped off Sally, things would have been better between us, but I didn't really understand it myself." Ridge dipped his chin. "I still don't know what Alexis has up her sleeve. All I can hope is that she doesn't hurt Sally trying to get back at me."

"Is that likely?"

"After the stunt Alexis pulled Friday night, and then disappearing without even visiting her daughter, I have to think hurting her is a distinct possibility."

"Are you sure Alexis left town?"

"I looked for her yesterday morning." Ridge blew out a frustrated breath. "None of the likely suspects admit to her staying with them."

"Would Beau lie to you?"

"Not when he's sober." Ridge exhaled noisily. "I'm going to have a long talk with him this afternoon or tomorrow about his drinking and his conduct toward you."

"I don't want you to risk a lifelong friendship over me." Sheri's expression shuttered. "After all, he lives here. I don't."

Sheri's statement was like a knife in the heart. Was she already thinking of leaving? Ridge could barely force out the next words without choking. "It's past time that he and I had a conversation about his actions."

The idea of what Beau and Alexis had put Sheri through tore at Ridge's insides. His supposed best friend had to be told that if he ever did anything like that again, he'd live to regret it.

"Just don't do it on my account." Sheri's tone was flat. "It would have been so much easier for everyone if I'd found a home health care worker for Errol right away and left town before I ever ran into you."

"Don't say that!" Ridge couldn't believe Sheri felt that way. Not after how loving she'd been the night before. An oddly primitive alarm sounded in his brain, and he closed the slight distance between them. "Easy is not better."

"True." Sheri nodded slowly and allowed him to take her in his arms. "But I can't help feeling my presence in Sutton Falls has stirred up something that might have been better left undisturbed."

"Would you really want to have never had this?" Ridge ran his thumb along Sheri's jaw.

"I guess not," Sheri sighed, leaning into his touch. "But—"

"Damn straight!" He cut her off, then changed the subject. "As it turns out, Harper also informed Sally that Alexis was mean to you at the party, and Sally is very concerned that you'll hate her for her mother's behavior."

"Of course I don't." Sheri frowned. "I'll have to tell her that ASAP."

"I assured her of that, but you're right." Pleased with Sheri's concern for his daughter, Ridge drew her even closer. "Sally probably needs to hear it from you."

"I should go talk to her right now." Sheri attempted to leave.

"Wait." Ridge kept a firm grip on her. "Before we go back, I need to ask you a question."

"Oh?" Sheri's voice was wary.

Ridge knew it was too soon. Knew that he was going too fast. But the fear of her leaving town again made him continue. "Are we together or was last night a one-off?" He struggled to keep his tone light, but his heart was hammering like an engine with a leaky intake valve. What if she didn't want to see him again? "When you go back to St. Louis, is that it for us?"

His gut clenched when the color drained from Sheri's face. He held her tighter. Was she going to faint?

"I don't know." Sheri closed her eyes. "I need some time to process. Which do you want it to be?"

Her hesitancy hit Ridge square in the chest, and he had trouble drawing his next breath.

He was tempted to play it cool, but he manned up and admitted, "To me, it already feels like there's an *us*."

Sheri's thick lashes had been lying on her cheeks, but at his words, they flew up.

Before she could speak, he continued, "Like we should have been together for the past thirteen years. Like I should have the right to take you in my arms and kiss you whenever I want, in front of everyone." He pressed his lips to hers as if to demonstrate.

"I..."

Sheri stuttered to a stop, and Ridge waited, challenging her to deny it. When she didn't, he persisted, "I want to make love to you every night and wake up with you beside me."

"Why now?" Sheri's big brown eyes were suspicious. "Why didn't you ever seek me out after the prom? It had to be several weeks before you learned that Alexis was pregnant."

"That was a terrible time. Rumors were swirling around that something bad had happened to you that night, but no one would tell me exactly what it was." He scowled. "And I wasn't sure if you blamed me. Hell! I wasn't entirely sure I hadn't participated. Or if you'd ever want to see me again."

Sheri opened her mouth but closed it without speaking.

Ridge nodded to himself. She needed to hear more.

He continued, "Then, when I finally screwed up my courage, your mother passed away, you left for college, and Alexis told me she was having my baby." Ridge shoved his fingers through his hair. "I convinced myself that my feelings for you had been just a teenage crush and I should do the honorable thing—marry Alexis and forget about you."

"And after your divorce?" Sheri's voice was so low he could hardly hear her.

"I was totally disillusioned about everything, especially myself." Ridge twisted his lips in disgust. "I was so weighed down with the expectations of the town that every time I looked at myself in the mirror, all I saw was failure. Then when I finally got myself back under control, your first book came out, and suddenly you were a big success. What right did I have to expect you even to remember me? Or if you did, to still have any feelings left for me?"

"I thought about you a lot," Sheri said slowly, tucking a stray curl behind her ear. "I always wondered what would have happened our senior year if I'd been brave enough to acknowledge how I felt about you."

Ridge absently noted that she had put her hair into a bun again. Too bad. He preferred it loose. Like she'd worn it for their date.

Pressing his lips to her temple, he whispered, "Something tells me that this might be my last chance for happiness. Our last chance to see if we can be together. If you go back to St. Louis before we find out, who knows what will happen?"

CHAPTER TWENTY-TWO

When Sheridan and her father arrived home, she found Merry sitting on the back step.

As soon as Sheridan opened the car door, Merry demanded, "Why did Ridge Sutton haul you off during fellowship? Does it have anything to do with the lip-lock I witnessed between you two Friday night?"

Shooting her cousin a censorious look, Sheridan said, "I'll meet you on the front porch. Just give me a minute to get Errol settled."

Errol protested that he wanted to hear the answer to those questions, too, but Sheridan wheeled him into the living room and handed him the remote.

Joining Merry outside, Sheridan snapped, "I spent the entire drive home avoiding Errol's questions about Ridge. Why would you mention me kissing him in front of my father?"

"Seriously?" Merry giggled. "You can't keep something like that a secret. Especially not after Ridge went all caveman and practically dragged you out of the church hall by your hair."

"Well..." She trailed off, recalling his searing kiss and his disturbing declaration.

She'd hated to upset him, but she wasn't anywhere near ready to commit to a long-term relationship. She was still trying to get her mind around the incredible sex.

"You should have seen the look on everyone's faces when you two disappeared."

"I—"

"Ridge was anything but subtle when he snatched you away from Mrs. B's tirade." Merry chortled. "From what I hear, he'd already made his intentions pretty darn clear when he defended you against Beau and Alexis at my party, then followed you out to the deck. And he never let go of your hand once you two came back inside." Merry's smile faded. "By the way, I am *so* sorry for what they did to you that night. I had no idea either of them would be there."

"It's not your fault." Sheridan hugged her cousin. "And in a way, I'm glad I finally got to deal with them face-to-face."

"I knew getting everyone together so you could see our classmates in a different light was a good idea." Merry beamed. "And your reward for dealing with your past is Ridge. When he walked you out to your car Friday night and didn't come back in, the whole party was buzzing."

"He was just being gallant." Even as she spoke, she realized how ridiculous she sounded but couldn't stop herself from adding, "He's always defended the underdog."

"Then what was dinner last night, an apology for his ex-wife being a witch?" Merry tsked when Sheridan's expression betrayed her surprise. "Did you really think Uncle Errol wouldn't call my mother to share the news?"

"Right." Sheridan hit her palm to her forehead. "How could I forget the Davis grapevine?"

"And today was the clincher." Merry crossed her arms. "That man is head over heels for you."

Warmth flooded through her. Her cousin's words were both exhilarating and terrifying.

"We've had precisely one date," Sheridan protested. "No one falls in love that fast."

There was no way she was telling her cousin what Ridge had said to her in the church lounge. At least, not before she'd had time to digest it herself.

"Unless that person was in love for the past thirteen years."

"Don't be silly." Panic, and something else, flickered in her chest. Sheridan crossed her arms. "Ridge just wanted to talk to me about Sally."

"What about her?"

Sheridan explained how she and the girl had grown closer, then said, "So he wanted to tell me about the fight she got into at the sleepover."

"Yeah." Merry pursed her mouth. "I heard about that. Harper Webster isn't usually so cruel." She grimaced. "But Alexis has always been pretty nasty to Prissy, so maybe Harper's mother planted those malicious seeds."

"You mean since Prissy never had the nerve to stand up to Alexis, she used her child to get back at Alexis's daughter?" Sheridan thought the whole thing sounded a little Machiavellian.

"I've seen parents weaponize their kids in divorces." Merry's lips curled. "So why not against their high school enemies?"

"I suppose." Sheridan hated the thought, but from the stories Delaney and Lucy had shared about their students, she knew it was true.

After several seconds of silence, Merry changed the subject and asked, "Why didn't you return any of my calls yesterday?"

Sheridan crossed her fingers. "I had a headache."

She hated fibbing to her cousin, but she hadn't been up to answering her questions. Instead, she'd talked to Delaney. It was somehow easier to share her hopes and doubts with her than with Merry. Her sorority sister had never met Ridge, Alexis, or Beau and didn't have any personal stake in the situation.

Merry rolled her eyes in disbelief, then drawled, "It's a good thing you recovered in time for your date with Ridge. Where did you go? During fellowship, I didn't hear anyone talking about seeing you at the country club."

"We, uh..." Sheridan's mind raced for an answer. "We ate at his place so we could talk privately. We had a lot of past issues to work out."

Last night might have been the start of something wonderful—or at least could be if she allowed it. And that would mean acknowledging that she and Ridge were seeing each other. They couldn't hide their relationship for long in a town as small as Sutton Falls.

"Interesting." Merry grinned. "So did his housekeeper cook for you?"

"No." Sheridan didn't elaborate. "Does Ridge have a housekeeper?"

"Not a live-in, but Les's mother cleans for him." Merry tilted her head. "I think she does the laundry and shopping, too."

"I remember her." Sheridan nodded. "She's a nice lady."

"Back to your date." Merry took Sheridan's hand and tried to tug her down onto the porch swing. "Spill."

"Fine." Sheridan surrendered. "Let me get us some coffee and sweet rolls, and I'll give you the scoop."

What the hell! She might as well tell Merry. Her cousin would just pester her until she gave in.

"Okay." Merry waved her finger in front of Sheridan's nose. "But don't try to sneak out the back door, because I'll be watching."

"Of course you will," Sheridan muttered as she hastily escaped inside.

On her way into the kitchen, she noticed that Errol had fallen asleep on the couch. She took the afghan from the chair and spread it over him. His handsome face was relaxed, and his color was back to normal. He really did seem to be getting better.

Maybe she could leave for New York in a couple of days. But did she still want to go? Her book was number one on the *Times* bestseller list for the second straight week. It didn't look as if her not touring had harmed sales at all. And she had to admit that it was immensely satisfying to be with Ridge after all her fantasies about him. Still, he was her past. Could he really be her future?

As Sheridan waited for the Keurig to make the coffee, she stuck two frozen cinnamon rolls in the microwave. While the pastries warmed, an image of Ridge swooping her from the church hall popped into her mind, and a jumble of confused thoughts and feelings assailed her.

When he'd swept her into his arms, the possessive light in his eyes had sent a shiver of electricity through her. She'd attempted to throttle the dizzying current zipping between them, but when he'd focused all that intensity on her and looked at her as if she were the only woman he'd ever wanted, her control had slipped away.

An unfamiliar warmth had surged through her heart, and she'd been too startled to fight the dynamic vitality that emanated from every pore of his body. She couldn't afford to be distracted by romantic notions of happily ever after, but his tender expression had unleashed something inside of her.

Although she'd struggled to conquer her response to his touch, everything he'd said and the raw emotion in his voice as he'd said it had had her quivering with lust. Then, when he'd told her that he wanted more than a fling, her determination had faltered.

He'd caught her off guard, and she'd felt flattened by the realization of how much he already meant to her. His bluntness had stunned her, and she'd been too startled by his statement to answer him. Her mind had refused to register the significance of his words, and she'd hesitated, unwilling to face him and just as unwilling to turn away.

Sheridan hadn't expected Ridge to be so unpredictable or so direct, and a cynical inner voice had cut through her emotional state and whispered, *Are you sure this isn't all a trick to persuade you to hand over control of the levee to him?*

But a sense of conviction, which was a fundamental part of her character, had hushed that niggling doubt. If she was going to erect a wall of defense against her feelings for Ridge, it wouldn't be built from mistrust and suspicion.

At that moment when he'd declared that he wanted to wake up with her every morning, Ridge had looked so impossibly sexy that he'd stolen her ability to breathe. Any woman who walked away from a man like that without fighting for his love deserved to live out the rest of her lonely life by herself.

The ding of the microwave brought Sheridan back to the present, and after putting the coffee and rolls on a tray, she rejoined Merry on the porch. Once they had their plates and mugs, Sheridan told her cousin about her date.

"He remembered you liked peonies." Merry clasped her cup to her chest. "How romantic."

"That was sweet of him." Sheridan took a sip of her French roast.

This was the first chance she'd had to have a cup of coffee. Maybe the caffeine would help her think straight.

"And to cook for you and serve it in front of a roaring fire." Merry shook her head. "That is just swoon-worthy."

"It was pretty dreamy," Sheridan admitted.

"Did he explain his part in what Alexis did to you at prom?"

"He was drunk and unaware of Alexis's schemes."

Sheridan had to be careful. She couldn't tell her cousin anything that would betray Ridge's confidence regarding his daughter's conception. She also had no plans to tell anyone else, including Merry, about being assaulted that night.

"So you believe him?" Merry tipped her head. "And the whole prom incident is behind you?"

"Yes." Sheridan took a deep breath. "It's a part of my past. It made me stronger, but now I'm over it."

The weight she'd carried for so many years really was gone.

She felt lighter and more optimistic. Her assailant was dead. Ridge hadn't been involved. And her classmates were sorry for what they'd done—at least all but Alexis and Beau. And Beau was probably sorry when he was sober.

"Yeah!" Merry put down her cup and hugged Sheridan. "What happened after Ridge explained everything?" Merry's eyes glowed, and then just before she took a big bite of cinnamon roll, she asked, "Did you...?"

"I'm not going there." Sheridan drew the line at discussing intimate details with anyone. Okay. Occasionally, she and Delaney compared notes. But Lucy was married to a minister, and Darcy had always been too much of a good girl to talk about sex.

"So you did!" Merry squealed. "Was Ridge as good as he looks?"

"Better." Sheridan couldn't hide her smile. "And that's all I'm going to say, so let's change the subject."

"Are you going to keep seeing Ridge?" Merry asked, then added, "Don't give me that look. You said you didn't want to talk about sex. This is about a relationship."

"Fine." Sheridan wrinkled her nose fondly. Merry was as persistent as a squirrel digging for acorns. "I don't know. In truth, we don't have much in common. My life is in St. Louis. His is here. He wants to buy the levee, and I'm not sure that I'm willing to give up the land that meant so much to my mother. He has a daughter to raise, and the thought of being a part of that scares the crap out of me."

"As always, you're overthinking it." Merry smacked Sheridan's knee. "You need to open yourself up and explore the possibilities."

Merry's words were jagged darts to Sheridan's heart, finding their target with absolute precision. Her cousin was right. Overthinking was Sheridan's specialty, and the results were

SMART GIRL SWEPT AWAY

never good.

Instinctively, Sheridan went on the defensive and retorted, "Like you and Beau?"

She had always wondered why her cousin hadn't gone after the guy. She'd had a crush on him for years. Way before his drinking had gotten out of hand.

"The timing was never right for us." Merry twisted a ringlet around her finger. "When I wasn't seeing someone, he was, and vice versa." She smiled sadly. "Just a little bit ago, he asked me for a date, and I told him if he stopped drinking, I'd go out with him."

"And?"

"And he refused." Merry sighed. "He claimed he didn't have a problem with alcohol." She shook her head. "Still, he has so much potential. I still wonder what he could be if straightened himself out..." She trailed off. "If he were clean and sober, I'd want to find out if there was something real between us, so I'd definitely date him."

"It's easy for you to say 'go for it.'" Sheridan tapped her cousin's arm. "You're an optimist and you bounce back. But I don't. If it turns out that I fall for Ridge...okay...fall harder, what do I do if it doesn't work out?"

"You cope." Merry drained her coffee, put down the cup, and turned so she could look Sheridan in the eye. "You've managed in the past, and you can do it again."

"Maybe I don't want to manage by myself anymore," Sheridan blurted out, then wondered what that said about her so-called independence and feminist beliefs.

"You're emotionally stronger than you think. It's time to follow your heart."

"What if being with Ridge means that I'd have to move back to Sutton Falls?"

"Would that be so bad? To be home? To be near your

237

family?" Merry asked. "You can write anywhere."

"Not anywhere," Sheridan objected.

"Hire a moving company and bring your office down here," Merry chided. "Love, real love, isn't something to toss aside over a certain desk or a fancy chair."

"What if he doesn't love me?" Sheridan ran through everything Ridge had said. Love hadn't been mentioned. "And I never said that I loved him."

"Right!" Merry snorted. "Like you haven't been in love with Ridge Sutton since you were twelve years old."

* * *

Some things never changed in Sutton Falls. The wealthy played golf and tennis at the Belladonna Country Club, swam in its pool, and sunned themselves on its patios. They had their first dates at the club's spring ball, their wedding receptions in its banquet room, and their funeral luncheons in its restaurant.

The affluent citizens of the area spent their whole social life behind the protected walls of that privileged establishment, and Ridge was more than a little sick of it all. After accomplishing tonight's mission, Ridge vowed that he'd no longer go there just because it was what everyone in his circle did.

He was tired of living up to other people's expectations. Tired of putting on a self-assured public face while feeling anything but confident. And most of all, tired of being without a woman's love.

A few hours ago, Sheri had rung his doorbell and handed him the keys to his Z4. She'd refused to come inside the house and declined his offer of a late lunch, saying that Merry and Errol were waiting for her in the driveway. They were on their way to a family dinner at Merry's parents' place, and she didn't have time to talk.

It was embarrassing how much he'd wanted Sheri to stay. How much he'd missed her when she'd left. How the scent of her in his bedroom made him ache for her.

Sheri had seemed cool toward him, almost aloof. Was she already rebuilding the fortress around her heart? He wondered if she realized that when he held her, she nestled into him, her body instinctively seeking his. If she didn't, he needed to demonstrate. And he needed to do it before she added any more bricks to that wall.

He didn't want Sheri to regulate their relationship to just fun in the sack. He wanted a future with her. Or at least a chance to see if they had a future together.

Shoving thoughts of Sheri aside, Ridge had spent the afternoon working on the Mustang with his daughter. Around four, he'd received a call from his admin assistant, Wendy Gibson, inviting Sally to accompany her and her daughter, Jaylynn, to the movies in Mt. Morrison.

Wendy had heard about the fight at the fundraiser, and although Jaylynn was a year older, she thought his daughter might need a friend. After consulting with Sally, Ridge gratefully accepted Wendy's offer.

With Sally gone and Sheridan occupied with her family, Ridge had decided this was the perfect time to speak to Beau. And unfortunately, he knew just where to find him.

Pushing through the frosted glass door, Ridge stepped into the upscale atmosphere of the country club bar. He wrinkled his nose at the odor of the centerpieces and the oppressive scent of the overly cologned men. The one-two punch of the familiar smells reminded him that his life had fallen into a rut. A rut he was determined to step out of for good.

Ridge paused, waiting for his eyes to adjust. Pendant lamps over the pool table, candles flickering in the booths, and muted neon over the bar were the only illumination. The lighting was kept dim in order to allow the aging debutants like his mother to maintain their illusions of youth.

The place was just starting to fill up with self-indulgent men escaping after mandatory Sunday dinners with their families. The few females in the room were recent divorcées on the prowl. Ridge avoided eye contact with the predators as he crossed to the bar.

Beau was on his usual stool, and probably had been there since the bar had opened. Like Ridge, Beau had been on the high school football team. While Ridge had made an effort to keep himself in shape, Beau had added a layer of padding over his muscles.

Unless he felt ignored, as had happened at Merry's party, Beau was a happy drunk who everyone liked. And despite his drinking, he did an adequate job as the city attorney. But Ridge knew that his friend was capable of a lot more if he'd only sober up.

Ridge ordered a dry vodka martini, then took the stool next to his friend.

"Bro!" Beau swiveled toward him and said with a wide smile, "How's it hanging?"

"Not too great," he answered, then accepted his drink and thanked the bartender. Refocusing on Beau, Ridge said, "I'd like you to apologize to Sheri."

"For what?" Beau took a gulp of his beer. "She's not still harping about what happened back in the dark ages, is she?"

Ridge bit the inside of his cheek, realizing that he should have waited until tomorrow to speak to Beau. He knew better than to expect his friend to discuss anything rational once he'd started drinking for the day. It would have been like expecting Mrs. Bunson's Siamese cat to play chess. The best you could hope for was for him to accidently nudge a pawn in the right direction.

Still, he was here and he would say his piece. Especially since finding Beau completely sober was becoming more and more difficult to achieve.

Ridge kept his voice even but gave Beau a hard stare. "Alexis and you were beyond criminally responsible for what happened to Sheri that night. She could have been raped." He held up his hand when Beau started to protest. "Yes. I know you told me you had no idea what Alexis had planned with Newtsen, but we both know it was actually that you were too drunk to care."

"Dude! That whole deal is on Alexis, not me." Beau finished his beer and signaled for another one, then narrowed his bloodshot eyes and said, "It sounds to me like Ms. High-and-Mighty Davis has you by the short hairs. What is it? Won't she let you into her panties until we all play nice?"

With a considerable effort, Ridge throttled back his anger, reminding himself that Beau was drunk.

"I'd like you to apologize because it's the right thing to do," Ridge said calmly. "It's time for us all to bury the hatchet and start over again. We're all grown up and should start acting like it."

"That doesn't sound like fun." Beau looked at Ridge as if he'd suggested they both tear off their clothes and streak down the main drag of Sutton Falls in a blizzard. "And you know, buddy, that I'm all about a good time."

The cynicism of Beau's words grated on Ridge's last nerve, and his hand fisted, itching to wipe that smirk off his friend's face.

"Then let me put it to you this way." Ridge's tone was razor-edged. "If you aren't willing to man up and say you're sorry for what you did to Sheri, I'll beat the living shit out of you."

He stood up, hanging on to his temper by a thread. He'd

revisit the topic of an apology with Beau first thing tomorrow. Before Beau's morning bloody Mary.

But Ridge hadn't even taken a step away when he heard Beau mutter, "If that bi—"

Before Beau could finish the word, Ridge whirled around and punched him in the nose.

CHAPTER TWENTY-THREE

The next morning, Sheridan listened intently as Doc Brown leaned across his desk and said, "As the hospital informed you, the results of the tests that they ran were all within acceptable limits." He looked at Errol. "How have you been feeling? Any more dizziness?"

"I've been doing great." Errol pointed to his injured ankle with his broken wrist and said, "If it weren't for these, I'd be back to normal."

"Good." Doc Brown tented his fingers. "For now, we'll chalk up your fainting spell to low blood sugar or a mild case of the flu." He typed a note into his iPad. "You suffered two non-displaced fractures, both of which appear to be healing surprisingly well." The doctor glanced at Sheridan. "Plan to bring your father back to see me in about six weeks, and I'll remove the casts."

"Otherwise Errol's fine?" Sheridan asked, the lingering anxiety she'd felt since receiving the initial hospital call finally lessening.

"As far as medical science can determine, yes." Doc Brown rose from his seat and winked at Errol. "Maybe all you needed was Sheri back home."

"I prefer Sheridan," she corrected.

When the old family doctor grunted his reluctant acknowledgment, Sheridan gritted her teeth. Clearly, getting the good folks of Sutton Falls to call her by her full name would be more difficult than she'd imagined.

After a late breakfast at Pinky's Diner, Sheridan drove Errol home. He told her that since his right hand was fine, he intended to spend the rest of the day painting in his studio. She set up his easel at a height he could reach from his wheelchair, then assembled the necessary supplies—including a cooler filled with sandwiches, snacks, and soda—and left him in the garage with instructions to use his cell to call the house phone if he needed her.

Once Sheridan had her father settled, she turned her attention to her own work in progress. Her writer's block was gone, and her fingers flew on the keyboard. She wrote straight through until she heard Merry's voice from the laundry room. Glancing at the clock, Sheridan realized that it was close to five p.m. Except for a couple of brief coffee and bathroom breaks, she'd been at it for six hours.

Merry breezed into the kitchen and asked, "Am I interrupting?"

"Nope." Sheridan clicked save and turned to her cousin. "It's time to think about supper."

"That's why I came by." Merry put a cardboard carton onto the table. "Mom sent leftovers from Sunday dinner. She said that she forgot to give them to you yesterday."

"Yum!" Sheridan peered into the box, the smell of fried chicken making her mouth water. "Please thank Aunt Flora for me. I had no idea what we'd eat tonight."

"No problem." Merry pulled out a chair. "Mom always makes enough food to feed an army."

"How was school today?" Sheridan asked, noting the lines of worry between her cousin's eyebrows.

"Okay, I guess. But I'm concerned about Sally."

"Oh?" Sheridan's stomach rolled. Had the girl been in another fight?

"Her scuffle with Harper has isolated her from her classmates even more than before. They seem to have picked sides, and most of them chose Harper." Merry tapped her fingers on the Formica tabletop. "A part of the problem is that Sally resents kids only being nice to her because she's a Sutton. And she isn't shy about letting them know her feelings."

"I can see that." Sheridan took plates from the cupboard. Her father would want to eat soon. "Does she have any friends?"

"Sally said she went to the movies with Wendy Gibson and her daughter." Merry pursed her mouth. "But Jaylynn is a seventh grader, so she and Sally don't share any classes or a lunch period."

"Are there any special teacher tricks to help Sally make friends?"

Sheridan hadn't been very good at socializing herself, until she'd gotten to college and joined Alpha Sigma Alpha, and since she was pretty darn sure there weren't any sororities at Sutton Falls Middle School, she was stumped as to what to do to help the girl fit in.

"Alas, although I'm the mighty, the all-powerful, the Educator, I don't have that magical power," Merry said glumly, then brightened. "The best thing would be if Sally would sign up for some of the extracurricular activities, but she refuses."

"Any of those coming up soon?" Sheridan turned on the oven, a glimmer of an idea simmering in the back of her mind.

"There's a class car wash tomorrow afternoon." Merry gazed heavenwards. "That is, if the weatherman is right and there's no rain."

"The three-day forecast this morning said we should be in the clear through Wednesday." Sheridan crossed her fingers. If the damn rain would just stop, she and Errol wouldn't have to face the awful decision about selling their land to the city.

"Let's hope so."

Sheridan popped the chicken into the oven along with the mashed potatoes. A plan was forming, and she turned back toward her cousin and said, "Tell me about this car wash."

"It's a fundraiser for the class trip," Merry explained. "Kids and parents who take part get points against the cost of the hotel and bus."

"Okay." Sheridan nodded to herself. She could work with that. "I'll talk to Sally and see if I can persuade her to participate."

"She might do it if you offer to help, too."

"I can do that. With Errol's good doctor report, I feel okay with leaving him alone for longer periods."

"Mom said all his tests and stuff were fine." Merry tilted her head speculatively. "Does that mean you'll be going back to St. Louis soon?"

"Errol will be in the wheelchair and won't be able to drive for six more weeks," Sheridan hedged. "I have a couple more interviews with home health care workers set up for tomorrow, so whether I can leave or not will depend on how they go."

She was surprised that the prospect of returning to her normally scheduled life didn't seem more attractive. Just as she'd feared, leaving town, leaving Ridge, was no longer nearly as appealing as it had been when she'd first gotten to Sutton Falls.

"Good luck." Merry stood up and headed toward the back door. "On whichever way you want the interviews to go."

After Errol and Sheridan finished supper, he retired to his room saying that the painting had gone well, but he was bushed. Once the kitchen was clean and the dishes washed, Sheridan dug her cell from her purse to check her messages. There was one from Ridge, so she quickly closed herself into her bedroom and returned his call.

He answered on the first ring. "I was beginning to wonder if you were avoiding me."

"Of course not." Sheridan smiled at his anxious tone. "I muted my cell while I was writing."

"Well, yesterday when you hurried off after returning my

car, I worried that what I said to you in the church lounge scared you."

"It did." Sheridan hated how breathless she sounded. Hated how thrilled she was to be talking to him. "But in a good way."

"That's a relief." Ridge's voice was a low rasp and Sheridan shivered. "Do you want to know how I spent my day?"

"Okay." Sheridan hoped Ridge hadn't been with Alexis.

"I hired Les York's mother as my live-in housekeeper."

"Merry said she occasionally cleaned for you." Sheridan wrinkled her brow. Why did Ridge sound so happy about his new employee?

"Yeah. With only Sally and me, the house doesn't get that dirty, and I like to cook, so we really only needed part-time help before."

"What changed?" Sheridan sat down on her bed.

"I fired my mother." Ridge's tone was rueful. "I concluded that Sally was better off with a stranger than a grandmother who didn't stand up for her and kept trying to change her into somebody else."

"How did Sally take your decision?"

Sheridan fully agreed with his reasoning but wondered how the twelve-year-old had reacted. Figuring out what a child that age wanted could be tricky. At least, that's what Merry always told her.

"She was relieved. She likes Mrs. York." Ridge's voice was husky. "She hugged me and thanked me for taking her side."

"That's great." Sheridan was delighted that Ridge and his daughter seemed to be mending their relationship. "Will you miss your privacy?"

"Somewhat." Ridge hesitated. "But Mrs. York seems pretty discreet, and there're two apartments over the garage. My groundskeeper, Odell Voss, lives in one, and Mrs. York agreed to move into the second."

"Which solves your childcare problem." Sheridan tried not to feel jealous but couldn't resist and said, "I'm shocked how easily you found someone to take care of Sally when I can't seem to locate anyone for Errol."

"Don't you know that I put the word out around town that I didn't want anyone to apply for your job?" Ridge teased.

"Why?" Sheridan chuckled, leaning back against the headboard. This conversation felt so right. Like she and Ridge had always been a couple. And suddenly, she yearned for that so badly that the force of that wanting shocked her.

"Because if you don't find a home health care worker, you can't leave me."

His words sent a spike of joy whizzing through her, and Sheridan had to swallow the lump in her throat before she could ask, "Did Evelyn give you a hard time?"

"She's not happy," Ridge admitted. "I told her she had until Wednesday, but she moved out today. And frankly, it feels as if Captain Bligh has left the ship."

"Understandable."

Sheridan stuffed a pillow behind her head, marveling that she was chatting with Ridge as if they were a true twosome. None of the men she'd previously dated had made her feel this way. Made her feel as if she didn't have anything to prove. Made her feel comfortable with being her true self rather than her feminist author persona.

"What are you doing tomorrow?"

"In the morning, I have two interviews scheduled with prospective home health workers." Tension at the thought of what hiring someone to take care of Errol would mean tightened her shoulders, and Sheridan squirmed to find a comfortable position. "And in the afternoon, I may be helping out at the sixth grade car wash, but my calendar is open for the evening."

"Can I pencil my name in?"

SMART GIRL SWEPT AWAY

"How about I write it in ink?" Sheridan was already counting the hours until she could see him, and she had never, ever done that with any other guys that she'd dated.

"Even better," Ridge answered. "Do you want to go out to dinner and maybe see a movie?"

"I'd rather spend the time alone with you." Sheridan hurriedly added, "And it's not that I want to hide our relationship. I just don't want to share you. We have so much to talk about."

"That's how I feel, too." Ridge's voice deepened. "I need to feel you..."

He trailed off as if he'd decided not to go there, then asked, "So, did Merry drag you into the sixth grade fundraiser?"

"In a way." Sheridan frowned. This would be better if she was face-to-face with him, but tomorrow night would be too late. "Merry mentioned to me that she believes that Sally would have an easier time making friends at school if she would participate in the extracurricular activities."

"Merry and you were talking about Sally?" Ridge's voice was suddenly sharp.

"Why are you so angry? It's not as if we were hashing over her faults. We both care about her and are worried that she seems so unhappy."

"Sorry." Ridge sighed. "I truly appreciate your concern. My thou-shalt-not-be-the-subject-of-gossip kicked in."

"I understand." Sheridan liked him even more for his protectiveness of his daughter and his quickness to apologize when he was wrong.

"I've been meaning to talk to Sally about that. Mrs. Warner, her homeroom teacher, said the same thing to me."

"Well..." Sheridan paused, hesitant that Ridge might think she was interfering or, worse, trying to worm her way into his life via his daughter. "Merry said that Sally thinks the kids are only nice to her because she's a Sutton. Not because they really like her."

"Oh?" His tone was guarded.

"And some of what Sally has said to me leads me to believe that her classmates haven't seen what a great girl she is, no matter what her last name."

"Which leaves things at an impasse."

"Exactly." Sheridan drew her knees up and rested her chin on them. "My thinking is that if I can persuade Sally to go with me to the car wash, and maybe guide her a little through the fundraiser, she might find one or two other kids with similar interests."

"That would be wonderful."

"Would it be okay for me to pick up Sally from school?" Sheridan asked.

"Definitely. I'll call the principal to let her know that Sally has my permission to go with you. And I'll tell Sally that it's okay, too."

"If I can talk her into it, I'll drive her to the car wash, lend a hand with the fundraiser, and then bring her home."

"You'd do all that for Alexis's daughter?" There was an incredulous tone in his voice.

"No." Sheridan tucked a curl behind her ear. "I'd do it for *your* daughter. But mostly, I'd do it for Sally."

CHAPTER TWENTY-FOUR

Sheridan spent Tuesday morning interviewing two prospective home health care assistants. Both were huge improvements over the previous candidates, and it was clear that her father liked the applicants. However, when Sheridan had found fault with each of them, Errol had quickly agreed that neither were the perfect person for the job.

Sheridan told herself that both workers had flaws, but she knew in her heart that their imperfections weren't the real reason she hadn't hired them. Her true motivation hadn't had anything to do with their qualifications and everything to do with the fact that she wasn't ready to leave Sutton Falls.

If she found someone to care for Errol, she wouldn't have any excuse to stay. And she wasn't ready to admit that she didn't want to go.

During lunch, her father pestered Sheridan for details on her budding relationship with Ridge. When she refused to discuss her love life, Errol pouted, quickly finished his soup, and returned to his painting.

Relieved that she had avoided adding fruit to the family grapevine, Sheridan buckled down to produce her daily page count. At two thirty, she saved her efforts, grabbed her purse, and headed out.

Sheridan stopped by the garage to tell Errol she was leaving and remind him that she would be with Sally all afternoon at the car wash and with Ridge that evening. He informed her that Flora was dropping off a pan of lasagna and a loaf of garlic bread for his dinner, so he was all set.

As Sheridan waved good-bye to her father, she said, "Call my cell if you need me."

"Will do." Errol barely glanced from the canvas on the easel in front of him. "Have a good time."

During the short drive into town, Sheridan thought about her plan. If she read Sally correctly, the key would be to convince her that participating in the fundraiser was the honorable thing to do.

A few minutes later, Sheridan saw Sally walk out of the school building. The girl looked around, spotted Sheridan's car, and ran toward it.

Sheridan leaned over, opened the passenger door, and when Sally slid inside, said, "How about we head to the drive-in for a snack."

"That would be amazing." Sally buckled her seat belt. "Can I have a Rocket Man Special?"

"Sure." Sheridan smiled.

The special was a banana split supreme—five different ice creams and toppings, sprinkles, nuts, whipped cream, and half a jar of maraschino cherries. She hoped Ridge didn't mind that she was about to feed his daughter enough sugar to keep her wired up for a week.

On the way to the drive-in, Sally chatted about the movie she had been to Sunday evening. She had enjoyed the outing and liked Jaylynn, who was also interested in writing.

After Sheridan parked, rolled down her window, and gave the carhop their order, she said, "Ms. Mac and I think you should help out with this afternoon's class fundraiser."

"Why?" Sally crossed her arms. "None of the kids like me."

"I'm sure that's not true." Sheridan kept her voice neutral.

"Well, they don't like the real me." Sally's bottom lip poked out. "The ones who pretend to like me only do it because I'm a Sutton."

"That may be true of some of them," Sheridan agreed. "Once my books became successful, suddenly people who had never given me the time of day were announcing that we were BFFs."

"What did you do?"

"By that time, I'd realized that when I was in high school, I'd rejected a lot of possible friends because of a few mean ones. I made it a point to give everyone the benefit of the doubt. It became obvious pretty quickly who only wanted to hang out with me because of my fame."

"And you think if I give my classmates a chance, I'll figure out who is real and who isn't?" Sally's voice was subdued and more than a little forlorn.

"Yes." *So far so good.*

Sheridan paused to pay the carhop and accept their order. She put her chocolate milkshake in the cup holder and passed Sally the Rocket Man Special. Watching as the girl dug into the gigantic banana split, Sheridan allowed the silence to lengthen, giving Sally a chance to think about what they'd discussed.

When Sally remained quiet, Sheridan said, "Here's the thing. One of my writer friends faced a similar situation to mine when his books were made into movies. He chose to withdraw from everyone rather than to weed out the bad apples, and he ended up looking like a snob."

"Do you think the kids believe that about me?" Sally scooped a bite of crushed-pineapple-covered strawberry ice cream into her mouth.

"I'm afraid they might." Sheridan tilted her head. "This car wash is to raise money to go on the class trip. If you blow it off, it looks as if you feel that you don't have to work to go on the trip. That your father will pay the entire fee for you."

"Oh." Sally's eyes rounded. "That's not it at all." Her shoulders drooped and her lips quivered. "I'm just so tired of the kids being mean to me."

"Sadly, some people will always be cruel." Sheridan's

thoughts flickered to Alexis, but she brushed those aside. "I've actually given the idea of popularity a lot of thought." She gave Sally a wry smile. "Probably too much thought."

"And?" Sally returned Sheridan's smile, then shoved a spoonful of chocolate-covered vanilla ice cream into her mouth.

"And what I've concluded is that the whole notion of popularity is a fluid concept. It's ambiguous at best, and more often than not, it's a self-fulfilling prophecy."

For a moment, Sheridan wondered if she should have simplified her vocabulary for the twelve-year-old, but Sally nodded and said, "Go on."

"If we feel good about ourselves, then we are more open to the folks around us—to others who could use a friend," Sheridan explained her theory. "And before you know it, you've formed your own group."

"Easier said than done." Sally licked whipped cream from her red plastic spoon.

"True." Sheridan nodded. "It's definitely scary to open up yourself like that. And I've certainly been guilty of choosing to protect myself rather than put myself out there. Of trying to make myself invisible so the mean kids would forget that I existed and leave me alone."

"But that doesn't work." Sally spoke around the maraschino cherry she'd just bitten into. "I heard about how awful Mom was to you at Ms. Mac's party."

"I'm sure your mother is fighting her own demons." Sheridan would have liked to avoid talking about Alexis, but she knew that wasn't possible. She reached across the console and laid her hand on Sally's arm. "I would never hold your mom's behavior against you."

"Or my dad?"

"Or your father," Sheridan said, hiding her smile. She definitely wasn't holding anything against Ridge, except herself.

Sally and Sheridan finished their treats in silence, then, after the carhop took away their tray, Sally said, "I'll go to the car wash, but we're supposed to have an adult with us. Dad has a meeting with the engineers about the flood threat, and I'm not taking Grandmother."

"I asked your father if I could be your adult, and he said yes. Is that okay with you?"

"Okay?" Sally flung her arms around Sheridan's neck. "That would be awesome."

Sheridan drove them from the drive-in straight to the car wash. It started at four, and the kids had been asked to be at the school parking lot by three forty-five. With a meaningful look at her cousin, Merry assigned Sheridan and Sally to a team with two mothers and their daughters. As Sheridan and the moms chatted, she kept an eye on Sally, who seemed to be making an effort to interact with the other girls.

The weather was beautiful—warm and sunny—and as the afternoon went by and the fundraiser wound down, Sally appeared to have made a couple of friends. There had been one incident when Harper Webster's team had attempted to steal a car from Sally's crew, but the owner of the vehicle had suggested that one group do the interior and the other the exterior, then paid both squads equally.

One of the last customers to arrive was Ridge. He gave his daughter a hug, then turned his BMW over to her and her new friends for a super deluxe wash.

While he and Sheridan watched the girls work, he whispered, "Thank you for doing this. Sally looks happier than I've seen her in a long time. How did you get her here?"

"I explained the mechanics of popularity versus being thought a snob," Sheridan explained.

The warmth in Ridge's expression sucked the air from her lungs, and she struggled to inhale.

"Obviously whatever you said was brilliant." Ridge laced his fingers with hers. "Not that I'm surprised by that."

"Sweet talker." Sheridan could feel the blush creeping down her neck, and trying to keep her emotions in check, she playfully swatted his bicep.

"Just the facts, ma'am." His eyes darkened as he met her gaze, and his free hand reached out to tuck a curl behind her ear, lingering on her cheek.

The awareness she'd been fighting since his arrival bubbled to the surface. But this wasn't the time or place to let him guess her arousal. She licked her lips, searching for something to distract herself, but before she could think of anything, a stream of water hit Ridge in the face.

Sally, her eyes huge, dropped the hose and said, "I am so sorry, Dad. I was trying to unscrew the sprayer, and it just slipped."

"It's okay, honey." He walked over to his daughter, his shoes squishing with every step. "I'll get it off for you."

At the sight of water dripping from his chin and the dye from his red tie oozing down his white dress shirt, Sheridan burst out laughing. It was the first time she'd ever seen Ridge less than immaculate.

He looked at her and asked in a deceptively mild voice, "So you think this is funny?"

Sheridan nodded, still giggling hysterically.

Without hesitating, Ridge picked up the hose, aimed the nozzle at Sheridan, and squeezed. The girls squealed with glee, and their mothers quickly moved out of the path of the spray.

"So you'd shoot an unarmed woman?" Sheridan asked, leaning down and grabbing a bucket of soapy water.

As she advanced, Ridge backed up, then abruptly halted. Sheridan, determined to douse him, didn't see why he'd stopped, only that he was now in range. Shouting triumphantly, she launched the water at his head.

Ridge jumped aside, and Sheridan watched helplessly as the dirty stream hit Principal Boutte instead. Sheridan closed her eyes and covered her mouth. What had she done?

Ms. Boutte accepted Ridge's and Sheridan's apologies, then, as she moved on to the next group, she winked at them and said, "I always knew if you two ever got together, you'd shake up this town."

While the kids cleaned up the area, Ridge turned to Sheridan and said, "I'll pick you up at seven."

"What about Sally?"

"Mrs. York is watching her." Ridge grinned.

"Where are we going?"

"I have a surprise for you." His eyes twinkled.

The control freak in Sheridan wanted to ask for details, but Ridge looked so much like a little boy with a wonderful secret she squelched her need to know the details and said, "Sounds great."

Sheridan had seen Ridge in a lot of moods. The serious mayor. The caring father. The sensual lover. But this hint of playfulness was a side of him she'd rarely witnessed. She squeezed his hand and smiled tenderly at him.

Ridge leaned closer and whispered in Sheridan's ear, "Tell Errol not to wait up."

* * *

Ridge drove Sally home, amazed at the change in his daughter. The time she'd spent outdoors at the car wash had put some pink in her cheeks, and she was actually smiling. While she chattered on about her new friends and their plans for the next day at school, his thoughts turned to Sheri.

When he'd arrived at the fundraiser and seen her bending

over a bucket of soapy water, it had been all he could do to stop himself from hauling her into his car and driving off with her. Never had denim molded an ass so enticingly, and it had looked even better soaked and clinging to her body. She wasn't a skinny woman, and every wonderful curve beckoned him.

As he and Sheri had stood together watching his daughter giggle with the other girls, he'd felt a sense of connection with Sheri, and a rightness that he'd never experienced with anyone else.

He couldn't even imagine how his ex would have reacted if she'd been sprayed with water and had her hair and makeup ruined. Sheri had laughed it off, drying her face with the bottom of her shirt and joining in on the fun.

Every time he'd looked into her big brown eyes, he'd gotten the strangest sensation that he was seeing into his future. Or at least, what his future could be if he didn't screw things up.

"So can I go over to Cyndi's tomorrow after school?" Sally asked, interrupting his thoughts. "We'll do our homework together, have dinner, and then watch TV."

"It's fine with me as long as Cyndi's mom agrees." "Mrs. Pearson said to tell you it was okay with her and she'll have me home by eight thirty."

"Sounds like a plan." Ridge turned into his driveway, and while he and Sally were walking inside, he said, "Is it okay with you if I go out with Sheri tonight and Mrs. York watches you?"

"Uh-huh." Sally turned to look at him. "You like Sheridan a lot, don't you?"

"Yes, I do."

"Me, too." Sally wrinkled her nose. "Do you think she might stay in Sutton Falls?"

"I hope so."

"Me, too."

Sally headed up the stairs, then stopped, whirled around,

and pointed her finger at her father. "Don't blow it, Dad."

CHAPTER TWENTY-FIVE

The tires of Sheridan's car squealed as she turned into the driveway. Stomping on the brakes, she threw it in park and cut the engine, then leaped out and ran over to the garage. When she peeked into the window, she was relieved to see that Errol was still engrossed in his painting.

Good! She didn't have time to chat.

Tiptoeing away, she let herself into the house and sprinted toward her bedroom. She shed her wet jeans and shirt, then ran into the bathroom. Ridge would be there in a little over half an hour, and she really needed a shower.

Once she was clean, Sheridan contemplated her wardrobe choices. Thankful that the care package from her assistant had arrived yesterday, she slipped on her sexiest bra and panty set, a flirty pink circle skirt, and a black lace T-shirt.

There wasn't enough time to dry her damp hair. Instead, she twisted it on top of her head and secured it with a rosewood comb. She was just finishing her makeup when she heard a car pull into the driveway.

Grabbing her purse, she flew through the living room and out the door. As soon as the BMW came to a stop, she opened the passenger door and slid inside.

When Ridge shot her a bemused look, she explained, "Errol has been dying to know how things are going with us. If he catches you, he'll put you through the third degree."

"Then let's get out of here." Ridge put the Z4 in gear and reversed onto the road. "I have big plans for us tonight, and they don't include your father."

His lips curled up in a smile that flooded her with heat and made her press together her thighs in an attempt to ease the sudden ache between her legs.

"Mine don't, either," Sheridan barely managed to whisper.

"Good." Ridge floored the gas pedal, and the car raced down the blacktop.

A few minutes later, he swung the car into his driveway, and Sheridan worried that her sexy evening would be chaperoned by Ridge's daughter and housekeeper. But instead of stopping in front of the house, he continued around to the back and parked next to a small cottage.

She had forgotten that in addition to the main building and Evelyn's place, the Sutton Estate included a guesthouse next to the in-ground pool. It was hard to remember details like that when she'd never been a part of the high school crowd that hung out there during the summers.

Interrupting Sheridan's not-so-happy trip down memory lane, Ridge suddenly hauled her across the Z4's console. How had he managed that in such a small space?

Before she could figure it out, she was in his lap and aware of his arousal. A flash of anticipation trickled down her spine. His nearness made her senses reel. Immediately, the tight confines of the car's interior no longer registered, and she was carried away to a place where only Ridge existed.

"I can't wait another second for this," he muttered, then pressed his mouth to hers.

Ridge's low moan, almost a growl, inflamed her. She opened her lips to his probing tongue, and a delicious shudder warmed her body.

When he finally allowed her to inhale, she dragged in a shuddering breath. If anything, this kiss was more intoxicating than the ones they'd shared before.

"I... That was..." Sheridan tried to form a coherent sentence but drifted into silence.

After a long moment, Ridge rested his forehead against hers and said, "My marriage and the inevitable divorce did something to me, left me empty inside, but with you I feel something again."

Once again, his bluntness surprised her. The men she'd dated in the past had rarely spoken about their feelings and then only after being poked and prodded to talk. She was deeply touched by Ridge's willingness to open up to her, and it gave her the courage to allow him to see that part of her, as well.

"I've felt hollow for a long time, too." Sheridan ran a fingertip along his jaw.

She never revealed her innermost thoughts to men, which was probably why she hadn't gone out with anyone more than once or twice. But she wanted to share her feelings with Ridge. It wouldn't be easy to change the habits of a lifetime, but she'd try.

"Have you considered what we talked about Sunday after church?" Ridge stroked her hair. "About what's going to happen to us when you go back to St. Louis?"

"A little." Sheridan stiffened. "But no decisions."

"I won't pressure you." Ridge kissed her temple. "I don't want to ruin our evening. All I've been able to think about is getting you alone again."

"So it would seem." Sheridan wiggled her butt, and his erection pressed against her ass. She was glad to drop the subject of the future and concentrate on the present. "Maybe we should move to somewhere with a little more space to maneuver."

"My thought exactly." Ridge threw open the car door and deposited her on the sidewalk.

Together they hurried up to the guesthouse. After fumbling with his keys, he pulled her across the threshold and locked the door behind them.

He gestured to a large space containing a living room, kitchen, and dining area, and a doorway she sure as hell hoped led to a bedroom, and asked, "What do you think?"

Sheridan melted against him and said, "I think it's perfect."

* * *

The sensation of Sheri's soft breasts pressed against his chest shoved his erection into overdrive. He could see her pulse hammering at the base of her throat, and when he leaned a little away from her, the outline of her nipples pushing against her pretty lace T-shirt enticed him.

A savage triumph arrowed through his heart. She was as turned on as he was.

Wanting this to be a true date and not just a hook-up, he got himself under control and asked, "Are you hungry?"

He'd spent an hour that afternoon getting the guesthouse ready for their evening together. There was a deli platter of meats and cheeses in the refrigerator, a loaf of crusty French bread on the counter, and wine ready to open. Romantic music was queued up on the sound system, and he'd put a box of condoms in the nightstand drawer.

"Later." Sheri took his hand and yanked him toward the bedroom.

Even though her low, sexy voice made him instantly harder, Ridge teased, "How about a drink?"

He allowed her to tow him across the hardwood floor. He was enjoying her impatience, but she hadn't made it easy for him when he was the pursuer, so he wouldn't make it easy for her. Or at least, not too easy.

"After." Sheri's smile was predatory as she flung open the oak door and headed straight for the king-size bed.

"Are you sure you don't want some Merlot?" He was primed and ready. It wouldn't take much to fire him off, so he had to fight to keep his voice casual. "I bought the brand you said you liked."

"What?" Sheri swept the duvet from the mattress and glanced back at him.

Confusion and then a hint of anxiety shone from her big brown eyes. The animation drained from her face, and Ridge's gut twisted. What had he done?

"I... I thought..." She stuttered to a stop. "If you'd rather—"

Ridge swiftly closed the gap between them. Something flickered far back in her eyes. He was a jackass for giving her a hard time.

"I was teasing you." He tried to hug her, but she shrugged him away.

"Really, maybe a glass of wine would be a good idea." Sheri's voice had lost its confidence, and she stared at her feet. "After all, there's no rush."

"I'm an idiot." Ridge silently swore at his own stupidity.

"No." Her laugh was shaky. "I don't know what got into me."

Sheri was so self-assured in most ways that he'd forgotten that their relationship was too new for the kind of stunt he'd just pulled.

Putting his arms around her, he drew her against him and said, "Does this feel like I don't want you right this instant?"

"Maybe." She raised an eyebrow, clearly recovering from her momentary insecurity. "But the moment's been lost for me."

His gaze drifted downward, settling on her pebbled nipples, and he silently called her a liar.

Sheri's lips quirked upward. "Of course, I'm open to persuasion."

"And I'm just the man for the job." Still holding her, Ridge moved his hand around to her hip and slid down the zipper of her skirt. "Let's get rid of this." The silky pink fabric pooled at her feet.

He'd intended to undress her slowly, like that special gift saved for last on Christmas Day. He'd wanted to build the desire in both of them until they burned for completion. But once her creamy thighs and sexy lacy panties were revealed, his plan was forgotten.

"And this." Her T-shirt landed somewhere behind them. "And definitely this."

Anticipation thrummed through his veins as he removed her bra and stepped back to enjoy the view. Her skin shimmered like a flawless pearl, gleaming in polished perfection. When he continued to gaze at her, she wrapped her arms around her waist. The defensive gesture made his heart ache. She really had no idea that he loved everything about her.

Noticing that Sheri was sucking in her stomach, Ridge growled in frustration. She was perfect the way she was. From her sweet orange toenails to the gorgeous golden-brown curls that she'd gathered on the top of her head, she was the sexiest woman he'd ever seen.

He'd been hard since she'd slid into his car. He was worried that if he didn't open his zipper soon, there would be permanent damage to his equipment.

"When we're apart, your eyes haunt me," Ridge murmured, wanting her to know how much he cared about her. "And I dream about running my fingers through your hair." He removed the wooden comb from her topknot and spread the waves over her shoulders. "But it's your spirit that makes me want you. It's what makes you so extraordinary."

He claimed her mouth with a wildness that was foreign to him, and she kissed him back with equal ferocity. Backing her up until she bumped against the mattress, he broke their kiss and guided her down onto the bed.

As he looked at her, his breath seemed to solidify in his throat. She was so damn beautiful.

"You know what I think?" Sheri tilted her head back and gazed at him, a smile curling lips that were swollen from his kisses. "I think you have on way too many clothes." She reached for his belt buckle. "Let's see what we can do about that."

Once he was down to his boxer briefs, Ridge lay down and said hoarsely, "Come here."

Gathering her into his arms, he cupped her cheek in one hand. Her eyes were closed, and her lashes rested like dark lace against her porcelain skin. He took a second to cherish the image, then moved her onto the mattress.

Ridge gazed at her as she stared up at him. She was spread out before him like a feast. He had never seen such gorgeous breasts. The pale globes were flawless and gleamed like satin. And her pale pink nipples beckoned him, waiting to be devoured.

Her tantalizingly spicy perfume enveloped him, and his erection throbbed in response. Although he'd always prided himself on his ability to stay in control, he didn't think he could with her.

He had planned to take it slow, explore every inch of her body. He wanted to learn all her likes and dislikes, but he was wild to feel all the heat and wetness between her legs. He needed to be inside of her right now or he thought he might die. This time, there just was no way he could pace himself.

But before he could act, Sheri sat up, pushed him down, and purred, "Last time, you were in charge." Her voice was husky with determination, the voice of a woman who'd overcome any inhibitions that had previously held her back. "It's my turn."

The thought of Sheri taking control, of lying there and allowing her to do what she wanted to him made Ridge's erection turn to granite. Surrendering to her ministrations, Ridge gritted his teeth. He would not ruin this by coming too soon.

Kneeling between his thighs, she bent her head, and the second her lips brushed his hard length, his entire body tightened. Ridge clamped his teeth together and moaned. He reached down and tucked her hair behind her ears, wanting to see her moist pink lips gliding down his erection. The image was so hot, he nearly went off right then.

Like a flame flickering along his skin, the heat of her tongue ignited his nerve endings. She licked him from tip to root, repeating the process until he was out of his mind with desire. Finally, she took him fully into her mouth, and his body clenched in a pleasure that bordered on pain.

He loved watching her, and her lips on his hard length were incredible, but what he really wanted was to sink into her warm, soft body and plummet over the edge of oblivion while he was inside of her.

Gritting his teeth, Ridge drew his erection out of that amazing mouth, flipped her on her back, and said, "Time for me to play."

Sheri's eyes widened, color flooded her cheeks, and she echoed, "Play?"

He slid his hand between her legs. She was wet and ready for him. He fastened his lips to her breast, and while stroking her honeyed folds, he sucked hard on her nipple. He increased the rhythm of his fingers and mouth, until she was clawing at him. This was better. He'd wanted the evening to be all about her.

He loved watching her muscles tremble with every touch of his hand. Kissing his way down her stomach, Ridge took his time reaching his goal, then he licked inside of her. She moved against his mouth, her breath stuttering. He could tell she was close, so he swirled his tongue against her sweet spot and watched as she broke. Her back arched off the mattress, and she cried out his name.

He held her until the shudders stopped and she floated back to earth, then grabbed a condom from the nightstand. Once he was sheathed, he fit himself against her opening.

Sheri's face was a study in passionate need and desire when she said, "I want you now, hard and fast."

At her husky admission, Ridge lost all control and plunged into her. The scent of her recent orgasm surrounded him, increasing his hunger for her. Being inside of her was heavenly, and each time he pistoned into her, she grew hotter and wetter.

With every thrust, her internal muscles pulsed around his hard length, and her nails dug into his back. The sexy words she whispered into his ear drove him to the brink.

Ridge stared into her lust-filled brown eyes, his gaze taking in her plump lips and the rosy color on her usually creamy cheeks. Sheri was close to going over the edge again.

Removing any last restraint, he slammed into her, once, twice, and finally found paradise. Pleasure surged through his body. A split second later, she sobbed his name, and her climax rolled over him, intensifying the sensations of his own until he thought he might break into pieces from the force of it.

Unwilling to sacrifice one exquisite moment of the ecstatic experience, Ridge continued to pound into her as his orgasm went on and on.

His bliss was so overpowering that it pulled the breath from his lungs. And in his heart, he knew this moment had joined their souls. A sense of serenity settled around him. This was right. This was how it should have been all along.

He disposed of the condom, then, while they both recovered, Ridge held Sheri, trying to memorize the shape and weight of her cuddled against him. The rhythm of her heart beating in sync with his soothed him and helped ease his worries.

The anxiety over the fate of the town, his fear that someone was targeting the family businesses, and his concern that he wasn't up to raising his daughter alone, all melted away. Doubtlessly they would be back, but for the moment, with Sheri's head resting against his chest, he was finally at peace.

She dozed off in his arms, and he smoothed a stray curl from her eyes. He loved being inside her sweet body, bringing her to climax and watching her come apart for him. But what he really wanted was her heart. Would he ever claim that part of her?

Sheri had years and years of creating extensive defenses against her feelings. Given enough time apart from him, would she overanalyze what was happening between them? Would she decide that their relationship was too difficult, too messy to bother continuing?

He felt Sheri wake with a start, and when he looked down at her, her brown eyes were full of hot desire. He immediately hardened. What was it with this woman? He was still drenched in sweat, and his muscles ached from their first round of lovemaking. Yet all he could think of was sinking into her again.

CHAPTER TWENTY-SIX

When Sheridan woke for the second time, it was to the sound of Ridge's steady breathing. They'd showered together, then fallen asleep again.

What time is it? There wasn't a clock on the nightstand, and in her haste to get dressed for their date, she'd forgotten her watch. She twisted her neck until she could see Ridge's wrist. Nearly ten o'clock.

Sheridan eased out of his arms and immediately missed his warmth. Swinging her legs over the side of the mattress, she padded into the bathroom, splashed her face with water, and peered into the mirror.

Who was that woman grinning back at her?

Her typically pale complexion glowed pinkly, and her usually serious brown eyes sparkled. Joy had crept into her heart, cracking the walls of her usual detachment.

When she'd left Sutton Falls, she'd been determined never to allow anyone close enough to hurt her. Instead of pursuing any kind of personal life, she'd spent years putting everything she had into her profession.

But a couple of nights in Ridge's arms and she'd reclaimed her ability to feel. To hope. To risk being vulnerable.

It wasn't only that he was gorgeous. Or that his erotically raw words rumbling against her throat had brought her to a fever pitch of desire. Or that he'd made her come embarrassingly fast. It was the connection they shared.

In only a few days, he knew her. He'd reached into her heart and her mind, uncovering everything she kept hidden from the rest of the world.

A sense of serenity and bone-deep satisfaction settled over her. With Ridge, the shadows that had darkened her soul for so long were gone. A newly awakened sense of purpose brought the world around her into a sharper focus.

She was tired of the iron control that she'd always imposed on her emotions. It was past time to allow herself the luxury of her own emotions.

Humming, Sheridan opened the medicine cabinet and found an assortment of travel-sized toiletries. Grabbing a plastic-wrapped comb, she disposed of the cellophane and ran it through her hair and then misted herself with lavender body spray.

When she exited the bathroom, she heard Ridge whistling in the kitchen. He'd left an oversize terry robe draped across the foot of the bed. Smiling, she slipped into it, ready to begin the next chapter in her life.

Ridge wore a matching bathrobe. Clearly, he didn't want either of them to get dressed just yet. She hoped it was because he had plans for the rest of the evening that required them both to be naked.

When she walked over to him, he cupped her face in his big hands, gave her a sweet kiss, and said, "You're fantastic. I always knew you were special, but I had no idea of just how wonderful we would be together."

His words made her feel infinitely treasured. She rejoiced in his open admiration, but she was caught off guard by his tender expression. A tiny shard of hope stole through her. Maybe they could have something long term. *No.* She ruthlessly quashed that thought. It was too soon even to consider the idea of forever.

Lowering her gaze in confusion, she murmured, "Thank you. It was sort of amazing."

"More than just 'sort of' for me." He kissed her nose, then led her over to the sofa, where a plate of food and a glass of wine waited for her on the coffee table. Sitting down, he scooped up a

271

remote, pressed a button, and Antonín Dvořák's *Serenade for Strings in E Major* poured out of the speakers.

Sheridan's heart turned over. During one of their tutoring sessions, she'd told him that this was the most romantic music she'd ever heard. How had he remembered?

Smiling, she leaned forward to pick up her plate, but Ridge stopped her. He lifted the dish onto his lap and fed her morsels of cheese, bites of crusty bread spread with creamy butter, and sips of Merlot. When she'd had enough, she insisted on returning the favor, enjoying the sensation of his lips brushing against her fingers as he ate.

Once both plates were empty, Ridge put his arm around her, and they sat drinking their wine. They chatted about their lives during the years they were apart and laughed at each other's stories.

When Ridge asked about her book tours, she wasn't sure if he was really interested or just thought as a public figure she liked to talk about herself. The truth was that she was a bit shy about the whole idea of fame. But with his encouragement, she described speaking to large crowds at university campuses, appearing on talk shows, and being wined and dined in various cities.

As she spoke, she remembered the excitement of those occasions. Along with the large advances and hefty royalty checks, those experiences were the validation of the success she had worked so hard to achieve.

Eventually, Sheridan trailed off and they both grew quiet. After a few minutes, she turned to look at Ridge and saw an expression of reluctant resolve on his handsome face. Apparently, the fun portion of their evening was about to end. Maybe she should go put her clothes on for this next part.

Before she could drag herself from his warm embrace, Ridge released her and stood up. He returned with a fresh bottle of Merlot, sat down, and refilled their glasses. A muscle twitched in his jaw, and his knuckles were white as he gripped the arm of the sofa.

His continued silence was too much for Sheridan, and to her dismay, her voice broke slightly when she asked, "Is something wrong?"

"I just wish we could have this night without me having to bring this up."

"What?" A weight settled on her chest, and she almost couldn't inhale.

Was he about to tell her that he was getting back together with Alexis for Sally's sake? He wouldn't be the first parent to return to a miserable marriage in order to ensure his child's happiness.

Ridge answered slowly, "This afternoon, I met with someone from the U.S. Army Corps of Engineers." His expression made it clear that this was the last thing he wanted to discuss tonight. "The rain we had Saturday and Sunday has pushed the flood control system to its limits. He warned me that one more heavy downpour and the system won't be able to handle the excess water."

"I see." Sheridan pulled the lapels of her robe more snugly closed and tightened the belt. *Yep.* She should have gotten dressed. "And you need our levee."

"It's the town's only hope." Ridge took her hand. "I understand that that land has been in your mother's family for generations and it's your connection to her, but would she want you to sacrifice people's homes and possibly their lives in order to save it?"

"My father and I have talked about this a lot, but I just don't know."

Sheridan slipped her fingers from Ridge's and put her elbows on her knees. A painful arrow of doubt ripped through her. Had his whole pursuit of her been leading up to this conversation?

"Will Errol listen to you?"

"Actually, he has to." Sheridan stared at the fire. "I own a part of the land."

"Dammit!" Ridge seemed shocked by her statement. "How in the hell did Beau miss that? He was supposed to have researched the legalities of the sale."

"Like everyone else, I'm guessing he just assumed Errol had inherited the whole thing from my mother." Sheridan sighed, then explained, "When Vivian's father died, Mom and Dad bought out her brother's half so that my parents owned the whole farm, and she left me a thirty percent share. I think she did that to ensure my father couldn't sell it without someone with her family's bloodline having a say."

"What would it take to convince you?" Ridge tried to recapture her hand, but she scooted over, putting several feet between them.

"I have no idea," Sheridan admitted.

All the pleasure of the evening drained from her. It felt more and more as if Ridge's interest in her was solely due to his need for her family's levee.

"It's essential that you make a decision right away. Delaying any longer isn't an option. If you don't agree to sell the town the levee, we'll have to start evacuations." Ridge's voice was soft and persuasive. "Will you go with your head or your heart?"

The irony was not lost on her. Sheridan glanced at him. In permitting herself to believe that Ridge cared for her, had her heart already led her astray?

Inwardly cringing at the idea that she'd been such a sap, she kept her voice expressionless and said, "It's not just the sentimental value of the land that makes me hesitate. If the levee comes down, it isn't only our southeast fields that will be flooded. It's also the property of a lot of other farmers in that direction."

"Believe me, I understand." Ridge moved closer and cupped her cheek. "It's a hellish choice to make. But from a purely logical perspective, it's fifty houses versus fifteen hundred. It's the livelihood of six or seven families versus all of the downtown businesses."

"I'm aware of that." She hunched her shoulders against the hurt.

She'd allowed herself to indulge in a relationship with Ridge, ignoring that there was a good chance he was only after her family's property. Allowed herself to dream of a future, when her head said their relationship was never meant to be. Allowed herself to feel something for him, realizing that she was opening herself up to the pain of betrayal.

Sheridan had always known that giving the town control of the levee was the right thing to do. She'd fooled herself into thinking that she could handle the repercussions of being selfish. Of saving her mother's land and sacrificing so many others.

But she wasn't that kind of person. She had never been as hardhearted as she pretended to be. A flaw that had often worked against her in the ruthlessly competitive publishing business.

She couldn't bear to let Ridge see her cry, so she took a shaky breath and said, "I promise to tell Errol that I think we should sell the land to the city."

"When?" Ridge asked, clearly intent on pinning down an answer tonight.

"He's probably already asleep tonight, but I can go home right now and check," Sheridan said thickly, dropping her lashes to hide the hurt in her eyes. "At the latest, I'll talk to him first thing in the morning. I'm sure he'll agree, and I'll have him call you and confirm tomorrow."

The ache in her heart was so intense she could barely move, but she forced herself to her feet. She needed to put on her clothes and get out of there before she said or did something stupid. Now that Ridge had gotten what he wanted, he probably couldn't wait to get rid of her, and she didn't think she could stand hearing his excuse to end the evening early.

"No need to leave right away. The next possibility of rain isn't until Thursday, so tomorrow's fine." Ridge tugged her back down to the sofa and traced a curl that lay against her cleavage. "And I have a much better idea of how to spend the rest of this evening."

"Oh?" The implication sent waves of excitement through her, but she tamped them down. Determined to keep a grip on her emotions, she gazed at the floor and whispered, "You've got my word, and I don't go back on my promises, so you don't have to pretend you want to be with me anymore."

"Son of a bitch!" Ridge tipped her chin up and made her look at him. "Do you truly think that I brought you here to seduce you into giving up your land?"

"Of course I do." She couldn't expose any more of her weaknesses to him, so she summoned her courage and infused her voice with disdain. "It's fairly obvious that you used sex to ensure my cooperation."

"How can you think so little of yourself?" Ridge's voice cracked with suppressed emotion. "The last thing that I wanted to do tonight was talk to you about the goddamn levee. I knew you'd think the worst. That you didn't fully trust me yet. But I'd put off this conversation for so long that I had no choice."

"You mean you ran out of time to wine and dine me," Sheridan corrected, refusing to allow herself to believe him. "So you had to bring out the big guns sooner than you wanted."

"That's not true!" Ridge shouted, making Sheridan jump. "I should have talked to you Saturday night or Sunday when I saw you at church or even yesterday on the phone, but my fear of losing you over this issue made me hesitate. And now I've put the town at risk."

"Losing me?" Even though she didn't believe him for a second, her pulse ratcheted into overdrive. "You're trying to tell me that you cared so much about me, about having a relationship with me, you were afraid to ask about the land?"

"Hell yes!" Ridge tried to gather her close to him, but she jerked away. He scowled and said, "I even considered letting the deputy mayor handle the negotiations with your father. But I was afraid Mrs. Bunson would put a bullet in Errol if he refused."

"I can see how that might happen since it appears that Mrs. B is one of the few women immune to my dad's charms." Sheridan tried to look away, but Ridge held her gaze and she murmured, "Thank you for saving Errol from her rifle."

"I figured getting him shot was not a good way to say, gee, I hope you don't mind if I date your daughter."

"You're probably right about that." Sheridan chewed her bottom lip.

Should she believe him? Was Ridge really as interested in her as he claimed? She'd promised him the levee. Unless he was afraid she'd go back on her word, he didn't have anything more to gain from pretending to be interested in her. Was she using his poor timing in asking her about the land as an excuse to put the barriers back up around her heart?

"I don't think you have to worry about Errol objecting to us seeing each other," Sheridan said, then added, as a test of Ridge's sincerity, "Still, it might be best if we call it a night, go back to my place, wake him up, and get this levee business settled."

"Why?" Ridge asked, a guarded expression on his face. "Are you tired?"

"No." Sheridan shook her head. She'd give him one more

chance to bail on her. "But it's getting late, and we both have a lot to do tomorrow."

"I'm not ready to end our evening." Ridge's voice was husky. "I looked forward all day to this time with you."

"Me, too," Sheridan admitted, her mood suddenly buoyant. For once, she would believe the best about someone instead of allowing her past hurts to convince her otherwise.

"So, you'll stay a while longer?" Ridge asked.

When she nodded, he scooped her into his lap and nuzzled her throat, pushing Sheridan's robe down her shoulder and exposing the creamy slopes of her breast.

"Mmm." Sheridan was lost in the sensation of his lips closing around her nipple when the sound of a door slamming open penetrated her fog.

Shocked to see Evelyn Sutton marching across the floor, Sheridan yanked her robe closed. The woman's high heels clicked angrily on the hardwood, and she stopped a few feet from the sofa and scowled.

Evelyn pointed a finger at Sheridan and hissed at her son, "I thought we agreed that you were going to stay away from this woman."

"Never." Ridge tucked Sheridan against his side, then turned a fury-filled gaze at Evelyn. "What are you doing here, Mother?"

"I was coming home from a dinner party and saw your car parked outside." Evelyn threw each word like a stone. "Since I had no idea what in the world you'd be doing in the guesthouse in the middle of the night, I stopped to see if you were okay."

"How did you get in?" Ridge's tone was frosty. "The door was locked."

"I have keys to all the doors on the estate," Evelyn informed him.

"No. You *had* keys. I'm having every damn lock on the

place changed first thing tomorrow." Ridge tenderly moved
Sheridan aside and stood. "Until you show some respect for
Sheri, you are no longer welcome on my property."

Sheridan told herself that she shouldn't be so thrilled to
have Ridge defend her. She didn't need a man to protect her. In
the past, she'd have been turned off by a guy assuming she
couldn't take care of herself. But Ridge's words were oddly
comforting. They made her feel cared about.

"How can you speak that way to me?" Evelyn huffed.

Ridge didn't respond to his mother's outrage, and Sheridan
watched as he stepped toward Evelyn, crowding her personal
space, and said, "Now, get the hell out of here before I have you
arrested for trespassing."

"You wouldn't," Evelyn faltered. "This is as much my
home as yours."

"No. It. Isn't." Ridge took his mother's elbow and towed
her to the door. "As you very well know, the estate came to me
when I turned thirty. The only part of it you have any legal right
to is the house you live in and the acre of land around it."

"But...but..." Evelyn sputtered. "You're choosing someone
like Sheridan Davis over your own mother."

"Not someone *like* Sheri." Ridge opened the door, pushed
his mother over the threshold, and said emphatically, "I'm
choosing *her*."

Sheridan's heart soared at his words. He'd defended her
against his mother and made his intentions crystal clear. After
the hurt of him asking for the levee during such an intimate
moment, it was a balm to her soul.

CHAPTER TWENTY-SEVEN

The weatherman had been wrong. The rain didn't wait until Thursday. It started drizzling late Wednesday afternoon. Errol had already informed Ridge that he and Sheridan would cede control of the levee to Sutton Falls, but when the downpour intensified, Ridge had called and asked them to meet him in the mayor's office as soon as possible to sign the papers.

By the time Sheridan and Errol arrived at city hall, there was already standing water on the street. As she pushed him into the lobby and toward the elevator, she wondered if they'd waited too long to give Ridge the land.

Guilt made her stomach churn. Would they lose the town? If they did, she was to blame. Her father had been ready to turn over the property last week. Sheridan was the one who hadn't been able to make up her mind.

When she and Errol entered Ridge's reception area, Wendy was busy on the telephone. The admin paused to wave them through, then went back to taking notes.

The mayor's office was full of people vying to be heard over each other. From what Sheridan could gather, several communities along the river were already underwater, and the National Guard was now attempting to rescue residents who had refused to leave their homes in time.

Using her father's wheelchair to part the crowd, Sheridan managed to get to the desk, where Ridge stood surrounded by an agitated mob. He greeted her with a quick hug and kiss, thanked her and Errol for their generosity to the town, and turned them over to Beau Bunson, who fanned out the necessary paperwork and showed them where to sign.

Sheridan noticed the antagonistic body language between Ridge and his best friend, and she suspected that at least some of the hostility was due to her. She hoped that Ridge's relationship with her hadn't cost him a childhood pal.

Turning her attention to the contracts, Sheridan signed and initialed the various pages. Then, while Errol did the same, she listened as Ridge called the U.S. Army Corps of Engineers.

"We have written consent," Ridge said into the phone. "Your men can get in position to blast the breach in the levee. When everyone in the flood's path is evacuated, I'll give you the signal to go ahead."

Sheridan felt a twinge. This was it. A good portion of her family's property was about to become a lake. The previously rich farmland would lay fallow for many, many years.

"What!" Ridge shouted. "Yes. Of course, I know other towns also need your assistance, but—" He listened, then argued some more. Finally, he said, "Let me know when your guys are free to head to the levee." He slammed down the receiver.

"I take it we're not first on the list?" Beau said.

"Not by a long shot." Ridge shoved his hands through his hair. "According to the engineer in charge, there are several other towns that are in more imminent danger. Once their situations are resolved, he'll route his men to our levee."

"In the meantime, did he have any suggestions?" Mick asked from the back of the crowd.

Sheridan hadn't realized her cousin was there. Now, she gave him a little wave, and he nodded to her and Errol.

"Start sandbagging," Ridge sighed.

"Like we haven't already been doing that," Beau snapped.

"Time to kick it into high gear." Ridge flicked his friend an annoyed glance, then began issuing orders.

Sheridan said to Errol, "I'll drive you home and then come back here to fill sandbags."

"No way." Errol shook his head vehemently. "Push me over to the diner. I'm sure there's something I can do there to help. They're going to need coffee and food for everyone working. I can sure as hell make sandwiches and fill cups."

"You're right," Sheridan agreed. "It's better if we stay put and keep the roads clear for emergency vehicles."

Ridge was hemmed in by men and women yelling questions at him, but when Sheridan started to wheel Errol out of the room, he broke free and joined her by the door. "Where are you two going?"

She explained their plans, then said, "I noticed the water is already rising downstairs. Are you planning to transfer your headquarters to higher ground?"

"I'm staying at city hall as long as possible. We've turned off the gas, but we should be okay up here. And once you get Errol down the elevator, we're shutting off the first floor's electricity," Ridge answered grimly. "The storm is causing a lot of dead zones for cell phones, but the landline in my office is still working, and we also have a CB system we're using to communicate with some of the farmers in the area that will be flooded when the levee is breached."

"Have you notified them all to evacuate?" Sheridan asked, troubled that it was her decision that was causing other families' losses.

"Most of them have already cleared out." Ridge glanced over his shoulder at the people waiting for him to return to his desk. "But we're still trying to reach a handful."

"Then I'd better let you get to it." Although Sheridan hated to leave him, there wasn't anything she could do at city hall except get in the way. "I've got my cell."

"Me, too, but remember most coverage is spotty, so don't depend on it." Ridge hesitated, then asked, "As long as you're going to fill sandbags, can you keep an eye on Sally? She and her classmates are working on Merry's team."

"Of course."

Ridge kissed her and whispered, "Be careful."

"You, too." Sheridan waved good-bye as he disappeared back into the throng.

Errol had been right. Pinky's was the official rest spot for the volunteers. The diner was being manned by the folks who weren't physically able to be on the front lines, and Sheridan's father was immediately set to work dispensing coffee next to Evelyn Sutton. The older woman scowled, hissed something at Errol, and stepped a few inches away from him.

Sheridan frowned. What was up with Ridge's mother? Was she holding her son's relationship with Sheridan against Errol? If so, he seemed unperturbed by her disapproval.

Shrugging, Sheridan helped herself to one of the rain slickers from the pile that Sutton's department store had donated and left her dad with instructions to have someone find her if he needed her.

A few seconds later, she reported for duty at the sandbag filling station. Merry was in charge of the high school and junior high students who had volunteered, and she drafted Sheridan as her second-in-command.

Noticing Sally chatting away with her two new friends, Sheridan joined the girls. Her car wash plan had been a success, and she was glad there was at least one reason to smile.

Townsfolk had contributed whatever materials and equipment they had. There was everything from rakes and spades to Bobcats. The nursery had donated piles of burlap bags, and the highway patrol had sent trucks full of sand, dumping it as close to the water's edge as possible.

As they worked, Merry explained that there were personnel attempting to divert the water upriver, and downriver roads were already submerged. Reports came in of drivers trying to go through the flooded areas, and there were already stories of cars being washed away.

Throughout the evening and into the night, they filled sandbag after sandbag, stacking them several feet high, striving to ensure the town's safety. Sheridan hadn't heard anything from Ridge, but rumors circulated that there were still folks unaccounted for who lived in the homes that would be in the water's path once the levee was blown.

Evidently, they hadn't been reached by telephone or answered during the door-to-door search, and time was running out. As soon as the engineers were ready, the levee would be breached. Messages had been left for the remainder of the people in the water's path, and the best they could do now was pray for their safety.

At midnight, the Red Cross arrived with lunch wagons and portable lighting. People from inland communities surrounding Sutton Falls poured in to relieve the exhausted residents on the front lines.

But it seemed that no matter how many sandbags they stacked, the water kept rising. This was the worst flood anyone could remember. Far more severe than the one fifty years ago that had caused significant structural damage up and down the main street.

Errol and the others at Pinky's had been relocated to the high school evacuation center. It was on one of the uppermost points around Sutton Falls and the safest place for folks to stay.

Finally, word arrived that the Army Corps of Engineers had pumped two types of liquid explosives into the embankment. When mixed together, they would explode, blowing up the levee. Unfortunately, the breaching might be too little too late. The first floors of the houses and businesses closest to the river already had standing water, and folks were helping the owners move what they could either out or to the top levels.

When the news about the flooding in the buildings along the main street came through, Sally approached the adults and said, "I'm going over to my father's office to see if he's all right."

Sheridan and Merry exchanged a concerned glance, and Sheridan put her hand on Sally's shoulder. "Okay if I come, too? I could use a restroom break."

"Sure." Sally linked her arm with Sheridan's, and the two headed to the city hall.

Sheridan was thankful that the streetlamps were still on. She'd been afraid that the power would be off and they'd have to make their way through the dark using only the flashlight that she'd requisitioned from Merry's supply.

When she and Sally entered the lobby, they had to wade through ankle-deep water to get to the stairway. Once they climbed to the top floor, they made a beeline for the restroom.

As they took off their dripping raincoats and hung them on the hooks beside the door, they heard the sound of a muffled explosion. The levee had been breached, and the river would soon erase hundreds of acres of fields along with the farmers' homes. Sheridan shivered. Whatever happened today, many people's lives had permanently changed.

After using the facilities, they washed their hands and faces, and while Sheridan refastened her ponytail, Sally said, "I'll meet you in Dad's office."

"I'm right behind you." As Sheridan turned to follow Sally, she glimpsed herself in the mirror. No makeup, frizzy hair, and mud-spattered clothing—her reflection revealed a totally different woman than she was used to seeing.

A couple of weeks ago, she would have been appalled to be spotted in public looking so unkempt. Why didn't it bother her now? Was it the situation, or had something deep inside of her changed? Had she gained the self-confidence that before she had only pretended to possess?

Taking one last glance at the new Sheridan, she grabbed both rain slickers, exited the bathroom, and stepped into the hallway. As she did, she heard someone call Sally's name and watched the girl step inside the city clerk's office. Had Ridge moved into that space for some reason?

Sheridan hurried down the corridor, skidding to a stop when Sally shrieked, "Mom!"

What was Ridge's nasty ex doing back in town?

Sheridan stood in the open door, but neither Sally nor Alexis acknowledged her.

As Sally hugged her mother, she asked, "Did you come to help save the town?"

"I've been here all along, darling," Alexis giggled. "But Daddy asked me to hide until he'd charmed Ms. Davis into giving her family's levee to him."

All the breath in Sheridan's body whooshed out, leaving her dizzy. Had Ridge been pretending to care for her all along? Were his assurances last night because he hadn't had her signature yet?

No! Sheridan reassured herself. Alexis was lying.

"You mean Dad tricked her?" Sally asked. "That isn't right. Why would he do that?"

"Sweetheart, it was the only way to make sure Sutton Falls got control of that land." Alexis's tone was soothing. "The Davises were being greedy and holding out for more money. They would have bankrupted the town."

"I don't believe you." Sally backed away from her mother. "Sheridan isn't like that."

"Sometimes grown-ups don't allow children to see their true colors." Alexis gave her daughter a peck on the cheek, then smiled brightly. "But since everything is settled and your Daddy has gotten the levee from the Davises, I'm finally able to come out of hiding and move back home with you both."

With each word that Alexis spoke, Sheridan's soul shredded

into fragments. The woman was a liar, but even liars occasionally told the truth. Had Sheridan allowed her desire for a relationship with Ridge to burrow itself into her heart and make her careless?

"So you and Dad are getting remarried?" Sally's voice held a mixture of hope and doubt. "But he said—"

"Listen," Alexis interrupted her daughter. "We'll discuss this all later. Daddy asked me to pick you up and take you to where I've been staying. Just in case blowing up the levee doesn't work, he wants you to be safe. He'll meet us there in a little while."

Sheridan hesitated. Even if Alexis was telling the truth and Ridge had deceived her, all of her instincts screamed that Sally shouldn't leave with her mother.

Pushing herself to be brave, Sheridan walked into the room and said coolly, "Sally's father entrusted her to my care. I'm afraid that I'll need to check with him before allowing you to take her anywhere."

Alexis's icy blue eyes narrowed. "In what fantasy world does someone like you have any influence on what I do with my own daughter?"

"All I'm saying is that we need to clear it with her father before you leave," Sheridan answered evenly.

She couldn't make herself say Ridge's name. The bitter taste of betrayal in her mouth was too strong. She needed time to process what she'd overheard before condemning him, but it was hard to remain reasonable in the face of such hurt.

Alexis gripped her daughter's hand and tried to push past Sheridan. "If you think for one moment that you were ever in the running to be Sally's stepmother, you're even more pathetic than I thought." Alexis smoothed her palms over her Burberry trench coat, then glanced pointedly from Sheridan's filthy sneakers to her own Michael Kors rain boots. "Ridge was never truly interested in you. It was all an act and you fell for it."

"Why should I believe a liar like you?" Sheridan blocked Alexis's exit, refusing to allow the cruel woman to see how she really felt.

"Because you know in your heart it's the truth." Alexis showed her blindingly white teeth in a fake sympathetic smile. "Admit it. There is no way that Ridge would ever love someone as fat and ugly as you." She patted her perfectly coiffed hair. "Why would he settle for tuna casserole when he can have lobster thermidor every night?"

"Not everyone enjoys rich food." Sheridan forced herself to stand her ground as self-doubt washed over her. "It gives some people indigestion."

"Think about it." Alexis continued to try to get to the doorway. "Wasn't it quite a coincidence that Ridge and I both showed up at a party you were attending?"

"No." Sheridan managed to answer in a voice that didn't sound as if she'd been punched in the stomach. "It's a small town, and Merry had invited everyone from our class who was around."

"It was a setup, you cretin," Alexis sneered. "So he could rescue you from his horrible ex-wife and seduce you into giving him the levee. He told me all about how grateful you were and how easy it was to convince you that he was nothing but my pawn. I can't believe you fell for that roofie story that he fed you."

How would Alexis know that Ridge had told her about being roofied if they hadn't hatched the scheme together? According to Ridge's explanation to Sheridan, he'd only found out last Saturday from Beau, so Alexis shouldn't even be aware that Ridge knew he'd been drugged.

The fragile bubble of hope Sheridan had kept alive throughout the other woman's diatribe shattered. She questioned everything she'd come to believe in the past few days. Searching for another plausible explanation, she came up empty. Alexis might be a liar, but there was a good chance that this was the one time she was telling the truth.

Although anxious to escape Alexis's disturbing presence and regroup, Sheridan gathered the tatters of her dignity around her and said, "Fine. You and Ridge can celebrate duping me once the danger is over, but since he has full custody of Sally, I still want to hear it from him that it's okay for her to go with you."

Despite everything, Sheridan's intuition insisted that she shouldn't allow the girl to leave with Alexis.

"You win." Alexis held up the hand that wasn't holding on to her daughter's fingers. "Let's go find him and get this over with."

With Alexis's capitulation, a raw and primitive grief overwhelmed Sheridan. No way would the conniving woman agree to request permission from Ridge if she'd been lying about his scheme to get the levee from Sheridan's family. If his ex was being untruthful, he'd reveal her deception, and Alexis wouldn't risk that.

Sheridan had to accept that Ridge didn't really care for her. It all had been an act.

Alexis led the way to the mayoral suite. The reception area was empty, and the whole place was eerily quiet. Sheridan opened the door to the inner office and found it unoccupied, too.

"Looks like they've already evacuated." Alexis pressed her lips together. "Now, can I take my daughter to safety?"

"Let me try Ridge's cell."

"There's no signal." Alexis crossed her arms. "Quit wasting my time."

Ignoring the evil woman, Sheridan dug her phone from her pocket and swept her finger across the screen. Her shoulders slumped. Alexis was right. There was no service.

"It's okay, Sheridan." Sally moved away from her mother. "I'll go with Mom, and when you find Dad, you can tell him where I am." She turned to leave, then came back and said softly, "I'm really sorry about what my parents did to you. I hope you don't hate me."

"Of course not." Sheridan hugged her and helped her into her raincoat. "You and I will always be friends."

She looked over at Alexis, who was clearly anxious to get out of there. Sheridan still didn't like it, but she really had no choice but to let the girl go with her mother. It wasn't as if Sheridan had any legal standing. It wasn't as if Sally was her stepdaughter—or ever likely to be.

CHAPTER TWENTY-EIGHT

After Alexis and Sally left, Sheridan collapsed on a nearby chair. How had she not seen that coming? She was pathetically foolish and excruciatingly dimwitted to have trusted Ridge so quickly last night, so completely.

She should have known better. After all, he was a politician. Who better to lie without batting an eyelash? The recognition that he was a professional deceiver did nothing to douse her pain. If anything, it only made it worse that she'd been so naïve as to trust him.

Sheridan had allowed herself to pretend that she could have a life here in Sutton Falls. That she and her father could forget the past and move forward. That Ridge truly cared for her.

She'd been an idiot to believe in a fairy-tale ending. When had her feelings ever meant anything to the men in her life? None of the guys she'd dated had ever worried about hurting her. Her own father chose to keep his word to some strange woman rather than save their relationship. And evidently, Ridge felt so little for her that he was willing to use her attraction to him to get what he wanted from her family.

Why were Ridge's actions the most devastating? Because she loved him.

Sheridan gave a choked, desperate laugh. This was a fine time to admit to herself that she had always loved Ridge. Their time together had brought the emotions that she'd denied for years bubbling to the surface. She had opened up her heart to him, and he'd ripped it apart.

The years of numbness had been better than this. Why had she allowed Ridge to tear down the walls that she'd built around her feelings? Why had she allowed herself to love him? Why had she allowed him to turn something so beautiful into something so agonizing she thought she might die from the pain?

Ice crept up Sheridan's spine as a desperate sense of loss swept through her. She doubled over. Her stomach ached as if she'd been punched in the gut by Evander Holyfield.

Ridge had betrayed her in the worst way a man could betray a woman. The knowledge of his utter duplicity churned inside of her. He had taken her love, her body, her trust and used them all against her for his own gain.

She was gasping for air, and her vision was blurry with tears when anguish shattered the last slivers of her self-control, and she howled her misery. Overcome by a horrific sense of bitterness and facing a loveless future, she buried her head in her trembling hands and wept.

The sound of a ringing telephone finally infiltrated her desolation. Swallowing her sobs, she rose to her feet. Her legs trembled, and the inside of her mouth felt like the pages of an old book—dry and dusty.

Making her way to Wendy's desk, she snatched up the receiver, cleared her aching throat, and said, "Mayor's office. May I help you?"

"This is Lucille Wilson. Thank God I finally got through to someone. There's no answer at the police station or the fire department." The voice on the other end of the phone cut in and out, indicating a bad connection. "My aunt and I are trapped. We need help."

"This is Sheridan Davis." She clutched the handset. She had forgotten that her high school English teacher had moved in with her elderly aunt. The Wilson farmhouse was directly in the path of the water released by the breached levee. "Why didn't you get out earlier?"

"Aunt Albie hid my car keys and my cell phone," Lucille explained. "The dementia made her believe that I was trying to put her in a nursing home."

"What's your situation?"

"Grim. We're in the attic, but the water is rising rapidly, and I doubt I can get Aunt Albie up onto the roof." Lucille's next words were lost in the static, then Sheridan heard her say, "If someone doesn't come for us soon, I doubt we'll survive."

"Hang on," Sheridan shouted into the phone as the line went dead.

Although Sheridan jabbed the button with her index finger until her nail broke, she couldn't get a dial tone. She tried her cell, but there was still no signal. Spotting the CB radio, she snatched the mike and said, "Anybody there?"

Silence. Spinning the dial, she tried every channel, but nothing. Maybe the antenna had blown down. She needed to do something. But what?

Her only option was to find someone to help the Wilsons. If she didn't, both women might die.

When Sheridan ran down the city hall's staircase and stepped into the lobby, she discovered that the water was now up to her knees. Making her way out the door, she was relieved to see that the streetlights were still on. The rain had finally stopped, but the road was completely deserted.

Everyone must have left for higher ground. If Lucille and her aunt were going to be saved, it would have to be Sheridan who went for them. The best place to find transportation would be the marina. Could she make it there, locate a boat, and get it started?

It was tough walking into the gusting wind, and when she heard the sound of a motor, she paused to get her breath. A few seconds later, a jacked-up truck towing a bright red Chris-Craft on a boat trailer squealed to a stop beside her. The driver had on a neon yellow slicker similar to the one Sheridan wore.

The Chevy idled as Beau Bunson rolled down his window

and grinned. "Need a lift?"

Beau wasn't exactly the knight in shining armor she was hoping for, but Sheridan knew she was in no position to be picky about who rescued the Wilsons.

Hurrying around the pickup, she opened the passenger door, hopped inside, and said, "We need to get out to the Wilson farm right away. Lucille and her aunt are trapped in the attic, and she says that the water is still rising."

"Sorry. No can do." Beau shook his head regretfully. "When I spotted you, I was on my way to launch my boat. My cousin is stranded on the roof with her two boys and her newborn daughter."

"Shit!" Sheridan sure couldn't expect him to choose the Wilsons over his own family. "Why did everyone evacuate downtown? Didn't breaching the levee work?"

"It seems to have, but they can't be certain, so as a precaution, everyone was ordered to higher ground."

"Smart." Sheridan nodded, then asked, "Do you know if there's another boat that I could use?"

"I bet there'll be at least one or two floating around at the dock." Beau put the Ford in gear. "Most will have sunk and be under the water, but a few will have broken free from the cleats they were tied to."

"So you'll take me with you and help me get one?"

"Sure." Beau swung the wheel and headed in the direction he'd come from. "Do you know how to operate a boat? Maybe we should find Ridge and have him take you out to the Wilson farm."

"No!" Pain shot through Sheridan's chest. She wasn't ready to face Ridge yet. "I don't want his help." At Beau's perplexed expression, she swallowed and said, "I mean, there's no time to locate him."

"Let's at least try to call him." Beau whipped out his cell

phone, gazed at it, and announced, "Shit! Still no signal." He shook his head and said, "Ridge was looking for you and Sally. When Merry told him you two were at the city hall, he said that he'd left a note on his office door to meet him at the high school evacuation center so he'd head there." Beau's eyes widened, "Where *is* Sally?"

"Alexis was at the city hall and took her," Sheridan explained, then murmured, half to herself, "I didn't see any note."

"Oh." Beau slowed down to avoid a patio umbrella twirling down the road. "How about if I drive you over to the high school to find Ridge?"

"We can't afford to waste the time going back and forth." Sheridan wasn't about to ask a favor from a man who had used her for his own gain.

"You're right. We need to hustle." Beau sped up. "By the way, I've been thinking about what we did to you at the prom and everything I said to you Friday night. I just wanted to say that I'm sorry about it all. Alexis always brought out the worst in me, but it was my fault for not standing up to her."

"Really?" Sheridan raised an eyebrow.

Where was his sudden contrition coming from? Did he think she was going to die and he wanted a clear conscience?

"Yeah." A flush crept across his cheeks. "I can be an asshole when I drink, and I need to stop." He hunched his shoulders. "I attended my first AA meeting on Monday. And I learned that one of the steps to sobriety is to make amends to people you've harmed."

"Well, I hope AA works for you." Sheridan gave him an encouraging smile.

She wasn't quite ready to forgive him for his past cruelty, but she wished him the best. Everyone deserved a second chance. Even if hers had ended up breaking her heart.

Beau stopped the pickup at the top of a slope that normally led down to the riverbank, but because the water had risen so far, the incline was no longer visible, and the river was spilling into the street.

As Beau helped Sheridan get down from the jacked-up truck, she asked, "What made you decide it was time to quit drinking?"

"Ridge had a talk with me Sunday night"—Beau fingered a fading bruise on his cheek—"and I realized he was right. My life was spinning out of control, and if I didn't make a change, someone was going to get hurt."

"That's true for a lot of us." Sheridan flinched again at the mention of Ridge's name. It would be a long while before she could handle hearing about him without her heart shattering.

"I suppose." Beau went to work getting his Chris-Craft off its trailer. "I see a couple of familiar boats floating around nearby. I'll take you out to one."

"Thanks."

Sheridan hoped she could remember what Darcy's husband had taught her the last time she'd visited her sorority sister in Ft. Lauderdale. As a former cruise ship captain, Mitch had insisted that she learn the basics of boating during her stay, saying it was always good to be prepared in an emergency. And this certainly qualified.

Sheridan and Beau got into his Chris-Craft, and he powered it up, then steered it toward a boat whose lines had caught in a bobbing mass of debris.

He pointed at it and said, "This belongs to a friend of mine. He won't mind if you use it. The key is in a magnetic box under the driver's seat."

Once she was on board, Beau handed her an extra flashlight and waited while she started the motor, then said, "Use the radio to call me if you get into trouble."

"Thanks for everything." She waved at Beau and headed out into the river toward the Wilson farm.

* * *

Where the hell were they? Ridge hurried through the gymnasium searching for Sally and Sheri. Twenty minutes earlier, when Merry had said they'd left to look for him at the city hall, he was sure that he'd find them at the evacuation center. After all, he'd thumbtacked a note to both the front entrance and on his office door stating that the mayor's office was relocating to the high school.

But he'd been through the gym several times and couldn't find them. Errol and Evelyn were present, but neither of them had seen either Sheridan or Sally. Ridge had noticed that both Sheri's father and his mother were frantic with worry, and Evelyn was clinging to Errol's hand, which was out of character for the Ice Queen.

After a final, more thorough examination of the evacuation center, Ridge sucked in a lungful of air trying to still the panic creeping into his chest. Sheri and Sally weren't there. The two most important people in his life were missing. Were they trapped downtown?

Ridge had one arm in his raincoat, walking toward the exit to head back to city hall, when his phone rang. He hadn't had a signal in so long the cheery tones sounded foreign to him. It startled him so much that he almost dropped the cell as he fumbled it out of his pocket.

He breathed a sigh of relief when he saw the call was from his daughter, and he quickly answered, "Sally, are you okay?"

"I'm fine. I can't believe I finally got through to you. I've been hitting redial, like, forever." Sally's voice seemed to be coming from the inside of a barrel. "Mom and I are at her friend

Jeff's."

"What are you doing with your mother?" Ridge had a bad feeling. Jeff was the personal trainer Alexis had been messing around with behind his back.

"She was at the city hall when Sheridan and I got there," Sally answered. "Mom said that you asked her to pick me up."

"I haven't spoken to your mother since Ms. Mac's party." Ridge felt his chest tighten. "Put your mom on the phone."

Was Alexis kidnapping Sally? He had full legal custody, and without going back to court, his ex-wife had no right to take their daughter without his permission.

"I...I don't think that's a good idea." Sally hesitated, then blurted out, "Mom doesn't know that I'm calling you. She took my phone and said not to bother you. That you were too busy saving the town. But something didn't seem right, so I snuck my cell from her purse and told her I was going to take a bath."

"Good thinking." Ridge fought to keep his anger toward Alexis out of his voice and remain calm. "Do you know the address where you are?"

"Not exactly." Sally said. "We're in the county seat, and it's the big pink building next to the Wal-Mart. It's apartment number sixty-six."

"You were very smart to call me." Ridge wedged the phone between his ear and shoulder, zipped his slicker, and dug through his pockets for his keys. "I'll be there as soon as I can. Hide your phone so your mother doesn't know you have it, and call me if she takes you somewhere else."

"Okay."

When Sally didn't hang up, Ridge asked, "Do you know where Sheri is?"

He jogged to his truck, thankful he'd driven the 1940 Ford. Since he had only begun the restoration process, it didn't look like much yet, but it ran like a dream.

"She tried to stop Mom from taking me, but when we couldn't find you, Sheridan had to let me go."

"Didn't you and Sheri see the signs I left tacked to the doors?" Ridge slid into the driver's seat and turned on the engine.

"There were no notes when we got there."

"They must have blown away." Ridge gritted his teeth to stop himself from exposing Alexis to their daughter. Clearly, his ex-wife had removed the notices. What was she up to? "So you have no idea where Sheri was going after you left with your mother?"

"No. Mom said that you were getting back together with her and that you only dated Sheridan to trick her into giving you the levee." Sally's voice quivered. "Is that true?"

"Son of a bitch!" Ridge swore, then apologized for his language and said, "No. That is pure fantasy on your mother's part. She and I are certainly not getting back together, and I would never use Sheri or any other woman that way."

"I thought so." Sally's tone was thoughtful. "Especially since Mom and Jeff are making out in the living room. Why would she be kissing him if you two were going to get married again?"

"An excellent observation," Ridge said, then added, "If you're all right, I need to hang up now and try to call Sheri."

"I'm fine, Dad." There was a pause before Sally added, "Sheridan tried to hide it, but I could tell she was really upset. I hope she's okay."

"Me, too, sweetie." Ridge's chest tightened. "Me, too." He took a breath and cleared his throat. "Lock the door and stay in the bathroom until I get there."

"Hurry, Dad."

"I'm on my way. I'll be there in twenty minutes. I'll send you a text when I get to the parking lot."

As Ridge sped toward his daughter, his headlights illuminating the empty road, he dialed Sheri's number. When his call went to her voice mail, he left her a message assuring her that Alexis had been lying. He hung up and immediately sent her a text saying the same thing.

Ridge's entire body was tense with the thought of what Alexis might do to Sally, what she'd already done to Sheri. He should have made sure that Sheri knew how much he loved her. How much she meant to him, but he'd thought he'd have time after the flooding situation was resolved to tell her. Clearly, he'd been wrong.

With a strangled sound of despair, he prayed that wherever she was, Sheri was safe. And that when he found her, she'd believe him.

CHAPTER TWENTY-NINE

Sheridan pushed thoughts of Ridge's betrayal away, telling herself that the Wilsons' survival was far more important than her own messed up love life. She was doing pretty well navigating the borrowed boat, ignoring the ache in her chest and the regret curdling in her stomach, until, out of nowhere, Alexis's cruel words popped into her head once again.

Suddenly, hopelessness washed over her. The pain swept away her concentration until she realized that she'd somehow gotten turned around. She had no idea what direction she was heading.

She knew she had to suck up the hurt and pay attention to what she was doing. There really was no choice. She'd used up her share of stupid when she'd believed that Ridge truly cared for her and wasn't just using her to gain control of the levee. It was time to pull herself together and focus on saving Lucille and her aunt.

There was a sort of GPS attached near the steering wheel, but when Sheridan activated it, the device indicated that she needed to enter the latitude and longitude of her destination. Who had that kind of info on hand?

Next, she looked for the radio, searching until she remembered Darcy's husband mentioning handheld units were getting more popular among pleasure boaters. The owners were able to keep them at home and avoid costly losses due to thefts.

Great! She was alone on the river without a usable navigational system or a way to communicate with the outside world. Crossing her fingers, she turned the boat toward where she thought the shore should be located.

A few seconds later, she spotted the railroad trestle bridge.

She was halfway to the Wilson farm.

Thank goodness! Although the rain had stopped, the current was strong, and the water was full of debris. Fortunately, the sky had cleared enough for the full moon to help her see where she was going.

Just as she thought she might be lost again, Sheridan recognized the Wilsons' distinctive old concrete silo. She had made it. Now to pick up Lucille and her aunt and get them to safety.

After several attempts, Sheridan managed to pull the boat next to the weathered gray farmhouse. Only the very top peak stuck out of the water.

Sheridan yelled her teacher's name. Her pulse raced when there was no response. What if something had happened to the women? Lucille was in her late fifties, and her aunt had to be nearly a hundred. This kind of stress might have brought on a heart attack for either one of them.

Finally, Lucille appeared at the window and shouted, "Get back. I'm going to have to break the panes. The frames are painted shut."

Sheridan moved the boat and turned her head away from the house. When she heard the glass shatter, she looked back.

Lucille motioned her forward, calling out, "You need to come inside and help me with Aunt Albie. She's refusing to cooperate, and she's surprisingly strong for a ninety-seven-year-old. I can't handle her by myself."

"Okay." Sheridan looked around for a place to tie up the boat, but there was nothing. "Here." She tossed the line to Lucille and instructed, "Fasten this to something inside."

It was quite a balancing act, but Sheridan made it into the attic. Looking around, she saw that Lucille had tied the rope to the leg of an old couch.

Satisfied the boat was secure, she asked, "Where's your

aunt?"

"She's hiding in the other room." Lucille handed Sheridan a battery-operated lantern. "Back when the Wilsons were wealthy, the attic was divided into bedrooms—this one was for the male hired hands." She led her through a doorway. "This one was used by the female household help."

Sheridan glanced around the dusty space. "I still don't see her."

"She's in there." Lucille pointed to a pine cupboard against the opposite wall. "Aunt Albie's convinced it's the great depression and the bank is foreclosing on the house."

Sheridan eased open the wardrobe's door, found an elderly woman cowering inside, and said, gently, "Miss Albina, I've got a job for you. Will you come to work for me and save your home?"

"Cash money?" Albie's faded brown eyes radiated her suspicion.

"A dollar a day and room and board." Sheridan was thankful she'd just researched women's working conditions in the twenties and thirties.

"Meat at supper?"

"And bacon for breakfast." Sheridan held out her hand.

"I need my own bed."

"You can have a room all to yourself." Sheridan hid a grin. The old lady was a tough negotiator.

"Okay." Albie put her fingers into Sheridan's palm and allowed herself to be helped out of the armoire. "How are we getting to your place?"

Lucille had remained silent, but now she said, "We're going to take a boat ride. Won't that be fun?"

"Who are you?" Albie pointed at Lucille and said to Sheridan, "Is she working for you, too?"

"Yes. And we have to hurry. I'm having a party tonight, and

we need to get everything ready for my guests." Sheridan led the elderly woman into the next room and stopped dead.

Oh my God! The sofa was tipped on its side and missing a leg. She ran to the window and stuck her head out as far as she could. The boat was gone.

Lucille stood with her hand over her mouth, clearly holding back a sob. Swallowing, she said, "Sheridan, I am so sorry. What have I gotten you into?"

* * *

It was a little past three thirty in the morning when Ridge pulled into the apartment complex's lot. During the twenty-minute drive, his mind had ping-ponged between worry for his daughter and how he could fix things with Sheri.

He was confident that he'd be able to rescue Sally, but after all the lies that Alexis had told Sheri, would she even give him an opportunity to explain? Or would she think that a real man would have been able to protect her and his child from his crazy ex-wife?

Ridge texted Sally, took the elevator to the sixth floor, and marched down the hallway until he reached number sixty-six. His only goals were to get his daughter back and find a way to convince Sheri to give him one more chance. He needed to hear her laughter again and fill his soul with her smile.

Putting his finger on the bell, Ridge left it there until Alexis's boyfriend angrily flung open the door. If the idiot had bothered to look out of the peephole first, Ridge was certain he'd have never answered the buzzer. Before the asshole knew what was happening, Ridge bared his teeth in a feral grin and pushed his way inside.

When Ridge entered, Alexis was sitting on the couch, but as soon as she saw him, she jumped to her feet and demanded,

"What are you doing here? Shouldn't you be going down with the ship or something?"

Ridge ignored her and yelled for his daughter. Instantly, Sally bolted from the bathroom and flung herself into his arms.

He hugged her and whispered, "Be brave for just a little while longer." She nodded but kept her head buried in his chest.

As Ridge started to leave, Alexis grabbed his arm and, completely disregarding her lover's presence, begged, "Take me back. I promise never to be unfaithful again."

Ridge snorted and peeled her fingers from his bicep.

"Sally wants us all to be a family again, don't you, darling?" Alexis tried to smooth her daughter's hair, and the girl flinched.

Turning to look at her mother, Sally said carefully, "I'll always love you, Mom, but I think it's best if Dad and I live together without you." She narrowed her eyes. "You lied to me about Dad and you getting back together, and you lied to Sheridan about Dad using her for the land. And I bet when you were married, you lied to Dad a lot then, too."

"Sheridan!" Alexis's beautiful face filled with rage. "You care more about that woman than me!"

"No. But she's never lied to me." Sally's voice was mature beyond her years. "And I don't think you understand that you can't lie to get what you want. Honesty is important to me."

At that, Alexis shrieked at Ridge, "I don't know how you and that bitch brainwashed my daughter to go against me. But when I get custody of Sally again, I'm going to take you to the cleaners for child support." She sneered, "That is, if you have any money left after what I've done to your businesses."

Ridge had been ignoring his ex-wife's screeching as he headed to the door, but now he slowly turned and said, "So you're the one behind all the problems."

"Of course." Alexis's voice sounded as if she were clinging

to the edge of sanity. "If you were occupied with all the precious Sutton companies, you wouldn't have time for Sally." Eerily calm, Alexis explained, "She'd love me best. And she'd want to come with me." Alexis clasped her hands together and crooned, "You'd have to pay me lots and lots of lovely cash to keep her."

Sally cried out and collapsed against him. Turning his back on Alexis, Ridge swept his daughter into his arms and carried her out of the apartment.

Alexis followed them into the elevator, screaming, "You owe me. Without my magic potion, your precious daughter would never have been born."

Ridge freed one of his hands and put it over the ear Sally didn't have pressed to his chest. He prayed she hadn't heard or understood what her mother had just said.

As they descended to the lobby, Alexis alternately begged for another chance and threatened him. Rambling on and on about her family being broke and needing money.

He'd parked his truck in the circle of illumination provided by a halogen streetlamp, and when his ex-wife saw him tuck Sally into the passenger seat, lock the door, and walk around to the driver's side, she lost it.

Alexis pounded her fists against the hood and yelled, "Errol Davis was fed up with the vandalism." Tearing at her hair, Alexis screeched, "If your stupid girlfriend hadn't interfered, he would have sold his land to me."

"I thought you were broke." Ridge shook his head. "You're even more delusional than I thought."

"Daddy's old pals at the bank would have given me a loan." Alexis was sobbing so badly she was hard to understand. "I would have controlled the levee." She sank down onto the pavement and sprawled on the asphalt, beating the ground with her hands. "You would have had to marry me to save your beloved little town."

"Not in a million years," Ridge said. "I'd let the whole damn state flood before spending one more second as your husband. Sutton Falls comes a very distant second to what I feel for Sheridan."

He slammed his door, started the truck's engine, and floored it. How could he have ever been attracted for an instant to that toxic woman?

Twenty minutes later, Ridge pulled the pickup into the high school's parking lot and glanced at his sleeping daughter. Sally had been silent since witnessing her mother's nervous breakdown. At least she hadn't mentioned Alexis's comment about using a magic potion to get Ridge to have sex with her. Maybe Sally hadn't heard her mother's ranting or hadn't understood it. If she had, how much therapy would she need to get over that information?

While he sat there trying to formulate something to say to his daughter when she woke up, his cell chirped. Hoping it was Sheri, he snatched it from his pocket, but his heart plummeted when he saw it was only Beau.

For a few seconds, he contemplated allowing the call to go to voice mail. Things had been awkward between them since Sunday night, when he'd punched Beau in the face, and Ridge was not in the mood for a drunken diatribe.

Beau claimed that he'd quit drinking and was attending AA meetings, but Ridge was skeptical as to how long the guy would stay on the wagon. And as far as Ridge knew, Beau still hadn't apologized to Sheri, which was a deal breaker if he wanted them to remain friends.

Nevertheless, when the phone chirped again, Ridge realized that he had to answer. It could be something concerning the town, and he couldn't let his personal feelings toward Beau get in the way of his duty to Sutton Falls.

Sweeping his thumb across the screen, he grunted, "Yeah?"

"Bro, where you at?" Beau's voice sounded sober. "I can't believe I finally got a signal."

"I'm at the evacuation center." Ridge sagged back against the seat. He was so damn tired. "Where are you?"

"I'm on my boat. I just got my cousin and her kids off their roof and am bringing them into the shelter."

"Are they okay?" Ridge knew Beau's cousin. She was a sweet woman whose husband was serving overseas.

"Just cold and hungry." Beau hesitated, then said, "I'm really sorry I couldn't help Sheridan earlier."

"You saw Sheri? When? Is she okay?" Ridge jerked to attention. "Helped her with what?"

"That's the thing." Static crackled and Beau's next words were lost.

Frustrated beyond belief, Ridge yelled, "Get to the fucking point before you lose the signal!"

Beau hastily explained, "I picked Sheridan up in front of city hall about three a.m. I was heading to the marina to launch my Chris-Craft so I could go get my cousin. She told me that Lucille Wilson and her great aunt were trapped in their attic, and Sheridan wanted me to take her out to their farm."

Clenching his jaw, Ridge demanded, "What did Sheri do when you said you couldn't take her?"

He couldn't really fault Beau for putting his cousin first, but he sure as hell wanted to.

"Sheridan asked me to help her get a boat so she could go save them herself," Beau answered. "I got her into Joe's Bayliner. She's a sweet cruiser and easy to handle."

"You let her go all by herself?" Ridge thundered, his throat clogged with anxiety.

"I tried to call you, but I didn't have a signal, and Sheridan refused to let me drive her to the high school to look for you," Beau protested. "Man, I didn't know what to do. I couldn't reach you, and she was going with or without my help. I figured at least I could get her into a safe boat."

"So she's been on the river for the last hour or more?" Ridge gritted his teeth in frustration.

"I told her to use the radio and call me if she got into trouble," Beau bleated. "And I haven't heard anything, so that's got to be a good sign, right?"

"Yeah." Ridge didn't bother to keep the sarcasm out of his voice. "Unless she couldn't figure out how a marine radio worked, or it was broken, or she flipped the boat and drowned."

"Oh." Beau was silent, then said, "Hey, I'm almost downtown now. You want to meet me there and take my Chris-Craft to go look for her?"

"Wait for me," Ridge ordered. "I'll be there in ten."

It took him a few minutes to wake his daughter, but when Sally heard that Sheri was in danger and Ridge convinced Sally that there was no way in hell she was going with him to look for Sheri, his daughter nearly beat Ridge into the school. Ridge found Evelyn drinking coffee with Errol and told them what was happening.

When he asked Errol to keep an eye on Sally, the older man's voice cracked as he said, "You go save my baby, and I'll take care of yours."

Ridge nodded and said, "Under no circumstances are you to permit Alexis to take Sally anywhere. In fact, if she shows up, notify the police. She's the one behind all the vandalism on your farm and my businesses."

Evelyn clutched Ridge's arm. "But—"

"I'll explain later," Ridge interrupted, shaking off his mom. "And Mother, now is the time to choose sides. It's either Alexis or me. And I need to know right this second which way you're going to go."

"Well, of course I choose you," Evelyn said contritely. "I'm sorry if I ever gave you cause to think otherwise." She glanced at Errol. "I'm afraid that I've made a lot of mistakes, but I hope we can get past them."

"We'll see." Ridge hugged his daughter and said to Errol, "Take care of Sally."

Ridge ran to his truck and raced it into town, relieved to see that the water level on Main Street had already receded a few inches. Blowing the levee must have done the trick.

When he arrived at the riverfront, Beau was waiting in his truck with his cousin and her children. He tossed Ridge the keys to the Chris-Craft and said, "She's all yours."

"Great." Ridge immediately waded toward where the boat was secured to a downed tree.

"If you give me fifteen minutes, I'll take my bunch to the shelter, then come back and go with you."

"Thanks for the offer, but it's already been too damn long."

Ridge boarded the Chris-Craft, untied the line, and headed toward the Wilson farm, praying that Sheri was okay. He wasn't sure he could go on if something had happened to her.

Beau had mounted a searchlight to the bow of the boat, and Ridge continually swept the water and the shore looking for any sign of Sheri. The wind had died down, and the only sound was the waves lapping at the hull of the Chris-Craft.

Ridge had just passed the Wilsons' unique concrete silo when he spotted something big and white caught in a snarl of rubbish. As he maneuvered closer, he saw that it was Joe Martin's Bayliner. And it was empty.

His stomach clenched. Had Sheri run into the debris and, unable to free the boat, swum for help? Or had she fallen overboard and the vessel drifted into the snag by itself?

At the thought of the only woman he'd ever loved dead, he turned his face up to the sky and screamed, "Goddamn you to hell, Alexis!" If Sheri was dead, Ridge would spend the rest of his life making sure that his ex-wife was miserable.

After a long string of curses, Ridge pulled himself together. Falling apart wouldn't help matters. The Wilson place was less than a quarter mile away. Maybe Sheri had been able to swim there. She'd mentioned doing laps every morning in her condo building's indoor pool.

Clinging to the belief that she was strong enough to make it to safety, he wiped his face with the back of his hand. Then, calling Sheri's name over and over, he turned the Chris-Craft toward the house.

* * *

Sheridan had placed chairs for herself, Lucille, and Aunt Albie on the old dining room table. The two older women were dozing, but Sheridan's mind refused to stop churning.

She felt empty, hollow. She was tired of fighting, of trying so hard to be okay. All she wanted to do was rest. Once she got the Wilsons to safety, she'd hire one of those home health care workers for Errol and disappear for a while.

She'd gotten over Ridge once before, and she could do it again. Her shoulders sagged. But this time would be infinitely harder than the last one.

Coming back to the present, Sheridan noticed the water in the attic was now lapping the tabletop. Another millimeter and it would overflow. Before long, they'd need to move up to the roof, but she wasn't sure how they'd manage that feat.

Unless she could somehow break through the attic's ceiling, they'd have to wait for the river to rise high enough for Lucille and her to climb up via the outside. They could tie a sheet around Albie's waist, and between the two of them, they could haul the elderly woman onto the roof using the makeshift rope. At least, she hoped they could.

Lost in her plans, it took a second for her to realize that someone was shouting her name. She hopped off the table and half swam, half waded toward the broken window.

Leaning as far out as she could without falling into the water, she screamed, "Over here! We're trapped in the attic!"

A second later, Beau's bright red Chris-Craft appeared, and Sheridan smiled. He must have rescued his family, then come looking for her.

Sheridan waved both arms and shouted, "Beau! We're in the attic!"

As the boat pulled next to the window, the figure in the yellow slicker turned toward her and grinned. "I hope you don't mind if it's me and not Beau."

For a moment, Sheridan's heart leaped with joy at the sight of Ridge's handsome face, then she remembered his betrayal and nearly cried for what she'd never have.

Her throat was clogged with unshed tears, but she managed to say stiffly, "While I'd prefer a different rescuer, beggars can't be choosers. So once again, it seems like you have me exactly where you want me."

"Sheri"—the smile slipped from Ridge's lips, and the painful hope in his eyes dimmed—"I can explain everything." He held out his hands in a gesture of supplication. "Alexis—"

"Stop," Sheridan interrupted him, glancing behind her. Lucille and Albie had managed to join her at the window, and they were plainly engrossed in the conversation. "Let's get these ladies to safety, then you can tell me how you just had to do what you did for the town's good."

"That isn't—"

"Seriously," she interrupted him again. "I don't want to talk about it here. We're all cold, wet, and exhausted. Just take us to the shelter."

CHAPTER THIRTY

The boat ride back was a silent one. Everyone was tired and lost in their thoughts. It was excruciatingly obvious to Ridge that Sheri had chosen the seat as far as possible from him. Her expression was frozen into that detached, closed-off façade that she donned to hide herself from the world, but she kept her arms wrapped around her waist as if the pain inside of her was too much to bear.

Sheri's eyes met his. They were flat, empty, and his chest ached remembering the liveliness and passion that had been in them during their time together at the guesthouse. With every beat, Ridge's heart broke a little more.

He understood that she didn't want to talk in front of an audience, but he was afraid that she'd withdrawn to a place of no return. Would she just leave Sutton Falls like she had the last time she was hurt? He couldn't stand the thought of her disappearing from his life again.

Ridge blew out a thankful breath when he saw the lights of town emerge from the darkness. Once he got everyone to safety, he could concentrate on convincing Sheri that he loved her.

Securing the boat to the same tree Beau had used, Ridge carried Albie to dry ground. Sheri and Lucille followed behind him, but when they reached his truck, Sheri maneuvered Lucille into the cab, then stared at Ridge until he put Albie next to her niece. He could see in her eyes that Sheri was considering refusing to ride with him, but she exhaled noisily and squeezed into the remaining space on the 1940 Ford's bench seat.

As he drove the women toward the evacuation center, the sound of Sheri's forlorn sighs slashed into him like a scalpel. Each of her sad breaths broke him more and more. Winning her trust back might be impossible, and he couldn't stand the thought of being without her for the rest of his life.

Ridge parked at the high school and carried Albie inside. He brought her to the Red Cross first aid station, and when Lucille joined them, he told her to find him if she needed anything, then went in search of Sheri.

While he'd been occupied with the two older women, Sheri had vanished. His pulse sped up until he realized she'd probably gone to find her father. Rushing through the gym, he took a relieved lungful of air when he saw Sheri being hugged by her dad and Sally. Nearby, Evelyn sat quietly staring at her hands.

When he approached the group, Sally broke away and threw herself in his arms. "You did it, Dad! You saved Sheridan, and we can all be together again."

At his daughter's words, Sheri made a strangled sound, but before he could respond, Evelyn said, "Sally, dear, I'm sure your father and Sheridan are chilled to the bone. Could you get them a cup of cocoa from the cafeteria?"

"Right away." Sally turned to go, then whirled back and said to her grandmother, "You called me Sally, not Sarah Ann."

"I know you prefer the diminutive." Evelyn stood and walked over to her granddaughter. "I should have respected your wishes."

"Awesome!" Sally hugged Evelyn, then said, "Two cups of hot chocolate coming up."

* * *

Once Sally was out of earshot, Sheridan was startled when Evelyn approached her and said, "I owe you an apology."

"Oh?" What had the woman done? Sheridan braced herself. How much worse could this day get?

"I'm the one who commissioned your father to paint my

314

portrait. It was just before my husband passed away, and I intended it as an anniversary gift for him. He had always asked me to pose in the nude." Evelyn blushed and glanced quickly at Ridge, then added, "I wanted to please my husband, but I was afraid that my social standing in town would be hurt if anyone found out, so I hired Errol, had him sign a confidentiality agreement, and demanded that he do the work in my home."

"Go on." Sheridan's voice was tight.

Was Evelyn about to confess to having an affair with Errol? Sheridan was finally dry and warm, but she'd never been colder.

"Thirteen years ago, when I found out that my son was interested in you, I was determined to get you out of town as soon as possible." Evelyn's shoulders slumped. "I...I thought he'd be happier with Alexis, and if you were gone, he'd come to his senses and go back to her."

"So after my mother died you sent me the photograph hoping that I'd be so upset with my dad that I'd leave right away."

"Yes," Evelyn admitted, gazing at her shoes.

Dredging up the past, bringing it all to the surface where she could no longer ignore it made Sheridan's stomach ache, but she was starting to put together the pieces.

"Did you and my father—"

"No. Never." Evelyn shook her head. "It was always a professional relationship."

"You counted on the confidentiality agreement and Errol being a gentleman."

"Exactly," Evelyn whispered. "And after I sent the picture, I was always afraid Errol would retaliate and tell Ridge what I had done and how I was behind you leaving town. I avoided Errol and tried to poison Ridge's mind against him and you."

"How did you get the picture?" Sheridan asked, guilt over what she'd put her father through making her voice weak.

"Errol took several snapshots to use for the rough sketches, and when the portrait was completed, I insisted on keeping them all. The one I sent you didn't show my face and happened to have caught his reflection in the mirror." Evelyn looked between Sheridan and Errol. "I am so sorry for what I did. I know you can never forgive me, but nearly losing my granddaughter to her crazy mother has taught me that family is the most important thing." She stepped over to Ridge and said, "And if you and Sheridan are in love, you have my blessing."

Sheridan strangled the painful moan that threatened to bubble from her lips. Clearly, Evelyn hadn't known about the plan Ridge and Alexis had concocted to charm Sheridan into giving up the levee.

"Thank you, Mother." Ridge's voice was cold, but Evelyn put her arms around him and held on until he returned her embrace. It would take a long time to mend that relationship, but Evelyn was obviously determined to do whatever it took to repair it.

Knowing that she needed to work just as hard to fix things with her father, Sheridan turned to him, squatted down in front of his wheelchair, and said, "I am so sorry for doubting you, Dad. Can you forgive me?"

"Of course." Errol leaned forward and gathered Sheridan into a hug. "I'm sorry that I was too stubborn to explain. But although I suspected Evelyn had been the one to send the picture, I was never sure. She denied it, claiming it must have been the housekeeper she had recently fired." He kissed Sheridan's cheek, then added, "Evelyn begged me not to reveal her identity to you, reminding me that I had promised complete secrecy, and in my day, a man was raised to keep his word to a woman."

"Too bad that isn't the way it is now."

As she spoke, Sheridan glanced at Ridge over her father's shoulder. Their eyes locked, and it took every ounce of strength she possessed to look away. Ignoring the regret curling around her heart, she focused on her dad.

*   *   *

Ridge saw Sheri's strained smile as she whispered something into her father's ear and then left. Before he could follow her, Sally returned with the hot chocolate. After asking his daughter to stay with Errol and Evelyn, Ridge hurried to catch up with Sheri.

She was heading toward the exit when he grasped her hand and said, "You promised to let me explain."

"Why should I keep my word when all you do is lie?" Sheri jerked her fingers from his.

"I've always told you the truth." Ridge moved closer as she edged down the hallway. "Just hear me out."

Sheri avoided his gaze, but he noticed that her hands were clasped together so tightly her fingertips were white.

"Please." Ridge caressed her cheek with his thumb, trying to convey how much he loved her. Somehow, he knew that she'd reject his words, but maybe she'd accept the truth in his touch. He watched the battle waging behind her eyes, and when she stepped away from him, he grabbed her arm and begged, "Just give me a chance."

"I can't." Her voice shook.

"Why won't you fight for us?" He growled in frustration. "For what's between us? For the life we could have with each other?"

Sheri hesitated, and Ridge sagged with relief when she said, "You have five minutes." He started to speak, but she held up her palm and said, "Not in the middle of the corridor. Somewhere we can't be overheard."

"I know just the place." Ridge led her through the building.

He turned into an isolated hallway, opened the door at the end, flicked on the overhead lights, and pulled her inside the spacious faculty lounge. "How's this?"

Sheri glanced around. "Fine." She perched on one of the leather club chairs and said, as if she could care less, "Let's just get this over with so I can get on with my life."

Ridge flinched. He could see in her eyes that she was already planning to leave him and never return. He couldn't let that happen.

After closing and locking the door, he sat on the coffee table in front of Sheri's chair, took both her hands in his, and said, "Alexis lied about everything."

"How do you know what she said?" Sheri yanked her fingers free and crossed her arms. "Unless, of course, she repeated the conversation to you because you two are still a couple."

"Sally told me when she called me to come get her at Alexis's lover's apartment."

* * *

Sheridan's mind raced. Alexis had taken Sally to her boyfriend's place? Hadn't she said that she was taking her daughter to where she'd been staying? If she and Ridge were getting remarried, surely she wouldn't be shacking up with another guy. Had she lied about everything?

No! Sheridan wasn't falling for any more of Ridge's fairy tales. She slid her chair back, away from the invisible force field that seemed to draw her under his spell. Being near him cut the power to her brain. If she was too close to him, she might do something stupid, like trust him.

When she remained silent, Ridge continued, "Sally was extremely upset that her mother had confiscated her cell phone and refused to allow her to contact me."

Sheridan's heart tried to argue, but she scooted her seat back a few additional inches. The more distance between them, the better she could think.

When Sheridan was sure she could speak without revealing her churning emotions, she said, "I tried to keep Sally with me, but Alexis pointed out that I had no right to stop her from taking her daughter."

"Thank you for trying to protect Sally." He pulled the coffee table forward until, once again, their knees were touching. "When Sally called me to pick her up, she told me how you fought to prevent Alexis from taking her."

For a second, hope flickered in Sheridan's chest. If Ridge had had to rescue his daughter from his ex, maybe he hadn't done the things Alexis had claimed he had.

No! Sheridan quickly dismissed that treacherous thought and said, "Just because you found out that once again your wife was sleeping with another man doesn't mean Alexis wasn't telling me the truth."

"Ex-wife. And she wasn't." Ridge traced a fingertip down Sheridan's cheek.

His butterfly-soft touch burned her skin, and Sheridan had to stop herself from leaning into his hand.

"Whatever." Sheridan shrugged.

Attempting to keep an edge on her anger, she tried to ignore the sensation of his legs pressed against hers. Why did her body still respond to the man who had used her?

"My guess is that Alexis played you like you played me, and now that she's gone back to her lover"—Sheridan held on to her resolve and moved her chair back until she was out of his reach— "you've decided that good old Sheri can warm your bed until you find a more suitable girlfriend."

"Goddammit!" Ridge roared, then, taking a deep breath, his

voice ragged, he begged, "Don't let that bitch ruin what's between us. She won before. You can't let her do it again."

Sheridan stared into Ridge's beautiful green eyes. His words seemed so genuine. But he was a politician. He had a lot of practice lying through his teeth while oozing sincerity. She had to protect herself. If she believed him and he was just stringing her along, she wasn't sure she'd survive the devastation.

At her continued silence, Ridge pleaded, "What in the hell would I have to gain by lying now? You've signed the papers. The money's been wired into Errol's bank account. The levee has been breached. What other possible ulterior motive could I have? If I just wanted sex, there are a lot of women who have made it abundantly clear to me that they're available."

Recoiling from the picture of Ridge with anyone else, Sheridan made a decision and said, "Let's look at this logically. Examine it lie by lie."

"However you need to do this is fine with me." Ridge scooted the coffee table forward, recapturing her hands. "What do you want to know?"

"Were you aware that Alexis was staying in the area?"

At the intensity of Ridge's stare, every millimeter of Sheridan's skin tightened. Her muscles stiffened and she shuddered. It was as if he were looking through her body all the way to her soul.

"Absolutely not. The morning after Merry's party, I left messages on her cell, but she never returned my calls. And although I tried to find her, no one around here admitted to any knowledge of her whereabouts." Ridge's thumb stroked Sheridan's palm. "Don't you think I would have insisted that she visit our daughter if I knew she was around?"

"Yes." Sheridan had no doubt about that.

Sally certainly hadn't been aware of her mother's presence.

And whatever else she thought about Ridge, she was certain that if he'd known his ex was in town, he loved his daughter too much to put her through what had happened at the sleepover.

"Next." Ridge brought their joined hands to his lips and kissed her knuckles.

Sheridan forced herself to ignore his mouth caressing her skin and tamp down the bubble of optimism trying to float free.

"Alexis told me that it wasn't a coincidence that you and she showed up at Merry's party within minutes of each other. She said that it was all a setup so you could come to my rescue and seduce me into giving you the levee."

"I swear that I had no idea she would be at that party." Ridge placed Sheridan's palm against his chest and covered it with his own. "Beau told me the party was for you. That's why I went. I wanted to see you and ask you out."

"She said the roofie story was a lie, too," Sheridan whispered. His rapid heartbeat stole her breath way. "How did she know you had told me that you were drugged if you two hadn't made up the whole thing together? You claimed to have no idea about the Rohypnol before you spoke to Beau, so how did she know you had found out?"

"I'm sure that as soon as I grilled him about what happened prom night, Beau reported back to her." Ridge let go of one of Sheridan's hands and dug out his cell. "Call him and ask him. If you phone him right now, you can be sure that I haven't contacted him and asked him to lie for me."

"Maybe later." Sheridan tucked the cell back into Ridge's pocket.

She could see the flash of frustration in his eyes, and she knew that she was pushing him away. Why couldn't she just accept his innocence? Perhaps because, deep down, locked away in a dark, dark place, was that seventeen-year-old girl who had reached for the shining star of his affections, and when she'd failed to grasp it, the fall to earth had almost killed her.

Sheridan wanted desperately to believe that Ridge was being honest with her, but there was one more question bothering her. She had to have his answer before she could allow her doubts to be dispelled.

Taking a deep breath, she asked, "If everything you've said is true, why was Alexis willing to let me try to find you when I insisted we talk to you before she took Sally? Surely she was aware that you'd have exposed her lies."

"Because, my sweet, darling girl, Alexis knew that I wasn't *at* the city hall."

"The missing note." Sheridan sagged, joy sweeping through her body. "Alexis read your message and took the sign down. She knew you had moved the mayor's office to the high school, so it was safe to pretend to look for you."

"Bingo."

"If Alexis is sleeping with another guy, she obviously doesn't care about you, so why would she go to all this trouble?" Sheridan's head ached with all of Alexis's deceit. "Why would she try to ruin things between us?"

"Because she's like a lot of folks." Ridge stood and drew Sheridan into his arms. "She needs to destroy anything that glitters, and you outshine her by a million kilowatts, so she wants to destroy you."

"How sad."

"It is." Ridge tucked a curl behind Sheridan's ear and vowed, "I will swear on a stack of Bibles, take a lie detector test, do anything you want me to do to convince you that the only reason I asked you out, the only reason I was ever with you, was because I love you."

With his words, Sheridan's heart opened, and all the hopes, dreams, and feelings she'd been repressing blossomed in her chest.

Ridge kissed her softly, then more thoroughly, branding her with his possession.

CHAPTER THIRTY-ONE

Sheri believed him! Ridge pressed his lips to hers, putting all his relief and love into the kiss.

Coming so close to losing her again had shaken him to his core. Without her, he was dead inside. Just going through the motions and not really living. But now, with her in his arms, he was alive.

When he lifted his mouth from hers, she traced a finger over his lips, and that slight touch roused all of his nerve endings. She wound her arms around his neck and rested her face against his shoulder, her warm breath stirring his hair. As she snuggled closer, the exquisite softness of her breasts set him on fire.

He kissed her tenderly, intending to go slowly, to savor their reunion, but desire sparked between them, sizzling out of control. The heat was so sweet, so intense, that Ridge struggled to rein in his response. But then Sheri arched against him, and he lost the fight.

* * *

The adoration in Ridge's eyes melted away any lingering doubts in Sheridan's mind. He truly cared for her. This wasn't about the levee or the town. This was solely a man and a woman who loved each other.

Breathing in his scent, she allowed it to soothe her. She pressed a kiss to the corner of his mouth, but he turned and captured her lips, nibbling and sucking until she opened and allowed him to lick inside. He tasted of the anguish and terror he'd felt when he thought he'd lost her, and the lingering fears inside of her were reduced to ashes in a flash of desire and love.

His leisurely assault on her senses drained all the stress and unhappiness of the day from her body, until only her need for him remained.

"Sheri."

Her name was all he said, but Ridge's low, sexy growl slid over her skin like silk, assuring her that she was all he ever wanted or needed. And with that single word, her body caught fire.

With one last swipe of his tongue, Ridge broke their kiss. Putting a fraction of an inch between them, he grasped the bottom of her sweatshirt and pulled it over her head. She returned the favor and stared at his magnificent chest. How did someone who sat behind a desk all day get such amazing muscles?

Before she could ponder further, Ridge flicked open the clasp of her bra, drew it off her shoulders, and fastened his mouth on her breast. Sheridan gasped for air, panting as his talented tongue drove her out of her mind.

While he teased her nipples to pebble hardness, he whispered all the sexy and mind-boggling things he had in store for her—right this minute, later when they got home, and for the rest of their lives.

She felt her cheeks redden at the erotic pictures he painted, which was a little silly, considering she was half-naked in the faculty lounge with most of the town only a few walls away. Still, she had a hunch that no matter how long they were together, Ridge would always make her blush. With one meaningful glance, he'd always set the butterflies fluttering in her stomach.

Then, when he reached down, unzipped her jeans, and used his fingers to take her breath away, any further thoughts were lost in the sensation.

Somehow, they both discarded the rest of their clothes and moved to the couch. The sensation of Ridge's tongue and fingers as he stroked her wet folds made Sheridan feel like she was about to burn up. It built to a point of delightful torture that threatened to consume her soul.

She clawed at him, fearing she was about to fly over the brink without him, and was grateful when he paused to snatch his pants from the floor and dig out a condom from his wallet.

Sheridan licked her lips as Ridge sheathed himself, admiring his strong male beauty. Then he nudged her thighs apart with his knee, and in one fierce stroke, he buried himself inside of her.

With a scream of pleasure, Sheridan felt herself filled and stretched farther than she had dreamed possible. Shuddering, she pulsed around him and his body tightened.

Her lashes flew up and she saw him staring at her. Then he rocked in and out of her, moving purposefully, watching her as she teetered on the edge.

Giving over all control to him, she luxuriated in the rhythm he set and allowed herself to savor the delicious friction of his hardness stroking inside her.

She wanted his special brand of joy in her life. He had the ability to make her feel safe enough to laugh at herself. To open herself to new experiences. To forgive and forget. He was the perfect therapy when her serious nature threatened to bring her down into the blackness of depression. With him, she could face anything.

Ridge's eyes had darkened and she trembled. He was wild with wanting her. She pressed more closely against him, and he reacted by thrusting harder, higher inside of her.

All the love and desire she felt for him coiled into one tight, hot eddy. And then, when she couldn't hold on any longer, she convulsed, the tremors making her thrash against him while he pinned her to the couch.

* * *

Ridge rode out Sheri's climax—every twitch and clench of her squeezing heat bringing him closer to his own release. Wanting this moment to continue forever, he held out as long as he could. Finally, as Sheri's spasms faded away, he allowed himself to free-fall into his own completion.

* * *

Sheridan held Ridge against her until his shuddering breath calmed. Then he moved, cradling her into his body and stroking her hair. Her heart pounded against his, and she felt wetness on her cheeks.

It didn't matter if the tears were hers, his, or both. Ridge had broken down all the barriers she'd built around her heart. She was far better with him than she could ever be alone.

He tilted her chin up and gazed at her, a look of concern in his warm green eyes. "Are you okay?"

She nodded, but the lump in her throat wouldn't allow her to speak.

"You're not thinking of running away? Of leaving me again, are you?"

Shaking her head, she swallowed and said, "I wouldn't have a chance in hell of ever being able to say good-bye to you. You have me body and soul."

"It's a good thing." Ridge gathered her even closer. "Because you have me body and soul, too. If I had to, I'd follow you to the ends of the earth."

"You'd leave Sutton Falls for me?" Sheridan was humbled that he'd give up everything he'd worked for his whole life to be with her.

"In a heartbeat," Ridge vowed. "If that's what it took to have you, I'd pack up my daughter and go wherever you needed to be."

"Considering that I can write anywhere"—Sheridan grinned— "I guess it's time I permanently move back home."

"As long as that home is mine." Ridge clasped her hand and said, "Will you marry me, Sheri Davis?"

Sheridan was stunned. She hadn't thought that far ahead. But suddenly, there was nothing she wanted more than to be Ridge's wife.

"I will," she answered. "On one condition."

"Anything."

"You remember to call me by my real name. Sheri was an unhappy girl who was too weak to face her own demons." She pressed a kiss to his lips. "Sheridan is a woman who is strong enough to love you and fight for you and be by your side through thick and thin."

"It's a deal." Ridge grinned, then said, "I always thought Sheridan Davis Sutton had a nice ring to it."

EPILOGUE

Sheridan stood with her new husband watching the Fourth of July parade wind its way down the main street of Sutton Falls. Spring had passed without any more rain, and although many buildings still bore high-water marks, the town had recovered from the flooding.

The levee had been rebuilt, and the land that the river had claimed was slowly drying out. Still, it would be years before it was ready to be farmed again.

Sunlight haloed Ridge's head, turning his auburn hair to golden red. He smiled at Sheridan and slid an arm around her waist, putting the other one around his daughter's shoulders. Sally had shown a remarkable resilience in the face of her mother's attempt to kidnap her and the resulting knowledge of Alexis's other misdeeds.

In exchange for Alexis relinquishing any future claims regarding custody of Sally and signing a contract never to set foot in Sutton Falls again, Ridge and Errol had agreed not to press charges against her for her vandalism spree.

Rumor had it that Alexis's father had scraped up the money to send his daughter for psychiatric treatment. And both Ridge and Sheridan believed therapy would do more good than any jail time Alexis might get if she were convicted of her crimes.

Sheridan glanced over to her father. Errol had fully recovered from his accident and stood next to Evelyn, who was smiling at one of his remarks. Although Ridge was careful to keep his mother from spending too much time with Sally, so far Evelyn had ceased her efforts to manipulate the girl into becoming the next Sutton princess.

A burst of laughter across the street drew Sheridan's

attention. Beau had caught a candy necklace thrown from the Lions Club float and was draping it around Merry's throat. He had been clean and sober since the flood, and Merry had promised him a date when he reached his one-year anniversary.

Sheridan sincerely hoped that he achieved that goal. Despite everything, Merry looked at Beau in a way she never had at any other man.

When the parade ended, Sally begged to be allowed to go with her friends to the carnival, assuring her father that one of the other girls' mothers was chaperoning the group. Ridge gave his permission, and Sheridan watched her stepdaughter walk away laughing with her pals.

When Sally was out of sight, Ridge leaned close to Sheridan and asked, "What would you like to do, sweetheart?"

"Let's go home." She slipped her arm through his.

"Sounds like the perfect afternoon to me," Ridge agreed and hurried her toward the city hall parking lot.

As they drove up the lane to their house, Sheridan squinted and said, "I really like the shade of red you had Odell paint the shutters. It gives the place some pizazz."

"Me, too." Ridge clasped her hand in his. "It was time for a change."

"Time for lots of changes." Sheridan smiled contentedly.

Her life had been in a rut. But between marriage and suddenly having a twelve-year-old stepdaughter, she found that every day brought something new and exciting. She'd opened up herself to love, and everything broken inside of her had healed.

"So what do you have in mind for our day off?" Ridge asked.

"It's so hot today, how about a dip in the pool?"

"Will you wear your new swimsuit?" Ridge whispered in her ear.

"No." Sheridan shook her head. He'd finally talked her into

a two-piece and now hounded her to wear it every time they swam. "Actually, since Sally is away, I was thinking that we didn't really need our suits."

"Why didn't you say so before?" Ridge stepped on the gas, and the Z4 roared toward the pool. "And after our swim, we can recreate our evening together in the guesthouse."

"That sounds heavenly." Sheridan paused, then frowned. "You did change the locks, right?"

"Absolutely." Ridge grinned. "This time there won't be any interruptions."

THE END

Thank you for reading Smart Girl Swept Away. I'm thrilled you chose to spend your time with my characters and I hope you enjoyed their story.

To receive an e-mail postcard when the next book in the Change of Heart series is released, sign up here.
[http://www.DeniseSwanson.com]

Reviews help other readers find the books they want to read. So before you go, please leave a review [link to Amazon or Nook], tweet, share or recommend it to your friends [link].

Join me on Facebook [http://www.facebook.com/#!/DeniseSwansonAuthor] or visit my website [http://www.DeniseSwanson.com] or follow me on Twitter [DeniseSwansonAu].

ABOUT THE AUTHOR

New York Times Bestseller author Denise Swanson was a practicing school psychologist for twenty-two years. Good Girl Overboard is her first romance and begins the Change of Heart contemporary romance series, which continues with Lucky Girl Wins the Lottery and Smart Girl Swept Away. She also writes the Scumble River and Devereaux's Dime Store mysteries. Her books all feature small-town heroines with lots of heart.

Denise's books have been finalists for the Agatha, Mary Higgins Clark, RT Magazine's Career Achievement, and Daphne du Maurier Awards. She has won the Reviewers Choice Award and was a BookSense 76 Top Pick.

Denise Swanson lives in Illinois with her husband, classical composer David Stybr, and their cool black cat Boomerang.

For more information, please check her website http://www.DeniseSwanson.com or find Denise on Facebook at http://www.facebook.com/#!/DeniseSwansonAuthor or follow her on Twitter at DeniseSwansonAu

51706037R00188

Made in the USA
Charleston, SC
02 February 2016